****

Into the Fire

Rise of the Republic – Book Five

By
James Rosone

with
T.C. Manning

****

Illustration © Tom Edwards
Tom EdwardsDesign.com

****

Published in conjunction with Front Line Publishing, Inc.

Manuscript Copyright Notice

Table of Contents

Chapter One
Silent Night

Two Weeks Post-Zodark Invasion
312th Battalion Command Post
Alfheim

Frigid air swept down the side of the ridge, bringing with it a swirling blast of snow and another cold front. Every evening, like a well-oiled machine, the sun would fade, and the two moons would appear at the two o'clock and five o'clock positions in the sky. Then the temperature would drop precipitously from the daily high of around twenty to forty degrees Fahrenheit to the nighttime average, somewhere around five degrees. The cold fronts would bring even more frigid weather.

Major Jakub Pilecki rubbed his temples. His head was killing him—a side effect of the kinetic strikes from the battleships in orbit above them. The shockwaves and concussive blasts from the hits were starting to have an adverse effect on him and his men. One could only handle so many overpressure impacts.

"Sir, General Bakshi is trying to reach you on the secured video teleconference," a staff NCO called out to him.

Pilecki nodded. He stood slowly and walked over to the communications room—a small side room in the cave tunnel they'd turned into a secured room. It wasn't amazing, but it was a private place to confer with his officers out of earshot of everyone else.

When he entered the room, he saw the digital image of General Veer Bakshi on the monitor. Bakshi was the head of the Republic ground forces and had opted to stay with his forces rather than flee off-world when the rest of the fleet had to withdraw. His face looked tired; his eyes had deep circles under them, likely from stress and a serious lack of sleep. "You look like hell, Major," the general commented.

"I could say the same about you, sir."

Bakshi laughed. "We're all going to need some sleep after this campaign."

"True enough. Sir, any word on how last night's attack went?" asked Pilecki, cutting to the chase. "My guys hit their targets, but we took an orbital strike in the process. Lost an entire platoon."

The general's face looked grim. "The attack was successful. Your men did a brilliant job. Two of the ten Orions made it through the enemy air defenses and successfully delivered their payload. We took the bridge out, and with it, the enemy's ability to move freely between the two provinces."

Pilecki felt good about that. At least his platoon hadn't died in vain. Their job had been a tough one—get in close and assault several laser and missile batteries so the Orions could deliver a series of smart missiles to take the massive structure out. They'd tried for more than a week to blow that bridge, to no avail, so this was a huge jump forward.

"Judging by the look on your face, General, you don't seem satisfied with the results," Pilecki commented.

Bakshi shrugged. "The cost of these attacks continues to grow, Major. Yesterday, we lost contact with the 192nd. They launched a large counterattack against a Zodark base, near the ruins of FOB Troy. Near as we can tell, they destroyed most of the enemy aircraft and ground vehicles when they hit the flight line and the vehicle depot—but during their withdrawal to the tunnels, they just went dark."

Pilecki had a sick feeling in his stomach. FOB Troy was maybe thirty kilometers from his own position. When that attack had taken place the other day, his own forces had heard it and turned some of their surveillance cameras in its direction. They had hoped to capture some footage of it that might help them down the road. As they were watching everything unfold, they heard a thundering boom, and then a plume of smoke rose into the sky in that direction.

"I think I know what happened to them, General. On our way back from our own mission, we had our surveillance cameras watching us and the 192nd. Pretty much any operations in our area, we observe. What we saw looked like an orbital strike somewhere in their general direction. It's likely they were taken out by it. If you'd like, I can dispatch some scouts to try and make contact with their base camp and see what happened," Pilecki offered.

"Yes, please do. If there are survivors, have them consolidate with your battalion. Oh, I'm also sending Dog Company from the 313th your way. I hate to be the bearer of bad news, but the Orbots launched a series of attacks on the 313th this morning. Near as I can tell, Dog Company and just a few remnants of the others are the only survivors."

Pilecki sighed at the news. *It just keeps getting worse. Each day, each week of this occupation, we lose more and more of our comrades.* He looked back at the general. "Sir, when these other units eventually make their way to our AO, it'll essentially plus me up to preinvasion levels. What more can my unit do to aid the overall effort?"

"I'm glad you asked, Pilecki. I'd like you to start creating sniper, IED, and IDF teams. Spread them out a bit. Have your teams make the roads dangerous to travel on. Use your snipers to create fear of leaving their bases. Your IDF attacks, have them focus on the enemy supply depots. We want these guys to constantly be short on supplies and scared of departing their bases.

"Have all your units that aren't participating in these kinds of attacks focus on staying out of sight and staying alive. There's going to come a time when reinforcements arrive. When the Republic returns to take this system back, we're going to need units left to help with the invasion. So, whatever you do, please try to keep as much of your battalion intact as possible. I can't let up on the attacks against the enemy, but I also can't lose my entire ground force, either. We just have to hold out a few more weeks, another month tops, and the fleet will be back with reinforcements. Just do what you can, Major, and don't risk more of your people than absolutely necessary."

They talked for a few more minutes before the general ended the call. He likely had a few more battalion and brigade commanders to talk with. Normally, a major wouldn't have this kind of direct access to a general, let alone the commanding general for all Republic forces on the planet, but General Bakshi had a vested interest in Major Pilecki's battalion since his youngest son was a sergeant in the 312th.

To the chagrin of Bakshi, his son had joined the RA as an enlisted soldier instead of following in his father's shoes as an officer. The general had been adamant about his son not receiving any special treatment, but Pilecki wasn't about to let the young man die on his watch if he could avoid it. He'd made the sergeant one of the battalion operations NCOs. It kept him away from the fighting but still involved in the action.

I just have to keep my men alive long enough for reinforcements to arrive, Pilecki told himself.
****

Three Weeks into the Zodark Occupation
Apollo Company, 1-331st Infantry Battalion

Deep below the surface of Alfheim, in their makeshift command and control room, First Lieutenant Henry Magnussen slammed his fist down on the table, causing the items on it to bounce. "I am telling you— I do not have the manpower or the resources to conduct such an operation, Hamza," he barked in frustration to the Primord commander.

Shortly after the massacre at Forward Operating Base McHenry, Commander Hamza had linked up with the human and synthetic survivors. They had all taken refuge in one of the many caves below the planet's surface, shielding them from the Zodark and Orbot scanners.

Hamza and his VikkSkein Continental Guard began working closely with the remaining Republic soldiers, carrying out hit-and-run attacks against the Zodark and Orbot ground forces as they continued to spread out on the planet. But as more time passed, Hamza grew impatient with the small pinprick attacks. In his eyes, the IEDs, sniper attacks, and small-unit ambushes just weren't enough.

According to Hamza's informant network, the Zodarks and Orbots had begun construction on several new orbital defensive platforms to replace the ones the Republic forces had destroyed a month ago. At least one of them was being built on the continent of VikkSkein, within striking distance of their location. The closer the thing got to being completed, the more anxious everyone became.

First Lieutenant Singletary looked at the rest of the platoon leaders of Apollo Company before stepping forward. "Henry, can we at least hear Hamza out? The fact of the matter is, if they're able to build those defensive platforms before help arrives, then you can kiss any rescue mission goodbye."

Lieutenant Henry Magnussen closed his eyes. It looked as if another outburst was going to follow, but then he took a very deep breath. He glanced at Singletary and then back to Hamza. "Go on, then, Commander."

Hamza removed a small circular disc and placed it on the table. Lights sprang from its face and created a three-dimensional blueprint of the defense platform that was being constructed in orbit above them in VikkShein. A large rectangular spaceport hovered in low orbit above the continent, with four long tubular elevators reaching into the atmosphere and down to the planet's surface.

"Each of these platforms will hold several orbital defensive weapons with early-warning capabilities that will help the enemy seek out and destroy any ship approaching the planet. Once completed, they'll be able to destroy our Republic ships before they can get within range of their weapons. If the weapons on these platforms are all allowed to come online, Lieutenant, the enemy will be able to defend this planet with impunity. My compatriots are working hard to gather more intel from their people on the inside, and they're convinced we can destroy the one here in VikkShein before it becomes operational, which will leave an opening for Republic forces when they come to liberate us. However, time is not on our side."

Magnussen walked around the table, looking at the blueprint. "Hamza, I have *one* company of Republic soldiers, two mech squads, and four hundred synthetic soldiers. I have three Cougars, three all-terrain vehicles—which are weaponless, mind you—and absolutely no air assets. I understand what the issue is, but I'm finding it more and more impossible of a feat to accomplish. How many Primords do you have in your Continental Guard? A thousand? We simply do not have the manpower nor the firepower to travel up those elevators and destroy the platform. We're just spread too thin."

Hamza smiled. "We won't have to go up the elevators and capture the platform. We just need to destroy their anchors here on the ground before their construction is complete. It will disrupt their supply lines and hurt their ability to send reinforcements through the space elevators. But even more than that—destroying the anchors won't just prevent them from using the elevators, it will destabilize the platform above and cause it to fall out of orbit—"

"And what, may I ask, would stop them from fixing the elevators and continuing construction?" Magnussen pressed. "After the attack, we will no doubt have lost hundreds of soldiers, our element of surprise, and our ability to hide. What then? We die knowing we took those elevators down with us?"

"Destroying those elevators will buy us time, Lieutenant— precious time we are running out of," Hamza insisted. "If we destroy those elevators, it could be in vain. We could lose everything—but if we are able to destroy them and your fleet is able to come back with a larger force, we could be the ones who turned the tide. It's simple: either we destroy the elevators and buy ourselves more time, or we sit in these caves and eventually starve to death."

Magnussen was silent for a moment, absorbing what the Primord commander had just told him. When he spoke again, he was much more measured in his response. "My big concern right now is trying to figure out how our forces wouldn't just get zapped from space. You heard what happened to the 312th Battalion, right? On the fourth day of the invasion, they reorganized and emerged from their bunkers and caves and launched a massive assault against an Orbot base. Minutes into their advance, nearly all their armored vehicles were turned into slag. Then an entire company was wiped out by a couple of zaps from their powerful lasers. The bastards had moved one of their cruisers into the atmosphere and used it for close-air support. So, that brings me back to my original question. How do we carry out a complex attack like this without losing what forces we have?"

Hamza also did not respond right away. "You bring up a good point," he conceded. "Still, I believe it is possible. Maybe we can look to break the attacking teams down into smaller elements, making it tougher for them to target our teams."

Magnussen's gaze had returned to the blueprint turning slowly in the air above the table. He flicked his fingers, moving the image to a certain spot he wanted to get a closer look at, and let out a sigh. "I have one of my squads heading out on an operation right now to destroy a mining facility. I could FRAGO that order and send them to a nearby supply depot and slow down the construction of this platform." He looked over to Singletary, who nodded and walked out of the room to inform Third Squad of the change. "In the meantime, Hamza, I want you to come up with a real, actionable plan on how we can take out those elevators, knowing the enemy will likely have a cruiser on standby to destroy our vehicles and zap any large clusters of troops. No hypotheticals—give me realistic plans with real solutions to the problem we face. The operation tonight should buy you some time to get it done, yes?"

Hamza nodded. "Yes, Lieutenant, that would be satisfactory. Thank you."

Magnussen nodded, and Hamza and his men left the room.

Magnussen looked back to his NCOs. "While Hamza is working on that, we need to keep trying to find other battalions out there. I know we can't be the only ones left. We need to coordinate our efforts with these other units. If we don't act alone, then we'll have a much better chance of survival."

****

The night sky was magnificent. It was hard to believe that a world filled with so much violence and ugliness could spawn such beautiful sights. Andre Bastille pulled his eyes away from the long-range viewfinder and stared up into the night sky. Hundreds of thousands of stars winked at him as the cold air of the ice planet bit into his exposed skin. Even in the most remote parts of the French countryside, he would never dream of seeing that many stars, let alone in Saint-Etienne, where he was from. It made the trips he'd taken with his mother to the Ardennes Mountains even more special.

Andre peered through the viewfinder again, setting his gaze on the enemy outpost that was being constructed a few miles away from where his unit was in refuge.

It had been three weeks since the battles in orbit and at their forward operating base. They'd been left stranded when the fleet had had to retreat from the system. It had been a *long* three weeks, with little rest and a lot of hardships. But they were still alive and kicking.

Unfortunately, there had been no word from any Republic or allied forces to let them know help was on the way. For the time being, the surviving members of the 331st Infantry Battalion were flying blind. Andre and the rest of Apollo Company had been working hard, building their underground network, working with locals who had chanced to meet them in the dark, and initiating hit-and-run raids on Zodark supply lines. It was about all they could do, given the circumstances.

The enemy knew they were still alive; what they didn't know was where they were hiding or how many of them had survived. The Zodarks sent out hunter scout drones regularly—nasty little two-meter drones that would fly over the tree canopies, using a thermal lens to identify their heat signatures. Once one of the drones located an allied soldier, it usually just kept going and seemed to ignore them...but a much larger drone would usually show up less than an hour later and prosecute the hunt.

11

If the Zodarks and Orbots had figured out just how few their numbers were and where they had been hiding, they would've wiped them out already. Instead, Andre lay prone in the rising snowbanks alongside his squad leader, Sergeant Tahlia Jones, as they watched the enemy push their area of control closer to the last bastion of Republic defense on Alfheim.

"Takata has been doing well," Andre said into his headset.

Akito Takata had come to Alfheim as a fresh-faced replacement only an hour before the attack on FOB McHenry had begun. When Staff Sergeant Otto Krauss had been killed in the attack, it had left the mech squad with one less member. Takata hadn't come down the well to be a mech operator; he was just a regular grunt that had yet to be assigned. However, when the company had taken shelter in the cave systems, Takata had practically fallen into the mech squad's lap. The young soldier had spent hours helping repair and find ammunition for the surviving mechs, and when no one had come from the line platoons asking for him, Jones had adopted him into their ranks.

From what Andre had seen, Otto Krauss had been a fantastic leader, beloved by Jones and Abede, but he was a hard man. Even though Andre hadn't known Krauss well, Jones seemed torn up by his death. Andre thought perhaps Krauss's thick German accent had given his words a harsher tone. Jones had told Andre that the military was made of hard people—some showed it on the battlefield, and some wore it all the time. It was hard men and women who would win this war and the many wars to come. She was right as far as Andre was concerned.

Jones looked over her shoulder to him. "He is doing pretty damn well; I'll give him that."

"It's a shame we cannot give him a mech to use," Andre bemoaned.

"You're more than happy to give him yours if you want."

Andre almost laughed. "I don't think that would be a very good idea."

Jones looked back to him again. "Why is that? Isn't it a shame that he doesn't get to drive a mech?"

Andre rolled his eyes. It was another lecture from Jones. She could never just say, "No, you can't do that, and this is why." She always had to kill him with sarcasm until he got the hint. Sometimes he wondered what was better, getting yelled at for being stupid or having it explained to him nicely that he was stupid. He concluded that Tahlia Jones was no Otto Krauss, and that was OK.

"It would be a bad idea to put him in a mech with no prior training and just thrust him into combat when we are already heavily outmatched. Given we only have a few mechs, we need the most skilled operators in them. Plus, we have no air support."

Jones nodded and looked back down her own viewfinder, satisfied to have received the answer she was looking for.

Andre wasn't satisfied with the conversation, though. "Jones, I could teach him. We could all teach him when we have downtime. We almost never come above ground when it's daylight, and even at night, we almost never bring the mechs out. I could teach him how to pilot one, and if the time ever comes where he is ready, he can be a pilot for the squad. You know, in case one of us ends up getting killed or unable to use our mech."

Jones sighed, her breath making a short cloud near her mouth. "Maybe you're right. I'm personally not planning on getting killed anytime soon, and I don't believe the rest of you are, but if you want to train him, then go ahead. If nothing else, it'll keep you guys busy."

Andre smiled. There would likely never be a free mech, but he was glad she'd at least let him plan for it in case something did happen. Krauss and Fujii had been dead for three weeks. While their deaths hadn't hit him too hard, it was acting like a leech on Jones, sucking the life and light right out of her. He wished he could do or say something to comfort her or help her through the grieving process. But Jones was a tough cookie—no matter what was going on with her, she was hell-bent on handling it herself.

Andre pitied her in that regard—not that he would ever tell her that. Despite having been in the Army for a few years, Andre hadn't lost any friends yet. This was the first unit he'd been assigned to that had seen real combat. Andre considered himself fortunate that he hadn't lost a lot of friends in this war. Heck, for all he knew, his family, including his grandparents, were all still alive on Earth. His grandparents were in their early hundreds, and his great-grandparents were in their 130s. It boggled his mind that they were still tilling their fields and pruning their vineyards in the South of France.

When Andre had arrived at FOB McHenry, the mech squad had already lost Fujii, and Andre was his replacement. The platoon had taken a lot of losses. It was always hard for a new guy to join any platoon, knowing their very presence was the result of one of his new platoonmates' friends having been killed or seriously wounded. However, at the end of the day, they would all just end up a statistic— either they'd be among those who'd fought on this godforsaken frozen planet and lived to tell about it, or they'd join the faceless multitude who never made it home.

In the lead-up to the Zodark and Orbot invasion, Andre had fought well with his new platoon. He'd shown he could follow orders and hadn't hesitated to take charge and lead in the midst of a battle if it was required. When their home away from home had started getting plastered from space, he'd rallied some soldiers to fight with him while they covered a retreat from the base into the forested hills and caves nearby. That retreat had saved lives and allowed many platoons and companies the time they'd needed to scatter to their predetermined bunkers and tunnel systems. From their new redoubts, they'd go on to carry out hit-and-run attacks against the enemy as they worked with the locals as best they could on building up an insurgency. Now, nearly three weeks later, Andre really felt like he was a part of the nucleus of the platoon, one of the old-timers.

"Friendlies on your six," came a voice in their headsets, breaking his train of thought.

Andre looked away from the viewfinders to see Abede and Takata slowly crawling their way up the snowbank until they drew even with Jones and Andre. Akito Takata wore a heavy cloth around his neck and face. All that was visible was his dark eyes, which smiled at Andre as they approached. Andre patted him on the shoulder.

"Welcome to overwatch," Andre announced as he pushed back and let Takata take his place at the viewfinder.

Jones did the same with her position and briefed Abede. "Same activity we've seen the past week. The Zodarks are continuing to build an outpost on the edge of that village. They started bringing in more supplies and dismantling those bundles near the road. I believe they're trying to expand the walls of the outpost to create a roadblock they can control. Two Orbots showed up to watch over the Zodarks, but hell only knows if it's the same ones from the last visit or new ones. Other than that, it's been a quiet night. Your relief, as always, will be here in the next eight hours—if you have any problems, call for help using the tones, and we'll be on our way."

The tones were a set of rhythmic audio blasts that sounded like keys on a piano being played: three short beeps and three long ones. Whenever that melody went out over the communications network, a QRF, or quick reaction force, would be sent out to its origin. The signal was only to be used in extreme situations.

"We got it from here, Jones. Thanks," Abede confirmed.

Now relieved, Jones and Andre pushed their way below the sightline of the snowbanks and stood, making their way to the two-person all-terrain vehicle at the bottom of the hill. Andre took his rifle and snapped it into the magnetic gun rack attached to the side of the vehicle before swinging his legs over and starting the machine up. Jones did the same and climbed behind him.

"Will Third Squad's mission tonight compromise Abede and Takata's position?" Andre asked.

Jones's grip on his waist tightened slightly. "I've been asking myself that question all night. It shouldn't—but honestly, nothing really surprises me anymore. If it happens, they'll be ready."

Chapter Two
Depot

It had been half an hour since Eva Jorgenson had watched the mouth of the cave slowly fade away from her sight. Third Squad had been tasked with infiltrating and destroying a mining operation five miles away, and Jorgensen had volunteered herself and Sam to be the medics for the op.

Usually, Mac would go, seeing as he was the medic for Third Squad, but the squad was the most battle-ready, and they received the bulk of the missions as a result. For the grunts, that was normal, but since they had a pool of medics to choose from and the ability to swap them out, after four missions in a row, Jorgensen thought it'd be nice to give Mac a break.

"Did you get enough rest, Eva?" the synthetic medic named Sam asked.

"Enough."

"Same," he deadpanned.

It was Sam's attempt at a joke. Since his time on Alfheim, he'd begun mimicking human behavior. Usually, it was something small like trying to make a joke or even the occasional attempt at laughing. However, during an ambush, Sam had somehow pushed past his programming and been able to kill an attack animal the Zodarks were known to have used. It wasn't an act of malice—he'd saved Eva's life when she'd been surprised by the beastly Ravager. She hadn't brought the event up to anyone…in fact, she and Sam both acted as if it had never happened.

Jorgensen smiled at her counterpart. "That was a good one, Sam. You're getting better at the jokes."

"Thank you, Eva."

Looking through the night vision built into her helmet, Jorgensen increased the exposure slightly. Visibility had dropped dramatically since they had stepped off as the snowstorm grew in intensity. The last mission that had gone out had seen three soldiers killed. Two of them had held on long enough to make it back to their cave systems, but with no ships in orbit and nothing resembling a hospital nearby, they had succumbed to their wounds. It was a rare sight nowadays. Modern medicine had come so far in the last few centuries. If a soldier survived getting taken off the battlefield, no matter how horrific the wound, their chance of survival skyrocketed to more than ninety-two percent. The system still wasn't perfect, but it was good enough that when someone died before being able to get on a transfer shuttle back into orbit, it was a big deal.

The soldier in front of Jorgensen put his fist up and knelt. The infantry soldiers began to peel off and face either side of the trail they had been on or had made—she couldn't tell which at this point. Jorgensen and Sam ducked down into the snow, staying as low as they could but positioned to jump back up and sprint for cover or to the aid of the grunts should one get injured.

Someone near the front, or perhaps the point man himself, had seen something that had forced them to take cover. However, as the minutes dragged on and no shooting or explosions erupted, Jorgensen realized this wasn't just a stop along the way to go over land navigation.

"Ah hell," the solider next to Jorgensen hissed.

"What's up, Jacobs?" she asked.

"They're calling leadership up to the front. Change of plans, apparently."

Jorgensen looked up to the front of the column and began to make her way with the rest of the team leaders that had peeled off from their teams. When she got to the front and knelt, she saw the squad leader, Staff Sergeant Osman Mahmoud, and the other sergeants conversing.

"Well, friends, HQ just sent us a FRAGO," Mahmoud said. He called everyone friend. "Lieutenant Magnussen wants us to peel off for a new objective. Bright side is it's closer to us than the mining facility."

"And the other side of that coin?" asked the Bravo Team leader, Sergeant Harrison Kodiak.

"It's a supply depot, which means there are a lot more enemy soldiers to deal with. There won't be any Prims on target working as laborers, so we won't have to be strict on weapons discipline, but those cyborg things might be there," Mahmoud explained, indicating there might be Orbots lurking ahead.

"Then what the hell are we even doing this for?" pressed the Alpha Team leader, Sergeant Kamel Patel. "We don't even have the right gear for an operation like that."

Mahmoud looked at the team leader disapprovingly. "Not with that attitude, you don't." Removing a disclike puck from his helmet,

Mahmoud placed it gently in the snow. A soft blue projection of the supply depot floated a couple inches above the puck. "Alpha Team will begin the attack with accurate covering fire from here." He pointed to a hill on the east side of the compound. "You'll draw the enemies, but I need you to provide enough cover for Charlie Team to begin taking out the guards in the towers as well as at the gate.

"Bravo will hit the west with mortars to take out the gate there and then will breach the compound. Once they've breached, Charlie will break off and assault the gate of the compound. Bravo, it's your job to ID the ammunition and weapon storage buildings. Once you've found them, I want those charges that were meant for the mining equipment placed on those caches.

"Charlie, you will locate the stockpile of building material here"— Mahmoud pointed at a structure near the front of the compound—"and will use your charges on that building. Once all our charges have been placed, we'll fall back out of the compound and conduct a tactical withdrawal back to a rally point here. Any questions?"

"Damn. You make it sound so simple, Sarge," Kodiak smirked.

"Sergeant, where do you want me?" Jorgensen asked.

"With me. You'll set up a casualty collection point on our location and wait to be called in. Your Synth will go in with Bravo Team. It'll be Sam's job to bring the casualties with the squads in the compound."

"I ain't going in with a synthetic, Osman. He's liable to leave my ass if I'm not statistically able to survive by his calculations," Kodiak huffed. A few of the other soldiers nodded in agreement. The C200 or medical synthetic had not exactly endeared itself to the unit it was serving with when it calculated likely chance of survival.

"It's *Staff Sergeant*, not Osman. And, yes, you *will* have the Synth going with you. He can take damage and keep going." Mahmoud glanced at Jorgensen and nodded. Kodiak didn't look happy, but he also didn't speak up again.

Mahmoud surveyed all his team leaders and nodded. "OK. Let's go, my friends."
****

Depot Attack
Alfheim

The drifting snow clouded Jorgensen's vision, and her eyes strained to pinpoint their objective. She had immediately set up a CCP upon arriving at the rally point with Mahmoud and Sam. The three squads had filed into the rally area like ants marching from their hill in different directions. Sam had gone off with Bravo Team toward the west of the compound, under the watchful eye of Sergeant Kodiak.

Jorgensen understood his reservations about the synthetic; she had them as well. But the machine was growing on her. So much so that she sometimes forgot he wasn't a human. Kodiak and the others just needed to give Sam some more time. In all reality, they hadn't actually operated alongside the synthetic medic—they just knew Sam wasn't human and that was enough for them.

When a soldier was wounded in combat and saw a medic coming, it brought comfort. There was a knowledge that this person was going to do their absolute best to save a soldier's life, even if their vision was already beginning to fade. With Sam, it all came down to his programming. If someone had a low survivability rate due to their injury and there was another wounded soldier nearby, then the synthetic would move on. It wasn't personal; it was a cold calculation that the military brass was OK making. That was why leaders got paid the big bucks and Jorgensen was knee-deep in the snow, waiting for a battle to kick off.

"Alpha Team is in position," Sergeant Patel announced over the intrasquad communications. The other teams soon followed suit.

Jorgensen looked intently toward the walls of the supply depot. A road wrapped around the perimeter of the walls and connected with the main highway system in the area. When Jorgensen stared at the buildings and followed the road long enough, she could almost trick herself into thinking she was back on Earth. But when she examined the scene more closely, she could make out the subtle details that reminded her she was not at home. In the distance, the soft glow of towns and cities danced in the dark night sky as snow fell across the planet. There was something peaceful about the scene, like a picture from a Christmas card. Then the peace was broken.

"All teams go," Mahmoud ordered.

Jorgensen watched as laser fire danced through the darkness toward the compound and enemy fire answered back. In the pitch darkness of night, all she saw was blue and red leaping into the night, trying to find its resting place in soft tissue or hardened skin.

"One-Three, this is One-Three Alpha. We need Doc up here ASAP," Sergeant Patel called over the net.

Jorgensen leapt to her feet, her medical bag strapped to her back, and sprang toward the crest of the hill Alpha Team was currently perched on. As she closed the distance to Alpha Team's position, explosions erupted from the depot in the valley. She looked to her right and watched as mortars hit the compound and the walls on the west end of the depot. Bravo Team had breached the walls and were heading toward their objective.

Apparently, the suppressing fire from Alpha Team had worked perfectly. Jorgensen had yet to hear any mass casualty event being called out from the assaulting team below as they entered the compound. The bulk of incoming enemy fire was crashing into the hillside to her front, just as they had intended.

Jorgensen slid into the protective shadow of the rocks Alpha Team was using as their cover and assessed the situation. Private Agnes Gunnar was propped up with her back against a rock and her rifle on the ground next to her. The rest of Alpha were in their positions, continuing to fire down into the compound. It was obvious who'd been wounded.

"Where are you hit, Gunnar?" Jorgensen asked as she swung her pack around and opened it up.

Gunnar's eyes opened and Jorgensen noticed she had been wincing in immense pain. "My left arm, Doc."

Jorgensen moved forward and assessed the wound, finding a fist-sized hole had pulverized Gunnar's armor in her left bicep. Checking behind the arm, she had a feeling what she'd find. Sure enough, she saw the laser had, in fact, gone all the way through. Removing a coagulant container, Jorgensen inserted the nozzle into the hole on both sides of the wound and pumped the cavity full of fluid. The gel would warm and stop the flow of blood while simultaneously cauterizing the veins the laser bolt hadn't. It was a quick fix, nothing permanent—but it would stop the bleeding for the duration of the battle and might even give her enough time to get back to the caves after the operation before having to apply another tube.

"OK, now let's take care of the pain, shall we?" Jorgensen smiled. She inserted her data pad's tether into the medical port on Gunnar's armor, giving her administrative access to her medical equipment. Jorgensen saw Gunnar's readings normalize as the bleeding subsided.

The next step was to access the fentanyl injectors within the suit. After Jorgensen typed her authorization code, Gunnar was pumped full of the medication. It would keep her as pain-free as possible until they got back to base.

"Oh, that's better, Doc. Thank you," Gunnar sighed as the powerful painkiller began doing its work.

"If you can get back in the fight, then you're good to go. If you can't, just wait until we move back to the rally point, OK?"

"OK, Doc. Thanks," Gunnar replied slowly, her speech slurred from the medication.

Jorgensen turned and approached Sergeant Patel's location as bolts of light crashed into the stones around her. The distant thwumps of explosions continued inside the compound, and she stole a glance down into the valley to see if she could make out any humans running around. She couldn't. She hoped Sam and the teams down there were OK.

"Sergeant, Gunnar received a wound to her upper left arm. I stopped the bleeding and gave her a shot of fentanyl, but that's all we can do from here. Anyone else down?"

"We're all good for right now, Doc. Head back to the CCP with Gunnar if you can."

Jorgensen nodded and turned back to grab her casualty. When she arrived, Gunnar had rolled over and was firing from the prone position, using her weapons with her right arm while trying to stabilize the front of the rifle with her left. Jorgensen couldn't help but shake her head. She ran into soldiers like that more often than not—they'd been wounded, some gravely, but after getting treated and being granted a ticket to the rear, they would continue the fight. It was the very embodiment of why she was proud to be serving in the RA.

She tapped Gunnar on the back. "Sergeant said you can head to the CCP with me."

"I'm good, Doc." Gunnar looked back. "Seriously, I'm fine. Help someone else who needs it."

Jorgensen nodded and began to make her trek back to the CCP, where Sergeant Mahmoud was.
****

Andre's eyes had just closed when he was shaken awake by Jones. As he adjusted to the low light in the cave system, Andre noticed soldiers running around. Something big was happening. He instinctually grabbed his rifle before asking, "What's going on?"

"Third Squad is in contact, and apparently they have some casualties. You and I are heading out to Abede and Takata to check on things and make sure whatever's happening with Third Squad isn't stirring the hornet's nest."

Andre almost rolled his eyes but checked the urge as he stood. He followed Sergeant Jones down the cave toward the exit that would let them out to the woods. As they exited the cave, Jones swung herself onto the vehicle and Andre took his place behind her, grabbing her waist and holding on tight.

"Don't get used to that," Jones teased as she gave it some gas and they sped off.

Andre ignored her, mostly because he didn't know what exactly to say to that. He had a sly remark to shoot back with, one of the ones that worked on the girls back home, but he wasn't a hundred percent ready to take a right hook from his sergeant just yet.

The all-terrain vehicle bounded through the snow, its studded tires digging tracks into the freshly fallen powder. The muffler system on the front dampened the engine's noise, but even though they'd used the vehicle a hundred times already, it still made him clench his teeth when the machine revved its engine.

After rolling to a stop, the two soldiers disembarked and slowly crawled up behind Takata and Abede, who were right where they'd left them a couple hours before, still lying in the snow and watching the outpost.

"What's the word?" Jones asked as she pulled herself alongside Abede.

"Yeah, we figured something was going down when we saw the activity at the outpost spike like crazy," Abede replied. "Orbots and Zodarks were rushing out of their buildings and appeared to be loading up into some air and ground transports. Then the call came out about Third Squad hitting a supply depot. After that, the storm kicked in, and as you can see, or rather can't see, the air units look like they're grounded for the moment."

Jones used her viewfinder and scanned the area below. Andre squinted and even tried to use his helmet's camera to zoom in on the outpost. The snow had picked up and visibility was near zero for his helmet cam.

"Move." Jones nudged Abede over as she got to her knees and cleared the snow in between them, revealing the circle-shaped hatch of a mech. They had buried the machine a few weeks prior, creating the snow drift they now sat upon. If they needed the mechanical killing machines, they could quickly access them and get them into the fight.

Jones disappeared down into the machine and lights began to pulsate from below before Abede closed the hatch. "Damnit, Jones! You just lit our position up like a Christmas tree!"

"Ah hell, Jones! You just blew our position!" Takata angrily chastised before sharing a few more choice words. When he'd finished letting off some steam, he turned to Abede. "Do you think they saw us?"

"Oh, chill out, guys. You're acting like a bunch of old women," Jones shot back. She was still running through the mech's start-up procedures and getting it ready to fight.

"I think they saw us."

"Look through the viewfinder, Takata, and verify. I gotta dig this thing out so we can get it moving."

There was a brief silence as Takata scanned the outpost below. "Oh, yeah. You blew it, Jones—they spotted you. We've got eleven tangos moving across the road headed right for us."

Now it was Jones's turn to curse. "Move, please. I need to get this thing ready to fight."

The three others on top of the snowbank rolled to the side as the mech roared to life and stood up. The snow puffed into the air around the machine as it revealed itself. Andre stood back and looked up at the hulking machine as its cannons lowered and the Gatling gun began to spin up.

"Apollo Actual, this is Overwatch Two. Troops in contact," Abede was able to get out before all hell broke loose.

Bullets sawed across the broken silence and ripped the Zodarks to pieces as they slowly moved up the embankment. Loud roaring noises came from the outpost. The Zodarks were going answer the buzzsaw of the machine guns with their own attack aircraft.

With their cover blown, Andre plopped himself next to Takata and raised his weapon. He switched his HUD over to thermals so he could see through the snow better and started looking for some targets to shoot at. Seeing the heat signatures of the attack aircraft getting ready to take to the skies, Andre flicked his selector switch from blaster to magrail. Finding the hottest part of the aircraft, he proceeded to place a few dozen penetrator rounds right into it. He was rewarded moments later with a large flash and explosion as the aircraft blew apart.

Looking to his right, Andre saw Takata still fixated on the viewfinder. "Takata, fire your weapon already, damn it!"

****

"Is your position tenable?" Lieutenant Magnussen asked the soldier at overwatch position two.

"We're engaging with our mech. Wait one," came the reply.

Magnussen held the hand mic for a moment longer before putting it down. He moved over to the table in the middle of the CIC and brought up the three-dimensional scans of their surroundings. Zooming over to where OP2's position was and then tracking back to where Third Squad reported in, he turned to the only other officer in the room.

"How did the enemy at the outpost know about our attack at the supply depot?" he asked.

First Platoon's leader, Lieutenant Singletary, stepped up to the table. "Could be a variety of ways. OP2 didn't report hearing the gunfire from the assault on the supply depot, but that doesn't mean the sound didn't make it to their position. The Zodarks may have also just sent out a distress call, or maybe one of their ships in orbit spotted some flashes on the ground and zoomed in to get a better look."

Magnussen sighed. "This is getting out of hand. Have Overwatch Two collapse back to the cave system and make sure they don't get tracked." He turned to the platoon sergeant, Master Sergeant Woods. "Woods, as soon as you receive a status update on Third Squad, let me know."

The two men nodded and left the CIC. Magnussen continued to monitor the map. Enemy markers popped up as they were tagged by friendly units on the ground. The fight at the supply depot seemed to be going off well enough. The medical squad had been awakened and made aware of casualties that would be coming in. All that was left was to receive word of the building supplies and ammunition caches being destroyed.

****

Jorgensen had only been back at the CCP for a couple moments when two large explosions turned the night into day. The blinding light caused her to switch off her night vision as orange and red fires shot skywards. The blasts detonated on opposite sides of the compound, and the light from the inferno cast shadows across the valley that allowed her to see humans running away from the scene of the crime.

"One-Three, this is One-Three Bravo. We are jackpot. Collapsing back to rally point. No casualties at this time," Kodiak reported from below.

"One-Three, this is One-Three Charlie. We are jackpot as well. Collapsing back to rally point at this time. One times casualty with us."

The voice that came through from Charlie Team was not the voice of their team leader, Sergeant Riccardo. Jorgensen knew that was most likely because he was the casualty they had. The fact that they hadn't given him a designation wasn't boding well for him either. Usually, the soldiers in the fight would let the medic know what shape the casualty was in so they could get prepared. When no designation was given, it usually meant they were dead.

When the teams pulled back to the CCP and rally point, Charlie Team's machine gunner, Private Dominik Cerny, was carrying Sergeant Riccardo over his shoulder. There were blood streaks running down Cerny's armor from the sergeant's wounds.

Jorgensen had started to approach him when she caught the private's eye. Cerny shook his head. Jorgensen knew then that Sergeant Riccardo was gone. All in all, on a major assault of this size and without the proper equipment for it, they had done great. The fact that they had one killed in action was exceptionally good. Jorgensen took the wins any way she could at this point.

The squad began moving out, Cerny still carrying their sergeant on his back. He wouldn't allow anyone to take their leader from him. Jorgensen always marveled at the bond soldiers created between each another; it was like the more severe the circumstances they were in together, the deeper that bond was. It was the kind of connection that led men and women to throw themselves willingly into harm's way, often into scenarios where they knew they were going to die, if it would save the life of one of their friends.

When the Republic had begun integrating soldiers from the *many* countries around Earth, there had been pushback. People who had once been sworn enemies now fought side by side for the survival of humanity. Jorgensen remembered her feelings when her own Army unit inside the Greater European Union had merged with the Asian Alliance. It had been a tough transition. Then a few years later, their new TPA alliance and military force had gone through the entire process again, this time merging with the Republic. In the span of a few years, she'd gone from viewing the Asian Alliance and the Republic as possible adversaries to seeing them as comrades and brothers-in-arms. It had been challenging to go from being near-enemies to suddenly having to fight and die alongside each other in this war across the stars. But if they didn't find a way to put aside their differences and learn to work together, like they were now, their home world and everything they held dear could be wiped out next.

Now, after nearly a decade of war and more than a few combat operations under her own belt, when Jorgensen looked at her fellow soldiers, she no longer identified them by their nationalities but by their species. She would be lying if she said she didn't miss Abba's jollof rice, though, or Ibrahim's grandmother's recipe for chicken shawarma. But life moved on, just like she had to.

As the mouth of the cave came into view thirty minutes later, Jorgensen let out a breath as if she had been holding it in the entire time. Safety was only a few feet away. The comfort of her cot, the comfort of her friends, the comfort of Sam. She looked over to the Synth, who had once again come out of the fray without a scratch, and smiled. Sam looked behind him confused and then realized she was smiling at him, and he grinned back—well, he tried to grin back. It came out as more of a pained grimace, and for the first time since the battle, she laughed.

****

Rockets let loose from the mech and careened downward toward the outpost. The explosive-tipped projectiles smashed into the buildings the Zodarks and Orbots had been working on for weeks. They now stood on fire, smoke and ash spewing into the space around them.

Andre knelt and tapped Takata on the shoulder. Then Andre began firing to allow Takata to fall back down the hill. As Takata turned to run, a laser hit him and spun him around viciously before slamming him into the ground. Andre nearly screamed as he grabbed on to Takata and tried to pull the man up. As he looked down, he noticed his buddy's gun in two pieces on the ground.

"You are one lucky son of a—" Andre started to say before being cut off.

"Fall back to the cave system now!" Jones screamed over the communications net. "Abede, get on my back. Bastille, take Takata on the ATV and get the hell out of here!"

Andre watched over his shoulder as Abede jumped on the back of the mech and began firing, using the hulking machine to hold his rifle steady. Andre leapt onto the ATV and started it up, letting Takata climb on board behind him. As Andre flipped the throttle back, the vehicle shot off, the increase in speed almost yanking him off the ATV.

"Watch it!" Andre yelled over the wind.

"Slow it down, then!" Takata yelled back, holding on for dear life.

Andre laughed at the absurdity of it all. Moments before, he had been in a firefight, a mech he hadn't thought they would have to use was letting loose its rocket pods, and the man who had grown to be his friend had almost just been killed. Yet here Andre was, laughing into the wind as he maneuvered the ATV around trees toward the mouth of the cave. As they pulled under the reflective camouflage netting, he idled and shut the machine off. A few soldiers secured the flap and waited for the mech to come inside.

"They're coming, right?" Takata asked.

Andre gave him a sidewards glance. "They are. Now go get a new rifle and be ready, just in case. I'll stay here."

Takata hesitated for a moment before nodding and turning toward where the armory had been set up. Andre's gaze moved back to the netting, and he strained to listen for any movement, especially the sound of a giant machine. Finally, after what was probably only a few minutes but felt more like an hour, the mechanical thud of a mech's leg became audible. The soldiers nearby scrambled to pull the netting away so the mech could get inside the cave. Once in, the soldiers covered the entrance up again and activated their electronic shielding system.

Abede hopped down from the machine when it came to a rest and punched Andre in the shoulder playfully yet painfully. "Miss us?"

"Would you be mad if I said no?" Andre smirked.

"Not at all, Legion, not at all," Abede replied, using Andre's nickname.

That made Andre light up. His nickname was rarely used, usually only when they were in their mechs together. Whenever someone called him "Legion," especially Jones or Abede, it seemed to take his worry away, which was exactly what he needed at this time.

As Jones stepped out of the mech and down the ladder, Andre walked up to her. "I sent Takata to go get another rifle; his was shot in half on the way down the snowbank."

"You and Takata did well, Andre. Grab some chow and shut-eye while I figure out what the hell happened. I'll wake ya all up to do some cleaning later."

Andre nodded. "Thanks, Sarge."

Jones walked past him and looked over her shoulder. "Good work, kid."

Chapter Three
Between a Rock

Apollo Company, 1-331st Infantry Battalion
Alfheim

First Lieutenant Henry Magnussen had been spending the majority of his time these last few weeks staring at map projections, trying to keep his meager force still in the fight while not getting wiped out by the ever-increasing number of Zodark and Orbot soldiers arriving on the planet.

In the Officers' Academy, Magnussen had excelled at land navigation and zero-gravity navigation, trying to get the best marks possible. Everything was a competition to him when his class trained. He looked at scores as an indicator of how good a leader he might be. In his eyes, his commanding officer should be tenacious and driven, someone who would always get the job done, no matter what—at least, that was what he told himself back then, when he was young and naive.

Thinking on it, Magnussen still considered himself young; he was only four years removed from the Academy. Then again, a lot had transpired in that time. After the Alfheim campaign, any naivety he might have had was thoroughly destroyed.

It was because of his good marks that Magnussen had become the company's executive officer when he'd arrived at Apollo Company all those years ago. Of course, his unwavering loyalty to the Republic and, most importantly, to Captain Fenti, played a role in that as well. When Fenti had gone back up the well on a routine meeting with the battalion commander just prior to the Zodark invasion, Magnussen had suddenly found himself in charge of the company when Fenti wasn't able to return. The burden of the entire responsibility—every decision, every life—it was weighing on him. It was his sink-or-swim moment.

The day of the invasion had been rough. They had been surrounded on all sides and looked like they were going to be overrun until the synthetics reinforcing their position had finished the fight. After that initial attack was over, the company had been so thoroughly decimated, Magnussen hadn't had much of a force left. They'd suffered nearly fifty percent casualties and their C100 reinforcements had been all but wiped out in the counterattack to save their hides.

It wasn't until they were on their way into the cave systems of Alfheim that Magnussen had received word that all other commanders had been killed in the fighting. He was now in charge of a little more than a company as soldiers from nearby units joined them, their parent units having been wiped out. Despite the initial losses, they weren't alone. There were other forces on Alfheim—some working with the Prims like he was, and some that remained in the dark. At least, that was what Magnussen had learned from the Prim intelligence reports.

Now Magnussen stood between a rock and a hard place, deciding whether he was going to go along with the Prims' insane idea of attacking the orbital elevators or wait to be rescued. Either choice might reduce his command to carrying out hit-and-run missions like they had been, only with few viable teams to carry out them out with. That would be a war of attrition, one he had no chance of winning.

He tried to filter every decision through pros and cons. On one hand, if they were successful, they would open up a major hole in the planetary defenses so the alliance could come sweeping in to save the day. But that only worked *if* the alliance was ready to come sweeping in to save them. On the other hand, if they went ahead with the attack and were all killed for it, then what help would they be to the Republic when they did finally show up?

Turning to face Lieutenant Adam Singletary, Magnussen asked, "Are you sure they have no clue where we came from? If too many ants stray too far from the hill, the enemy could be led to their home. I'm not about to be responsible for this company ending up on the bottom of the Zodarks' boots."

"We've sent patrols out to cover every inch of ground within a five-mile radius over the past couple of days," replied Singletary. "No one has seen or run into the enemy. I'd have to assume if they knew where we were, then we'd already know it."

"What if that's exactly what they want us to think?" Magnussen pressed. "What if the moment we walk out of that cave, they drop an orbital bombardment on us, killing any chance of retaking this place?"

Singletary stifled a laugh. "Henry, we can sit here and debate what-ifs all day. The fact of the matter is we hurt their supply lines—we destroyed an outpost that was placed a little too close for comfort, and if anything, the Zodarks have taken a step back. I mean, if the Zodarks or Orbots were really hunting for us, then why are we not encountering any patrols? Why are we not detecting any surveillance flights or drones covering the area? This planet is a very big place, Henry. They can't be everywhere at once. We have to take advantage of that fact."

The two of them stared at each other for a moment before Singletary asked, "You don't like the Prims' plan, do you? The one to attack the spaceport."

Magnussen sighed. He'd lost so many people up to this point. *I just don't want to lose more people on a fool's errand that has no chance of success...*

"No. I don't," Magnussen admitted. "I get why they want to do it. Tactically, it even makes sense. But strategically, it's a mistake."

"Oh. How so?" Singletary pressed. "I'd think taking an orbital platform and spaceport down would be a pretty good strategic plan."

Magnussen shook his head. "Let me try and break it down for you, Adam. Suppose we get lucky and manage to destroy the spaceport, and we somehow take down the platform. Then what? We don't know when or even *if* the Republic is going to send another invasion force. If we attack this spaceport and we lose, say, half our people, or worse, we get wiped out trying, then what? What did we accomplish? I think our best bet is to continue hitting these bastards with hit-and-run attacks like we've been doing. You know, death by a thousand cuts."

"I thought you were trying to stay away from the what-ifs, Henry," Singletary replied. He'd known Magnussen since their days back at the Academy, when Magnussen had been a year ahead of him. "It's been over a week since our last operation. The guys are getting restless, and the Prims are pushing for us to do something."

"I know, I know. I've been thinking the same thing, but after that last raid we conducted...I just wanted us to lie low for a little while. I know your scouts haven't come across anything near our base camp, but that doesn't mean they aren't looking for us. Maybe we need to expand our perimeter—get some scouts further out, get eyes on some of the larger roads in the region."

Singletary stared at Magnussen for a moment and then nodded in agreement. Death by a thousand cuts still resulted in death. "You're right, as usual. I'll send some additional scout teams out. We'll take a look at Junger's Pass. It's the only road through the mountains that large enough for the enemy to transport large numbers of troops on that's still close enough that we could consider ambushing it."

"Whoa. If that's the case, Adam, why haven't you already scouted it out?" Magnussen challenged.

"Henry, it's nearly fifteen kilometers away, and the scouts would have to travel on foot most of the way. It's rough terrain. Since we can't really use our primary coms gear, it's nearly impossible to communicate with any forces we send. It'll take close to twenty-five hours for the scouts to get there and come back with any credible intelligence."

"Damn. That's going to make coordination a problem. Still, I like this a lot more than the Prim plan. Get your teams on the move. Let's see if we can identify some juicy targets that travel down that road. Maybe we can get the Prims to agree to this instead."

Singletary nodded and walked out of the CIC. Magnussen placed his palms over his face and rubbed at his bloodshot eyes. So far, he had been awake for more than forty-eight hours with only stimulants from the medics keeping him going. His eyes longingly gravitated to the cot in the corner of the room.

Magnussen sighed to himself. "A couple of hours won't hurt."
****

Sergeant Harrison Kodiak sat with his back against the warm rocks of the cavern his squad was bunking in. Looking to his left, he watched his squad leader, Mahmoud, checking on a couple of Charlie Team's soldiers. Losing a leader was always hard, especially when they were NCOs.

Noncommissioned officers were called the backbone of the military for a reason: they were usually the ones on the battlefield that knew what to do and led the execution of the mission. When fresh-faced privates showed up to a unit, they clung to the sergeants like sponges and soaked up any knowledge they could. Kodiak remembered the first time he'd been shot at. The sizzle and burn a laser made were indescribable.

Training always kicked in at moments like those. Instinctually, Kodiak had slammed himself to the ground and found cover. When his team leader, Sergeant Sosa, had knelt and returned fire, Kodiak had followed suit. A lot of time had passed since then. Kodiak had lost friends to promotions, reassignments, and death. He had been promoted himself and moved up the ranks and now led his own team.

"Sergeant Kodiak," said a voice next to him.

Kodiak looked up at the face of Lieutenant Singletary and he quickly stood and saluted. "Yes, sir."

Staff Sergeant Mahmoud noticed the platoon leader had entered the room. "How can we help you, sir?" he asked.

Singletary turned his head toward Sergeant Kodiak. "You're sniper-qualified, correct?"

"Yes, sir," Kodiak responded.

"Good," he replied. He turned back to Staff Sergeant Mahmoud. "I want Sergeant Kodiak to lead a sniper team into Junger's Pass." Singletary took out his data pad and sent the operation order to Kodiak and Mahmoud.

"That's fifteen kilometers from here, sir," Kodiak remarked, surprised by the orders.

"It is. Bring enough equipment for seventy-two hours. You'll be in the bush for two nights, then out of there and back to base. The XO thinks the Zodarks may still be looking for us. He thinks they may be bringing in soldiers from further away before they kick the bushes in our direction. If he's wrong and they aren't, then he wants to see what kind of traffic is using the highway—we may look to ambush it.

"Oh, and before you leave, I want to impress upon you that you are to gather intelligence on that route. If you see the enemy, take note of how many and where their locations are. But do not engage them unless you've been compromised. If they find you, then they'll know for certain we have a camp somewhere nearby."

Kodiak nodded to his platoon leader. "Yes, sir. We'll get it done."

Singletary turned back for a moment after returning their salutes and looked at Kodiak. "You won't have any support. No air, no QRF, and no mechs. You will be alone. So try and stay hidden."

Kodiak just nodded.

When Singletary left the cavern, Kodiak turned to Mahmoud. "Who else you thinking?"

"Josef from Second Squad is a crack shot—he can be your second."

Kodiak sighed. "Josef was dusted about two weeks ago, shortly after we got here."

"Oh, damn. That's right. That's a shame."

"He was a good kid…knew his stuff."

Mahmoud smiled. "Always used to tie down what's his name—"

"Fritzy," Kodiak replied, laughing. "Oh, he sure was an idiot."

"Good kid, though. Man, I tell ya, he always smiled. Was always grinning and I couldn't understand it. A bolt could've taken the bark off a tree next to him and he'd just shrug and say, 'Best job I ever had.' Whatever happened to him?"

"He bought it at the FOB. Cougar he was in took a big hit. Thing went up so fast." Kodiak shook his head. "I didn't see anyone get out of that."

Mahmoud clicked his tongue. "Yeah, it's been a hell of a ride."

"I want Kumar from Charlie Team to be my second—he's got good eyes. Jacobs from my team will spot for our second shooter—"

"Which is who?" Mahmoud interrupted.

Kodiak shook his head. "I don't know. Does it really matter? We aren't planning on assassinating a target, and I'd feel much more comfortable if I had another rifle on the ground with me instead of another long gun."

Mahmoud thought on it. "What about Staff Sergeant Moreau from First Squad?"

Kodiak stared at Mahmoud, chewing his lip for a moment. "As long as a squad leader doesn't mind being ordered around by a team leader," he finally spat out.

"Oh, please," Mahmoud replied. "You both came up as sergeants together. Just because her squad leader was killed and I luckily was not doesn't mean you have to get territorial. You both can make decisions together and once you break off into your teams, Jacobs will have a competent leader by his side. Correct?"

"Correct," Kodiak conceded.

Mahmoud was right after all. Moreau and Kodiak had graduated basic training together, they'd both been assigned to 331st Infantry Battalion, and they'd both been promoted up through the ranks around the same time. Moreau was a fantastic soldier—even if she really did enjoy being in charge.

"I'll start getting everyone saddled up," Mahmoud said. "Get the ATVs ready to roll out and get your gear together as well. You're going to want to head out as soon as the sun sets."

"Let's get it done," Kodiak replied as he grabbed his bag.

****

Three Hours Later

For the first time in several weeks, the wind had died down, blanketing the snow-covered mountainside with an eerie silence. Kodiak finished stowing his ATV in the depths of one of the many caves found in the region and made his way to the mouth. The sun was well below the horizon by now, and they were mostly covered in darkness. He looked out across the valley below and took in a rare sight for Alfheim.

Usually, storms darkened the skies in all directions, with wind and violent snowfalls following behind. Kodiak remembered the lightning storms and shuddered. However, tonight, the sky glowed in the waning light, spreading an array of purples and pinks across the skyline. It made him forget where he was for a moment.

"You ready to move out?" The question came from Staff Sergeant Moreau.

Kodiak turned to her. "Just admiring the sunset. You have to admit, the sky hasn't been that beautiful since we got here."

"That's a sign from Surya, the sun god. He is giving us a good omen," interjected Private First Class Deepak Kumar.

"Or it's a sunset, my guy," Jacobs responded as he walked from the mouth of the cave and checked his rifle.

"Well, regardless of your beliefs, there's no denying its beauty." Kumar sighed.

"You got me there, Kumar, you got me there," Jacobs responded. "I'll take point." He stepped off and advanced up a trail toward the cliffs overlooking Junger's Pass.

Kodiak got into step next to Moreau and nudged her. "I tried to get ya a rifle instead of that thing," he said, motioning to the sniper rifle on her back. "Guess they didn't go for it."

"I don't mind. I haven't used one of these since New Eden, so it'll feel good getting some reps in."

Kodiak glanced at her; his visor was transparent, so he could look into her eyes. Ever since regular Army units had been issued helmets with full-face visors, he was finding conversations with others more difficult when on patrol. Before, he could see someone's eyes, tics, and facial expressions. He could see if they were joking or being serious. A lot of soldiers got into the habit of putting more emotion into the way they said certain things. Moreau was not one of them—on purpose, because she liked to torment people.

Thankfully, she laughed.

"You need to stop playing so much, Moreau," Kodiak said with a chuckle.

"When was the last time you fired one of these?" she asked, changing the subject.

"During the Intus campaign—we were sent forward to scout a Zodark outpost that controlled a supply line through the region. When we got on target, we went to work. Turns out, we got a pretty high-value target that was running operations for the enemy. When the rest of the company attacked, they fell into chaos."

"Sometimes it only takes one bullet," Moreau responded.

"Most of the time, it takes a lot more," Kodiak countered.

As the grade of the trail gradually climbed, the team focused on their footing more and more. Where the trail had been wide on both sides in the beginning, it now only allowed them to move one behind the other. Kodiak stole a glance down the steep cliff face into the darkness below and shuddered. He couldn't help but let his mind wander, envisioning himself stepping on a loose rock and hurtling downward to certain death.

Kodiak had known more than a few soldiers who had died not by enemy fire but by mistakes—whether they had fallen off a cliff or been killed in a training exercise. He'd even known a few soldiers who'd died because of the wildlife on some worlds. Humanity's military was in the unique space between the old world order and the new. When fighting had been restricted to their home world of Earth, everything had been close—soldiers would deploy for half a year and then go back home to whatever country they hailed from. Kodiak hadn't been back to Earth in years.

After graduating basic training, Kodiak had jumped from one planet to another. The Republic would build bases on those newfound worlds, so there was no reason to go back to Earth unless he won the leave lottery, which was a crapshoot. As Kodiak looked up at the night sky, he searched for the bright point that signified Earth's sun but gave up after a few seconds.

The line had stopped moving and Jacobs turned as he went to a knee. "We've reached Rome."

Kodiak brought up the map on his heads-up display and marked their location. Switching to a communication channel, he used an encrypted text channel to alert Lieutenant Magnussen that they had passed their first checkpoint.

He turned back to the others. "From here on out, we are radio silent. The Zodarks will no doubt be intercepting any traffic made over those lines, so if you need to report anything, if Moreau or I go down, do it over encrypted text channels. It's delayed, but it's what we've got to work with."

The others nodded in acknowledgment and the line began to move again. Their next stop was the peak overlooking Junger's Pass.
****

Magnussen didn't dream. He hadn't since the Intus campaign, since his first time in combat. When he was nudged awake, he stared into the face of Lieutenant Singletary. Swinging his legs over his cot, Magnussen strapped his boots up tight and stood, allowing the blood to start flowing through his limbs again.

He made his way over to the table and looked across to First Platoon's leader. "Where are we at with the scouting operation?"

Singletary flipped his data pad up, and the encrypted message from Sergeant Kodiak hovered over the table. "The team has reached Checkpoint Rome. Next stop is Junger's Pass, where they should arrive no later than 0100 hours, planet time."

"Any resistance so far?"

"Nothing yet, but they've moved further into enemy country than we have since the invasion. We're kind of flying blind on this one as far as enemy strength."

Magnussen looked to the platoon leader, his eyes heavy and serious. "Is Kodiak going to muck this up, Adam?"

Singletary looked taken aback for a moment but recovered. "He's a very good team leader and has extensive real-world experience with sniping during past campaigns. He's a vet, and I trust him."

Magnussen relaxed. "Hell, I'm sorry, Adam. It's been a rough couple of weeks. I'd be lying if I said I wasn't feeling in over my head."

Singletary sighed and sat down on a crate of equipment in the corner. "We're all struggling right now, Henry. The important thing is keeping our heads in the game now more than ever. I must believe these were the moments they prepared us for in the Academy."

Magnussen snorted. "What was it Colonel Forsythe always said?"

"'When going through hell, keep moving'? I think that's one of those sayings passed on through the military for the last hundred years."

"Doesn't make it any less true. Fenti is probably in another system. As far as officers go, we're it. So that brings me to the most important thing I need to talk to you about. If Kodiak and his team are overrun or if the Zodarks are in fact on their way to this base, I'm gonna need you to lead the company to our next location while I stay back and coordinate the tactical retreat."

Singletary nodded and that was all Magnussen needed from him, an understanding that if something were to go wrong, there always needed to be at least one officer able to lead what was left of Apollo Company.

Chapter Four
Innocence Lost

Junger's Pass
Alfheim

As Harrison Kodiak and his team continued their trek toward the pass, the weather took a turn. Slowly, clouds rolled in, blocking out the light from the moons. Wind and snow swirled around, reducing visibility. Every time a gust whipped down the trail, Kodiak felt as if he would be pushed over the edge.

Their tactical map showed their progress was still on schedule, and the cliffs overlooking the pass were only three more miles along the winding trail. The path had widened more, and their movements were being masked by the forest that seemed to have sprouted out of nowhere. One minute they had been surrounded by nothing but rocks and snow, then trees had risen on either side of them. Then their movement stopped.

Moving up the line to Jacobs, Kodiak knelt beside him. "What'd ya see?"

"I can't see a damn thing, to be honest, Sarge. But I heard something, like a shuffling of feet," Jacobs replied tensely, his rifle aimed in the general direction of the disturbance.

Kodiak silently waited for a few moments and heard what sounded like four feet crunching through the freshly fallen snow. He motioned to the three others to get into cover and watched them place their backs to the rock embankment on their left.

Slowly, Kodiak crawled up the rocks. He switched his night vision to thermal imaging and scanned the forests ahead. The mountain wasn't terribly steep anymore as they had moved closer to its summit. On the other side of the embankment was a thick forest that seemed to stretch for kilometers into a valley surrounded by the same forest and high cliffs.

As he scanned in front of him, a bright orange-and-red figure crept into his sight. He instinctively lowered his head again to keep out of the enemy's line of sight while also keeping whatever it was in his field of vision. It was one of the four-legged beasts called Ravagers the Zodarks used to patrol and sniff out enemies. A cold shiver went down his spine. The beast was accompanied by two Zodarks who walked behind the animal. Their body language looked lazy and not alert.

Kodiak waved his arm behind him, and Moreau slowly made her way up and took a spot next to him. When he heard her gasp a little, Kodiak knew she too was looking through her thermal imaging.

"We can't take 'em, Harrison. It'll compromise the mission," she reminded him.

"Don't have to tell me twice. We'll wait for them to pass and then continue moving," Kodiak responded.

He watched as the enemy continued its slow patrol southward. Suddenly, the four-legged beast stopped. Kodiak was about to slide back down the embankment when he noticed the change in attitude. He watched as the animal turned toward his location and crouched slightly, the spikes on its back bristling and clicking together in warning. The two Zodarks looked alert now as they held on to their rifles more tightly and followed the Ravager as it walked toward their position.

Kodiak turned to the others and called on their helmet's internal communications, "The bastards picked up our scent. I saw some brush a few meters back that could conceal us. Move."

The team turned and quickly but carefully found a cluster of waist-high brush. They pushed themselves into the shadows. Moreau removed an environmental camouflage tarp and placed it over the bushes. The tarp acted as a chameleon did, mimicking the environment it touched and digitally recreating an undisturbed area around it. Whether the Zodarks had the technology to detect it, he didn't know, but he was sure it didn't matter as long as they had the beast with them.

The crunch of snow, the growling, and the low guttural voices of the Zodarks continued to push closer until it sounded as if the patrol was right on top of their position. Kodiak had his rifle placed on the ground with its bipod. He lined up a shot on the beast as it came around the corner but held his fire. He only wanted to use it if he had no other choice.

What was that? Kodiak asked himself. There was a sound he didn't recognize, something akin to a dinner bell being rung back home in Texas. Feet shuffled. Something made of wood creaked. There was a strange animal sound that seemed to be a cross between a cow and a goat.

A figure with two legs, but not as tall as a Zodark, appeared around the bend to their north, walking alongside what looked like a cart being pulled by a beast. The animal had three distinct horns on its head and the body of a bull from Earth. As the figure drew closer, its features became clearer.

A Prim, probably heading home after foraging all day, was walking into their area of operations and right into the path of the patrolling Zodarks. Kodiak's blood pressure spiked. He switched his selector switch from safe to fire and followed the Zodark patrol as it crested the hill and walked down onto the path.

Moreau rested her hand on Kodiak's shoulder. "Don't," she whispered.

Kodiak tensed. He didn't flip the selector back to its safety position, but his finger slowly moved from the trigger well and rested on the side of the rifle. He understood why Moreau had stopped him. If he fired, even to save the Prim, he would jeopardize the mission.

The Zodarks saw the Prim walking and raised their rifles, yelling at him in their guttural language. Kodiak switched on his translator and tried to listen to the conversation, turning the sensitivity on his helmet's microphone up. The two Zodarks and their beast approached the Prim, who had already stepped away from his cart and frantically put his arms into the air. Kodiak strained to listen to their conversation.

"What are you doing out here?" one of the Zodarks barked.

The Prim just stood there with his hands in the air, visibly shaking.

Kodiak's finger went back into the trigger well and rested softly on the metal. The moral dilemma presented by the situation was beginning to weigh on his shoulders. If he fired and they ambushed the Zodarks, even managed to kill them and save the Prim, they would compromise their mission without getting to the objective. If he held his fire, the Prim would undoubtedly be killed. It wasn't fair, but nothing about war ever was.

"Damn," Kodiak hissed to himself as his finger moved away from the trigger once again.

Deepak shifted next to Kodiak. "We have to save the Prim, right?" he asked through their internal comms.

"If we kill them, the mission is over before it began," Moreau interjected.

"So, what? We just watch him die? You have to be kidding me, Sarge," Jacobs butted in.

"This is not up for discussion. Fall in line and shut up. I don't like this any more than you," Kodiak hissed back.

That was all they needed. Everyone remained quiet.

The Zodarks remained where they had stopped on the trail, but the beast moved slowly toward the Prim. The terrified Prim didn't run—why would he? There was no conceivable way he could outrun one of those dogs. The Prim slowly knelt on the snow and bowed its head in what Kodiak thought resembled prayer.

One of the Zodarks laughed. "A species so weak it would rather pray than fight. Pathetic."

"End this. We don't have time for games," the other Zodark ordered.

The Zodark who had laughed shrieked loudly, the echo bouncing off the mountains around them. The beast lunged forward and clasped its teeth around the Prim's head, crushing it with a savage bite before carrying the body up the embankment. The two Zodarks moved past Kodiak's position, pausing momentarily, and Kodiak thought they had been caught. They turned, however, and continued down the bend and out of sight.

The team waited under the tarp for several more minutes before hurriedly wrapping it up and continuing up the trail toward the summit. Kodiak looked back into the darkness, wondering if he could have done anything that would have saved the Prim and not compromised their mission. As they crested the top of the trail and approached the cliff's edge, he concluded there was, in fact, nothing he could've done, and that was what bothered him the most.

For the next twenty minutes, Kodiak continuously ran the scenario through his head. Every possible detail came back to him. Some he dismissed, not knowing if they were real or if his brain was compensating for the missing pieces. War was messy even when it was confined to a single planet. Kodiak had now fought on three different worlds. He had experienced different alien species, animals, and plant life. He had killed and had friends killed through the years, and it had never gotten any easier.

Kodiak might have been social with his soldiers, but he had always been a bit of a loner in his personal life. He would always watch as soldiers under his command wrote home almost every night. They talked to their sweethearts or spouses and made promises of seeing them again, even though they knew they couldn't keep a promise like that. He didn't have to worry about any of it. Sure, he'd met a woman from time to time since he had been in, but he never really looked for anything more than a one-night stand. Less chance of being disappointed when she'd eventually leave, or he redeployed for another campaign.

The real reason he didn't look for companionship, though, was the thought of losing it all. If he had a steady girlfriend, fiancée, or wife, then he'd have something to lose, something he cared about more than himself or his soldiers. Replacements came and died all the time in his platoon, even in his squad, and he hated getting to know them only to see them get killed. He couldn't imagine doing that to someone else.

The hill leveled out as the scout team approached what looked like the cliffs above Junger's Pass. Jacobs was the first to lie prone, and the rest followed suit as Kodiak made his way over to him. Faint light glowed throughout the mountain pass below, but Kodiak wouldn't have any sense of what he was looking at until they dug in.

He activated their internal comms. "I want Jacobs and Deepak to set up security to our rear. Moreau will stay up here with me. I'll message back to Lieutenant Magnussen and see what he has to say."

Jacobs and Deepak moved back toward their rear to set up the security positions to protect Moreau and Kodiak from anyone or anything that might wander up on them. The cliff's edge was only feet away from Kodiak as he removed the long sniper rifle from his back armor plate and brought it to his front. The bipod clicked loose and snapped downward to prop the muzzle of the rifle skyward. The sight acted more as a camera, relaying the information to his helmet visor's HUD. The rifle's reticle was currently pointing skyward, but soon a picture formed as he lowered the rifle into his shoulder and scanned below.

In the mountain pass, the faint light gave way to kilometers and kilometers of enemy vehicles and camps. Kodiak used the magnification on his visor to look closely at the enemy position and gasped audibly. Thousands of Zodark and Orbots were camped inside the mountain pass. If the Republic still had air superiority, it would've been a costly mistake for the enemy. However, the Zodarks ruled the skies of Alfheim, so they felt perfectly safe congregating in large numbers.

Zodark armored vehicles were parked in makeshift motor pools among each section of the camp. It had to be a brigade-sized element. Kodiak observed Zodarks pulling down shelters and packing up supplies. Some of the vehicles were already congregated toward the crest of Junger's Pass. *Crap! They're headed for the base*, he realized. Junger's

Pass had been a major highway system for the Primords before the war. Now the roads were being used to move soldiers rapidly through the mountain instead of losing time going around.

Kodiak remembered that when they'd first arrived on Alfheim, the initial plan had been to seize the dam and then push the entire battalion through Junger's Pass and use it as a solid launching point for further operations. After the dam had been destroyed, the plan had changed, and then the invasion had put it to rest for good. The Zodarks were now using the pass for that same reason. After the operation the other week, their scopes in orbit must have picked up the human movement. It was possible they had watched the Republic soldiers waltz right into the caves.

Kodiak took picture after picture and added them all to the same encrypted message, which he then sent out to Lieutenant Magnussen:

Sir,

Zodark brigade-sized element gathering to maneuver through Junger's Pass. Enemy has armored vehicles, line infantry, and support elements. Location of base possibly compromised. Please advise.

Sergeant Harrison Kodiak

****

When Magnussen's data pad beeped, brightening the dimly lit cavern, he snapped to his feet and retrieved it from the table. The message sent by Sergeant Kodiak was as clear as the ice on the planet surface. The Zodarks were coming. As he swiped through the different pictures attached to the message, the overall size of the enemy army was staggering. They had thousands of Zodark and Orbot soldiers and vehicles preparing to bear down on them. It was only a matter of time before they began moving toward their base camp.

A commotion behind Magnussen took him away from the pictures. Singletary marched in after the Prim commander, Hamza. The Prim was smiling, his pointed ears standing noticeably straighter than usual. His appearance and demeanor aggravated Magnussen because he was no doubt about to tell him that the plan to attack the orbital elevators was ready.

Despite how he felt, Magnussen put on a smile as he handed his data pad to Singletary. "Commander Hamza, thank you for coming. What can we help you with?"

"It is a good day, Lieutenant Magnussen. I have received word shortly before coming out here that your Republic Delta soldiers have somehow found a way they'll be able to insert onto the planet and are currently coordinating efforts for a reinvasion of the planet by Republic forces."

That was not the news Magnussen had been expecting, and it momentarily put him off-balance in the conversation. He had been about to tell Hamza that they couldn't talk at the moment, but now he was being reeled in.

Damn.

"We have a situation of our own currently, Commander," Magnussen revealed. "I've sent a scouting party to Junger's Pass. After the other week, we assumed that our position could have been compromised."

Hamza's face changed. "Junger's Pass is a long way from here. Have you received any information from your team?"

"We did, and I'm afraid it's not good news. They've spotted what appears to be a combined Zodark and Orbot force gearing up to go through the pass. My estimates put them less than a day away from us. We don't have time to pull our team at the pass back before we have to relocate, which needs to happen now."

"Relocate?" Hamza asked in disbelief. "Relocate where? What about the operation to take out the elevators?"

"If we don't move from this cave system immediately, you aren't going to have an operation. So please, for the sake of your planet, find me somewhere to take my soldiers."

Hamza looked at Magnussen with his piercing black eyes, emotionless, hard to read, but he finally made his way over to the table in the CIC. He removed his own data pad and sent a three-dimensional map hovering over the table. He spun the map and looked thoughtfully for a moment before drawing a path in the air between two sections.

"This is the most direct route to another cave system. It'll be able to house your vehicles and your soldiers, but it can only be temporary. If what you say is true and the Zodarks do attack here, then the next logical position would be those caves."

"If you can get us there, then we will immediately begin plans for the operation to destroy those elevators, but we need to start this now."

Hamza closed the map and removed his pad from the table, sliding it into his armor. "You have my word, Lieutenant."

Magnussen went into overdrive and turned to Singletary. "I want you to prepare everyone to move right now. I'll send word to Kodiak with the location of our new base of operations, but they'll be on their own to get there. You'll lead the first group out of the cave's back. They'll have to move out in intervals—we can't let the Zodarks see a massive group of humans leaving this area, so make sure you keep the groups spaced out. It'll take most of the night, but it's the only way."

"Where will you be during the movement, sir?" asked Master Sergeant Woods, the platoon sergeant.

"I'll move out with the last group. This is not up for discussion. Lieutenant Singletary will take the first group. This way, there will be at least one officer able to take charge of things on that end."

"Then I'm staying with you," said Woods, his senior NCO. *That's nonnegotiable.*"

Magnussen didn't have the time or the strength to fight the old war dog on that, so he let it go. "Let's get this done, men." He turned to Hamza. "And thank you, Commander."

"If this works out, it will be I who is thanking you, Lieutenant. These Zodark and Orbot hibtors won't know what hits them when our combined fleets arrive."

Magnussen let out a small chuckle. He'd learned what the Primord word *hibtors* meant, and now whenever someone said it, it made him laugh. Hibtor was a cross between calling someone a bastard and someone who practiced bestiality. It was just one of those words that didn't translate really well in English, so it amused the humans who heard it. In this particular case, it was aptly used. The Zodarks and Orbots had no idea what would be showing up if the Deltas managed to get planetside.

Chapter Five
Fire on the Mountain

Alfheim

After sending his message about their situation to Lieutenant Magnussen, Sergeant Harrison Kodiak waited nervously to see if the Zodarks would begin to mobilize below. In theory, it had yet to be proven whether they could intercept human text transmissions, but Kodiak didn't want to be the first to find out they could. For an hour, he sat beside Moreau, waiting for a laser bolt to come flying up to their position from below, but as time passed, he relaxed. Then he saw Magnussen's response.

Kodiak cussed under his breath as he read the message. He forwarded it to Moreau.

"He can't be serious," Moreau remarked incredulously through their internal comms.

"Those are our orders, Angeline," Kodiak responded, using her first name to emphasize the seriousness of it all. He then turned behind him and made eye contact with Jacobs and Kumar, who were lying low. "Rally on me, team."

Kumar and Jacobs moved out of the darkness up toward Kodiak's position and took a knee next to him.

"What's the word, boss?" Kumar asked as he shouldered his rifle.

"Apparently, our Prim allies have identified some high-value targets amongst the enemy force moving toward us. In light of this new intelligence, Lieutenant Magnussen has ordered us to take them out. The HVTs are an Orbot and Zodark senior commander. They appear to be traveling with that force down there—"

Interrupting him, Kumar blurted out, "Bloody hell! They're really trying to get us killed on this mission."

"Cut that crap out, Deepak," Kodiak shot back hotly. "I don't do suicide missions." He took a deep breath and recalibrated. "Looking at the maps, everything points toward the enemy using this pass to get to our base in the cave. This is the ideal place for us to take these guys out. Plus, we need to buy more time for Lieutenant Magnussen to move the remainder of our people to another cave system with the assistance of the Prims. I'm uploading the coordinates of the new base to your heads-up display; this is where we'll be heading once we start the festivities on our end. You'll have to use that encryption tool we talked about."

"OK, so what's the plan? Take these HVTs out and move back to the ATVs?" Kumar inquired.

"To be honest, I don't think we'll have time to move back to the vehicles," Moreau said, jumping in. "Most likely, we'll move to our south, down the slope and into the trees to get away from these guys."

"I agree," Kodiak chimed in. "Once we zap these guys, you can bet they'll be madder than a hornet. Once we're safely hidden in the forest, we'll start our movement to the new base and stay as hidden as possible."

"When's this going down?" Jacobs asked, a pensive look on his face.

"The targets are down there right now, so let's get ready to do this," Kodiak answered, a devilish grin spreading across his face.

Jacobs and Kumar smirked and nodded. Then they began preparing some fun little surprises for the soldiers who would invariably pursue them. It was their job to buy everyone enough time to get away, and they'd brought just the tools to make it happen.

Kodiak was sure Alfheim was the first campaign where Jacobs and Kumar had fought. They'd survived that horrible attack on their base, and they'd endured everything else the enemy had thrown at them. If they all lived long enough to be rescued, he was going to make a point of ensuring they received a couple of valor medals for everything they'd done. The fact that they had volunteered to be in the military only added to his level of respect for them.

When the war with the Zodarks had first broken out, the Republic Armed Forces had been an all-volunteer force. It had stayed an all-volunteer force for the first couple of years, but when the Altairians had invited them into their protectorate, it had come with certain strings—like consolidating the world's governments into one, same with the military. Then came the military quotas. They needed to grow and contribute a ground force of twenty million and a space force of nearly a thousand ships. In time, these numbers wouldn't be a problem to reach, but as casualties mounted from major battles, it became incredibly hard to maintain this quota. That was when the draft had been initiated, as well as the ten-year service terms.

Still, many people from Sol had volunteered. People like Jacobs and Kumar who'd joined, knowing they might never see Earth again, or at least during the term of their enlistment. Everyone knew the odds of returning to Earth were slim. In a way, it made people fight harder than they otherwise might have. Too much was riding on them achieving victory and protecting Earth from these terrible beasts.

As Kodiak set up the tripod to his rifle, he quietly expressed some of his frustration with this mission privately to a fellow NCO. "This is utter crap, Moreau."

She patted him on the shoulder as he looked over the barrel of his rifle. "Look at it this way, big guy. If we pull these shots off, we can give our people a real chance of escaping and continuing the fight," Moreau countered. "Taking these two commanders out just might give our people the edge we need to outfox them one more time."

"You're right, as usual. Let's do this thing and hope we live to tell about it," Kodiak grumbled through gritted teeth as he pulled the rifle's stock into his shoulder, lowering his cheek to peer through his scope.

As Moreau searched for her target, she laughed. "Bet you're glad I brought this rifle now, aren't you?"

"Understatement of the deployment goes to you, Angie."

Kodiak watched the Zodarks through his scope. Without too much effort, he was able to pick out the Zodark and Orbot commanders, surrounded by a circle of bodyguards. The Orbots didn't have distinguishing uniforms like the Zodarks did, but it was still clear that these were the two in charge. The hulking Zodark waved his arms theatrically in the air as they discussed something. Trying to figure out what the Orbot was doing was a bit more difficult since Kodiak couldn't really get a read on their facial expressions like he could with a Zodark.

"On target," Kodiak reported, flicking his safety to the fire position.

"On target," Moreau replied, confirming her own sight picture.

"On me," Kodiak said as he moved his trigger finger into the trigger well and slowly depressed the trigger.

The rifle barked and was followed less than a second later by Moreau's rifle report. The magrail slug left the rifle, its magnetic force keeping the solid piece of tungsten rod from dropping too much due to the massive range.

Kodiak watched through his scope as the head of the Zodark disintegrated and his body fell like a puppet having its strings cut. The Orbot didn't have a chance to move before Moreau's round impacted center mass into its bulbous body. Sparks flew and a dark liquid sprayed the white snow around the area before the Orbot collapsed to the ground, dead.

Kodiak smiled and took his eyes away from the scope to look at Moreau. "Mission accomplished." The words typed themselves on his helmet's HUD, which sent the encrypted message to Lieutenant Magnussen back in their underground base.

The celebration was short-lived, however. Enemy laser bolts slammed into the rock face in front of them. The rifle reports had echoed through the pass, letting the Zodarks know some human soldiers were nearby. In seconds, they were on them. Small units fired at them while others bounded forward at lightning speed, rapidly closing the distance between them.

Kodiak jumped to his feet with Moreau. They raced down the slope toward Jacobs and Kumar, who had come out from their hides at the sound of their teammates' rifle fire.

Kodiak patted Jacobs on the shoulder as he ran past. "Time to go! Get to the tree line!"

The green cover was some three hundred meters down the side of the ridge they'd just fired from. It was an easy run when no one was being shot at, but the added danger gave the team an extra boost as they sprinted downslope.

The enemy fire had stopped. The Zodarks and Orbots likely realized their human foes were racing down the other side of the ridge, zigzagging down the steep decline.

Kodiak felt a low rumble in the air, and the ground around him vibrated. He turned to look over his shoulder at what could be headed toward them when his eyes caught sight of something that caused his heart to skip a beat. Three Zodark fighters were sweeping down from the clouds above them as they flew over top of the vehicles and soldiers on the opposite side of the ridge. The fighters had locked on to them, angling themselves for an attack run.

"Run! Get to that damn tree line or we're dead!" Kodiak roared.

The night turned darker as Kodiak escaped into the safety of the trees' canopy, the thick branches shielding him. He ran at least twenty meters into the forest before he spun around, leveraging the trunk of a nearby tree as a shield. He watched as Moreau and Jacobs bounded into the trees and ran toward him. But Kumar had fallen further behind them. He'd lost his footing on the loose soil and tumbled to the ground.

By the time Kumar regained his footing and began running again, the Zodark fighters had lined up for their gun run and opened fire. Two lines of blue laser fire scorched the ground behind Kumar as they raced after him. A look of terror spread across his face.

"Come on, Deepak! Keep running!" Jacobs yelled from the safety of the tree line.

Moreau and Jacobs had their rifles up. They fired at the nearest fighter, but their blaster bolts caused no damage to the fighter.

"Switch to magrails!" Kodiak yelled, urgency in his voice as Kumar ran toward them for all he was worth.

Kodiak tried to will Kumar's feet to go faster as they switched their rifles from blaster to magrail. Kodiak watched as one of his slugs impacted against the cockpit of the lead fighter. The glass windshield shattered from the impact. As the third, fourth, and fifth slugs punched their way into the pilot's seat, Kodiak saw a blue splotch splatter across the remains of the windshield. The fighter lost control, and it careened into the ground as it cartwheeled. It rotated wildly, with some pieces falling off it as it tumbled, until it rolled right on top of Kumar. Then it crashed to a halt against the first line of tree trunks.

"No, no, no! This can't be happening!" Kodiak railed as he dropped his rifle to the ground, sinking to his knees in sheer frustration and anger. Tears streamed down his face as he lost it emotionally.

"Come on, Kodiak. We have to get out of here. It's what he would have wanted," Moreau said to him as she and Jacobs pulled him back to his feet.

The two remaining fighters flew overhead but were unable to locate them visually in the forest. The three of them activated the stealth mode on their combat suits, temporarily spoofing their aerial sensors to prevent the Zodark fighters from tracking them. If Kodiak, Moreau and Jacobs were lucky, they'd slip away from the Zodarks and live to fight another day.

****

Lieutenant Magnussen had just walked back from the rear exit of the cave with the mech soldiers after checking to see that they were ready to pull out. They were securing the exit with demolition charges as the platoons lined up for their long walks to the next base. Meanwhile, Magnussen kept his data pad clutched in his hands, waiting for the familiar buzz to let him know how his scouting party had made out. When he returned to the CIC, he put his pad on the table and sat down.

Lieutenant Singletary walked in. "The medics and their wounded will head out with two mechs as their security. First Platoon will follow, then Second, and so on and so forth."

Magnussen looked up to his friend and executive officer. Singletary appeared to be very tired. Magnussen realized he probably looked just as tired—there were bags under his bloodshot eyes, and his unshaved face was beginning to itch. The war was already taking its toll on him and the one other officer still alive in what was left of their company, a mere shell of what he had once been.

"Adam," Magnussen began as he stood, "I was being serious about you moving out first. I need you to go with the medics and mechs as soon as we receive word from the scouting party. It's imperative these soldiers have at least one officer in case this whole thing goes south."

"I know. It doesn't mean I have to be happy about it, Henry," Singletary replied.

"Hell, Adam, you think I'm happy about any of this? We're beyond having our backs against a wall. We've been pushed up against the wall and beaten within an inch of our lives. But as long as we're breathing, we can fight."

"And we will," Singletary confirmed with a grim nod.

The data pad buzzed on the table and Magnussen grabbed it. As soon as he read the message, he breathed a sigh of relief. "Mission accomplished." He held up the screen. "Begin your movement. We're leaving."

****

Medic Platoon

Corporal Eva Jorgensen looked out of the cave's exit and into the cold night. Wind whipped flurries of snow into tiny tornadoes that danced around the idle medical Cougar. The back ramp was lowered and the last of the critically injured were being loaded aboard and stabilized in preparation for departure. The back was filled with wounded lying on the floor in some places.

Because of the tight fit inside the vehicle, Jorgensen was going to brave the journey on foot next to the hulking mechs that were coming along to provide security. Inside the Cougar, their platoon medic, Staff Sergeant Oliver Moore, would make sure the patients were cared for.

Jorgensen slapped her hand on the outside of the hulking armored personnel carrier and shouted over the engine. "All right. Let's move out!"

The door in the back slowly rose, and Moore's strained face disappeared behind it as he continued to monitor some of the more seriously wounded soldiers. Jorgensen took her first steps out of the cave and into the night. The Cougar's engine noise was muffled as it left the small confines of the cavern and moved into the open air, flanked on both sides by a mech. A mech operator she wasn't too familiar with gave her a thumbs-up as the mech's big legs pushed past her, and then she felt eerily alone.

She wasn't by herself, though. Jorgensen looked around her. Numerous walking wounded trudged along in the snow, their armor helping to push their wounded limbs to their limits while injecting them with adrenaline. They were the first wave to brave the long trek to the new base of operations. They were the guinea pigs. If their convoy was attacked, there would be little the mechs and Cougar could do to hold back the onslaught that would take place. When Zodarks attacked, they swarmed an area, favoring brute strength over tactical brilliance.

"Doing all right, Corporal Jorgensen?" a voice called from beside her. Lieutenant Singletary, the de facto executive officer of what was left of Apollo Company, moved like a phantom in the night.

"I'll be doing a lot better once we make it to the new cave," Jorgensen replied.

"I'm with you there." The lieutenant sighed. "At our current pace, we should make it there with a lot of time to spare for the other squads, but we'll be pushing it."

"I can tell Sergeant Moore to pick up the pace of the vehicle, sir," Jorgensen offered.

"No. That won't be necessary. If we push the wounded too hard through these conditions, we may arrive in better time, but at what cost? This movement will be for nothing if we lose people along the way. Keep their spirits up and keep them moving. That's all there is to it."

Jorgensen nodded. The lieutenant patted her on the shoulder and left to check on the rest of the soldiers.

Jorgensen thought back to when she had arrived with the unit, just before the Intus campaign. In her rush to make a good impression, she had forgotten her paperwork. The master sergeant behind the desk, a mean-looking man with a missing leg, had berated her and threatened to write her up before she'd even reported to the company. Lieutenant Singletary, only a second lieutenant at the time, had stepped forward and dealt with the situation. He was a good man and always tried to do right by his platoon.

The war had become a revolving door of newly enlisted and officers from the Academy. When the newer soldiers met someone from the battles of New Eden, or at this point even Intus, they quickly figured out to follow them, or died because they didn't figure it out in time. Singletary was an officer everyone looked to when wondering what to do next. Ever since he had come to Apollo Company, through every engagement they'd had, he'd been in the thick of it. The fact he was still alive was a testament to who the man was: a true warrior.

"Doing all right, love?" came the smooth Irish accent of Mac from behind her.

He had made her jump. She looked behind herself and watched him walk alongside. "I'll be fine compared to the others with us. How are you?"

"Right as rain," he replied.

A silence fell over them. They hadn't talked in a while, not because they were mad at each other but because they had both been preoccupied with their squads since their FOB had been overrun. Jorgensen stole the occasional glance or two at Mac and would catch him doing the same, but with the odd hours they were putting in, their paths rarely crossed.

"I wish I knew how Kodiak's team was doing," Jorgensen said, breaking the silence.

"He's a tough man—he'll think of something. Plus, he's got Sergeant Moreau with him, and she's as solid as anyone left alive."

Jorgensen was surprised and a bit unsettled. She hadn't known that Sergeant Moreau had gone with Kodiak's scouting party. They were both very good NCOs, and losing just one of them would leave a serious experience vacuum. But both? She didn't want to think about that. Their situation already seemed so helpless; she didn't think she could handle one more blow.

****

Sergeant Harrison Kodiak grabbed a few fallen branches and covered the cylindrical explosive he had placed near a tree. The bouncing betties activated when an organic creature passed within a couple meters of the object. Then they would shoot into the air, about chest level for a Zodark, and explode into thousands of deadly pieces of shrapnel. Kodiak's scout team, or what was left of it, had littered their path with tons of the explosive devices, and he had just placed their final one.

"Let's keep moving," Kodiak ordered as he stood and continued south toward the edge of the forest.

The woodland ended in ten more miles. Looking at the map on his heads-up display, Kodiak saw a river that snaked through the forest's edge. If they followed that path, they could reach the new base. If his plan worked, they could be home before daybreak, but he knew that almost no plan survived first contact. Kodiak still had to account for the Zodarks chasing them down.

After Deepak Kumar had been killed, the team had watched the remaining Zodark aircraft break off and climb away into the distance. Soon, more Zodark craft had come into view from below the cliff's lip above them, and they'd watched as transport vehicles landed a couple of Zodark squads on the slope. Kodiak, Moreau, and Jacobs had seen all they needed to, and they fell back deeper into the thick Alfheim trees.

Kodiak looked over to Moreau, who was now carrying Kumar's rifle. "Where's *your* rifle?"

She glanced at him from the corner of her eye but didn't turn her head. "Give me a break. They aren't going to give a damn about my rifle when we get back. *If* we get back."

He reached out and punched her arm lightly. "I'm just giving you a hard time. You threw it in my face about bringing it along, and now look at you, you ditched it for a smaller model."

"What would you rather carry for miles while being chased by Zodarks?"

Kodiak looked down at the long rifle he still carried. "You're right about that."

"You can have mine when I die," Jacobs chimed in.

Kodiak stopped, and so did the other two. "Both of you listen up. Stop saying *if we get back* and *when I die*. That helps absolutely no one and makes my job harder. We did our job, Kumar did his job, and I intend on having us complete this godforsaken mission. I'll be damned if we're going to let Kumar die for no reason."

"He *did* die for no reason," Jacobs snapped back. "You think killing a couple of generals is going to win this war? Win this damn planet back? We're outgunned and outmanned. What do you think is going to happen if we do get to this new base? The big blue men are just gonna give up and go back home? No, they're going to continue to look for us until they slaughter every one of us."

Moreau stepped forward, but Kodiak raised his hand. "You know how many campaigns I've fought in, Jacobs? I've fought on Eden twice, Intus, and now Alfheim. I've been doing this for twelve years. How old are you? Eighteen? I was your age when I enlisted. That's right—I wasn't drafted into this, I *enlisted* for this crap. I'm thirty now, and in the time I've been in, I've seen amazing soldiers ripped in two and innocents get a harsh lesson in the true evils of this universe. I haven't seen Earth for more than a decade. I'm tired, so damn tired. I'm tired of seeing good soldiers die for no good reason other than *take that hill* and still I drive on, and you know why? Because I still have hope and sometimes that's *all* you need."

Jacobs stood silent, unmoving, and because of his helmet, Kodiak couldn't read the young man's face to guess what he was thinking.

"I'm sorry," Jacobs finally said, his voice trembling a bit. "I'm just—" He took a step forward but then leaned against a tree and squatted down. "I'm just so damn scared."

Kodiak knelt next to him and put his arm on his shoulder. "We all are. If anyone tells you differently, they're lying. That's what makes you human. That's what makes you more than those savage blue beasts. Use that fear to push you forward. Use your emotions to your advantage because *that* is why I'm still here twelve years later."

Suddenly, an explosion pierced the night in the distance. The Zodarks had run into the first field of mines. Kodiak stood and looked toward where the detonation had come from. He focused but didn't see any movement, either with his night vision or his thermals. They hadn't been found, at least not yet.

"That's it. We need to move. You good?" he asked, looking back to Jacobs, who was now standing.

"No, but I'll manage."

"Good man," Kodiak responded, turning and marching south, toward the river.

****

Private First Class Andre Bastille had set the grid location of the new base into his mech's navigation, reduced its automatic speed to five miles per hour, and engaged his auto-walk. Now he sat back and watched the snow flurries bounce off his canopy and melt against the six-inch-thick glass. Andre had fired his mech's weapons only once during the attack on the FOB. Before that, he had come down the well and trained with the machine that would become his home away from home.

Home, Andre thought. France seemed so far right now. It was starting to feel like a lifetime ago, though it had only been two years. Just the very thought of home still made him sick. A lot of the soldiers he'd met on his way to Alfheim had been drafted or enlisted near the same time he'd been—all replacements headed for the killing fields. When he was down on Alfheim, though, he'd met a lot of veterans, and every single one of them had the same story of not having been back to Earth since they'd entered service. Of course, some with the most grievous of wounds had gone back home, but those were few and far between. The only ones he had personally seen leave to return to Earth were the soldiers in body bags.

He glanced at Jones. "Do you miss Australia?" he asked over his team's internal comms.

The question was obviously intended for their Australian sergeant. She responded, "I find myself thinking about her every once in a while, mate, but don't dwell on home for too long. Pretty soon that's all you'll think about—"

"And then you're dead," Abede cut in sarcastically. The obvious grin he had could be heard through his words.

"It'll distract you from the mission," Jones retorted. "At that point, you might as well be dead. I've seen a lot of privates succumb to the slip-space blues, Bastille. Even more once they get dirtside. Best thing to do is hope you make it through this crap and end up at a fully sick base on New Eden or something."

"What's the best place you've been stationed?" Andre pressed.

"New Eden for sure. I got there after we took it, of course, but it was still absolutely deadly."

"Deadly? How so?"

"It's Aussie for *really awesome*, mate. Don't get lost in translation."

Andre paused. "Well. Here's hoping," he finally replied.

"When we do go back up the well and get to an outpost somewhere, I'll buy the first rounds. How's that sound?" asked Abede.

Andre's ears perked up. "Sounds like a plan."

With all his focus pointing itself toward the negatives like homesickness, death, and combat, it had become increasingly difficult to see a future past Alfheim. Even in the tough spot his team was in, they remained optimistic, or at least gave the appearance of optimism, and regardless of whether it was the former or the latter, Andre didn't care. What mattered now was getting to that cave and then back home.
****

Mac had shifted over to the other side of the slowly moving Cougar, leaving Jorgensen alone with her thoughts once more. She had been walking alongside the vehicle for the past hour. By now, another squad had already left the cave and should be trailing at a safe distance in the rear. When she chanced a look behind her, she saw a few stragglers, walking wounded, but everything beyond them faded into the blackness of the night.

This had turned into the loneliest forced march she had ever taken part in. Back at the garrison, she had music playing in her ears on ruck marches to help pass the time; in combat, the occasional radio chatter echoed in her comms. Tonight, the comms were dark while they attempted to cover their movement to a new hideout.

For the past week, reports had indicated that there were other Republic platoons scattered around the planet, fighting to maintain some sort of foothold. The majority sounded like they were in the same situation as they were, forced into guerrilla tactics to remain in the fight. She had heard rumors about entire platoons being vaporized by orbital bombardments. It was the reason they were moving out one squad at a time—the Zodarks only used those types of strikes on large pockets of resistance. Still, she chanced a glance upward into the starry night sky every once in a while, wondering if one would drop on her.

"Hey, Doc," a soldier who didn't seem injured called out to her. He was carrying his rifle at the low ready as he had made his way to her.

Jorgensen looked at the nameplate engraved on his armor: *Takata.* "Hello," she replied, wondering why he had chosen to start a conversation with her.

"I'm Private Takata. I'm with the mech platoon."

"I've seen you around. I'm Corporal Jorgenson."

Takata looked around them, acting like a Zodark might jump out from around a bush or tree. "I know who you are, Doc."

"Feeling nervous, Private?" she asked. *He certainly looks nervous.*

He looked down at his rifle and she saw his grip relax a little. "We are outnumbered, vulnerable, and stumbling into the night to who knows where. Not to mention I'm not even in a mech. So, yes, I am a little nervous."

"Why don't you have a mech? Did you lose it in the attack on our FOB?"

Takata chuckled and shook his head. "No. I'm not even technically mech-qualified. I had only been planetside for a few hours before the attack happened. I was in the middle of in-processing to my assigned squad when they attacked. After we fell back to the caves, they didn't know where to put me, so Sergeant Jones took me in."

"She's a good leader. Losing Krauss was a huge blow to that platoon—"

"Yeah, I heard," Takata cut in.

"But Jones is good. Learned everything from Krauss and probably some more. You'll do fine," Jorgensen replied reassuringly.

"See, I don't know if I will," Takata said, speaking as if confessing to a priest. "I didn't fire a single round during the entire attack on the FOB. I was so busy running around trying to find people to fight with, I didn't really know what to do. Then suddenly, we were falling back to the caves. I've fired my weapon since then—just not in direct combat."

Jorgensen looked at the cherry and shook her head. "You were there at the base all the same. You might not have fired a shot during the battle, but you still experienced it. You had the same likelihood of getting killed as anyone else. Keep yourself focused, because this all seems to be coming to a head, and I'd hate for you to miss out." She smiled behind her visor but knew he couldn't see it.

"Thanks, Doc. I appreciate that," Takata replied, picking up his pace a little as he walked ahead.

Sometimes a person just needs to hear that it's going to be all right, she thought.

Jorgensen watched the private move up in the gaggle formation as they continued to push toward their new home. She flipped through different screens on her helmet's HUD by flicking her eyes to the left and right. The coordinates of their new home glowed underneath an orange dot. Their destination was only a mile away now. That meant the final squad was about to disembark from the network of caves that had been their home. Deep down, she hoped this would be the last time they needed to move before reinforcements eventually started arriving.

Chapter Six
Sacrificium

Alfheim

Harrison Kodiak and the remainder of his team had been in a constant state of falling back for over two hours. The glow of sunrise hadn't yet pierced the horizon, but after taking a chance to glance at the time, he realized the cover of darkness was about to fade. They had reached the river and begun to head south, following the rapidly moving water toward their final destination.

The explosions from their antipersonnel mines had stopped about thirty minutes earlier. With how close each blast had sounded, one right after the other, Kodiak believed the Zodarks had reached the end of the minefield they'd left in their wake. Now there would be nothing to slow the vicious blue beasts chasing them down, unless the bastards couldn't swim.

"You think Zodarks can swim?" Kodiak asked.

"What?" Jacobs queried, sounding a little winded.

"Zodarks. The big blue—" Moreau began.

"Yeah, yeah, I know who you're talking about," Jacobs groaned, which slowly turned into laughter from the three of them.

"All right, then. Do you think they can swim?" Kodiak pressed. "Do Zodarks have pools where they come from? Do they even have a life outside of mindlessly fighting? Or is their existence exactly this— killing for their Orbot overlords?"

"Everyone's got a mother, right?" Jacobs shot back. "We all come from somewhere."

Moreau cut in. "There are some animal species on New Eden where the male has the babies."

"What are you going on about?" Jacobs retorted.

"I'm saying that as we continue to move deeper and deeper into the big unknown, a lot of the things we took for granted back home have broadened or taken on an entirely new meaning. For instance, fourteen years ago, we didn't even know aliens existed. Sure, we always had a feeling there might be something out there. Still, we had no idea that we'd come across even one race of aliens, let alone additional humans. As time went on, we came to learn we weren't the only ones blessed with existence in the galaxy. And now here we are, fighting in an alliance with aliens against another alliance full of aliens as well. Who would have thought so much could happen in such a short time frame? I mean, think about it—we're now in some sort of galactic and even intergalactic war. Who could have imagined that?"

"Oh, you've done it now," Kodiak remarked with a laugh as he pushed himself over a boulder that had blocked his route.

"Our perception of the greater existence of beings was narrow-minded," Moreau continued. "We had *laws of physics* and other things that told us this is the way it is, and nothing can move off that path. Now we have ships that run on a power source we never thought possible. Our understanding of the greater galaxy is no longer bound by the speed of a ship's propulsion."

"Hell, Sergeant—forget I asked." Jacobs scoffed at how philosophical she was suddenly becoming.

Moreau trotted past Jacobs and tapped him on the shoulder. "Jacobs, you don't even know the half of it. You'll see. In time you'll start questioning everything."

Kodiak looked over as Jacobs and Moreau advanced past him, stepping from rock to rock and making sure they didn't slip into the raging water to their left. He smiled, letting the prospect of making it back to the new base with his team creep its way into his mind. It was a mistake.

His grin faded as the hair rose on the back of his neck—not because he sensed danger but because he felt the electric charge of a passing laser bolt. The deadly blue bolt passed by him, and Kodiak watched helplessly in slow motion as it pierced Jacobs's back, exited the front of his armor, and embedded itself into the snow. Jacobs's legs buckled and his body crashed down on one of the rocks before slipping into the water and floating away.

"Contact rear!" Kodiak yelled as he dropped behind the nearest boulder. "You still with me, Angie?"

"I'm up! I think Jacobs is gone!" she shouted back from a pile of rocks behind his position.

Swinging his rifle up and bracing it against the rock, Kodiak used his helmet's HUD to search for targets in his rifle's scope. The first Zodark bounded from behind a tree on the other side of the river. Kodiak matched his speed and led the shot, firing a magrail slug. The tungsten rod spun the Zodark around from the force of its impact. Kodiak immediately looked for another target and squeezed the trigger.

The enemy hadn't been able to flank their position yet, but they were sure trying to. Kodiak and Moreau were lucky to have crossed the river when they had. It had created a natural barrier between their position and the ambushing Zodarks.

"Reloading!" Moreau roared.

Kodiak checked his own ammo count as he slammed another magazine into his rifle and brought it up. He couldn't tell how many enemies were on the other side of the river. So far, he'd killed the three that had exposed themselves, but heavier laser fire kept coming down on their position and it was getting harder to bring his rifle to bear.

"I'm moving!" he yelled, pushing off and joining Moreau.

When Kodiak slid behind the rock, he saw his teammate sealing a hole in her thigh armor. "How bad is it, Angie?" he asked.

"I'll live," she responded through clenched teeth.

Kodiak raised his rifle and fired a few more times, taking down two more Zodarks. Their position was becoming untenable. If they stayed there any longer, the Zodarks would eventually find a way to flank them.

"Can you move?" Kodiak inquired.

"Stop asking me questions, Harrison, and just get us out of here," she shot back.

Kodiak nodded. "Then let's move. Can you swim?"
****

Lieutenant Henry Magnussen looked out the rear exit of the cave that had been their base ever since Alfheim had fallen. The last squad had begun their journey into the night. All that was left in their cave system now were the remaining combat Synths and the platoon sergeant, Master Sergeant Woods, who refused to leave the company commander alone.

"Well, Woods, looks like it's about that time," Magnussen sighed as he turned and began making his way back to the formation of combat Synths that waited patiently for his orders.

Woods didn't reply, which was strange for him. Magnussen turned when he noticed Woods wasn't following him and saw him frantically scrolling over several tabs on his data pad. Magnussen began examining his own data pad, going through the multiple tabs of camera relays, unit status markers, and even the blue force trackers that marked his units making the dangerous trek toward the new base.

First Squad had arrived safely behind the medics, who were already setting up a new triage bay. Second Squad was only a mile away, and Third Squad, together with the surviving members of Fourth, continued through the snowy night. Nothing seemed out of the ordinary until Magnussen received an alert from their sensor map.

Motion sensors had been placed around the entire vicinity of the cave, from fifty meters to five hundred meters out—the two-hundred-meter sensor blinked red, warning Magnussen of movement. "They're here. Woods, take half the Synths and start setting up positions around the entrance. We must hold them back for as long as possible. We need to buy the others time!"

Master Sergeant Woods nodded and took off at a modest pace down the cave's corridors with several Synths in tow. Magnussen grabbed twenty more and began securing the rear exit of the caves. As the Synths scaled the walls and placed explosive devices around the mouths of the caves, Magnussen's eyes focused on a Synth that stood out among the others.

He walked over to the medical synthetic and touched its shoulder. "Sam, why aren't you with the rest of the medics?" he asked.

"Sergeant Moore instructed me to stay with you, sir," Sam replied tightly.

Magnussen wanted to mutter a bunch of curses to himself but realized it wouldn't do any good. He looked back out the mouth of the cave and then up to the explosives lining the exit. *It's too late now.*

"All right, Sam. Thank you. Just stay near me because it's about to get really bad."

A deep rumbling shook the caves, dropping rocks and debris onto their heads. Next came a concussive rush of air down the tunnels that kicked dust up everywhere and almost threw Magnussen on his back. Shaking the dust from his face, he called through his comms, "Woods, SITREP!"

"Zodark armored, air, and foot mobiles are at our perimeter about a hundred meters out. It's not looking good, sir."

Magnussen wasn't shocked. He didn't feel a sag in his shoulders or a tinge of regret for not doing enough. In the back of his mind, he had always known this was going to happen; he just hadn't known when. It was why he'd sent all his human soldiers to the next base. It was why he'd kept the Synths behind, and it was why he'd rigged the back exit to explode, blocking the exit for the Zodarks to follow. With that entrance sealed, the enemy would have to traverse the steep mountain range to get to their new location, which would buy the Republic just enough time to finish the fight at their next target, the space elevator.

****

Kodiak looked at his team's status icons one more time to see if Jacobs had any vitals. He was dead. The only solace Kodiak had was that Jacobs hadn't seen it coming, and it had most likely happened too fast for his brain to register any suffering.

More enemy fire slammed into the rocks he and Moreau were utilizing as cover. "It's now or never, Angie. We need to jump," Kodiak said, looking down into the dark, churning water.

"What am I gonna say? No, I'll stay here?" she asked sarcastically before she leaped over the edge into the icy river.

Kodiak watched her armor disappear beneath the rapids, but he chose to take the plunge as well. When his body hit the water, he immediately felt the tug of the current pulling him below the surface. His armor didn't leak, and it tried to adjust its internal temperature to keep him warm, but the water was too cold. Alerts blared on his helmet's HUD, warning him of the cold temperatures, but all he felt now was relief. His helmet had its own supply of reserve oxygen and he had escaped the onslaught of Zodark fire. For the moment, suspended in the fast-moving water, he was safe.

Ice crystals formed on his helmet's visor as he keyed his mic. "How are you holding up?" he asked.

Moreau replied immediately. "My helmet's icing over and the warnings are giving me a headache, but other than that, I'm fine."

Kodiak checked his map and saw the current was pulling them south toward the new coordinates he'd been given. His plan was working perfectly. At some point, they would have to get out of the water before their armored suits locked up from the ice, but his alarms hadn't sent that warning just yet.

"It's a shame about Jacobs," Moreau said. "He seemed like a good kid."

"I didn't know him well. He was in another squad, but he knew his stuff. Just new, that's all."

"At some point in this war, they'll all be new and we'll either be dead, broken, or still wishing we'd never signed up for this crap." Moreau laughed.

"I hated it at first. You know, in basic?" Kodiak said. "You helped keep my head above water."

"We were a pretty good team." Moreau smiled.

"Yeah. We still are, believe it or not," Kodiak remarked. "Even if you did leave me to go be a squad leader."

"People die and others fill their shoes. You of all people should know that."

"Yeah," he sighed. "Doesn't make it any easier. Listen, we'll float like this for another mile or so or until our suits can't take it anymore, but after that, we need to get out and hoof it to those coordinates. Time is no longer on our side. Sunup in two hours."
****

Magnussen jumped behind a wall as a Zodark laser sliced through the air where he had once stood. The enemy had broken through the lines and entered the cave systems, cutting off Magnussen and his Synths from Woods and his. The past few minutes, Woods had been radio silent, despite Magnussen's calls to him, but the gunfire and explosions raged on in that area of the caves, so someone still had to be fighting.

Magnussen looked to his right and saw Sam kneeling behind a wall, his face emotionless as he seemed to stare off into the distance. It made him feel uneasy. He turned the corner and fired a blind burst toward the enemy location. The exit to the cave was only a few meters behind them. Magnussen and his Synths continued to get pushed back—it was a miracle he'd been able to keep the fight going this long against such incredible odds.

Magnussen's ammunition was almost depleted by now. He'd been waiting to give an all-out charge order to the Synths until the last possible moment. Now it seemed to be about that time. Grabbing his comms and keying the mic, he ordered, "All remaining C100s, charge and destroy the enemy until the last one stands. This is my final order. Magnussen out."

Magnussen glanced back over at Sam as his combat Synths rushed past his position and into the fray. He smiled. "Let's get to the exit, Sam. Get me there at all costs."

Sam nodded and grabbed onto Magnussen, which he was not expecting. The medical Synth slung the lieutenant over his shoulder and sprinted at breakneck speed. From his newfound vantage point, Magnussen watched his combat Synths tearing into the charging Zodarks, who in turn were ripping Synths limb from limb. It was a horrible sight. Magnussen had left the cave exit open, just in case a miracle occurred, but by this point, he knew this would be his final stand.

A laser slammed into Sam, sending both Magnussen and the Synth to the ground, hard. Magnussen rolled and somehow caught the ground with his feet and pulled himself up. Sam also pulled himself to his feet, despite a smoking black hole in his midsection.

"Sam, look out!" Magnussen yelled as a Zodark came from the shadows with its sword raised high.

Sam turned and spun his leg underneath the Zodark, causing the aggressive beast to lose its footing. Taking advantage of the fumble, Sam grabbed the rifle Magnussen had dropped from the ground and fired the last magrail into the head of the Zodark.

Magnussen stood in disbelief. There must have been something wrong with Sam's programming because a medical Synth should not, under any circumstances, be able to fight or show violence in any way.

Sam turned to Magnussen, who still sat on the ground with his back against the wall. "Do it, sir," he directed. "I can't hold them much longer."

Magnussen watched as three more Zodarks charged into the cavern. Sam raised the sword the previous Zodark had been carrying and gave it a swing but missed the blue beast he was aiming for. That Zodark grabbed Sam by the throat and lifted the Synth into the air.

What was Magnussen supposed to do? He went to push himself to his feet, but his hand brushed something metallic next to him. Looking down, he clasped his hand around the metal detonator and smiled. The blast would be large enough to cave in this entire tunnel, including the exit. They'd be trapped.

"I would advise you to do it, sir," Sam said calmly before the Zodark ripped the medical Synth in half.

Magnussen regarded the destroyed Synth with sadness; Sam was a being with no soul, no brain, no emotions, yet here he was, sacrificing himself for a species that, at the moment, didn't honestly give a damn about him.

Then Magnussen looked back up at the Zodarks and smiled again. Not a lot of people got to choose how they went out. Even fewer got to choose to go out as some sort of hero. He didn't know what future history books would say about him, or if he'd even be mentioned at all—what he *did* know was that, by pushing on the detonator, he would give his soldiers another day to fight, another day to live, and that was enough.
****

Kodiak's armor triggered a new alarm in his helmet. His eyes shot open, and for a moment of panic, he didn't know where he was. Somehow, Kodiak had managed to fall asleep underneath the rushing water of the river he and Moreau had jumped into. The warning lights flashing on his heads-up display told him that his armor was no longer able to keep his body temperature regulated. If he didn't get out soon, it would freeze up.

Foggy vapor was expelled from Kodiak's nostrils and mouth, filling his helmet with haze, but he was still able to read his HUD. The map showed they had floated farther than he had wanted to. The new base of operations was closer, but he could tell from the faint light coming above the water that the sun was beginning to rise over the continent.

"Moreau, you still with me?" Kodiak asked through his internal comms.

He could see her floating body just beyond him, skipping across the smooth pebbles of the river floor. He pushed his arms out and swam to her. Pain shot up his arms and legs as he kicked; his whole body felt as if it would break into pieces from the cold. When Kodiak reached her body, he pressed his helmet to hers and saw it was completely iced over.

Squad leaders and those certified in advanced combat lifesaving had access to the same medical devices the medics carried into combat. Kodiak wanted badly to check her vitals, but the current kept pulling him downstream, and he realized they would both die if he didn't get them out of this frigid water. Not knowing what was above the surface terrified him. In his momentary lapse into sleep, Kodiak had lost his rifle. Moreau no longer carried hers, either. They had no weapons to defend themselves, but if he didn't get her out of the water soon, she was dead anyway, and he might not be far behind.

Wrapping his arms underneath Moreau's, Kodiak kicked off the bottom and breached the surface. The sky was a brilliant blue. Alfheim's sky almost never lost its gray, overcast hue, but today there was not a cloud to be seen. There was no snow falling, although it still clung loyally to the ground.

Kodiak pulled as hard as he could toward the shoreline and miraculously felt his arms grip the edge. His feet kicked against the rocky riverbed, pushing himself and Moreau onto the shore. Immediately, he tried to open her medical compartment, but it was iced over. Kodiak needed to break or melt the ice off, but as he frantically searched, he couldn't find anything that would be able to do it.

Kodiak suddenly remembered his survival kit. Attached to his right gauntlet was a box that contained wilderness survival essentials. It was useless on Alfheim with its weather conditions, more suited to a drier climate or even a humid forest region, but inside was something he could use to melt the ice.

He removed three small cylindrical tubes and placed them on the ground. The flares were meant to mark one's location for a search party or the members of one's squad in the event of separation. They would shoot a red ball of burning phosphorous hundreds of meters in the air, deploy a parachute, and slowly float to the ground. They were tools that had been used by the military for hundreds of years.

Picking up the first flare, Kodiak slammed the bottom, sending a bright red orb into the clear sky. *Yes! They work.* He took a second one and popped it toward the ground. The red-burning chemical hit the snow and instantly began melting through. Without thinking, he picked up the phosphorous and pressed it against the frozen pieces of Moreau's armor

The ice began to melt easily from all the vital areas he needed to clear, but the intense heat was also damaging the armor on the hand Kodiak held it in. The warmth was pleasant at first, but within seconds, the burning chemical actually began to melt his gauntlet. The hot metal and fibers woven into his armor burned his skin. Alarms blared in his ear, warning him of the damage he was doing, but on he went, melting away the ice. The pain he could deal with, but he'd be damned if he lost another soldier on this mission—especially one he was so close to.

When Kodiak dropped the burning flare to the ground, he was satisfied. Even though he was in immense pain, he tried to block it out so he could keep working on Moreau. Flipping open her medical compartment, he stuck in the toggle to his medical device and read her vitals. Things did not look good. Her pulse was very weak, and her heart was barely beating, but she was alive, which meant she still had a chance.

Immediately, Kodiak reactivated her environmental controls to warm her core temperature up again. He then initiated the medical drips, minus the fentanyl, into her bloodstream. Watching her vitals was torture—more so than the pain throbbing in his hand. As Moreau's core temperature rose, her brain activity continued, but her pulse and heartbeat remained low. Kodiak thought back to his ACLS class, trying to retrieve any piece of knowledge he might have missed, but he couldn't think of anything else he could do but wait. He could always hit her with another shot of epinephrine, but doing so could stop her heart altogether.

In anger, Kodiak slammed his fist down, sending pain shooting up his arm. He screamed in agony and ripped off his helmet. The biting cold wind hit his face, but the air was fresh. With his remaining strength, he grabbed the final flare and ignited it, sending the red orb into the sky.

Kodiak was spent. His body was numb, and his adrenaline was wearing off. All he felt was tired. His body slumped to the ground, his back resting against a large tree.

In the distance, through the haze that glossed over his vision, Kodiak saw movement. What looked like a white deer with large glowing antlers softly approached them. First it sniffed Moreau and then it turned to Kodiak. He wanted to yell at the animal, to tell it to get away from Moreau, but its beauty captivated him, and he had no strength to shout.

So, there he sat, with his back against a foreign tree on a foreign planet, taking in the beauty of its creation. Kodiak was tired. For more than a decade, he'd fought this war for humanity, for people back home he loved, for the people he served next to. But he was all used up, and all he wanted to do now was sleep.

Chapter Seven
Requiem

The Following Day
Alfheim

It had been a full day since they had occupied the new cave system and recovered what was left of the scouting party. Jorgensen had watched as Abba left with First Squad to try and recover the team when they hadn't returned from their mission. The last twenty-four hours had gone by without an ounce of sleep touching her. When the last squad had arrived in the night, the question had shifted from "Will we make it?" to "Who made it?"

Their commanding officer, First Lieutenant Magnussen, had been killed alongside their interim company first sergeant, Master Sergeant Mark Woods. They had perished with the remaining combat Synths and Sam. Sam's death, if you could call the destruction of an inorganic life form "death," really hit Jorgensen. When she had first been introduced to the medical synthetic, she'd hated it. However, after landing on Alfheim and literally fighting alongside Sam, she had grown attached, almost like one would become attached to their favorite dog.

Sam wasn't human; he didn't have the same qualities someone of flesh and blood had. He was cold and calculating, but he did his job. Not only that, Jorgensen thought she'd witnessed the birth of a personality coming from the Synth. She'd been saved by Sam once when he'd killed that beast that was attacking her, which was a direct violation of his protocol—yet it had happened anyway. She wondered if Sam had gone out fighting.

Was it quick? Did Sam know what was happening? Did he care? Those were all questions she knew she'd never get the answers to

When Abba and First Squad returned to the base, they had Staff Sergeant Moreau and Sergeant Kodiak with them. They had found the two by a river, miles away from their objective and with no vehicle in sight. When Moreau woke up, she reported the deaths of Kumar and Jacobs, making sure to detail their heroics and bravery. From what Jorgensen could tell, they had been through absolute hell.

Kodiak was worse off. When they ran diagnostics on Moreau's armor, they discovered that Kodiak had been the one to stabilize her.

They had found him lying against a tree a few meters away from Moreau, unresponsive. The medics had stabilized Kodiak, but he remained in a coma. He would most likely lose his hand—the phosphorous from the flare had burned through his skin, tendons, and even bone—but all indications pointed toward a full recovery. That was, if they ever made it off Alfheim.

"You doing OK, love?" Mac asked, a concerned look on his face.

Jorgensen turned to him, conscious of her puffy eyes, and kissed him. His response to her kiss wasn't overly aggressive but slow and compassionate, even loving. There was a time and a place for being aggressive. The fact that Mac knew that warmed her up to him even more. Jorgensen figured at this point, it didn't matter anymore if they fraternized openly. Half the company knew they were together. Heck, the entire medical platoon had figured it out before the invasion those many months ago.

"I'll be all right, Mac. Thank you for being there for me," she replied softly, a single tear escaping to fall down the side of her face.

"I never got a chance to work with Sam, but I knew you had grown attached to him, Eva, and I'm sorry for that loss."

Mac kept surprising Jorgensen. She had known the medical Synth the best out of anyone. Usually, Mac didn't call Sam by any gender, yet here he was trying his best to comfort her, even if it meant saying something he didn't believe.

She smiled and hugged him again. "It's getting harder, Mac. This is the first campaign where I've seen so many veterans be killed. A lot of people who have been fighting a lot longer than you or I have taken the long journey to Valhalla, and it makes me worry about the future."

"If you're worried about the future, then that means you haven't completely lost hope, Eva," Mac countered. "Think about the hell they've all been through and what they accomplished before their end— all the things they've done and seen. There are tactics being taught in basic training now that are based on the actions of people we fought with. It's hard to see more than a day into the future right now, but it's those thoughts that keep us goin'. I still think about what I'm gonna do when I get back to the Emerald Isle, despite the fact I'm most likely never going to see Earth again. But if there's a chance, and I mean a real chance, then I gotta hope one day it'll find me."

Jorgensen nudged him playfully with her shoulder and rested her head against his. "And what are you going to do when you go back home?"

"Introduce me mum to this beautiful lass that has ensnared me mind and captured me heart."

"You think she'd like me, Mac?" Jorgensen asked as her eyes began to fall shut.

"I think she's going to absolutely love you, Eva," Mac replied, kissing her forehead.

Jorgensen smiled as her head grew heavier. Soon her mind drifted off to sleep, dreaming of the Emerald Isle she'd most likely never see.
****

First Lieutenant Adam Singletary stared off into the dank darkness of the cave, which housed their newly established CIC. In a little over a month, he had gone from being a platoon leader with a full platoon to taking over as the company commander with only a platoon-strength element left. It was a jarring experience: one he was struggling to accept. He knew Magnussen had sent him with the first wave that had left their previous hideout so that, if things soured and didn't turn out like they had hoped, then at least one officer would remain to take charge of the rest of the soldiers in that gaggle they called a company. It still didn't make the increased responsibilities any easier to handle.

In addition to taking stock of who was left, Singletary now had to find a new platoon sergeant after the death of Master Sergeant Woods. His first choice was currently recovering from severe hypothermia.

Hearing someone coming up behind him, Singletary turned around to stare into the face of Staff Sergeant Lillian Murphy. She was the squad leader for Second Squad, and if Singletary was being honest, she wasn't getting the job because of her brilliant personality or skill on the battlefield. She had simply survived long enough to be the next one in line. Now he had to get her up to speed on the plan before the Prim commander, Hamza, arrived.

Singletary took a deep breath. "Effective immediately, Murphy, you'll be taking over duties as platoon sergeant for Master Sergeant Woods," he announced. "Your rank will remain the same and there are no guarantees you will hold the position when we are relieved, but for right now, I need you to step up and take charge. Is that understood?"

"Yes, sir. I understand," Murphy replied with a sharp nod.

"In a short while, we're going to get a visit by a local Prim commander by the name of Hamza. He's the man who was responsible for coordinating our tactical retreat to this new base of operations. When he gets here, he's going to explain to you and me what he needs from us for a major operation that's been in the works for some time.

"Hamza said some Deltas had infiltrated and linked up with some other RA and Prim units. They said a major offensive to retake the system and the planet was underway and would kick off soon. We haven't been given an ETA on when it'll start. In the meantime, we're going to get things ready for this operation once we've been given the go-ahead. Mind you, this is all 'need to know' until it's time to send out the operation order, is that understood?"

"Yes, sir," she replied again. She quickly followed that with a question. "What exactly is the mission, sir? Our company isn't anywhere near effective strength. What could we possibly do?"

Just then, Commander Hamza appeared in the doorway with his guards and walked over to Singletary and shook his hand. "Lieutenant Singletary, I am very sorry for the loss of Lieutenant Magnussen and Sergeant Woods. I am grateful that you and many of your soldiers were able to get away to this location."

"I appreciate that, Commander," Singletary replied. He turned to Murphy. "Sergeant Murphy, please go round up the other squad leaders."

Murphy nodded and left the room. Singletary wondered who she would even bring back. The rank structure was crippled, and he didn't know who could possibly fill the holes of some of the better leadership the platoon had. Still, he gave the order with confidence and turned back to Hamza with a smile.

Hamza grinned back. "I bring good news, Lieutenant. I promise."

Sergeant Murphy returned with a full complement of noncommissioned officers from the platoon. Behind her stood some very capable people and some Singletary had no idea about. He looked to the familiar face of Staff Sergeant Moreau from First Squad. Sergeant Haus would be Second Squad's squad leader with Murphy moving up, and Staff Sergeant Mahmoud would be heading up Third Squad. Fourth Squad had been decimated over the months of fighting, and its remnants had been folded into the other squads shortly before they'd moved locations again.

Lined up next to the squad leaders were the other leadership needed for such a meeting. The platoon medic, Sergeant Moore, stood with tired eyes, scanning the room. Next to him was Sergeant Jones from the mechanized platoon.

Singletary looked at his platoon's leadership and tried to maintain his best neutral expression, but inside he was terrified of now being the guy calling the shots. It'd be his orders that sent people to their deaths in the future. Whatever Magnussen had cooked up with Commander Hamza was a mystery he'd soon discover. For all Singletary knew, he was about to send all these men and women to an untimely demise, an order he wasn't sure he could issue.

The Primord commander seemed to sense Singletary's apprehension. "OK, Lieutenant, let me get you guys up to speed on what Lieutenant Magnussen and I had been putting together. My name, for those of you who do not know, is Commander Hamza. I'm a commander in the VikkSkein Continental Guard. My commandos have been moving between lines of Republic resistance, coordinating movements for a massive assault we are hoping to launch in the near future."

Hamza made his way to a table. "Before I start to explain things, are all of your translator devices still working properly?" he inquired.

Everyone nodded, so Hamza continued. "First, I want to thank you for meeting with me. What many of you may not know is that over the last couple of days, we've received several encrypted communiqués, letting us know that a large military operation to retake the system and Alfheim is currently underway. We've been informed that in less than a week, a few Delta units are going to make an orbital insertion. Once on the ground, their job is to identify and neutralize any potential planetary defensive weapons that may need to be destroyed prior to the main force showing up."

Several of the sergeants nodded and smiled. They were visibly relieved as they realized they hadn't been abandoned after all.

Hamza flicked his wrist lazily into the air, projecting images of a massive platform over the table. It appeared to house some massive guns, ship killers, and attached to the underside were the unmistakable tubes of an orbital elevator. "On our continent, one of these orbital platforms needs to be dealt with. Our intelligence suggests that there may be two more platforms on the other side of the planet, but this is the one we're concerned with.

"When the Delta units arrive, they are going to bring with them a tactical nuclear weapon that we can use to disable this platform—we need it neutralized it so that the Republic forces can safely reinvade. Our objective is to reach one of the elevators and then toss this nuclear device, which somehow fits into a duffel bag, onto the elevator and send it to the platform. Once it's at the top, it'll detonate, destroying the structure and clearing the area for your troopships to offload the new invasion force. With this platform down, this region of the planet will be left largely defenseless."

One of the sergeants asked, "What if we don't succeed in taking this platform down? Does that mean our reinforcements won't make it down to us?"

Singletary took this question. "Not necessarily. The key thing we have going for us right now is none of these platforms are finished. The Orbots and Zodarks have been working around the clock on them, but so far, these things are barely functional. That's not to say they're defenseless—they can still pose a threat to our forces. We're just not sure how big a threat. Regardless, we're going to come up with a plan to assault this platform and get that nuclear device loaded onto the elevator."

For the next twenty or thirty minutes, they took turns talking over some ideas and tactics for how they were going to assault the elevator their group had been assigned. They had a little bit of time before the Deltas arrived, but once they did, it was going to be go-time.
****

After Commander Hamza and his people left, the CIC remained silent. The squad leaders stayed behind, some sitting and some standing, waiting to be further briefed. Lieutenant Singletary took a seat on one of the rocks of the cavern and looked up at the NCOs. "Anyone got a smoke?" he asked.

A pack appeared in the air, and he caught it. Inside was one final cigarette. Cigars, cigarettes, and other forms of smoking tobacco were rare nowadays with the invention of other forms of injectable performance-enhancing substances, but they could still be found in line infantry units. Nothing did the trick better after high-stress moments than taking a drag from an old-fashioned cigarette. Singletary lit the rolled parchment and took a long pull, letting the acrid smoke fill his lungs before letting it out.

He sighed. "I wouldn't ask you to do this, and neither would Magnussen, if we didn't think it could work. The invasion force is coming, whether we take those orbital platforms out or not. If we can destroy them, we can save a lot of lives."

Mahmoud, a veteran of multiple campaigns, smiled. "It's our job, sir. I think I speak for everyone here when I say we've come too damn far to just throw in the towel now."

Grunts of agreement came up from the others.

"Thanks, Mahmoud." Singletary stood and took another drag. "So, here's the deal. First and Third Squads will take our two remaining Cougars. I want a driver, a vehicle commander, and a gunner on board. The rest of the squads will follow on foot once we get to our rally point. Second Squad will set up our mortar tubes in this tree line." He motioned to a holographic map that showed the battlefield.

Open ground stretched for two miles in every direction, with the orbital elevator complex in the middle. Around the complex stood several more buildings for Zodark barracks, ammunition supplies, and a vehicle depot. To its south, there was a large forest they'd use to conceal their approach. Commander Hamza had assured him the Prim commandos would create a diversion to the west through a mountain pass, which would be the most direct path for an attack on the facility. He was confident that once the Zodarks saw them approaching from the mountain entrance, they'd rally to attack his forces, thereby drawing off defenders who otherwise might have been able to respond to Singletary's force when they launched their own assault. If this worked, they'd catch the defenders by surprise when they emerged from the forest on the opposite side of the base.

Singletary took a final drag on the cigarette before dropping it on the ground and putting it out with his boot. "When it comes time for the attack, I want the mortars to focus on hitting the barracks, the ammo dumps at these two locations, and then these three defensive positions. My Cougar gunners—you need to use your smart missiles to take out these guard towers along this area here." He pointed to six structures that all had some sort of heavy blaster on them.

"In addition to taking those guard towers out, these four defensive bunkers need to be destroyed. As for your remaining six missiles, hold them in reserve. If you see a Zodark vehicle start up or one of their ground attack aircraft suddenly show up, you need to take 'em out. Remember, you guys need to defend these vehicles while keeping them in the fight. Do not use up all the ammo we have for them right away.

"Once we've cleared a path through the base to the elevator, that's when First Squad's vehicle will look to board it. When you've gotten the vehicle on the elevator, arm the nuke and get the hell out of Dodge. I'll fire a red signal flare in case you aren't able to hear the fallback order. It's important we do what we can to get back into the woods to disappear into the network of caves. Does everyone understand?" Singletary confirmed as he surveilled the room.

A hand went up as Sergeant Jones asked, "Where do you want my mechs, sir?"

"That's a good question, Sergeant. I want your mechs to advance with the vehicles, covering them as they approach the elevator. It's going to be your guys' job to keep the Zodarks off them as much as possible. It is imperative the vehicles make it to the elevator, Sergeant. If both Cougars are taken out, we'll be sitting dead in the water."

Singletary paused before looking over to his chief medical NCO. "Sergeant Moore, how many of the wounded are mission capable?"

"Under normal circumstances, sir, I would say none. These don't seem like normal circumstances, however, so I'd put the number at thirty percent that can fight."

"How is Sergeant Kodiak doing?" Singletary asked with honest concern.

"He's still in a medically induced coma to keep him stabilized, but he'll need to be evacuated as soon as possible."

"*Will* it be possible?" someone asked from the back.

Singletary sat on the question for a moment. He knew everyone else was thinking the same thing—would any of them be rescued or make it out of this thing alive? He bit his lower lip as he nodded. "We've all been through hell since we landed on this godforsaken planet. But we're at the goal line now. We know help is on the way, and we know what they've asked us to do to help clear a path for them. If the mission is successful—no, *when* this mission succeeds—the invasion force will land and relieve us. Getting our wounded to the *Valkyrie* or a medical ship will be my first priority. As I said earlier, we're at the goal line. Apollo, let's finish this fight. Hooah!"

"Hooah!" came the quick reply from the others.

"Good. Get with your squads and let's get ready. Dismissed."

Chapter Eight
Grand Fleet of the Republic

Five Days Earlier
RNS *Freedom*
Sol System

Viceroy Miles Hunt stood at the center of the table in the wardroom and pored over the data before him. He was examining the number of ships that would comprise his fleet, especially the number of orbital assault ships and additional troop transports. He was pleasantly surprised to see that capability had continued to increase over the years. Fortunately, in all the major battles and skirmishes they'd fought, they hadn't been losing orbital assault ships like they had other warships.

The upcoming fight would be one of the last major engagements with their original human-built ships. The new Altairian-Human hybrid ships were starting to come off the assembly line in greater numbers. Soon, they'd be able to outfit the expeditionary fleets with them and not just the home guard.

"It's impressive, isn't it?" commented Fleet Admiral Chester Bailey as he joined him at the table.

"It is," Hunt replied with a nod. "I still can't believe how many ground forces we're able to bring to bear for this singular fight—nearly one million soldiers. Now that's impressive."

"Agreed. I had to strip Halsey's fleet of nearly all of her military transports to make it happen." Chester paused, not saying anything for a few seconds before he added softly, almost whispering, "This had better work, Miles. If this fails…it may be the end of us. We simply won't have much of a force left to beat back any sort of counterattack if they launch one."

"This won't fail," Hunt insisted confidently. "If we didn't have the *Freedom*, it might, but I think the firepower we'll be able to bring to this fight is going to change the dynamics of the war forever."

"You leave tomorrow?" Bailey queried.

Hunt turned to his friend and former mentor. "Yes. We're going to jump the fleet to Kita, where we'll form up with the Primords. Seventy-two hours later, we'll jump into the Sirius system and the battle will commence."

"When will you land the ground force? Our guys on the planet have to be in dire straits by now."

Miles grimaced at the thought of the soldiers still trapped on Alfheim. He could only imagine how tough that fight must be—surrounded by the Orbots and Zodarks, being relentlessly hunted on the ground and hit by orbital strikes whenever they gathered together.

"I'm sending some Special Forces in ahead of the fleet to make contact with our remaining forces. I believe the ground force should arrive in system a few days after we do. This should give us enough time to neutralize and disable the warships in system. I still want to try and capture a Zodark and an Orbot warship if possible—the more additional intelligence we can gather on their new systems, the better."

Bailey nodded in approval. He and Hunt had known each other now for a little more than half a century. He placed a gentle hand on Hunt's shoulder. "I believe that's a sound plan, Miles. I must say, you've grown into an incredible leader. Not everyone could handle what's been placed on your shoulders. I'm not sure I could handle it, either."

Hunt smiled. "I appreciate that, Chester. I really do. You've been a great friend and mentor. Having Lilly travel with me on the *Freedom* has helped me immensely. I couldn't imagine having been gone from her all these years. These new Gallentine warships are incredible. They really thought about everything; making sure the senior officers and NCOs had the ability to take their spouses with them on an extended deployment was brilliant."

"I can see that. Still, I'd be concerned about having my spouse with me on a deployment that might result in my ship being destroyed," Bailey countered. "This is certainly not an option we're looking to build into our human-built ships."

Hunt pursed his lips, deep in thought. Bailey changed the subject. "What I wish we could get access to are more of those enhanced neurolinks and the improved medical nanites the Gallentines gave you and some of your crew."

"I know. I'm still pressing them to let more of our people have the same combo they gave me," Hunt replied. "I think, in time, they'll come around."

Bailey grunted approvingly. "All right, Miles. I'm going to head back to the station. Tell Lilly I said hello. Good luck, my friend, and Godspeed."

The two shook hands, then embraced before Chester left the wardroom to head to the flight bay and the shuttle that would take him back to his own station.

The following twenty-four hours went by in a blur. The final supplies, soldiers, and ships were now ready to go make history and hopefully end this war, or at least bring about a pause to it.
****

Viceroy Miles Hunt's Personal Quarters
RNS *Freedom*

When Miles entered his private quarters, Lilly was lying down on the couch in their living room, reading a book. "Whatcha reading?" he asked as he took his uniform jacket off and made his way toward her. He had a little bit of time before he'd need to get ready for their themed dinner this evening.

Without taking her eyes off the e-reader, she replied, "A long time ago, someone put together a list of the hundred best books you should read from each century. Right now, I'm working my way through the best books of the twentieth and twenty-first centuries. It's actually quite fascinating to see the changes in writing styles and literature across a two-hundred-year span of history."

"That does sound interesting. Where are you on your list?" asked Miles.

"I'm nearly done with one hundred and forty-three of the two hundred. Why, you want to join me on my quest to read them all?" she asked with a wink.

Hunt laughed at the suggestion. "You know, I should. Send me the list, and I'll give it a go, but I'm going to start where you are and then go back and get caught up. I want to read the same book you are so we can talk about it together."

Lilly gave Miles a mischievous smile. "Look at us, reading the same books so we can talk about them over some wine and a delectable piece of chocolate like a couple of old farts."

Hunt put his arms around her. "Ah, I'm so glad you get to travel with me, Lilly. This would be an incredibly lonely job if you weren't by my side. I don't know how'd I'd get through all this on my own. You're my rock, my North Star."

Lilly eased into his embrace as she stared intently into his eyes. "I'll follow you to the gates of hell if I have to. Just let me be by your side, and I'll always be here for you."

The two kissed passionately before meandering to their bedroom. Sometime later, Miles received a message, reminding him of the dinner that evening. The officers and NCOs were bringing their wives for a 1940s-themed dinner and band performance that Lilly had organized. She was hell-bent on having one last amazing dinner on the ship before it left for battle—a final send-off before the ship embarked upon its first combat mission.

Some of the officers and NCOs had chosen to have their spouses stay behind, while others were letting them travel with the ship into battle. It was a tough decision—either taking one's spouse into the thick of danger or not seeing them for twelve to eighteen months.

Having the room to allow the senior officers and enlisted personnel to bring their spouses with them was a first for the fleet, limited to only the *Freedom*. This benefit, however, was restricted to lieutenant commanders and chief petty officers and above. The lower enlisted and officers still had to abide by the same restrictions that other sailors had to endure across the rest of the fleet.

That evening, Lilly ensured that the spouses staying behind and the ones traveling with their loved ones into war had an amazing evening. The military members all wore 1940s-style dress uniforms with their medals and awards affixed while their spouses wore clothes of the same era. Even the waitstaff participated in the themed outfits. The food, music, and drinks were of the same period, further adding to the ambience of the event.

The crew was preparing to leave for a battle that would either lead to an end of the war with the Zodarks or further prolong it. After more than twelve years, the Republic was growing weary of a war with no end. In the coming weeks, they'd learn whether a final battle could be fought that ended it.

****

RNS George Washington
Kita – Primord Space

Since the unceremonious withdrawal from the Sirius system nearly four weeks ago, Admiral Fran McKee had been working feverishly with Admiral Bvork Stavanger on organizing a way to retake the system. It had been an agonizing decision, leaving behind more than two hundred thousand Republic soldiers, contractors, and government civilians. She knew she was likely sentencing them to death. The longer they were left behind enemy lines, the more likely it was they'd be hunted down and killed.

Looking at the status update on her fleet, she shook her head. A quarter of her ships were still in the shipyards. *Heck, even the* GW *is going to take another two months to repair...there just isn't a way for us to return right now*, she lamented privately.

McKee would never admit it outwardly, but the decision to withdraw from the system was killing her. Never in all her time in the military as an officer and commander had so many people died under her command. The faces and names were now haunting her dreams, forcing her to wake up covered in sweat.

Then a message arrived on her tablet. It was from Viceroy Hunt. A slight smile crept across her face for the first time in months. She had a long history with Miles Hunt. She'd been his tactical operations officer on the *Rook* before it had been destroyed over New Eden. Then she'd been his executive officer on the *George Washington* before he'd been assigned to be on the Altairian war council. Now he was the Viceroy. She was still having a little trouble understanding his new role and how he fit in with the Republic military structure.

Once she opened the message, her eyes quickly scanned the text. Her smirk turned into a giant grin as she kept reading. *Help is on the way.*

As she perused the specs he'd sent along of his fleet, a tear streaked down McKee's face. Miles had somehow pulled every string possible to get nearly every Republic vessel assembled for this mission. He'd even convinced the Primords to do what Admiral Stavanger hadn't been able to—commit their entire fleet to one final battle. This would become a battle royale to end the war if it was possible. The message concluded by saying that Miles would be arriving in system in forty-eight hours. In the meantime, she was to prepare what ships and soldiers she could to participate in the final battle.

When she finished reading the message, Admiral McKee suddenly didn't feel quite as hopeless as she had before. Help was coming; the people on the ground just needed to hold out a little while longer.
****

4th Special Forces Group
SOCOM Headquarters
Tampa, Florida
Earth, Sol

Captain Brian Royce looked at the op order and then back to Major Jayden Hopper and Colonel William "Wild Bill" Hackworth, not saying a word. They stared back at him, waiting on his response. Finally, he said, "I thought slipping into the Qatana system to infiltrate Sumer was risky, but this seems like a suicide mission. Have there been some sort of modifications made to the Nighthawks or something else that's going to allow us to slip into the system unnoticed and then land a force on the ground undetected that I haven't been made aware of?"

Hackworth snorted. "As a matter of fact, there has been an upgrade to the Nighthawks' stealth capability, and there's a completely new ship that has finally come out of the shipyards, specially designed for SF stealth insertions just like this." A second later, Colonel Hackworth brought up an image of a ship. "This is a Type 001C stealth frigate. It's a human-Altairian hybrid ship, developed exclusively for Special Forces or HVI transportation between nonpermissive environments. Here, let me pull up the specs. Then you tell me if you think your mission is still a suicide one after you've seen it."

A second later, an image of the Type 001C model of the frigate floated on the table between them. The new ship had a lot of electronic wizardry on it and an enhanced troop compartment. The frigate was able to carry sixty-four operators and another forty C100s into a system along with their equipment to carry out a host of Special Forces missions.

Royce studied the ship. He found himself slowly nodding the more he read. "OK, I think this might work. It'll take at least four of these to get my entire company in place, though, unless you plan on making a few trips, which I do not recommend."

Colonel Hackworth declared, "We have twelve of these ships. They just came from the shipyards and completed their shakedown cruises. We've assigned them the best crews from the destroyer classes to fly 'em for us. They know they'll be ferrying Special Forces around and that every mission is likely to be deep behind enemy lines. So, Captain, do you still think it's a suicide mission or do you think we can get your people inserted?"

The invasion was going to take place soon. To make that happen, they needed someone to help reestablish coms with the soldiers that had been left behind and then identify any ground-based planetary weapon systems that might need to be destroyed before the main force arrived. The problem was, they didn't have a lot of time. The entire rescue mission was being hastily thrown together.

There was an awkward pause before Royce finally said, "I think this can work. If this ship can get my guys in orbit, we'll insert via a HALO jump. The ship can then deploy a couple of stealth com satellites for us and move to a position further away from the planet and relay our messages out of the system back to you guys."

"Good, then it's settled," said Hackworth. "Have your men report to the John Glenn and prepare to disembark in twenty-four hours. The RNS *Freedom* is going to create a temporary wormhole connecting our system with Sirius. Your ships will jump through and head off to your individual missions." He stood up taller. "Good luck, Captain Royce. You guys are going to need a lot of it this time around."

With the meeting ended, Royce got to work. Using his neurolink, he sent out the alerts to his soldiers, letting them know they had twelve hours to report to the John Glenn. From there, they'd go over the equipment loadouts they'd be taking with them for the mission. They'd likely be operating on their own for at least two to three weeks, but they could only bring with them whatever they could jump with.

A few hours later, Royce and a handful of officers and generals from SOCOM all headed over to Bern's Steakhouse. Anyone who'd been to Tampa and asked about a steak joint likely would have been told about Bern's. What separated Bern's from its competitors was their dry-aged steaks. You could order a steak rare and not have to worry about how bloody it might be. Plus, the dry-aging process allowed the meat to become incredibly tender, almost to the point of being able to cut through a steak with a fork or a butter knife. Then there was the wine cellar, containing Earth's largest collection of private wines, cognacs, and other fine drinks, ranging from twelve Republic dollars or RDs to upwards of 250,000 RD for a glass of their most expensive bottle of wine.

Royce thanked Major General Trevor Morton, the deputy commander of SOCOM, for arranging what had to be a last-minute VIP reservation. Bern's was typically booked solid for close to two months straight. It was also an incredibly expensive dinner, with Royce's tab alone costing some 425 RDs. General Morton insisted on covering the bill for everyone.

"It's the least I can do," he'd insisted. "I know some of your operators may not make it back." Morton sighed. "I never get to go out on missions anymore now that I'm the deputy commander—it's one of the things I regret about this position. At least I can give you all one great night."

****

Thirty-Four Hours Later
RNS *Pathfinder*

Captain Brian Royce sat in an extra jump seat on the bridge, waiting like everyone else to see what would happen next. Their ship, along with seven others, was loaded down with eight platoons, two companies' worth of Special Forces soldiers. The huge Gallentine warship, the RNS *Freedom*, would soon open the wormhole, allowing them to travel through. Then the giant ship, along with the rest of the invasion force, would jump through another portal, taking them directly to Kita. All Royce knew of that part of the operation was that they'd spend a few days forming up there before they'd begin to deploy into Sirius.

"Captain, the portal is opening up," called out one of the crewmen.

Looking at the display, Royce saw the electrical anomaly form and then a hole appeared in space. It was odd—surrounded by a swirliness, almost like the top of a tornado or hurricane.

"Very well. Helm, bring us up to full power and guide us in. Time to earn our pay, boys," Commander Aylie Rogers, the captain of the *Pathfinder*, announced to her bridge crew.

Royce smiled at the bravado of the captain.

The ship moved forward, toward the swirling black hole. Then, in an instant, they were sucked inside. Being inside the wormhole was a strange feeling. Royce could almost see and feel the ship and then his own body stretching like Play-Doh before it all seemed to catch up. The transition took only seconds before they emerged on the other side.

"We're through, Captain. I'm activating the electronic shield," one of her other officers announced.

Royce hoped they knew what they were doing. This was his first time traveling in one of the new stealth ships. These bad boys had been specifically designed to infiltrate behind enemy lines and deploy Special Forces soldiers to hostile planets to carry out reconnaissance and surveillance operations. Until he'd seen a successful insertion or two, he was holding his comments on what he thought of the new ships. They certainly had a lot more room to stretch out in than the previous Nighthawks, though. Those things were cramped.

"Electronic shielding activated. We're in stealth mode, ma'am."

"Excellent. Helm, take us in toward Alfheim and get us into a position to drop our cargo," Commander Rogers announced before she turned in her chair to look at Royce. "OK, Captain. We should arrive in orbit in fourteen hours. We'll get you in position, then it'll be on you and your people."

Royce nodded. "Thank you for the ride, Commander. I fear we just completed the easiest part of our mission. Now comes the fun part."

"I know. I don't envy what's ahead of you, Captain. I don't know how you Deltas do it, but I'm sure glad you guys are on our side."

With nothing more to say, Royce got up and headed down to the troop compartment. It was time to brief his people one more time. He'd force everyone to try and get at least two hours of downtime to spend as they wished and then a mandatory six hours of sleep. Once they landed on the surface, it was going to be a twenty-four-hour nonstop operation.
****

RNS *Freedom*
Kita Station
Primord Core Worlds

When the RNS *Freedom* finally emerged from the wormhole, the sight of such an enormous fleet assembled on the other side almost took Miles Hunt's breath away. In addition to his fleet of twenty-six battleships, thirty-two battlecruisers, forty cruisers, and sixty destroyers, the Primords had assembled eighty-six of their own battleships—a ship class that far outweighed their own *Ryan*-class ships. They had an additional one hundred and ten cruisers and smaller escort ships traveling with them. It was an incredible display of raw power, unlike any he'd seen until now.

I can't wait to see what this ship can do in battle, Miles thought.

He turned to his Gallentine ship captain, whispering, "Wiyrkomi, how would the *Freedom* fare if it faced all the ships we see around us on its own?"

Hunt knew it was a foolish question to ask, but he had nothing to compare his own ship's fighting power against.

Speaking softly to match Hunt's tone, Captain Wiyrkomi replied, "If we deployed all our fighter and bomber wings, we might get lucky and destroy a third of these ships, but eventually they'd just overwhelm us. They'd destroy enough of our weapon batteries that'd we'd be defenseless." Wiyrkomi paused for a second before adding, "Miles, while I agree the *Freedom* will likely be the deciding factor in us winning this battle, please keep in mind we are not fighting with a fully trained crew. Your pilots have barely enough experience to fly their fighters and bombers, let alone be proficient with them. The sailors manning the hundreds of turrets and other weapon systems haven't had time to fully learn how their weapons work, let alone know what to do if one is damaged.

"My crew and pilots will do their best to aid and assist you, Miles, but make no mistake, this will be a tough battle—which means the *Freedom* will likely sustain some serious damage."

Miles winced a bit at Wiyrkomi's words. He knew he was right; he just didn't have many other alternatives. This battle had to be fought. They had to recapture Alfheim, if for no other reason than to recover their stranded force.

Wiyrkomi must have seen the look of concern written on Miles's face. "Remember, Miles, the *Freedom* is a capital support ship. It is not designed to go into a wild melee of a battle without a support fleet or even a fully trained crew like we're about to do," the Gallentine captain quickly added. "The *Freedom* combined with, say, ten of our Gallentine battleships would likely take this group of warships out. It is all the more reason why Alfheim needs to be captured. The Bronkis mineral is the key ingredient in the armor needed to produce a Gallentine warship."

"Viceroy, we're being hailed by the Primord flagship," Hunt's communications officer announced. "They're asking if their delegation has permission to come aboard."

Hunt turned to the young man and nodded his approval. He and Wiyrkomi headed down to the flight line. They'd greet the Primord delegation in person and then bring them to the wardroom to discuss things further. Hunt had to keep reminding himself that he was there as the Viceroy, the leader appointed by the Gallentine Emperor—not as the fleet commander for the Republic. The Primords would likely have a lot of questions about the alliance beyond just this battle.
****

When the Primord transport landed, the delegation that deboarded was a bit larger than Hunt was prepared for. It appeared the head of their navy and ground forces had arrived, along with the leader of their people, a man by the name of King Iona whose family had united the Primords nearly a thousand years ago. Under his family's leadership, their people had enjoyed an unparalleled time of peace and prosperity—until they'd run into the Zodarks.

The King walked up to Hunt. Once he reached him, he dropped to a knee, as did everyone in his entourage. They did this out of respect for Viceroy Hunt, but also for Captain Wiyrkomi, who was the first Gallentine they had ever seen.

"Your Majesty, please rise. Let us talk in my wardroom as newfound friends and allies. Come," Hunt declared loudly for everyone to hear.

The King stood and smiled. He offered a greeting in his own language and thanked Hunt for honoring the Primord people with his presence and this magnificent ship.

When they reached the wardroom, Hunt sat through what felt like an hour of niceties and conversations with the King before he was able to get down to the task at hand. He explained to King Iona the need for this battle, that this was the one time they could genuinely surprise and destroy the Zodark and Orbot fleets. They had no idea a Gallentine *Titan*-class ship was going to enter the battle and they had no defense against it. If this attack worked, then they might finally be able to sue for the peace they had all longed for but that had eluded them up to this point.

King Iona was a bit hesitant about committing so much of their naval force to a single battle. If things didn't work out, then it would leave them incredibly vulnerable. It might even place Kita in danger. The massive shipyard facilities were known far and wide within the alliance. They produced nearly half of all Primord warships. This system wasn't something that could be lost or traded away to buy more time.

Hunt assured him that if the battle went poorly and that scenario became a reality, he'd order the Tully and Altairians to dispatch a large enough fleet to stand in the breach long enough for them to be able to replace their losses.

By the time the meeting was over, the Primords had been won over. They came to the same realization that Hunt had—with the *Freedom*, they truly did have a chance to destroy the Zodark and Orbot fleets once and for all.

Looking at the Primord delegation in front of him, Viceroy Hunt declared, "Then it's settled. We launch the invasion in forty-eight hours."

King Iona nodded in agreement, sending the signal to his military leaders that they were to move forward with whatever plans the Viceroy put forth. For the time being, they'd operate under his authority.
****

RNS *Freedom*
4th Fighter Group "Death Rattlers"

Commander Ethan Hunt looked at his four squadron commanders, asking, "What hesitations do you have about the mission or your pilots' ability to perform it?"

The squadron commanders looked at Ethan and squirmed uncomfortably in their seats. Finally, Commander Tommy Rens, his executive officer and the commander of the Yellowjackets, replied, "What I think the others are afraid to say is all our pilots are still a little green and wet behind the ears when it comes to flying these Hellcats into combat. We wish we'd had more time to prepare our people for what's about to happen next."

Ethan sighed, more to himself than anything else. He'd thought the same thing.

"I don't disagree with any of your concerns. I share them as well," Ethan admitted. "But here's the deal—we're going to war with the pilots and weapons we have, not with what we wish we had. From the very first discovery of the Zodarks, we've been playing catch-up. We've been fighting down-and-dirty street brawls and winning—not because we have better technology or equipment, but because we're the meanest hellraisers in the galaxy.

"I know we're going to lose pilots because they aren't as trained or proficient as we'd like them to be. But I want you all to keep something in mind—we have more than two hundred thousand soldiers stranded down on Alfheim. How do you think they're holding up against the Zodarks and Orbots? Not only does the enemy have control of the high ground, they've also been able to ferry in reinforcements unabated for nearly a month."

Ethan let his words sink in before continuing. "I'm not trying to minimize the losses we're going to take. But know this—the pilots that emerge from this battle will be veterans. Their experiences will be shared and spread across the fleet.

"Is this the only concern you all have?" Ethan pressed. "Is there something else within my control that I can address?"

"I think you covered it, Commander, and you're right. We're going to take losses no matter what we do. The experiences we'll gain from this battle will make us even more deadly in any of the future battles we're sure to face against these bastards." Commander Rens paused for a second before adding candidly, "Maybe I'm speaking for myself or maybe the others feel the same way, but this is the first mission any of us will have led pilots on where, if our fighters get blown up, we're going to lose not just the fighter but likely the pilot as well. Up to this point, if a fighter was destroyed, we just grabbed another drone and jumped right back into the fight. This manned fighter thing is going to take a little adjusting to."

"That's a good point, Tommy," Ethan conceded. "You're right, this is going to be the first time those of us in leadership will have to deal with the loss of someone. This is also why we as leaders need to keep pushing our pilots hard during training. We need to drill them intensely because their survival may ultimately come down to that training."

When Ethan had first met Commander Tommy Rens several weeks ago, he hadn't been sure how things would work out between them. Tommy had earned his rank the old-fashioned way, through time in grade and service prior to the war with the Zodarks. He'd then gone on to form the initial cadre of remotely piloted drone or RPD squadrons that operated on the *Ryan*-class battleships. Despite the twenty-year age gap between them, they'd become fast friends.

Ethan brought up the mission parameters. "Let's go over the deployment plan one more time. Then I want you guys to have your squadrons spend as much time as you can in the cockpit, dogfighting and training. Twelve hours before we deploy, I want you to stand your pilots down—I want them as rested and relaxed as possible before we jump into system. It's going to be crazy as hell once we jump. Chances are, we'll be in constant combat until the battle is over. We can only push our pilots so far; once you start to see one of your people pushing beyond that breaking point, you have to be strong enough to ground them for twelve hours and insist they use that time for sleep. I don't want to lose pilots because we didn't cycle them through some crew rest. Am I clear?"

A chorus of "Yes, sirs" followed.

Ethan continued with the command brief. "The *Freedom* is going to open two wormholes near Alfheim. Eighty percent of the Prim and Terran fleets are going to jump through and initiate the battle here." Ethan pointed to a spot in the system near one of the moons. "This will draw the enemy to this area and hopefully pull some ships in orbit to join the battle. Approximately sixty minutes after the first fleet has arrived, the second portal will open here, on the opposite side of the planet. Once we're on the other side, our Hellcats and Devastators will deploy as our second fleet moves around the planet to join the main battle.

"Our objective is to push ahead of our fleet and clear a path for the bombers, who'll be following behind us to pulverize the battleships. Once the bombers finish their runs, they'll return home. We're going to stick around until we're relieved by Fighter Group Six.

"Any further questions? If not, then you all are dismissed. We have roughly thirty-two hours left to train our pilots before it's game time. So, let's take advantage of the time we have left."
****

Team Four, Sapper Platoon
Dog Company, 313th Battalion
Highway 210, Near Ridge 582
Alfheim

Sergeant Hidalgo shivered briefly. The temperature always got coldest once the sun had gone down. Fortunately, the evening hours only lasted six hours before the sun was back, and with it an increase of twenty to thirty degrees in temperature.

For the last forty-eight hours he'd been lying in wait for his time to strike. That time, as of five hours ago, had finally come.

When a critical bridge some forty kilometers away had been destroyed, it had forced the supplies arriving from the space elevator to be carted several hundred kilometers out of the way to another bridge. That other bridge meant the vehicle traffic had to travel down Highway 210 to reach their supply base.

Shrugging off the biting cold from the wind, Hidalgo grabbed for his spotting scope and looked down to the highway running through the valley. It was still dark, the dawn only thirty minutes away, when he spotted the headlights of the vehicles. The column was making its way toward him. Looking through the scope, he spotted the first vehicle pass by a marker he'd placed on a tree, which meant it was 300 meters away from his trap. When the lead vehicle entered the kill box, he let it pass. He waited until the fourth vehicle entered the kill box and then he triggered the explosives.

BOOM!

A bright flash illuminated the night sky, turning everything white in his scope until it automatically adjusted to the light. Pulling his eyes away from it, Hidalgo saw the flash dissipate and a fireball erupt before the flames washed over several additional vehicles. At first it was just two vehicles that blew up. Then five more joined the fiery cauldron as their cargo caught fire. In the span of a few seconds, Hidalgo had created an utter mess. As the chaos he'd just sown in the enemy ranks continued to spread, he readied his second ambush.

As the minutes ticked by, the shadows from the fires danced their dance of death just as a sliver of predawn light crept above the horizon. At first, Hidalgo didn't hear anything save the explosions that rippled across the convoy. But as the seconds turned to minutes, he heard a hideous new noise rise up from the convoy. He heard the cries of pain and agony coming from the vehicles.

Peering back through his spotting scope, he saw dozens of figures running toward the burnt and destroyed vehicles. It was in that moment that his eyes registered the bodies. Dozens of them had been strewn about the area. They covered the ground. Some of them just lay still, likely dead or knocked unconscious. Some looked like they had been torn to shreds. An arm ripped off, a leg or even a torso torn from the body. Amongst the bodies were the wounded.

The injured Zodarks cried out in pain and called for help from their comrades. Hidalgo saw one Zodark holding a nearly severed leg together as he screamed for help. One of his comrades came rushing toward him, placing some sort of bag on the ground next to him. Hidalgo watched in fascination as the Zodark treated the injured soldier. He placed what Hidalgo assumed must be a tourniquet on its leg, then gave him some sort of injection, which caused the Zodark to stop screeching and screaming in pain.

That Zodark is a medic, just like ours…

Hidalgo had fought against the Zodarks for many, many years, but in all that time, he'd never seen them interact with each other like this. He'd always seen them in the heat of a battle. In those circumstances, it was easy to think of the enemy in a single dimension. Deep down, he knew there had to be more to the Zodarks than what he'd seen up to this point. They were a spacefaring species, after all.

As more Zodarks rushed toward their wounded, Hidalgo almost felt bad about what he was about to do next. Then he remembered seeing the Zodark Christmas trees around his old base. His sadness changed to anger, and a smile spread across his lips as he depressed the button that would trigger his second surprise.

BOOM!

The second set of explosions weren't quite as thunderous as the first ones, but the damage they inflicted on the enemy soldiers who were now out of their armored vehicles was immense. The twelve claymore mines he'd hidden along both sides of the highway erupted, throwing thousands of small steel ball bearings into their ranks.

When the cloud of smoke cleared, the cries from the wounded began, only this time there had to be three or four times as many wounded as there had been from the first ambush. As the enemy reacted to his second ambush in less than five minutes, Hidalgo packed up his spotting scope and a few other items, placed them in his rucksack and then folded his special hide cover-up. He stayed low to the ground now that he didn't have the benefit of hiding under the electronic and IR protection of his hide, slithering and crawling away from the scene of the crime.

His job here was done. He'd ambushed the enemy, inflicting a lot of casualties, and gathered some additional intelligence. It was now time to get out of Dodge and put some distance between himself and this highway. Forty kilometers further down the highway, the next soldier would execute a similar type of attack. If all went according to plan, this convoy wouldn't even make it to the supply depot.

Chapter Nine
HALO Insertion

Alpha Company, 1st Battalion, 4th Special Forces
Alfheim

Captain Brian Royce stood near the bay doors, loaded out with his kit, waiting to receive the word to jump. The ship had to descend from low orbit down into the upper atmosphere first—a tricky thing to do.

The Altairians had helped them to mimic the appearance of a shooting star. If a ship tried to scan them, they'd look like a small piece of metal or a rock burning up in the atmosphere. It wasn't perfect by any means, but it was enough to fool a nominally attentive observer.

"We're in the upper atmosphere, Captain. Stand by for bay doors to open," announced the ship's captain, Commander Aylie Rogers.

"Thank you for the ride, ma'am. Good luck on your next mission. Royce out."

This was a pivotal mission. His company, along with one other, would be inserting at different points all around the planet. They were the preinvasion force being sent in to get things ready.

Standing behind him and preparing to jump were the men and women of First Platoon and Lieutenant Karen Williams, his platoon leader. He also had forty C100 combat Synths joining him on this jump. Adam and his combat synthetics had become an integral part of their Delta teams.

"We're approaching the designated drop zone, Captain. Prepare your people," directed Commander Rogers.

Turning his head, Royce barked, "This is it, folks. We're about to jump. Remember your training, stay alert, and stay alive. We're going into Indian country, so heads on a swivel at all times until we can get a lay of the land and link up with the resistance groups left on the planet."

Just then, the bay doors opened, allowing the limited atmosphere to swirl inside the compartment. Looking out into the abyss, Royce saw a small sprinkling of lights below, mostly wrapped around the equator of the planet, where the habitable zones of Alfheim were found.

Using his neurolink, Royce connected to the C100. *Adam, have your teams jump with the equipment. Once you land, get a perimeter*

*established and begin looking for a suitable base camp and get it set up.
We need to get under cover quickly.*

That's affirmative.

Seconds later, the forty C100s rushed forward and leapt off the back of the ship like it was nothing.

Royce motioned with his hand for his soldiers to follow him as he, too, jumped off into the abyss.

As he fell through the night sky, Royce felt the cool air whipping past his body. He kept his arms tucked in close to his core. His rucksack and smaller patrol pack were anchored near his legs, ready for him to drop them down once he'd deployed his parachute and was near the ground. For now, his body continued to slice through the crisp night air, his altimeter still showing him to be some seventy thousand feet above the ground.

Royce looked at his HUD; the rest of the platoon he'd jumped with had all made it out. The other three platoons in his company had likewise jumped and were headed toward their own designated locations. Royce hated breaking his command up like this, but he knew it would have been impossible for such a large force to operate together doing the kind of mission they'd been tasked with. As it was, operating at a platoon level was still too large.

As Royce continued to race through the atmosphere, small water droplets whipped past his visor. His HUD pointed him in the direction of the DZ they'd determined would be best to set up in. He angled his body slightly, causing it to fly in that direction. He was blowing through altitude at these speeds.

Ten seconds until automatic chute deployment, chimed the AI in his HUD.

In the distance, Royce saw several large encampments. He assumed those were Zodark camps. They were making no attempt at hiding their positions from the sky.

As the countdown until his chute deployed got closer to zero, Royce braced himself. Moments later, his parachute unfurled and his dramatic race to the ground came to an abrupt halt. The sudden stop jerked his body. Then he regained control of himself and continued toward the ground.

When he reached fifty feet above the ground, Royce released his drop bag, allowing it and his equipment to dangle below him. They connected with the ground just as Royce pulled tight on his guide wires, causing the chute to fill with air. His feet gently settled on the ground as he took a couple of steps forward, his chute collapsing and falling to the ground. At that point, he disconnected it from his harness and quickly wrapped it up. Royce already had his rifle strapped to him, so all he had to do now was retrieve his rucksack and patrol pack and he was ready to roll.

According to Royce's HUD, the other operators in his platoon had all made it to the ground, and so had the forty C100s. The synthetics had landed a few minutes ahead of them and had already fanned out in a wide circle, establishing a perimeter. Even now, a few of them were out scouting possible hide locations where they could set up their base camps.

Captain Royce, I have found the cave network previously identified by intelligence, Adam told him over the neurolink. *We are checking it out. This may work as a hide location.* Adam was still the C100 that was the overall leader of the combat synthetics. He was essentially the designated point of contact to communicate orders to all the other Synths.

Excellent. Find out where the tunnels lead and what other exit points there may be. Let's hope the caves are still abandoned. If you find any Zodarks, please try to take them out stealthily, if possible, Royce directed.

Affirmative.

Royce shivered and modified the climate control on his suit, cranking it up a couple of degrees. *Damn, they weren't joking about this planet being cold*, Royce realized.

Snow was starting to descend. That was both a blessing and a curse. On the one hand, it would help cover their landing and give them some concealment as they sought to get a lay of the land, but it would also make covering their tracks a bit trickier unless the snow continued long enough to cover them up.

Lieutenant Williams, get our drones deployed, Royce ordered over the neurolink. *I want to know what's in our immediate area. Also, have our coms guy establish communications with* Pathfinder *and let them know we've landed unopposed. We're proceeding to objective Bravo.*

Half an hour later, Adam reported back that the tunnel network was clear. It wasn't as large as they had first thought. It looked like it had been fought over at one time. They found the remains of a number of Republic Army soldiers as well as a few Zodarks. The C100s cleared the tunnels of the remains, burying them so they wouldn't continue to rot and attract predators or vermin.

Once inside the tunnels, Royce had his people do what they could to cover up the entrances and make the place as invisible as they could. For the time being, he'd establish his headquarters here. He didn't have a lot of time to get a lay of the land and figure out what resistance forces were left or what kind of planetary defensive systems the Zodarks or Orbots might have built.

Eight hours after they arrived, Royce finally got his first major status report. "Captain, we've managed to locate three Zodark base camps and a single Orbot camp," Lieutenant Williams reported. "I'm sending you their coordinates. I've got observation teams watching them while we continue to gather more intelligence on them. Um, there is something else I'm sending that ya need to see. It's...ah...pretty disturbing." Her files started to download on his tablet.

"Good job, Lieutenant. But what do you mean by disturb—" His voice suddenly broke off as a video file began to play. What he saw shocked him. He'd seen a lot of death and atrocities during this war, but this took things to an entirely new level.

One of Williams's scouts had come across the ruins of what had been a Republic base. The facility had been thoroughly destroyed, but that wasn't what caused his stomach to churn—it was the hundreds of bodies hanging from the nearby trees and exposed support structures of the destroyed base.

Zooming in closer to look at the images, Royce almost recoiled. He suddenly wanted to vomit. The Zodarks had not only killed these soldiers and then hung them naked from the nearby trees and structures, they'd also completely skinned them. In some cases, the bodies of the soldiers looked like they had been tortured before they'd been killed. More than a handful of them looked to have been disemboweled before they'd died. It was a gruesome and horrific scene.

"Jesus...how many bodies have you guys found like this?"

There was a momentary pause before Lieutenant Williams responded. "As of right now, we've found over three thousand."

"Williams, I need you to keep this under wraps for the time being. Don't let anyone else know what you've found, and make sure the scout team that discovered this doesn't share it with the rest of the platoon. It'll only distract them from the mission. We need to keep everyone focused on our primary tasks: locating the remaining Prim and Republic forces on the planet and getting ready to support the invasion."

"Yes, sir, I understand and agree," Williams confirmed. "I've already told them to keep this quiet. We've located a few enemy bases and we're starting our surveillance activities of them."

Royce closed the file with the gruesome images and opened the other files up. His HUD populated with the known enemy encampments they'd found and had under surveillance. Using his right hand, Royce made a grabbing motion in front of his HUD, throwing a projection of the map with the enemy bases down onto the ground in front of him, which gave him a much bigger image to examine.

Looking at the overall picture of what they had collected up to this point, Royce commented, "This is good work, Lieutenant. Your people have done a great job locating the enemy. Now we need to focus on finding the remaining RA units still out there. How is that part of things coming?"

"We're still working on it, sir. We're trying to see if we can locate them by scanning for any of their squads' communication nets," Williams explained. "We're hoping we may find a unit still using their coms in any capacity. If we do, it'll help us locate them pretty rapidly."

Royce nodded to himself. "That may work, but let's keep those scout drones moving. Remember, if we can use that to track them down, then chances are the Orbots are doing the same thing and passing that information to the Zodarks. We need to find our people and figure out if there's any sort of chain of command still functioning. The invasion is going to happen soon; we don't have a lot of time."

Lieutenant Williams sent her squads to task. They'd break down further into smaller teams to cover more distance. While that took place, Royce would keep most of his C100s hidden in the cave, ready to deploy when the time came. For now, he wanted to keep them hidden while his operators did what they did best.

I just hope there are soldiers still fighting and holding out, he worried.

Trying not to get distracted by what was going on, Royce turned his attention to one of the scout drone's images of an Orbot base. He'd fought against the Quadbots in the past, but this was the first time he'd seen so many of them. They also appeared to have military vehicles and aircraft of some sort with them.

Those could prove to be a problem.

When he thought back to the battle on the station over Rass, Captain Royce remembered how the Orbots had somehow managed to coopt the C100s. They'd nearly taken them over and turned them against their human masters.

I sure hope that latest software patch they gave us will work, he thought. *I'd hate to have to issue a kill code again. We need these synthetics...*

Royce sent a tasking over to one of the closest teams to the camp to have them focus on surveilling it and the surrounding area. He wanted as much detailed information on their equipment and numbers as possible.

I'd like to plaster that base from space before we have to battle them.

Several hours later, Royce finally got up and took two of his operators with him. He had found a spot on one of their drone scans that looked a little off, like it might be a hide site of some sort. His other teams were all tasked with missions, so rather than waiting for one to become free, he figured he'd set out to check it himself. The location was roughly twelve kilometers from their current location, so not too far. For this mission, Royce opted to bring Corporal Ellis and Sergeant Steve Mudrak—they were seasoned operators.

As they left their underground command post, Royce used his neurolink to tell his two guys to follow him but keep their spacing twenty meters apart and initiate their digital camouflage. They needed to do their best to blend into the surrounding area.

Moving through the snow-covered wooded forest reminded him of just how alien this planet really was. It was largely an ice planet with only a small portion of it being habitable along the equator. For some reason unknown to him, the Primords had settled this planet hundreds of years ago. Then the Zodarks had invaded and taken the planet from them nearly one hundred years ago. He still didn't understand the strategic importance of Alfheim, but orders were orders. They had to seize it and take it back from the Zodarks.

Royce stole a quick glance behind him. He knew his guys were there; he just couldn't see them, at least not with their digital camouflage on. As long as they didn't move too quickly, they essentially disappeared.

Four hours later, his team had come within a thousand meters of what they suspected was an underground RA base. Royce just hoped it was active and he'd be able to link up his teams with whatever remaining forces were still on the planet.

Let's approach the entrance from a wide angle, Royce directed over the neurolink. *I'll head down the middle—you guys take the flanks. Keep your eyes open for possible scouts. We don't want to spook them and end up getting lit up by our own forces. If you spot one of our guys, let me know, and we'll look to make contact.*

With nothing more to be said, the three of them advanced slowly and smoothly toward the cave entrance. As Royce crept closer, his eyes continued to scan everything in front of him, looking for any sign that this might be a trap or even a Zodark or Orbot base. When they came within three hundred meters, they detected their first signs of life. There were a handful of motion sensors positioned at varying levels. Some were near shoulder height, some near the ground, while more than a few had been placed high in the trees, likely to give the defenders time to figure out if they were going to fight or flee. These sensors were tiny little buggers. Unless someone knew what to look for, they'd likely miss them. However, Royce did know exactly what to look for and spotted them right away.

Halt. I think they've got some guards out here. I'm going to call out to them and see if I can talk with one of them, Royce explained over the neurolink. They were trying to minimize their radio chatter to decrease the likelihood of it being intercepted—or worse, having their location triangulated.

Royce turned his digital camouflage off. Then he activated the speaker on his helmet and turned it up just a bit more so his voice would carry.

"My name is Captain Brian Royce, 4th Special Forces Group. Please identify yourself!" he declared loudly. He was confident they were being watched and he wanted whoever was out there to know he knew they were there.

There was a momentary pause as an eerie silence fell across this wooded area. Then a voice called, "Give us the challenge word and we'll let you live."

He grunted. *Challenge word...I suppose that's a good sign if they're still using them.*

"I need to speak with someone in charge," he countered. "My unit just arrived on planet last night."

Another short pause ensued, then a figure emerged from under a camouflage blanket and cautiously stood, his rifle aimed out in front of him, ready to lay waste to whatever threat materialized.

Then Royce stood slowly, revealing himself to the other soldier.

"You're a Delta soldier?"

"I am."

The soldier turned briefly. "He's legit. Stand down, men."

A couple of other soldiers revealed themselves. The soldier standing closest to Royce approached him. "I'm Master Sergeant Corbyn, Fox Company, 312th Battalion."

Walking toward the man, Royce extended his hand. "I'm Captain Brian Royce, Alpha Company, 1st Battalion, 4th Special Forces. It's a pleasure to meet you. I need to speak with whoever's in charge immediately. It's critically important."

Looking around, the master sergeant leaned in, whispering, "Please tell me you're the advance party for our relief?"

"Let's just get inside and talk to whoever's in charge."

"Yes, sir. Follow me," Corbyn said as he led the way. Royce had to admit, they'd done a really good job of disguising their positions.

The three Delta soldiers passed through the RA lines. As they walked past the soldiers, he saw a lot of tired looks. Their uniforms were dirty, some were torn, but despite their obvious exhaustion, they still had a determined look in their eyes that said they weren't ready to give up yet.

Upon entering the cave entrance, they walked past a couple of bunkers that had been built and reinforced to hold an enemy at bay. Royce liked what he saw. If they had gone to this much trouble to build a fortified entrance, then chances were this was the command center he and his people had been searching for.

"Major Pilecki, I've got someone who needs to speak with you," called out the master sergeant as they made their way into a cavernous room further back in the tunnel.

The major turned, his eyes lit up at the sight of Royce and his two other soldiers. "I'll be damned. Help really is on the way, isn't it?" he said aloud. His Polish accent was very pronounced, possibly more so than usual due to the excitement. The other soldiers in the room all turned to look at the newcomers.

The Deltas wore slightly different uniforms and armor than their regular Army counterparts. Their body armor was a bit more flexible in nature and a hell of a lot stronger. It was also integrated with exoskeleton servos and parts that allowed them more agility and gave them considerably more strength than the average soldier.

Royce took his helmet off. "Help *is* on the way. My name is Captain Brian Royce. I'm the OIC for the invasion advance team. It's imperative that I get in touch with the various ground commanders still dirtside."

Several soldiers slapped each other on the shoulders, some high-fived each other, and a few hooted and hollered. The major approached Royce. "You have no idea how glad we are to hear that, Captain. This last month..." His voice trailed off and his eyes suddenly had that thousand-yard stare to them.

"It's OK, sir. Help *is* on the way. But we have a lot that needs to get done before that happens and not a lot of time to do it. Why don't we sit down and talk over your situation and start figuring out a game plan? I also need to try and get in touch with General Bakshi, if he's still alive."

"Yes, of course. Please, let's walk over to the map board, and I'll get you up to speed on our disposition. Then we can go to our coms room and talk with the general."

When they entered another connecting room, Royce saw a handful of soldiers monitoring various drone feeds, surveillance cameras, and some coms gear. A few soldiers were doing an inventory of some items while others cleaned their weapons.

"When the invasion happened, it forced everyone underground," Pilecki explained. "Anything of value on the surface was getting zapped from space or hit hard by the Zodarks and Orbots. When General Bakshi learned there was a chance we were going to be invaded, he ordered as much of our force and equipment to be dispersed as possible. Luckily for us, this planet appears to be crawling with caves and tunnels. Each battalion was given a certain geographic area to cause trouble in while we waited for help to arrive."

They approached a large holographic map being projected on a nearby wall. Pilecki pointed to the map. "This is us. We're responsible for this entire area."

A large swath of territory suddenly highlighted. Royce saw where his teams were looking, largely in the opposite direction, which might explain why they hadn't found anyone just yet.

"This area here had been the 192nd Battalion's AOR. One of their combat outposts got discovered three weeks ago by the Orbots. A few days later, the Orbots pretty much wiped out all the remaining COPs and the single command FOB for the region. I can't tell you for certain what's going on in that area anymore," Pilecki explained, a resigned sadness in his voice.

Damn, that would explain why my scout teams haven't found any RA units, just plenty of Zodarks and Orbots.

"I've got some scouting units up in that area right now. We've managed to locate a large Orbot base and three Zodark bases. One of the bases appears to be some sort of airfield or spaceport. They've got a lot of flying craft and vehicles there." Royce paused for a second before adding, "We, um, we found something rather disturbing near their base—"

"Let me guess—you found the Zodark Christmas tree?" Pilecki asked, stopping Royce from explaining any further.

"Yeah, I guess I could see how it'd be called that. Are you telling me there are more of them, or was that an isolated thing?"

Pilecki sighed briefly before he continued. "There are more. How many, I don't know. I just know any humans captured by the Zodarks likely faced a similar fate."

Royce shook his head in disgust. "OK, this is terrible and it's truly disgusting. Putting that aside, I've got a lot of scout teams gathering information on these enemy bases. When it comes time to launch some attacks, I'd like to have these bases plastered with mortars. We need to sow some chaos when the actual invasion starts."

Pilecki grunted at the news. "I agree. That information your scouts are gathering will come in handy for the mortar teams."

"Speaking of indirect fire attacks, my units have brought plenty of ammo for that kind of stuff," Royce informed.

"That's good. It's been hard for us to carry out any sort of large-scale attacks or ambushes on these bastards. Our most effective attacks at this point are IDF attacks against their bases and small IED or sniper attacks on their roving patrols and convoys."

They talked for a little while longer before Royce finally said, "Major, I need to talk to General Bakshi or whoever is currently in charge. Are you able to help me?"

Royce was getting the sense that these guys might actually be on their own, cut off from the larger network of FOBs and COPs.

Pilecki pointed to a couple of chairs and made his way over.

"I can put you in touch with General Bakshi, but before I do, I want to bring you up to speed on a few things. This way, you won't have to ask him about it. We try to keep our conversations to a minimum to lessen the chance of being triangulated. Six days into the invasion, I lost contact with my brigade commander. Near as I can tell, his position got hit by an orbital strike. He was a little too far away for me to send scouts to investigate, so I've been communicating directly with General Bakshi. His son is a sergeant in my battalion, so I think he likes to check in on us for that reason.

"What you need to understand about our current situation, Captain, is that once the Zodarks and Orbots had landed a substantial force on the planet, they really started hitting us with planetary bombardments. We started losing a *lot* of our battalion-level FOBs and COPs all over the equator. It was a very tough time to be in the Army."

Scrunching up his eyebrows, Royce asked, "Orbital strikes? We didn't detect any dust clouds in the atmosphere. Can you tell me a bit more about them?"

"Yeah, I thought the same thing as you until I saw what was happening with my own eyes," Pilecki commented. "Apparently, an Orbot ship came down from orbit to the upper atmosphere or something. Instead of hitting us with kinetic strikes like you'd normally expect, they've been using their laser turrets to hit command bunkers and locations. The damn lasers literally burn a hole right through the ice, dirt, and rocks into the bunkers, melting everything to slag and lava. There was no way anyone was going to survive that. I think this went on for a couple of weeks. Every time the enemy found one of our base camps or a cluster of soldiers, we'd get zapped by one of their ships."

These guys really have been put through hell, thought Royce. Whatever intelligence they'd received before insertions didn't seem to flesh out the reality of what life on the surface had been like.

"Major, are you aware of any sort of planetary defensive weapons they may have moved into place these last few weeks?" Royce asked. "If so, I need you to show me what you've found so we can try and take 'em out."

Major Pilecki looked at Royce for a moment before he responded, "They don't appear to have any built in our AOR. However, before our sister unit, the 315th Battalion, was wiped out, I saw in their report that a group of Orbots had started construction on some sort of large structure. It looked like it was part of a space elevator. Our understanding—and mind you, we could be completely wrong—but our belief was that this space elevator platform was going to be used as some sort of planetary defensive structure. Kind of like what we saw during the Rass campaign where the Orbots' space elevator platforms doubled as a planetary defensive system. The few images I saw of the structure looked just like the ones we saw on the Rass campaign a while back."

Royce grunted at the memory. "Yeah, I remember that. I was a newly minted captain. After my company took that station, we made our move on those other orbital platforms. It was one hell of a mission."

Pilecki nodded. "I was a baby-faced lieutenant during that campaign. I only remember that because my platoon fought around the base of it. That's how I kind of guessed at what they're building here, but again, that's over in the 192nd AOR.

"Captain Royce, once the Orbots started frying our guys with their lasers and dropping hunter-killer teams all over the place, I pulled my battalion back. We went dark. I ordered everyone into the caves. We went underground and did our best to hide and let the enemy pass over us. We stayed hidden for a week. I know we probably should have been out there trying to fight on and help the other battalions, but it would have been suicide. I just couldn't order my battalion to their deaths like that, not when we could lay low and reemerge to cause more problems."

Royce could tell the young officer was having a hard time with his decision. He reached across and placed a hand on his shoulder. "Major, you made the best decision you could with the information you had. No one's going to fault you for that. Staying alive has allowed you to pass on critical intelligence to me—intelligence that's going to greatly aid in the recapture of this planet. Now, let's try and figure out how we can get some eyes on that possible space elevator and plan our own little attack to take it out. But before we do that, I need to talk with General Bakshi."

In the coms room, it took them only a few minutes to connect with the general on a video call.

"Captain Royce, I must say I was hoping we would receive some reinforcements. Please, report," Bakshi ordered.

"Yes, General. Last night we inserted two Delta companies onto the planet. Tonight, two more will join us, along with our battalion commander, Major Jayden Hopper. We're the advance party for the main invasion force—"

Bakshi interrupted, "Captain, when can we expect help?"

"Sir, I'm not at liberty to say over coms. If we can somehow meet in person, I can relay that to you. What I *can* say is soon. I was told to relay to you from General McGinnis to have your forces standing by, ready to raise Cain and cause some problems for the enemy once the festivities do start."

General Bakshi smiled. The two of them talked for a few minutes longer before the call was ended. Despite the heavy levels of encryption and frequency hopping, they still tried to keep the calls concise.

Leaving the coms room, Royce and Pilecki walked back to the operations room and looked over the maps. For the next ten minutes, they strategized how best to stir up some trouble in the local area.

A short while later, two of Royce's other platoons reported in. They sent in their initial reports in, helping to paint a much broader picture of the area. They'd also managed to make contact with several other battalions who'd found themselves in a similar situation to Pilecki and his soldiers.

Pretty soon, the various battalions were sharing intelligence of what was going on in their AORs, which helped everyone to develop a better picture of what was really happening. They were down to thirty-one hours before the next phase of the invasion. That meant they didn't have a lot of time to figure out what targets they should hit and when they should hit them, and get units moved into position—all while not being detected by the enemy.

Chapter Ten
Fringe Science

Sol System
Nonaligned Space

Gunther Haas looked at the plans for the biosafety level six facility. He'd been responsible for overseeing a BSL-5 built on New Eden, but this would be the first level six facility he'd have designed and built. On top of the standard features in a BSL-5 facility, this facility would also be housing live species, prisoners they'd be experimenting on. So not only did the facility need all the standard containment protocols, they also had to build into the process a means of isolating and containing the test subjects.

Satisfied with the plans, Gunther passed them off to the engineer who'd begin work on the facility. Now came the tough part—finding the right people who'd be willing to work on this type of project. Combing through his Rolodex of contacts, he believed he'd found just the right person to lead this research project, a man by the name of Dr. Philip York from the Centers for Disease Control and Prevention out of Atlanta.

Dr. Philip York was one of the world's leading researchers when it came to studying extraterrestrial biologicals and their potential threats to humans. When Earth had suddenly had ten living Zodarks to study, Dr. York had rapidly become an expert in the differences between Zodark and human physiology. He'd authored dozens upon dozens of medical articles on the subject.

Next, Gunther stared at the name of Dr. Jim Peacock. Dr. Peacock was based out of Geelong, Australia. His background was in virology. Most of his research was based on understanding some of the unique viruses humans had been encountering and experiencing on New Eden and Alpha Centaurus. What drew Gunther to him was his research into something called gain of function—particularly with viruses and bacteria they had been encountering on the planets of New Eden, Intus, and Rass.

Having identified the two scientists he'd like to acquire for the project, Gunther now had to arrange a visit to see each of them and convince them to be a part of this secretive project.
****

The High Ground
John Glenn Orbital Station

Gunther Haas stood outside the entrance to the High Ground restaurant as he waited for Dr. Jim Peacock to arrive. He'd reserved a private room for them to eat and talk away from prying ears. Gunther had already met the day before with Dr. York, who'd immediately agreed to work on the project, and he was hoping to make this two for two.

Gunther spotted the doctor as he approached the restaurant and approached him. "Dr. Peacock, I'm Gunther Haas," he said as he extended his hand.

"Ah, Mr. Haas. It's good to meet you. Thank you for your invitation. I was pleasantly surprised to hear of your interest in funding some of my research."

As the pretext to this conversation, Gunther had offered a grant of ten million RD to help fund some of his research. But of course, he wanted to meet over lunch and discuss it first.

"Well, you've done some great work, and I want to see it continued. Come, let's go on in. I've reserved us a private room."

The two of them walked in and placed drink orders as they looked over the menu. Once they'd received their drinks and their order was taken, Gunther got down to business.

"Dr. Peacock—may I call you Jim?"

The scientist smiled. "Sure. Most of my friends and financial supporters do, Gunther."

"Excellent. Well, Jim, I'm afraid I may have asked you to come here under a bit of a false pretense, but before you get upset, please allow me to explain."

Jim grunted at the comment, his facial expression turning sour. "So, I take it you aren't providing my research team with a ten million RD grant?"

"No, I'll still provide you with the grant money," Gunther insisted. "As I said before, your research is incredibly important, and it should continue to be funded." Jim seemed confused, but he relaxed a bit at this comment. Gunther leaned forward and lowered his voice. "But what I want to offer you is something so much bigger, so much more important to humanity, if you are interested."

Jim's left eyebrow rose. "OK, I'm interested. But what's the catch?"

Gunther pulled something up on his tablet and slid it across the table. "Well, as a matter of fact, I'll need you to sign this before we go any further."

Jim took the tablet and briefly looked over the NDA before signing it. Once he had, the project revealed itself. After a moment of reading it, he looked up. "Wait a second, so you work for Viceroy Miles Hunt? I would report directly to him?"

"Yes, this would be a secretive, private research project for the Viceroy. You'll have an unlimited research budget for the duration of the project."

"When you say unlimited…"

"I mean *unlimited*—within means, of course, but yes. Money will not be an issue. I can also assure you that you and your staff will be well compensated."

The two of them talked briefly about the job and the lab being built in the Belt. When they started talking about the gain of function research Jim had been doing, and then Gunther mentioned how the lab would have a prison to hold a couple of dozen Zodark detainees, a light suddenly dawned, and Jim realized exactly what kind of research he was being asked to do.

"Gunther, I'm not opposed to doing the kind of research I believe you're proposing—but I have a couple of demands," Jim said, crossing his arms and leaning back. "First, I want a hundred million RD endowment established to permanently fund my research facility in Geelong. Second, I'm going to need some sort of blanket immunity, should this become public. Will that be a problem?"

Gunther smiled. He'd anticipated this and had a ready answer. He went over his arrangements with Jim, who appeared satisfied with what Viceroy Hunt had agreed to should things sour with the Republic. With his major concerns addressed, they started identifying who else would work on the project with him. Once an initial team had been put together, they went over more specifics for how they were going to make this work. They had to bring a lot of one-off supplies with them to this new lab. They also had to create an environment where the researchers could cut loose and relax when not working. It wasn't like they could go to the local bar and blow off steam. Everything had to be self-contained to the lab once a person entered.

When their lunch had ended, Gunther said he'd be in contact. Once the lab was finalized, he'd send for Jim and his team. In the meantime, Jim needed to identify who else would assist him on this project and finalize a list of supplies for the lab. If he needed things after the fact, they could be obtained; it would just take some time to acquire them.
****

Gaelic Outpost
Nonaligned Space
Sol

Gunther sat in the shuttle craft as they floated near the site of the lab.

"We had originally looked at some of the large asteroids nearby," the engineer explained. "Ultimately, we believe this crater on the main planetoid will provide you with the most secure location."

"Why are we not using one of the asteroids again?" Gunther asked. He wasn't keen on the idea of having their lab on the same rock as the Gaelic Outpost.

"These asteroids—they aren't exactly anchored to anything. Sure, they're large, but they have limited to no gravity of their own. If, say, a meteor or another asteroid bumps them, they can be thrown off course and set into a motion we may not be able to control. That can be a problem, and it's something we'd rather not have to plan for. Right now, when an object looks to be headed toward the Gaelic, our response is to destroy it if we can't nudge it out of the way. Our planetoid, however, is enormous, more than a hundred kilometers in circumference. It has point two gs of organic gravity When we add in our own artificial gravity generator, it jumps to point nine gs, even on the surface of the planetoid."

Gunther interrupted, "Meaning we'll have nearly the same gravity as we have on Earth by building the lab on the surface of the planetoid."

"Exactly," the engineer confirmed. "As to the location, we have multiple craters to choose from. This one we're looking at has the highest walls, so you could establish your lab facility here and it'd be largely hidden."

Gunther thought about the proposal. He glanced down at his blueprints and then back at the proposed site.

This could work...

"OK, let's assume we go with this location. How long until you think we could have this place completed?"

"Um, I've been allocated fifty synthetics for the project. We're not using any humans, which will limit the number of people who'll know about it. But with the workers I've got, I think we should have this place completed in maybe nine to twelve months."

Gunther frowned. He needed this lab built yesterday, not in nine to twelve months. "How about we bring in our own synthetics and materials to work the project? I've got a construction ship on standby, ready to start once we sign off on the location."

The engineer breathed a sigh of relief and nodded. "That would be excellent, Gunther. With the demands in the shipyards, I just don't have enough synthetics to meet the kind of timetable it sounds like you're after."

Gunther smiled understandingly. "I know. That's why we've brought our own small army of workers with us. Once we have the initial lab built, I think we'll probably build a dome over the entire crater to further hide our facility."

"Thank you, Gunther, for being understanding. Then if this site meets your expectations, I'll go ahead and let Sara and Liam know and we'll leave you guys to it." The engineer got their little shuttle moving again and they headed toward the shipyard and the port that would allow them to connect back to the station.

You'll get more accomplished using honey and money than you will vinegar and fear, Gunther kept telling himself.

He needed to be a nice understanding guy with this engineer, and a little kindness toward the overworked and likely underpaid man would go a long way toward making this guy an unofficial source of information and getting just about anything else he'd need from the people that ran this outpost.

As they approached the sprawling shipyard connected to the station, Gunther caught sight of everything going on there. For a small outpost, this place was humming with activity. In addition to the ever-present ten Republic frigates they were constantly building, there was a mix of half a dozen mining barges and some intersystem freighters under construction. Along the new shipyard extension were the keels of ten large transport ships.

These Belters aren't wasting any time gearing up to exit this place in favor of their new home world.

When Gunther had reached his office on the station, he sent a message to the construction ship nearby to start work on the lab. Next, he wrote up a detailed, comprehensive report to Viceroy Hunt, letting him know he'd found the location for the lab and explaining why it was going to be on the same planetoid as the station. Gunther also informed Hunt he'd secured their top two choices of scientists for the project. Everything was on schedule; they'd hopefully start the project in roughly six months.

Chapter Eleven
Once More Unto the Breach

Apollo Company, 1-331st Infantry Battalion
Alfheim

Snow started to fall. It wasn't a lot of snow, just some light flurries. *I can't decide if this snow will help or hinder our attack*, First Lieutenant Adam Singletary thought. He brushed that aside; he had a job to do regardless of the weather.

Maneuvering forward cautiously and slowly so as not to draw any attention, he crawled up to the very edge of the tree line that overlooked the spaceport and the orbital elevator. Using the magnification option on his HUD, he enhanced the zoom on his helmet's visor to give him a better view of the spaceport. Once Singletary identified what he was looking for, he started marking targets on the objective and then assigned them to different squad leaders to action. This kind of virtual intelligence tagging was a unique tool made available to platoon and company officers and their platoon or company sergeants. It allowed them to pick specific targets to be taken out in the opening seconds of an attack, something that was incredibly useful, particularly in a moment like this where timing was going to be everything.

With what he had determined as critical targets tagged, it was now just a matter of waiting for the timer synchronizing their attack with Commander Hamza's to reach zero. Then they'd find out really swiftly if their plan had some merit or if it was doomed to fail from the outset. Looking to the top-left corner of his HUD, Singletary saw the countdown getting closer to zero. With each second that ticked away, the butterflies bouncing around in his gut got stronger. He had the sudden urge to urinate.

Then he heard it. It was faint at first, but then it grew into a low rumble. Stealing a glance in the direction where Hamza's people were, Singletary spotted a plume of black smoke. Then his ears registered a loud thunderclap as the sound of the explosion reached him. Another column of smoke rose into the air, then another. Singletary smiled. Hamza's people were getting their licks in on these bastards.

Singletary suddenly felt a slight nudge on his left arm. He turned and saw Sergeant Corbyn point at something. Following where he was indicating, he saw swarms of Zodark and Orbot soldiers rushing out of their barracks buildings, running toward the vehicle park. Then the countdown on his HUD registered zero. It was their turn to bring the pain.

"Sergeant Corbyn, I think it's time to rain some steel, don't you?"

"Copy that, sir."

Seconds later, Singletary heard one of the soldiers a little further behind call out, "Hang it!"

The two mortarmen hung the smart rounds over the tubes, waiting for that final order. These rounds had all been preprogrammed to hit the targets Singletary had previously identified. Seconds after having the mortars hanging over the tubes, the sergeant shouted, "Fire!"

The rounds fell into the tubes and thumped into the air, journeying skyward as they arced through the small flurry of snow and toward their intended targets. No sooner had the first two rounds left the tube than the mortarmen had the next two dropping down, right behind them. The soldiers grabbed and dropped rounds as fast as they could, until all twenty of their remaining rounds had been fired. They were expending the last of their rounds on this mission.

It took approximately forty-two seconds for them to expend the ten rounds per tube. As the rounds reached their apex, little stubby wings and a rudder popped out, giving the mortars the ability to leverage their forward momentum to glide in a circular holding pattern until their targeting AI instructed them to begin their deadly approach on an unsuspected enemy. Once all twenty of the 81mm ten-pound high-explosive mortars were in position, they synchronized their descents, timing it so all the rounds would hit at exactly the same time.

What happened next was orchestrated chaos as the mortar rounds slammed into enemy vehicles, guard towers, bunkers, ammunition dumps, and clusters of Zodark and Orbot soldiers, tossing and throwing their bodies around like rag dolls. Singletary saw the explosions before he felt and heard the concussive blasts. He was beyond thrilled at the carnage unfolding. With each Zodark or Orbot thrashed and torn apart by the flames and shrapnel, it meant one less enemy combatant that could harm Singletary's people. The thundering explosions and geysers of flame and debris were also the signal to the rest of the squads to begin their attack on the base.

Both Cougars leapt forward out of their concealed positions now, closing the distance between themselves and the forest they had been hiding in. The mechs, controlled by their human operators, ran next to the armored vehicles, shooting at any soldier or machine that posed a possible risk to the Cougars. Right now, getting the Cougars to the space elevator with their tactical nuke was the only thing that mattered.

Enemy fire was already dancing across the snowy scene unfolding before them toward human targets. Some laser shots glanced off the vehicles with little to no effect, but soon enough, a few laser bolts hit some of Singletary's soldiers. At first, it was just one or two soldiers, but soon it was a handful as the enemy tried their best to reorganize and mount some sort of defense of the spaceport.

Singletary had only been in command of the company for a few days, and he'd just lost his first soldiers under his command as the acting commanding officer of Apollo Company.

****

"Stick close to your vehicle, Bastille!" shouted Jones over their internal comms.

Private First Class Andre Bastille noticed he'd drifted a little farther from the vehicle he was supposed to be following and moved closer. It was hard to discern what the proper distance should be. A couple of the rounds that impacted the vehicles had ricocheted off the Cougars and into his mech. His computer wasn't sending up any alarms yet, but why tempt fate?

Taking a deep breath, he said to himself, *It's combat, you're gonna be shot at. Stay focused.*

"Clear the channel!" Jones shouted again.

Andre cursed to himself before toggling off his microphone. The charge had moved halfway across the open field and was making good ground. Andre had let loose a string of rounds from his mech's Gatling gun, saving his missiles for when he got closer or found larger targets of opportunity. The key was not to damage the elevator so they could get the Cougar on board and send it up the well. However, with so much incoming and outgoing fire, he couldn't see how that was possible.

Another round pinged off his armor, and Andre grunted in frustration, letting loose another salvo from the Gatling gun. Next to him, he saw another Republic foot mobile fall in a heap and not get up.

Andre wondered how Takata was doing. Without enough mechs to go around in their squad, Takata had been forced to move on foot with the other squads. Andre hoped the kid hadn't caught a laser already.

"Legion, we have a Zodark rocket team setting up to the north. I've marked their location," came the voice of First Squad's leader, Staff Sergeant Moreau.

Pulling up the location on his HUD, Andre locked the building up and let loose three of his smart missiles. The rounds impacted and sent fire and debris in all directions, obliterating the antiarmor team before they could disable the Cougars.

"Good shot, Legion," came a cheer from his headset.

Andre smiled but continued to scan for more targets. That team wouldn't be the last.

****

Corporal Eva Jorgenson stayed in the rear with the other medics and Lieutenant Singletary. She hated it with every fiber of her being, even if she understood the reason why. Every time she saw a soldier go down, her muscles tensed as she wanted to stand and run into the fray, but she checked herself, against her instincts. The area was not clear. The ground was too open, and if they sent the medics out in the open like that, then chances were, they'd get shot themselves.

"This is bullsh—" Mac started to say.

Staff Sergeant Moore cut him off. "Enough, Mac."

"But, Sarge—"

"I said, that's enough," Moore responded through gritted teeth. "I don't like this any more than the rest of you, but we're all this company has, and if we go down because you want to be a hero, countless more will die."

"What about the ones down in the rear?" Corporal Kim asked. "The Zodarks are focusing their fire on the Cougars and mechs out front. We could easily move out there and start bringing the wounded back to safety."

Moore looked toward the chaos of the battlefield and moved over to where the lieutenant was monitoring it. The exchange looked heated, and Jorgensen waited for the moment Moore would give them the all clear.

"Eva, Abba, and Kim—get out there and start bringing back the wounded. If you can't stabilize them in a timely manner, just bring them to the CCP."

Moore turned to Mac, "Get a casualty collection point set up to my rear ASAP!"

Jorgensen knew Mac would be angry that he had been left behind to set up the CCP, but everyone went about their business as ordered without a word. This was the moment in combat when no one questioned anything; you were given an order and others' lives depended on you listening to it.

The three medics bounded into the open, running for the first soldiers they could see down in the snow. Jorgensen slid next to one who was lying facedown. Blood was pooling and melting the snow around the female soldier's head. She already knew what was going to greet her when she turned the body over. Still, she had to check. As Jorgensen flipped her over, pieces of hair, brain matter, and skull fragments fell out of the busted helmet visor, causing Jorgensen to shriek as she released the body. She fell back on her butt from the gruesome surprise.

As she fell back, several laser bolts flashed right where she'd just been, electrifying the air around her. "Holy crap! That was close," she stammered aloud.

Scrambling back to her feet, Jorgensen tried to put that person out of her mind and ran toward the next wounded soldier.

As she approached a group of three soldiers, she saw that one of them was writhing on the ground in awful pain while the other two were heavily engaged against a couple of Orbots. Jorgensen felt guilty about leaving the body of the other soldier. She deserved better than to just be passed over and abandoned. That soldier could have been someone's mother, sister, wife, or girlfriend. Someone knew and loved this person, despite them being halfway across the galaxy. Thoughts like that haunted her dreams. Still, Jorgensen had to push it aside and pull herself together. She was a Republic soldier, a medic, and a team leader.

As she kneeled beside the next wounded soldier, Jorgensen saw Abba run past her, a soldier thrown over her shoulder as she hastily moved him back to the casualty collection point Mac was manning. The soldier she was rushing back toward Mac was screaming wildly in pain. Judging by the looks of it, the man had one leg missing from the knee down. A streak of blood ran down the back of Abba's armor. The man's other foot looked like it was hanging on by a tangled mess of tendons, shredded muscles, and tissue.

"Watch out, Doc!" yelled a soldier near Jorgensen. "We've got an Orbot trying to flank us while these Zodarks keep us pinned down." A handful of laser flashes zipped over their heads and around them.

"Just keep 'em off my back while I get him stabilized and back to the rear."

Jorgensen read the wounded man's name tape. "Hang in there, Hodges. I'm going to see how bad you are and get some painkillers in you," she explained.

The soldier was thrashing about as he screamed relentlessly. She tried to plug her medical port into the man's armor to help him, but he kept squirming. Jorgensen grabbed him by his chest rig and yelled in his face, "Stop screaming and moving all over the place so I can help you!" Then she dropped him back on the ground.

The soldier seemed to have gotten the message and finally calmed down enough for her to start treating him. The obvious damage was from a laser blaster to his lower abdomen. He was also suffering from internal bleeding. Putting the correct information in, she sent a signal to the armor to begin plugging the holes with a bio-organic coagulant that would temporarily stop the bleeding, stabilizing him until they could get him to a higher-level trauma center. Next, she hit the soldier with a dose of fentanyl to kill the pain.

Now that he was stabilized, she leveraged the limited strength her exoskeleton combat suit gave her and lifted him up onto her shoulder. The medics' uniforms didn't have the same overly aggressive exoskeleton combat suit as the infantry soldiers or the Special Forces had, but it was just enough to help them carry a wounded soldier away from the battlefield. She remembered during training when they used to practice this without the exosuits. She'd have to pick a battle buddy up and run a hundred meters and back. Of course, the distance fluctuated sometimes based on what she'd gotten in trouble for. At the time, she'd hated it and thought she was being hazed. In retrospect, it was conditioning her to do exactly what she was doing now—saving someone's life.

As she ran with the soldier over her shoulder to carry him back to safety, he inexplicably let out a horrible scream of agony. She found that odd considering she'd just given him a dose of fentanyl. That stuff was usually strong enough to knock a horse out.

Cursing at him, she barked, "Stop screaming! I just hit you with the good stuff. You're going to get us shot if you keep yelling like that."

It was bad enough carrying the wounded man by herself. The last thing she needed was his screams clouding her judgment or getting them shot in the back by a Zodark. When she finally made it to the CCP, she laid the man down gently and returned to the battlefield to look for more wounded.

Rinse and repeat until we all come home, she thought.
****

RNS *Valkyrie*
Preparing to Jump into the Sirius System

Private First Class David Roberts was once again sitting around in the troop bay as they waited for their ship to join the melee that was the Sirius system. Word had passed through the PNN, the private news network of unofficial scuttlebutt, that the fleet had jumped nearly a hundred warships into the system to duke it out with an equally large Orbot and Zodark fleet. Meanwhile, dozens upon dozens of orbital assault ships and troop transports sat on the other side of the gate, waiting for the order to jump in and make their mad dash to Alfheim.

"Is it always like this before a battle?" said one of the privates to no one in particular.

One of the sergeants turned to him. "Like what?"

"Sitting around and waiting? The anticipation is killing me," squirmed the soldier.

A couple of the noncoms laughed. David did too. "It's an old military game," answered one of the NCOs. "You hurry up to one place or to get ready for something, only to wait for whatever to happen. Hurry up and wait. It's as old as the Army, kid."

"Just be glad we aren't with the fleet right now. Let them clear us a path. Then we'll follow in behind them," another soldier opined.

"Yeah, what would you know about that, Private?" chided one of the sergeants. "Isn't this your first combat tour?"

Not put off in the least, the young soldier stuck his chin out as he countered, "My older sis is a lieutenant commander in the fleet. She's aboard a battlecruiser. She told me how the fleet goes in ahead of the transports and clears a path. She's probably in with the fleet right now."

No one said anything for a moment. They were lost in their thoughts.

"What about you, David? You were here for the initial invasion, weren't you?" a staff sergeant asked as he passed out some snacks to the squad.

Taking one of the protein bars he was handing out, David looked at his feet for a second, then up at the others in his squad. They were staring at him, awaiting his response.

"Yeah, I was here for the first invasion," David confirmed. "I was in First Squad, First Platoon, Apollo Company. It was crazy and chaotic that first day. We went down in the first wave. Heck, a squad from Third Platoon didn't even make it to the landing zone. Their Osprey got nailed on the way in."

"What's it like? I mean, down on the planet?" another soldier asked. Now more of the soldiers were quieting down. For the first time in weeks, they were actually paying attention to him. Even a couple of the sergeants were listening. They'd been on Alfheim too, wounded like him, which was why they hadn't been trapped when the Zodarks had come back.

David shrugged. "I…I wasn't there long. What I do remember was the weather. It was cold. Bitterly cold. Cloudy, and it snowed a lot."

"What did you do? How'd you stub your foot?" chided Private Fischer sarcastically. "Sprain an ankle so you could get out on an evac?" Fischer wasn't liked by anyone. He was always smarting off to the NCOs and talking trash to anyone he could. At six foot five inches tall and built like an NFL lineman, the guy was a surly bully.

"Screw you, Fischer. You weren't there!" David shot back angrily.

Fischer stared daggers back at him. He was about to say something when Sergeant McAfee cut in. "Before you go making up lies, Fischer, David got wounded just like a lot of us did. He even got a valor medal and a Purple Heart for his actions that day. Maybe when it's our turn, you'll be so lucky as to earn a valor medal of your own, Fischer. Then you can talk smack. Until then, you're just a cherry like everyone else."

Fischer didn't smart off this time. He just sat there and stewed.

David had been days away from heading back to his unit on the surface when that fateful day had occurred. Instead, the RNS *Mercy* had jumped out of the system in retreat, back to Primord space. As he thought back to the invasion, the day he'd been wounded, David wondered how things might have turned out if he hadn't gotten injured. He still struggled with the bad dreams. However, other soldiers had told him that they would generally go away in time.

When his wounds had fully healed, David had been transferred back to the RNS *Valkyrie*, and from there they had cycled him into another unit the ship was taking on. Now, almost six weeks later, he was preparing to land back on Alfheim with a new squad and unit. Thankfully, the disputes he'd gotten into with that corporal had been shoved under the rug given the greater importance of the war.

Aside from his squad leader, Staff Sergeant Howell, and his team leader, Sergeant McAfee, David was the only one with combat experience. O'Connor, Fischer, and Valdez were good kids, but they were straight out of basic training. They hadn't even had time to get used to New Eden's gravity before their unit had shipped out.

"What if I get dusted before I even make it dirtside?" Private O'Connor asked as he squirmed. "David said one of his old platoon's squads didn't even make it to the surface. I didn't come all this way just to get plastered in the first couple seconds of battle." The guy's right knee was bouncing up and down rapidly as his hands fidgeted, his thumbs rubbing against the inside of this hands.

David turned to O'Connor. "Whoa—you need to calm down. Once we strap into that Osprey, none of us can control what happens next. If our shuttle gets nailed, it gets nailed. Chances are it'll be quick, and you won't know what happened. Just remember when you get on the ground, stick together and move. Find some cover, lay down a handful of aimed shots at the enemy and then advance to the next covered position and keep repeating."

O'Connor nodded. His fidgeting decreased after the pep talk.

After having been silent for a while, Fischer decided he wanted to insert himself back into the conversation. "Dave, you've been on one combat drop and got injured on the first day. Stop preaching to us all like you're some kind of combat veteran with all kinds of experience, because you aren't."

"That's one more combat drop than you, Private Fischer," Sergeant McAfee shot back in a harsh tone, "and I think it's about time for you to shut the hell up and sit down."

Fischer went back to sulking privately after this latest rebuke.

Sergeant McAfee leaned into David. "What you told O'Connor, that was good. Well said. Sometimes it takes a word or two to set the mind thinking straight again."

"Thanks," said David. "One of my old squad mates told me that before my first jump. Really helped me out."

"Huh, sounds like a smart guy. Think I might have known him?" asked McAfee.

"Don't know. You run across a guy named PFC Duncan Campbell?"

"That sack of bones?" McAfee laughed. "Hell yeah, I know who he is. We went through basic together. Did you say PFC? Jesus, you'd think he'd learn by now. He should be a staff sergeant. How's he doing, ya think?"

"I suppose we'll know soon enough," David replied.

Sometime in the next hour or so, the armada of troopships and transports would jump back into the Sirius system and the reinvasion would begin.

Chapter Twelve
Deadly Pawn Sacrifice

Spaceport Elevator
Alfheim

Adam Singletary watched as First and Second Squads' vehicles reached the outer perimeter of the orbital elevator base. The ground assault troops had suffered horrific losses, only compounding how savaged the company had been since the Orbots and Zodarks had thrown the fleet out of the system and reinvaded Alfheim. Looking at the losses and saying to oneself that it could have been worse, though that might have been true, did little to help Singletary cope with the losses he was taking. He knew this attack was necessary; still, he felt like a butcher sending his soldiers to their death.

As he scanned the battlefield, Singletary saw the medics were performing heroically, darting out into enemy fire to retrieve the wounded and get them back to the aid station. Looking deeper into the enemy base, Singletary saw that his mortar teams had thoroughly trashed the place, just like he'd hoped. They had hammered the hell out of the vehicle yard, the fortified positions, and the enemy barracks. Their precision hits had likely killed a solid third of the soldiers they would have had to fight. More than a handful of holes had been busted wide open in a few sections of the perimeter wall around the loading docks of the elevator. Many of his soldiers were rushing through those gaps.

Then Singletary spotted a strange movement near the left side of the wall. It was too far to focus his helmet's camera in on with the smoke obscuring his lens. What had been an organized assault suddenly looked to be collapsing into a chaotic mess.

"This is Cougar Two-One Delta to Apollo Six," came the voice of Private Takata, the transfer from the mech squad.

"This is Apollo Six." Singletary couldn't stop the worry rising in his voice.

Why is the driver of the Cougar calling? Why isn't it the vehicle commander, Sergeant Haus?

"Apollo Six, the vehicle was hit by some type of explosion. It's rolled over on its side. I have two KIA and I'm trapped inside. How copy?"

"Is the package secured?" Singletary asked.

"Yes, sir. I have it with me."

"Apollo Six, this is Legion, I'm on my way to Cougar Two to retrieve the payload."

"Get it on the elevator, Legion. Six out."

****

Andre "Legion" Bastille broke into a sprint toward the Cougar that had been hit and flipped over while Abede and Jones covered First Squad's Cougar, the only vehicle still operable and in the fight. The AI in his targeting computer automatically targeted any heads that poked above the tops of the concrete barriers surrounding the spaceport entrance.

BOOM!

An explosion erupted near one of the Cougars, showering Andre's mech with dirt, rocks, debris, and chunks of ice. Stabilizing himself, Andre spun around and watched as flame erupted around First Squad's Cougar as it was tossed over onto its side like a child's plaything. The explosion made him stagger backward to the point that he fell into Jones and Abede's mechs.

Andre tried to shake the effects of the concussion off as he searched through the smoke for signs of the two other mechs he'd bumped into, but he couldn't make anything out. Between the smoke from the nearby flames and the drifting snow falling across the battlefield, his field of vision was grossly obscured. Then Andre saw movement. Through the pillars of smoke, he saw the two hulking machines walk through the clouds of debris as they engaged targets to their front, not missing a beat in the action.

One of the mechs' arms with the Gatling gun swept across a forty-degree section in front of them, cutting down dozens of Orbots who tried to bum-rush their positions. Its fifty-caliber magrail slugs tore the cyborgs apart with the impact of each round. Then Andre saw the mech with the shield painted on the side of its bulky frame take a couple of laser bolts to its knee joint, causing the mech to buckle under its own weight and collapse to the ground.

Crap, with another mech down, how are we going to flip this Cougar back over so it can deliver the nuke?

He nearly turned his mech to go help Jones, but with the first vehicle destroyed, the bomb on board the overturned vehicle was their only remaining chance. Getting back to his feet and heading toward Second Squad's Cougar, Andre rounded the corner of the overturned vehicle and began lifting it onto its side. The driver's hatch suddenly popped open now that it wasn't obscured, and to Andre's surprise, Takata popped out.

"Where the hell have you been?" Takata yelled, holding the nuclear device in his arms.

Andre smiled and reached forward to let Takata place the device in his mech's outstretched hand, but a streak of blue caused him to flinch. He moved his head to the left as the blinding light suddenly flashed across his vision. That brief movement saved his life as a laser bolt sailed by, close enough that it scorched the paint job on his helmet. A second one tore through the glass of his helmet and then through the back of his mech and out the other end, barely missing his head.

As the mech fell to the ground, red and yellow warning lights flashed across his systems. Andre still had the presence of mind to let his targeting AI prioritize six targets for his remaining smart missiles. For the briefest of moments, time slowed as his mech collapsed in a heap.

Andre had no idea what the AI had targeted with his remaining missiles, only that they had zipped off and found their marks, judging by the explosions he heard. Peering through the shattered windshield of his mech, Andre saw Takata with the nuclear device close to his body. The young soldier turned and ran for all his worth toward the orbital elevator. Andre wanted to scream to him to stop or just throw the device into the elevator, but the words wouldn't form in his mouth. Instead, he saw Takata dodge flashes of lasers zipping all around as he jumped and dashed, running up the ramp to the space elevator. Takata took a giant leap and dove through the elevator door, crashing to the floor with the device.

The nearby Orbots and Zodarks knew something must be happening with this lone human soldier and whatever he was carrying because they now shifted their fire toward him. But before they could kill him or stop him from doing whatever it was he was about to do, Takata had hit the elevator button, closing the door and activating the lift. The giant elevator shot skyward through its magnetic rings, hurtling to the orbital station above at a rate of thousands of feet per second.

That was when Andre snapped out of his haze and shouted, "This is Mech Legion to all Apollo units. Jackpot. I repeat, jackpot!"

Andre could hear the responses from the units replying to his call that the device had been sent up the elevator. Lying in his half-destroyed mech, Andre craned his head to watch the lift race out of view at a startling pace. The last thing Andre saw after Takata jumped into the elevator was the platform being pummeled with laser bolts blanketing the space. He wasn't sure if a lone Zodark or Orbot had managed to jump on the platform with him. All he knew was that Takata had just knowingly sacrificed himself for every single person in the company. For the briefest of moments, he stared up until he saw the telltale sign that Takata had succeeded. A bright flash lit up the sky as a second sun momentarily appeared.

Well done, my friend. Well done, indeed…

****

Corporal Eva Jorgensen had just finished stabilizing another soldier brought to the CCP when radio traffic erupted in her ear. Looking up toward the battle, she tried to figure out what was happening in the chaos, but her senses were overloaded by the comms traffic. She stepped toward the tree line to see what was going on and was just in time to see one of the Cougars erupt in flames after being hit by something. Then, to her horror, the second Cougar ran over something and blew up. It was flipped onto its side. Jorgensen looked on as one of the mechs went down next to the Cougar that now was cooking off its onboard ammunition.

She turned to Moore. "Whose Cougar was hit?"

"They're both down," Moore replied.

"I know they're both down, but which one is on fire?"

"The nuclear device has a fail-safe in case of damage. The fire won't set it off."

"Damnit, Moore! Is it Second Squad's Cougar or not?" Jorgensen yelled back in frustration, her emotions starting to get the best of her.

She knew he was avoiding providing the specific information because Jorgensen was Second Squad's medic. She knew the soldiers of Second Squad well, and more importantly, she knew their acting squad leader, Sergeant Haus. When they went out on patrols, she would stick with either Staff Sergeant Murphy or Alpha Team's Sergeant Haus until she had to go do her job of saving a trooper's life.

"Jorgensen, it was First Squad's vehicle. There's been no word from the crew, and that includes Staff Sergeant Moreau."

"And the others?"

"I think their driver was Private Lancaster and their gunner was PFC Campbell. Both from Alpha Team." Moore looked at Jorgensen as he spoke.

A guilty relief set over Jorgensen, knowing that it wasn't her squad's Cougar that had erupted in flames. "See, was that so hard?" she hissed with a little more vitriol than she'd anticipated.

"More than you can know. Now get back to work, Corporal Jorgenson," Moore ordered.

Jorgensen knew that the vehicle flipped over on its side had to be Second Squad's Cougar. She had heard it mentioned over the comms but missed the traffic when she was talking to Moore. Now she wished she'd never argued with him.

Jorgensen knew her job was important; she was reminded of it every time they went into combat, but sometimes she despised being on the sidelines. All the action was in the front, and she never knew if her friends had made it out of the hellfire until either they came to her on a stretcher later or they just showed up, unharmed.

"Jackpot!" came the call over Jorgensen's radio. When she heard that, she knew what it meant.

She echoed the call to the other medics to make sure they heard that one of the nuclear devices had been sent up the elevator, and then she watched anxiously. The elevator was enormous, stretching into the clouds and out of sight.

She felt the others looking skywards as well. A hush came over the fighting, almost like it had been paused as they all watched for any sign that they had accomplished their mission. When it came, they looked away. A flash of brilliant white light erupted in the sky.

They'd done it. They'd done the impossible.

Chapter Thirteen
Incoming

Arriving in Orbit over Alfheim

After hours of waiting, the *Valkyrie* finally jumped into the Sirius system. The next ninety minutes went by in a blur of chaotic craziness and sheer terror. Their ship arrived near what they thought was going to be a cleared path directly to the planet. Instead, the *Valkyrie* jumped in within range of a few Orbot ships still battling it out with a handful of Primord ships. Needless to say, the dozens upon dozens of fat, juicy orbital assault ships and troop transports were just too big a target for the Orbots to pass on.

Suddenly, as David and his squad were moving from the troop bays to the flight deck, blinking yellow lights in the corridors changed to flashing red lights, indicating something was wrong. David's squad entered the flight deck and ran with the others toward the rows of waiting Ospreys. As they were racing toward the opened rear hatches, there was a loud boom. The ship shook a bit, but the crew chiefs and loadmasters continued to wave them on.

Then the *Valkyrie* took a second, much harder hit. This time, most of the soldiers running to the shuttles that would take them to the surface were thrown to the deck or stumbled and went flying. The soldiers suddenly had an entirely new fear to worry about—getting blown up in space before they even made it to the planet. Luckily for the soldiers, the attack on their ship ended about as swiftly as it had begun.

By the time they were loaded on the dozens of Osprey shuttles and dropships, the Orbot ships that had fired on them had been destroyed. Truth be told, David had no idea how many enemy warships were still nearby, shooting at the transports. All he knew for certain was that his squad was in their Osprey, waiting to be shot out the launch tube and on their way to the surface.

Sitting inside the Osprey, David felt something buffet the ship as the lights flickered and came back to life. The next thing he felt was momentary weightlessness as the Osprey launched away from their mothership. Being trapped in a confined space was the worst part of the journey. He had gotten over the fear of dying while in transit, but that didn't mean he wasn't concerned about what was going on around him, especially after their ship had just taken a few hard hits. That was a first for him.

Please, Lord, don't let me die in this can before I can even join the fight and help my friends.

Moments later, the voice of his squad leader, Staff Sergeant Howell, announced, "They did it! The orbital platforms nearest us have been destroyed! We're headed dirtside, troopers!"

The information was met with cheers around the cabin as the Osprey's thrusters kicked into high speed, rocketing them toward the atmosphere of the ice planet. Now it was all on them. When they hit the ground, David's team, led by Sergeant McAfee, would work on securing the perimeter of the spaceport and the space elevator. If the Zodarks followed their standard military doctrine, then they'd likely launch some sort of counterattack to overwhelm the landing zones and prevent them from establishing a foothold.

"Thirty seconds!" came the call over his internal communications from the pilot.

As the Osprey broke through the atmosphere, the crushing feeling of gravity returned to David's bones. Soon they would be touching down. As the Osprey banked and leveled out, the straps that kept him in his seat unlatched, allowing him to stand with the rest of his squad as they prepared to get off the shuttle once it landed.

David slapped O'Connor on the back. "Keep your head down, listen to Sergeant McAfee, and everything will be easy."

O'Connor didn't reply. Instead, he brought his rifle to the low ready and bent his knees for the landing. David felt the Osprey hit the ground and then the ramp lowered, letting in the blinding light that bounced off the snow. It was somehow more intense than the first time he'd landed on Alfheim. When he'd first landed, there had been overcast cloud cover, keeping most of the sun off the snow, but now there wasn't a cloud in the sky.

As David ran down the ramp and approached their rally point with his team, his eyes darted from one place to another, looking for possible locations a Zodark or Orbot could attack them from. What he saw all around them was sheer chaos. Vehicles were flipped over and on fire; bodies both friendly and enemy littered the ground. He saw torn-apart chunks of mechs strewn about and debris everywhere. The battle for the orbital elevator had clearly been a costly one.

From David's vantage point, it looked like the fighting had stopped around the elevator platform itself. Republic soldiers were gathering the wounded and bringing them to a triage point in the forests across the field a few hundred meters away. That was where his team was headed. They were positive a Zodark counterattack would be coming from the east to try to flank the newly captured position and retake the elevator. Looking up, David saw the hulking, twisted metal of the destroyed elevator. If the Zodarks came for it, it would be for nothing.

****

Lieutenant Adam Singletary surveyed the damage as the remnants of his company fell back to rally points around the battlefield. Staff Sergeant Moreau had been killed when her vehicle had taken a direct hit, and Sergeant Bankole was currently in charge of First Squad. Staff Sergeant Lillian Murphy, despite being his acting platoon sergeant, had retaken control of Second Squad after Sergeant Haus had been killed. The worst news came from Third Squad. They had incurred the heaviest losses and were only at five percent strength, with Private First Class Kathleen Clary acting as their squad leader. He had to start getting a feel for what was happening and called his squad leaders in.

He first looked to PFC Clary. "Take what's left of Third Squad and hold them in the rear as security, Private. Make sure they have water and enough ammunition, if they haven't already started dividing it up amongst themselves."

Clary, whose armor was scarred and blackened from intense combat, nodded. "Yes, sir. You can count on us."

Singletary smiled before turning to Murphy and Bankole. "We have reinforcements coming in from orbit as we reinvade this place, but now that communication with the fleet in orbit is back online, I'm being told we can expect a counterattack from the east." He sighed briefly, then asked carefully, "Which one of you is combat ready?"

Staff Sergeant Murphy spoke. "After losing Sergeant Haus, it's gonna take me a few to reorganize and get everyone ready for another go at it, if that's what you're asking."

Sergeant Rodriguez cut in, "Losing Moreau hurts, but it happened quickly, and I was able to get the squad into a better position. We've lost a lot, but we're organized and ready."

"How are you on ammo?" Singletary asked Rodriguez.

133

"We could use some more if you're sending us to defend against a counterattack. Mortars would be nice to have as well," Rodriguez replied.

"Then they're yours. Get with Private Clary and have her give you their ammunition. As soon as these reinforcements begin to rally up, I'll send them your way."

Rodriguez nodded and took off toward where his squad was waiting.

Singletary finally turned back to Murphy. "When you get reorganized, provide security here with Third Squad." A second later, everyone heard the unmistakable sound of Ospreys heading toward them. They also caught a quick glimpse of at least a dozen F-97 Reapers. They appeared to have been configured for ground combat as opposed to air threats.

Lieutenant Singletary returned his gaze back to his NCOs. "I'll get these reinforcements into the woods ASAP. As they send in a new platoon, I'm going to pull one of ours until they've fully taken over our positions. I'm going to see if I can get our company off this godforsaken planet. As far as I'm concerned, we're done with Alfheim."
****

Andre Bastille kicked again into the broken glass of his mech, trying to make a larger hole to fit through. The hatch was bent, and the hinges were stuck, so he couldn't escape; if the mech had been on fire, he would've been cooked alive.

"Stand back," came the voice of his squad leader, Staff Sergeant Tahlia Jones, from somewhere outside.

The Aussie's voice brought a smile to his face. Last time he had seen her, she'd been fighting alongside Abede, surrounded by Zodarks on all sides. He had seen Abede take a round but had lost Jones in the smoke. Slowly, the fingers of Jones's mech, using extreme finesse and precision, curled into the broken windshield. She then pulled gently, ripping the heavy glass away and creating an opening large enough for Andre to crawl out of.

He lunged forward for the fresh air and coughed out the smoke that was sticking to his lungs. "Thank you," he gasped, getting to his feet and surveying the scene around him.

Jones's mech was sparking and smoking from different joints. It made a horrific screeching sound when it moved, but it was still mobile.

"Where's Takata?" she asked.

Andre looked at the ground. "He handed the device to me, but I took a round that crippled my mech. I couldn't get out. I couldn't stop the damn idiot."

"What happened to Takata, Bastille?" Jones pressed, a look of concern registering on her face.

"He took the device into the elevator and went up with it. The doors slammed shut behind him. It must have been some lockdown the Zodarks initiated."

Jones must have reacted heavily because even the mech took a step back. "He did *what?*"

"Yeah. Crazy bastard rode a nuke into the sky." Andre almost laughed at the audacity.

"Then he was braver than you and I could ever hope to be. I've got to report this to the lieutenant. Are you good?"

"Other than a long walk back, I'll be fine. Is Abede—"

"Dead?" Jones cut him off. "He's gone." She turned and began to walk her damaged mech back to the tree line.

Andre regained his footing and walked over to the flipped vehicle, which he helped lift. Crawling inside the dark Cougar from the driver's hatch, he saw wires and insulation hanging and dangling all over the vehicle. It was thoroughly destroyed in his eyes. That wasn't to say a group of mechanics and technicians couldn't put Humpty-Dumpty back together if told to do so. A few wires sparked and small fires crackled, creating a devilish light throughout the hull. He saw Sergeant Haus, immobile and upside down in his vehicle commander seat. Next to him in a tangled mess was the gunner. He crawled over and flipped the soldier over but could tell that he was dead. Checking the name tape, he read aloud, "Winkler."

He sighed and climbed back out and into the bright day that now flooded the valley.

****

"I need volunteers!"

Corporal Eva Jorgensen heard the voice of Staff Sergeant Moore from across the CCP and made her way over. "What's up?" she asked.

Moore turned and faced Jorgensen. "First Squad needs a medic; they're moving to the eastern flank to repel a counterattack."

"Why can't Abba do it?" Abba was First Squad's medic, and it only made sense to Jorgensen that it should be her that went.

She watched as Moore's eyes glanced to his right from behind his transparent visor. Her eyes followed his until they fell on the lifeless body of Corporal Sade Abba. In that moment, sadness swept over Jorgensen. For a split second, she thought she was about to start crying, but she steeled herself. She could mourn the loss of her friend later, when it was safe to do so.

Abba and Jorgensen had gone through basic and advanced individual training together. They had been together since the beginning of their military career and had seen several engagements together. After a while, Jorgensen had fallen into a complacent state of watching friends who were infantry die on the front line, but even after the attack on their FOB, the medics had made it out unscathed. Jorgensen had always seen Abba as the most cautious of the entire group.

"What happened?" Jorgensen finally managed to ask.

Moore nodded to Corporal Kim. Once Kim ran off into the forest toward the east, Moore looked back to Jorgensen. "From what Mac told me, they had made it further down the line during the assault than the other medics and became pinned down behind one of the buildings."

"Behind the buildings? They weren't supposed to go that far!" Jorgensen shouted.

"I tried to stop her—" Mac interjected, but he was cut short by a solid punch to the chest from Jorgensen.

The Irishman staggered back from the hit before falling to the ground.

"I bet it was your idea! Always having to be in the thick of it!"

"You're one to talk," Mac snapped back, surprised she'd just decked him.

"He was following Abba, Jorgenson. She went too far ahead, and he chased her down to bring her back."

"When we started getting close, waves of interference were messing with the comms. I tried to call her back, but she kept going," Mac pleaded.

"He's right, Eva," Moore said, softening his tone. "She kept bounding up, and when Mac got there, she took a round directly to the chest."

Jorgensen heard what they were saying but refused to let it calm her anger. She stepped forward again and raised her fist to bring down on Mac's face when her wrist was caught, and she found herself hitting the ground next to him. Mac scrambled to his feet and Eva watched as the shadow of Moore stood over her.

"Get yourself together, Corporal Jorgenson. There's still a fight going on, and I can't have two of my medics at each other's throats over something none of them could've stopped. Abba is dead. There will be time to grieve, but right now is not that time."

Jorgensen stood and glared at Moore before heading back down the line to check on the wounded. Time would heal, but right now was not that time.

****

David Roberts followed his team leader, Sergeant McAfee, toward the tree line that ran against a road that wound its way through the canyon. That was where they expected the counterattack to come from, and by the looks of it, they had arrived just in time. Apollo Company looked in absolute disarray. He had even heard rumors from some of the men that they were almost completely wiped out. He hadn't served long enough in Apollo Company to truly get to know anyone besides his first team.

He had found out after he'd been wounded that Staff Sergeant Moreau had been promoted and put in charge of First Squad. That left Corporal Yeva Petrosian to take over Alpha Team. She, Aleksei, and Campbell had been great to him in the short time he had been on planet. Now he just hoped he would see them again.

"Set up along that line," Sergeant McAfee ordered as they moved into the area near the road.

David motioned with his left hand to signal to the rest to spread out along the tree line. "Don't expose yourselves. Get into cover and watch for any movement. If you see something, say something, but don't fire unless ordered."

"Is this farther than you made it last time?" Private Fischer asked.

David turned to him. "A lot farther than you would've made it. This landing was nothing like the first invasion."

"A lot farther than you would've made it," the German mocked. He was silenced by a palm into the back of his helmet from Private Valdez, who gave David a thumbs-up.

Staff Sergeant Howell had split his three teams along the road. Alpha Team, David's team, held the right flank. A hundred meters to his right were the remnants of Apollo Company, who had been ordered to hold the line as well. David heard they had been told to head back after being relieved, but they had stayed. That brought a smile to his face.

"Contact right!" Sergeant McAfee yelled.

David's head turned to his right just in time to see a blue jet of laser fire slam into McAfee's chest and spin him to the ground. David barely had time to move before an overwhelming amount of enemy fire poured down onto their position. Crawling over to McAfee's body, David checked to see if he was still alive, but the baseball-sized burn on his armor made it highly unlikely.

David turned back and watched his three other teammates huddling behind rocks and tree trunks, seeking cover from the incoming fire. He knelt and fired off a burst toward the enemy and then ducked back down. His team needed to start putting fire back onto the enemy before they all ended up the same as McAfee.

He keyed his mic. "One-Six, this is One-One Alpha."

Staff Sergeant Howell's voice responded, "One-One Alpha, this is One-Six. Send traffic."

"One-Six, we have troops in contact. One-One Alpha is down, and I am taking command of Alpha Team. How copy?"

"SITREP?"

"One KIA, but the rest are green," David replied.

"Solid copy, One-One Alpha. One-Six, out."

That was it. That was all David got out of his squad leader after letting him know McAfee had been killed and he was taking over. Now David had to put his money where his mouth was and get out of this situation. He immediately jumped up from his position and slid behind cover near the rest of the team. Tree branches and bark shattered and exploded under the heavy fire.

"McAfee is dead. If we don't start pouring it on 'em, we're dead too. Follow me!"

David broke off at a dead sprint back from the line and looked to see if they were following—and to his surprise, they were. As they traced back down the trail, David pushed further to the east, closer to where Apollo Company had started.

"We've flanked around, but we don't have the necessary angle yet. Valdez, get a grenade near those guys."

Valdez nodded and launched a grenade toward the heart of the enemy fire that had ambushed them. The explosion sent a shower of dirt and debris into the air.

"Hit 'em again!" David yelled.

"One-One Bravo, this is One-One Alpha," he called to Bravo Team's leader.

"One-One Bravo."

"You see those explosions to your two o'clock?"

"Grenade detonations? Yeah, we see it."

"Pour it on 'em. We're flanking around."

"Roger, One-One Alpha. Bravo out."

A roar of gunfire from what David guessed had to be both Bravo and Charlie Teams overwhelmed the area, and he noticed the Zodark fire lightening up. He got to his feet and threw his arm forward, signaling the others to follow him. Together, they moved across the snow-covered trail and scaled the gray rocks that overlooked the narrow strip the Zodarks were occupying.

When David peeked over the edge, he saw exactly how good their cover really was. The Zodarks had set up firing positions wedged into the sides of the rock face, allowing them to get a clear view of his men but keeping themselves hidden. That was how they had gotten the drop on them. If it wasn't for McAfee somehow seeing the movement, they could've all been cut down.

David removed a five-bang high-explosive grenade from its pouch on his armor and signaled the others to do the same. He mimicked the motion of dropping them below the ledge, and upon detonation, they would fire down onto the survivors. It was a bit like shooting fish in a barrel, but it was combat, and David knew the Zodarks would've done the same.

Pulling the pin and hitting the primer, he activated the grenade and dropped it over the wall with the rest. The five-bang grenade made a distinct popping noise when the five high-explosive charges broke apart and embedded themselves into their surroundings before exploding. When the first pop was heard, Private Fischer immediately raised his weapon and leaned over the edge.

"No, you idiot!" David tried to reach out and grab him, but it was too late.

One of the explosive charges ricocheted off the ground and slammed into the front of Fischer's armor, near the waist. He didn't even have time to spin away before the explosion threw his body back and over David's head. The blast had bisected him at the waist, spraying blood and gore everywhere. Below, the cries of the Zodarks were so loud they were heard above the detonations of the rest of the grenades.

David took one last look at Fischer's body and then raised his rifle over the edge and fired into the mortally wounded Zodarks below. When the dust had settled, a heap of six Zodarks lay in twisted displays of carnage.

He turned back to Valdez and O'Connor. "That," he said, pointing to Fischer's body, "is why you listen to orders!"

He walked back down the side and kicked Fischer's body. "Idiot," he muttered to himself.

David knew it was wrong, but at this point he didn't give a damn. He was frustrated. One man's ego had been his downfall and could've been the downfall of the entire team. Fischer reminded David of that corporal from the RNS *Mercy* who had given him such a hard time after he'd received his medal.

"Let's get going," David ordered. They scaled down the rest of the rocks and burrowed back into the forest.

"One-One Bravo, this is One-One Alpha. Thanks for that. We've destroyed their bunker. We have one KIA and six EKIA." David had no idea if he was supposed to report how many enemy were killed in action but thought he should add it on regardless.

However, the reply he got was not from One-One Bravo or even One-One Actual. "This is Tiger Six, cease fire and allow the Zodarks to withdraw from the field. I repeat: cease fire. All Tiger elements fall back to Rally Point X-Ray. Tiger Six out."

David looked toward the others, confused.

"Why did the battalion CO just tell us to stop fighting?" Valdez asked.

"Your guess is as good as mine. Let's get back to the rest of the squad and see what's going on."

Chapter Fourteen
Second Battle of Sirius

RNS *Freedom*
Kita System

Viceroy Miles Hunt looked at the latest intelligence summary from the Sirius system. It was almost as if the Zodarks and Orbots knew the humans and Primords were preparing to launch some sort of major offensive. They'd moved even more ships into the system over the last few days, including five Zodark battleships and one additional star carrier. The Orbots, not to be outdone, had moved three of their own star carriers along with two battleships in addition to the fleet currently there. The numbers were mind-boggling.

Are our fleet and this Gallentine warship even going to be enough?

"You look concerned, Miles," Wiyrkomi said as he walked closer to him.

"I was looking at the latest enemy reinforcements to have arrived in Sirius. Do we even have enough ships capable of defeating them?" Miles asked, concern in his voice.

Wiyrkomi had a look on his face like that of a father when a young son says he's scared of the dark. "Miles, you are aboard the most powerful warship in this galaxy, and you've managed to amass a rather convincing force to assist you," the Gallentine captain responded. "The enemy isn't going to know what hit them once we start. Your fighter and bomber wings alone will cause havoc unlike any they have seen before. Do not dismay, my friend. Tomorrow, we will brush aside the enemy force and victory will be achieved."

Miles knew Wiyrkomi was right. Still, it just seemed overwhelming. Then again, he'd never seen a Gallentine warship in action before, so he didn't have a frame of reference to compare it against. "You're right, Komi. I need to stop worrying about this. I need to focus on the task at hand—defeating the enemy."

"Miles," said Wirykomi softly. When it was just the two of them, Wiyrkomi did his best to be informal with him just as Miles did. "The key to this coming battle will be to take down the enemy warships that are causing the most damage first. In this case, if the enemy is attacking the Terran fleet, then the ships that will inflict the most initial damage are going to be the Zodark frigates and their new torpedo corvettes. I'd assign these targets to your fighters. Next, I'd have your bombers go after the battleships and star carriers."

"What about the cruisers?" Miles asked as he made a mental note.

"We'll use our primary weapons on them. You'll see—it'll be an easy one-shot and they'll be dead."

The way Wiyrkomi casually said that made Miles feel both good and nervous. If his Gallentine warship was this powerful, that meant the Collective's own ships were likely just as powerful. A scary thought indeed.

Miles looked at the internal clock his brain was able to magically make appear when he summoned it. *Not much longer. The first wave of the invasion starts in three hours.*

"Come, Miles, let us get some food together," Captain Wiyrkomi offered. "Once the invasion starts, we are going to be too busy to eat. We will need our energy to get us through the next couple of days."

Miles smiled at his friend. The two of them walked out of his private study to head toward the mess deck. As they passed through the decks of the massive warship and the various hallways, Gallentine and human crewmembers moved about the ship. Everyone was preparing for what would come next.

****

Alpha Company, 1st Battalion, 4th Special Forces
Alfheim

Captain Brian Royce looked at the disposition of the enemy force. It wasn't a large force, but it'd need to be dealt with before they launched the main attack. That SAM site and gun truck could seriously wreak havoc on an invading force.

"If you want to have your soldiers focus on some of those missile and gun truck positions, I can have my units focus on attacking the main base," Major Pilecki offered.

"Yeah, I was thinking the same thing, Major. What is your up-to-date count of C100s and regular ground soldiers?"

Royce hated asking questions like that. It reminded the commander of how many of his soldiers hadn't made it. That was a tough thing to deal with.

Pilecki looked at his data pad. "I have roughly three understrength companies, four hundred and sixty-eight soldiers total. That's across my entire AOR."

"C100s?"

"Not as many as I'd like. We've got thirty-six left. Honestly, we leveraged the hell out of them during the first few weeks of the war."

"It's OK, Major. That was a smart move. You likely saved a lot of soldiers by doing that. Each of my platoons brought forty C100s, so that gives us one hundred and fifty-six. Unless you're opposed, I'd like to have them attack the enemy base from these two points here. Once my operators start taking out these defensive positions along this ridge and inside the tree line here"—Royce pointed to the enemy positions—"then they'll attack here and here. This should cause the Orbots to send reinforcements to these positions."

"That's when we launch our mortar and missile attack along the perimeter here," Pilecki interjected.

"Exactly. Once we've breached the perimeter, then you start rushing your platoons forward into the mix. If all goes according to plan, we'll overwhelm them."

"And when the Orbots call for help, that's when you want my sapper team near Karelis City to start using their MANPADs and causing chaos near the spaceport?"

Royce nodded his head, a satisfied smile spreading across his face. "Exactly. If we're lucky, your sapper team will succeed in shooting down a few shuttles full of Orbots."

Pilecki grinned, the image of burning wrecks full of dead Orbots giving him warm fuzzies inside. "Are you sure about this invasion, Captain?" he prodded. "Because once we launch this attack, there won't be any going back. The enemy will know there's a sizable force in this area, and they'll relentlessly hunt us down."

"It's going to happen, Major."

"How do you know?" Pilecki asked. "I mean, sometimes things happen and missions get pushed a few hours or a few days or weeks—"

Royce cut him off before he could go down that line of thinking. "It'll happen, Major. Not everyone knows this, but I know the Viceroy personally. I served on his ship, the *Rook*. It was my platoon that saved his life on New Eden when he was about to be killed. When I say I know him, I really mean it. Just before we left on this mission, he told me his ships and force would be arriving at the time I've told you and for us to have things ready on our end. So that's what we're going do."

No one said anything for a moment. Finally, Major Pilecki nodded in agreement. "OK, then it's settled. We launch our attack fifteen minutes prior to the invasion. Let's get our people ready; we don't have much time left."

****

A Few Hours Later

Captain Brian Royce had never seen an alien surface-to-air missile or SAM truck before, but here he was on Alfheim, staring at one. Had he not seen a video of the thing in action, he likely wouldn't have believed it was real. Major Pilecki had shown him a clip of a handful of P-97 Orions trying to attack this base a few weeks ago and getting completely blown out of the sky. The remaining RA forces on the ground hadn't had a lot of air units left, so they'd used them sparingly. What they hadn't anticipated was running into an air-defense vehicle near the base.

"Strange looking, isn't it?" commented Master Sergeant Hanke, the platoon sergeant.

Royce shook his head. "Just when you think you've seen it all."

Lieutenant Williams, who was lying on the ground next to them, asked, "So one truck is a missile truck while the other is a laser truck? Just seems odd to have a laser blaster next to a missile battery."

"I may be wrong, but judging by what I saw in that video, these missile trucks essentially allow them to engage a *lot* of targets at one time whereas those laser trucks have to track and engage one target at a time," Royce commented.

"Yeah, makes sense, I suppose," Hanke countered, then added, "Ten minutes. Best be gettin' to my position." Then he scooted out of where he'd been and went to link up with the squad he was going to attack with.

For the last hour, the two squads of soldiers had stealthily made their way through the woods to get in close to this position. They had to move slow and steady, using the underbrush, fallen tree trunks, and any other objects they could as cover. The last thing they wanted to do was alert the Orbot sentries to their presence.

When Royce was roughly fifty meters from the sentry, he raised his rifle, placed his targeting reticle on the head of the cyborg and prepared to fire. One by one, the different soldiers called out their individual targets and stood by, waiting to hear him issue the order to fire.

Fire, Royce said over his neurolink as he squeezed the trigger on his M1 assault rifle. In the blink of an eye, the solid tungsten slug covered the distance, connecting with the head of the Orbot before the sonic boom could even be heard. Instantly, fourteen other Orbots dropped almost simultaneously.

Go, go, go! Royce yelled over the neurolink, leaping to his feet with his rifle tucked in his shoulder. He was moving fast, his eyes darting around as he looked for targets to shoot. More shots rang out—some of his soldiers had found targets and took them out before they could do anything else. Then his helmet's audio receivers started picking up the cracks and shots of his other squads hitting the air-defense units in the distance. The fight was on—taking these two sites out would open the main Orbot base up to the indirect fire and air attacks that would be starting soon.

Jumping over a fallen log, Royce found his footing and continued to race toward the two vehicles. A single Orbot exited one of the vehicles, maybe thirty meters in front of him. Royce already had his targeting reticle on the cyborg and fired a three-round burst right into the chest of the Orbot before it had a chance to react. Thinking the target was down, Royce went to find another target before he saw the Orbot get back up and raise its own rifle to fire back at his people.

Damn, how'd he survive that? Royce wondered. He fired a handful of rounds, making sure many of them slammed into the face and head of the cyborg this time.

Seconds later, his Deltas were inside the Orbot positions. Several soldiers had approached one of the vehicles. Two aimed their rifles at the vehicle door while a third pulled a hand grenade off his chest rig. After he removed the pin, a fellow soldier eased the door open, cracking it just a bit while the guy with the grenade tossed it in. It exploded, and moments later, the soldier that had opened the door the first time yanked it wide open and held it back while two of his comrades fired a barrage of bullets into the vehicle. His soldiers repeated this with the other vehicle as they finished clearing the nearby positions.

It took Royce's operators less than sixty seconds to clear the site and eliminate the air-defense vehicles. Now it was time to move on to phase two of the operation.

****

Team Fourteen, Sapper Platoon
Dog Company, 313th Battalion
Highway 19, near Karelis City

Corporal Wallace's data pad chirped. She'd received a secured communiqué. After she checked it, a smile spread across her face. *Finally...*

Wallace looked down at the flight line; it was suddenly springing to life. Ground crews were racing to their starfighters to get them ready while others began preflight checks for their shuttles. Near the main hangars, dozens and dozens of Orbot soldiers fell into formation. It was likely they were receiving their orders for what was about to happen.

Turning to her C100, which she'd named Tom, Wallace ordered, "I want you to head to point Alpha. There look to be four transports getting ready to take off. When you see them get airborne, I want you to engage them with your SAMs. Then head to firing point Charlie and use your sniper rifle to hit the engines of whatever aircraft they have left."

"Yes, Corporal." Tom then pointed down the flight line before adding, "It would appear they are bringing a truck over to fuel the shuttles. I would suggest shooting the truck while it's near the shuttles."

Turning to look at what he'd just pointed to, she saw it immediately. *Damn, those things have sharp eyes.* They saw everything, while still paying attention to a conversation or instructions.

"Good call, Tom. Head to your position," she confirmed. "I'm going to take that fuel truck out and sow some general chaos." She turned to grab for her sniper rifle, which was basically an M1 assault rifle with a four-inch barrel extension and an optical sight far superior to what the general infantry carried.

Looking through her optical sight, Wallace saw the activity around the flight line was only increasing. When the fuel truck finished fueling one shuttle, what appeared to be a platoon of Orbots climbed aboard. Clearly, they were being dispatched to reinforce another base or unit— likely a base or unit her comrades were in the process of attacking. She needed to take them out and stop those reinforcements from getting to where they were going.

Sighting in on the fuel truck, Wallace saw an Orbot attaching some sort of hose to the fuselage of the shuttle. She wasn't sure if the truck was even flammable, but she knew she had to try. Aiming at the center of the tank, she squeezed the trigger gently until it fired. At nearly three kilometers away, this would be the farthest shot she'd ever taken at a target. It took only a moment for the small projectile to travel that distance. When it hit, it looked like it hadn't caused any damage. At least for a moment. She was about to fire another round when the tanker truck exploded. The truck was suddenly enveloped in flames, along with the shuttle it was fueling and the nearby truck loading up with Orbots. In seconds, the entire area blew up as the other shuttles joined the conflagration.

With the base clearly under attack and the shuttles a burning wreck nearby, the fighters took to the air to try and escape whatever was coming next. Once they started heading to wherever they were headed, Tom, her C100, engaged them with the portable SAMs. Once the machine had fired off the missiles, it moved to its next attack location and started sniping at targets down on the flight line. Corporal Wallace and her C100 only stayed in their position for a few more minutes before they hightailed it out of there. No sense in sticking around when you knew the enemy would bring the pain down on your position at any moment. They'd done their part, now it was time to get to their next ambush location and get ready for whatever might come next.
******

100 Kilometers Away
312th Battalion, Republic Army

Major Pilecki smiled as he saw the Special Forces teams decimate the two air-defense positions. That was his cue to have his two P-97 Orions carry out their strike on the base. General Bakshi had given him control of two of the precious few that remained for this critical mission. The RA airwing supporting the ground forces had been destroyed in the last five weeks. What few they had left, they'd been holding back for a mission just like this. Chances were they'd only get one, maybe two passes over the enemy base before they'd get blown out of the sky by either a Zodark or Orbot fighter or one of the many air-defense sites the enemy had established in the region. These SAM sites had crippled the RA's ability to rely on fighter support during the occupation, which had made coordinating any sort of counterattack or resistance a lot harder.

"Send a message to the fighters that they're cleared to engage the base," Pilecki ordered. He then walked over to one of his other officers, directing, "Once the fighters hit the vehicle yard, I want your mortar and rocket teams to plaster those barrack buildings. Make sure you have your teams relocate once they fire off their volley. I don't want to lose them to one of those notorious counterbattery barrages those bastards like to launch."

"True that, I've jerry-rigged a nice surprise for them when they launch that counterbattery attack," the young officer replied with a mischievous grin.

The Orbots were known for launching horrific counterbattery attacks. Once they detected a rocket or mortar attack, they typically fired an enormous barrage of missiles at the launch point to flatten the area. The Republic Army had lost more than a few of their IDF or indirect fire teams to these barrages.

Time seemed to move fast and slow all at the same time. Small fire teams and squads of soldiers filtered toward their attack position, each of them hoping like hell the enemy wasn't moving one of their cruisers or battleships from orbit down into the atmosphere. They'd seen enough of their comrades get blasted to know that if one of these warships showed up, it'd likely doom their mission.

Major Pilecki turned to his operations officer. "Issue the order to all units—attack."

****

"That's it, we're cleared hot to engage. Let's drop our mortars and get the hell out of here," Corporal Blount barked to his team.

"On it, Corporal," came the quick replies.

The twelve soldiers of his squad manning their six 81mm mortar tubes grabbed the first rounds and started firing. The mortars they were using were nothing like the mortars used a hundred years ago. These used a unique propellant that could send these things as far as sixty kilometers away. They also had the ability to be programmed to loiter over an area for up to six hours, striking only if they spotted movement in the target box. They utilized a more advanced variable warhead, giving the user the option of a high-explosive warhead, the equivalent of up to a two-hundred-pound explosive device, or as low as a ten-pound device for close-in support. It could also be programmed to disperse an aerial shrapnel burst designed to shower an area with pellet-sized pieces of shrapnel.

Corporal Blount shouted, "Hang…drop."

Thump.

"Hang…drop."

Thump.

"Hang…drop."

Thump.

"All right, grab the gear and let's get the hell out of here!"

The soldiers took the tube and baseplate apart in seconds. They attached everything to their ATVs and sped away, putting as much distance as they could between themselves and the POO or point of origin of the attack. They'd now race to their next launch position some fifteen kilometers away and prepare to deliver whatever kind of support the infantry asked for.

****

Alpha Company, 1st Battalion, 4th Special Forces
Alfheim

"Hot damn! Would you look at that," one of the Delta operators said excitedly.

The P-97 Orion swooped in fast over the Orbot base, firing its laser blaster across the vehicle yard. A handful of ground vehicles erupted in flames and blew apart. When the Orion passed over the base, it released a series of six objects from under its wings. The cylindrical objects erupted in flames, dousing many of the nearby buildings with a sticky flammable substance. More than a handful of Orbot soldiers were engulfed in flames as it crested over top of them like an ocean wave.

"Man, you gotta love some good ol'-fashioned close-air support," Royce said to the soldiers around him.

The second Orion swooped in and delivered its own devastating attack with similar results. By now, Orbot soldiers were scurrying out of the buildings and shooting at the Orions as best they could. Then a barrage of mortar rounds started landing amongst their positions, decimating the groups of the cyborgs.

Along the far side of the northern perimeter, a string of smaller units started assaulting the base next. At first it was just three or four groups attacking the perimeter, then it grew into more than a dozen. Then another group started attacking along the eastern side of the base. The assault on the Orbot facility was now in full swing.

"Alpha Team, on me!" shouted Lieutenant Williams as she rose from her covered position and ran toward the enemy. She had her rifle in one hand while she waved her squad forward with the other.

That gal is fearless. I love it, Royce thought privately as he saw her team charge right alongside her.

Royce fell in behind Bravo Team. They were going to move to the left of Alpha and provide them covering fire as they moved to breach their part of the perimeter. The fighting around the large Orbot base had really escalated—brilliant flashes of light crisscrossed back and forth between the two sides, intermixed with explosions. Then in the sky above them, enemy fighters started to swoop down. As they did, the two Orion fighters engaged them. Some of the soldiers on the ground also fired off their own man-portable surface-to-air missiles.

Royce was trying not to get distracted by the aerial battle taking place in the sky above him. That was easier said than done, though. They didn't usually see aerial battles. Air combat was typically settled way before a ground operation or major attack started.

Approaching the base itself, Alpha Team had gotten itself drawn into a real zinger of a fight. A few dozen Orbots had rushed to plug the hole in the perimeter they were trying to press through. Now it was a race against time to take them out before reinforcements could be flown in from another base or one of the battleships in orbit.

Bringing his own rifle to bear, Royce sighted in on one of the cyborgs. He aimed for the head, the only shots that seemed to take them out. The problem was the damn things moved quick. They had these spiderlike lower bodies that allowed them to move rapidly over rugged and rough terrain. When it came to firing a rifle or pistol, they were quick and accurate. They weren't like the Zodarks, who'd fire relentlessly at times, just hoping one out of twenty shots hit something. They were much more deliberate in what they did. Royce thought that made them more dangerous than the Zodarks he'd spent most of his time fighting.

Aiming at the cyborg, he fired a three-round burst. All three rounds pounded into the face of the creature, dropping its body to the ground. *One down, tons more to go...*

Chapter Fifteen
The Alfheim Turkey Shoot

RNS *Freedom*
Near Alfheim
Sirius System

"We're exiting the wormhole now," the helmsman called out as the ship emerged from the blackness.

Moments later, the Gallentine *Titan*-class warship entered the Sirius system. It took only seconds for their suite of sensors to begin collecting data again and provide them a picture of what was going on around them. What their sensors showed was a complete and utterly chaotic mess.

Holy crap...this is a lot of ships, Viceroy Miles Hunt thought.

Wiyrkomi called out orders in a calm but assertive voice to the different sections of the ship. For the briefest of moments, Hunt stood by, listening and observing how effortlessly his Gallentine advisor began the process of fighting the ship. Wiyrkomi called out, "Flight Ops, I want our fighters deployed now. Tell the bomber squadrons to stand by and prepare to launch."

Hunt then joined the fray, ordering, "Weps, I want our secondary batteries to start taking those Zodark cruisers out now. Have the primaries identify the Orbot battleships and focus their fire on them."

"Viceroy," interrupted his coms officer. "Sir, we're receiving a message from Captain Brian Royce, from the Delta pathfinder group. He is requesting immediate support from us if at all possible."

Furrowing his brow at the vague request for support, Hunt said, "Ah, you're going to need to be a bit more descriptive than that. What kind of support is he asking for?"

A couple of seconds went by before he replied, "It would appear a Zodark battleship has descended into the upper atmosphere and looks to be headed toward them. It's lining up to use its laser batteries to wipe out the allied forces that are attacking the Zodark and Orbot bases. He's asking if it's possible for us to intercede."

Hunt looked at Wiyrkomi. "Suggestions?"

"I see the battleship they are talking about. It appears to be moving away from us. I'd recommend we divert one of our fighter groups and have them escort two of our bomber squadrons in to deal with the ship. This way we can stay focused on the larger battle at hand. Once we've cleared the high ground, we can then deploy our ground forces and additional fighter support as needed."

"I agree. Make it so," Hunt said as he looked at his flight operations officer.

"I'm on it," came the quick reply. "I'm redirecting fighter group four now. The fighters should intercept the battleship in the next twenty minutes, and the bombers will hit them in the next thirty-five minutes or so."

Hunt smiled at how smoothly his bridge crew was operating. Nearly a month of simulations and hard drilling was paying off.

"Damn, Miles. This is incredible," Admiral Fran McKee said softly as he took a seat in his command chair.

Prior to leaving Kita, he'd offered to let Fran travel with him on the *Freedom*. With the *George Washington* still down for repairs, the only option left to her was to transfer her flag to one of the battleships or join Admiral Bvork Stavanger on his flagship.

"It sure is. I'm excited and nervous to see our new ship in combat. I just hope we're able to save more of our people and put an end to this terrible war with it."

****

4th Fighter Group "Death Rattlers"

Commander Ethan Hunt, call sign Paladin, acknowledged the new change to his orders. Switching over to his command channel, he said, "Listen up, Death Rattlers. We just got our first FRAGO. It looks like a Zodark battleship has descended into the planet's atmosphere and is being used to wipe out our ground forces. We've been tasked with taking its fighters out and flying cover for a couple of bomber squadrons being dispatched to take the ship out.

"I want the Yellowjackets to go after the enemy fighters screening for the battleship. Greens, you've got the toughest job, protecting the bombers. You've got to keep these Orbot and Zodark fighters off our bombers."

"Whoa, did you say Orbot fighters, Paladin?" interrupted Lieutenant Khatri, the squadron commander for the Blues.

"I thought this was a Zodark battleship," Lieutenant Pushkin, Red Squadron leader, said.

Ethan tried not to get annoyed by their interruptions. He kept reminding himself that this was the first time any of them would be flying a physical fighter into combat. Until now, all their previous missions had been flown from the relative safety of their mothership as they operated a drone. Now, all of that had changed.

Paladin cleared his throat over the radio to let them know he was going to speak. "Hey, let's keep it together. This is a Zodark warship—however, the Orbots appear to have built a number of ground bases to help them hold the planet and repel any kind of invasion force. It's now our job to go in there and clear the area before our own invasion force arrives. I want the Reds to go low and try to intercept any squadrons looking to greet us. Blues, hang back with the bombers and stand by to fill in any gaps in our lines as they appear. Let's do this, Death Rattlers."

"Come to fight, come to win!" came the squadron motto.

Paladin changed over to Red Squadron's net. "Flattop, I'm going to fly with you guys. Lead the way."

Falling in formation with the Reds, Paladin saw his squadron commander lead his sixteen fighters down into the planet's atmosphere. When their Hellcats started to transition between the thermosphere and the mesosphere, the friction of the air passing over his wings buffeted his spacecraft pretty hard. A slight bubble formed around the front of his Hellcat and then enveloped it, the heat readings spiking as his airspeed increased.

Paladin pulled up on his flight controls just a bit, allowing the Hellcat to bleed off some airspeed. He now crossed over from the mesosphere and into the troposphere. At this point, the massive heat bubble around his starfighter had dissipated. He was still dropping altitude while at the same time traveling at an incredible rate of speed. His instruments indicated that, without the help of his inertial dampeners and the life support's ability to compensate for the massive g-forces pushing against him, he likely would have blacked out or gotten crushed from the weight of it bearing down on him.

Reaching his hand over, he extended the retractable wings for atmospheric combat and switched his combat controls and sensors over to atmospheric operations. Once he did that, his sensors started populating all kinds of ground contacts. They also identified and highlighted the approaching enemy fighters.

"Listen up, Reds. We've got multiple clusters of fighters approaching us. It looks like we've got one group of Zodark fighters closing in. Another three squadrons look to be heading toward the Yellowjackets. We've also got what looks like three Orbot squadrons that appear to have originated from the planet heading toward us as well."

"Outstanding, seven-to-one odds. Should be a walk in the park," Ensign Robert "Maverick" Bork opined sarcastically.

"Yeah, a walk in the park. Maverick, why don't you fly as Paladin's wingman? The rest of you all know what to do. Let's focus on the fighter in front of us and take 'em out, then move to the next fighter. Red Leader out."

A minute later, Ensign Bork's Hellcat settled into the wingman slot near Hunt's Hellcat. Opening a coms channel between them, Paladin said, "Maverick, just stay tight on me until we pass through their lines. Once that happens, I want you to figure out who you want to go after and do it. We've got a lot of fighters to try and thin out."

"Got it, Paladin. Sorry if I came across as cocky or being a jerk back there."

"It's OK, Maverick. No one really cares about that if you can back it up with actions. This is your chance to prove you've got what it takes to be a fighter jock. So let's put all that talk aside and show the others you know what you're doing, all right?"

Hunt hoped this kid was more than just good in a simulator. He was counting on him having some flying chops in this fight.

"Thank you, Paladin. I won't let you down."

The squadron flew on for another few minutes as they closed the gap between themselves and the waves of incoming fighters. They also caught sight of the Zodark battleship. Hunt wasn't sure why or how, but seeing that ship inside a planet's atmosphere with his own eyes seemed to make it so much larger and more real.

Then the warning systems on the Hellcat started going off. Checking to see what it was, he saw the Zodark ships rapidly approaching him had just fired off a volley of missiles. Paladin hit the electronic jamming system on the Hellcat and angled his fighter slightly toward the missiles. His targeting reticle found the first missile and he fired. He sent a couple of laser blasts right at the thing and then transitioned to the next missile, repeating the process. In seconds, he'd taken out the threats before they had a chance of becoming a problem.

Looking at his scanner, he was happy to see the other pilots in the squadron had done the same, just like in their training, just as their Gallentine advisors had told them to do. With the distance between them closing fast, Paladin moved into position to use his blasters on the incoming fighters. He lined up on one and depressed his firing stud. A couple of laser bolts shot forward and the Zodark fighter exploded. He moved to the next and repeated the process, taking it out as well before the fighters broke off their attack run and split into dozens of different directions.

So far, so good. It looks like their targeting computers can't get a solid lock on us.

Pulling hard on his flight controls, Paladin angled his Hellcat around and briefly gave chase to another Zodark fighter. He got in behind the guy, and despite the Zodarks' best efforts at jinking and zigzagging, they couldn't shake him. He fired again and was rewarded with his third kill in less than five minutes.

Suddenly, a string of bright flashes zipped right past him. Paladin pushed his flight controls down and applied more power to his engine, nearly doubling his speed in seconds. He pulled up hard on the flight controls as he'd lost half his altitude in less than sixty seconds. *Damn, I nearly dove right into the side of that mountain...*

Angling back toward the battle above him, Hunt looked for the fighter that had nearly taken him out. He found the guy moments later, already firing away at another one of the Reds. Then he saw the Red fighter take a couple of hits. The first three hits looked like they didn't cause much if any damage, but the fourth and fifth hits appeared to have nailed something important. The Hellcat emitted some smoke, and a small fire appeared to have broken out around one of its engines.

Tapping his coms unit, he synched up with the pilot. "Red Eight, hit your fire extinguisher now and then bank to the right and climb to gain some altitude. I'm coming up behind you on the guy that just shot you."

"Copy that, Paladin, thank you for the assist," the pilot replied. Hunt was impressed—the young ensign sounded cool as a cucumber despite nearly being killed.

The fire and smoke emanating from one of the engines puffed out. The pilot then banked hard to the right as he gave his one operational engine more power. As Red Eight sped out of the area, the Zodark fighter gave chase after him. He was oblivious to Hunt moving his aircraft into position behind him. Seconds later, he thumbed the firing stud and sent a string of blaster bolts into the rear section of the Zodark fighter. It exploded moments later, raining debris, smoke, and some small flames down to the ground below.

"Red Eight, I want you to head back to the *Freedom* and have the maintenance guys get to work on your fighter. Is that understood?"

"But, sir, I can still fight," the pilot said, almost pleading not to be sent back to the mothership.

"No, that's an order. I need your ship repaired for the next operation after this. Out." Hunt cut the line, not wanting to argue any further with the ensign about it. The kid might be mad about having to leave the battle, but Hunt had just saved his life.

Returning his attention to the rest of the fighting, he could see it was turning into a real furball. "Blue Leader, Paladin. I need you to deploy your squadron to support the Reds. We've got multiple Orbot squadrons inbound. How copy?"

A second later, the radio crackled to life. "About time you tagged us in. We're on it," Lieutenant "Spike" Khatri replied, his Indian accent more evident as his excitement increased.

Hunt switched over to the flight operations channel. "Redhawk Actual, Death Rattler Actual. How copy?"

Hunt was trying to get in touch with the head of the *Freedom*'s flight operations, Rear Admiral Aaron Blade, who went by the call sign Redhawk. He was the man in charge of all the space wings on the ship. It took a moment for the old crusty admiral to get on the radio. "What do you have, Paladin?"

"Sir, one of my squadrons just tore through a Zodark squadron, but we're about to encounter two more squadrons of fighters and what looks to be three squadrons of Orbot fighters with another three rising up to join us. The rest of my wing is fully deployed, so I can't request additional help from them. I'm hoping you may be able to dispatch some help."

Hunt wanted to run this request through his wing commander, but judging by what he was seeing on his tactical display, they were knee-deep in some major fighting around several of the star carriers and battleships.

"Paladin, are you telling me your group of cocky squadron leaders and pilots are in over their heads?" asked Admiral Blade, a slight edge to his voice. Hunt had allowed his pilots to get a little brash on the ship with their peers these past weeks, and it looked like that was coming back to bite him in the butt now.

Depressing his talk button, Paladin knew he'd need to eat a little humble pie. "It would appear so, sir."

A few seconds went by as he continued to race toward the rest of Red Squadron and prepared to join the fight. "I just reviewed your situation, Hunt. You made a good call asking for help now before your group became overwhelmed and started taking casualties. I'm going to order 7th Fighter Group to assist you. They'll be launching momentarily. Out."

Smiling, Paladin looked at his display. Help was on the way; they just had to hold out for the time being. "Flattop, I'm taking my wingman to go stir some stuff up with that Orbot squadron that's starting to get in range of us. I want you to finish these Zodark fighters off and then join me. How copy?"

"That's a good copy, Paladin. Happy hunting," came the quick reply.

"There you are, Paladin, I thought I'd lost you there for a moment," Maverick said as his fighter fell into formation next to him.

"Sorry about that, Maverick. Red Eight got in some trouble and needed help. Let's go tear into these Orbots. As we come into range, I want you to expend your missiles. We're each carrying eight of them— it's time we cut some of their numbers down."

"Sounds good, Paladin. Let's do it," Maverick replied excitedly. Ethan was becoming impressed with his flying abilities. He'd already scored four kills to Ethan's three.

As they angled their Hellcats down further into the lower atmosphere, the Orbot squadron seemed to know they were heading toward them and decided to rise up to meet them. The Orbots were still out of range of their own missiles, but they had just crossed into range of Paladin and Maverick's.

As his AI targeting computer locked up eight targets and deconflicted them with Maverick's targeting computer, Hunt got a good look at the bomber squadron as they approached the Zodark battleship. The bombers looked like they had just crossed into range of their own weapons and were now engaging the massive warship. The Yellowjackets had done a hell of a job tearing through the fighter screen protecting the battleship. They'd cleared a solid path for the bombers to swoop in and deliver their own death blow.

"We cleared hot to engage, Paladin?"

"Uh, yes, cleared hot to engage. Sorry, I was checking in with the bombers. They're going in for their attack run right now. Let's clear these guys out and move on to the next group of fighters."

"Engaging now, Maverick," he announced to his wingman.

He depressed his firing trigger, and the first missile dropped from his internal weapons bay. The engine ignited fractions of a second later, sending it racing toward its intended target. The process repeated seven more times until all eight missiles had been fired. They crossed the distance between the Hellcats and the Orbot ships in less than a minute. Six of the eight missiles scored hits. The enemy had somehow evaded two of the fast-moving missiles. One of Maverick's missiles also missed. All told, the two of them had just taken out thirteen fighters in one fell swoop.

"Hot damn! We're two-time Aces now, Paladin," Maverick exclaimed excitedly over their coms.

"We can celebrate back on the ship; we're coming into range of their missiles."

Then the Orbot fighters released their own missiles. The remaining fighters had fired four missiles at them, two at each of their fighters. Maverick and Paladin took evasive maneuvers, with Maverick diving for the deck as he increased speed while Paladin went high, increasing his speed exponentially. While they were trying to evade the missiles, the complex electronic defensive suite built into the Hellcat went to work, doing its best to jam the missiles' tracking systems. When a missile got in too close, the AI fired their close-in defensive laser. This was something their human-built drones had never had, nor did the Altairian-Human-built fighters. It made hitting the Hellcats with a missile incredibly hard.

As the distance between the swarm of Orbot fighters continued to close, Paladin switched from missiles, which he'd now expended, back to his blasters. They were powered up, and moments later, his AI targeting reticle began looking for a target. The Hellcats' quad blasters had the ability to move up and down or right to left by up to fifteen degrees. The weapons would follow the track of the pilot's eyes until the targeting AI lined up the targeting reticle to score a kill. The system worked a hell of a lot better in space, when the battles were fought at greater ranges, than in the atmosphere where the dogfighting was currently taking place.

Depressing the firing stud, Paladin watched as the first string of blaster bolts connected with the Orbot fighter. It ripped the wing clean off, causing the starfighter to spin out of control. Then a string of laser bolts flew past him. He jinked hard to the right, then pulled up hard, only to dive at a hard angle down as he gave the Hellcat more power. He was doing his best to maneuver with the altitude he had, something that took some getting used to when you spent nearly all your time flying and fighting in space.

The fighting lasted another ten minutes before the fighters of Blue Squadron joined the fray. By now, two more squadrons of Orbot fighters were rising from the surface to join the battle. Casting a quick glance in the direction of the Zodark battleship, Paladin saw the bombers had torn the battleship up pretty good.

The Yellowjackets were still fighting with the remnants of the ship's screening force while the bombers looked to be heading back to the *Freedom*. Paladin got in touch with Green Squadron and ordered them to leave the bombers at this point and hurry down to join the Reds and the Blues. The aerial battle taking place around and in the vicinity of the Zodark battleship was intense. What no one knew for certain was just how many Zodark and Orbot fighter squadrons they had on the surface. It was clear, though, that no matter how many they had, they'd need to be cleared before the invasion force landed. The landers would get slaughtered if they had to fly their way through this many fighters.

Another hour into the fight, Paladin finally had all four of his squadrons fully engaged. Fighter squadrons from the 7th Fighter Wing were also showing up, adding their own weight to the battle. As more of their squadrons showed up, Hunt was able to withdraw his own squadrons to head back to the *Freedom*. After more than five hours in the cockpit, his pilots needed a break and the chance to rearm their Hellcats.

Once Hunt's Hellcat had entered the hangar assigned to his fighter wing, his navigation AI guided his fighter to his landing pad. When his fighter had come to a halt, the ground crew rushed forward and started the process of getting him out of the fighter and servicing the Hellcat.

Climbing out of the cockpit, Ethan turned to look at his fighter. He saw half a dozen scorch marks on the fuselage. "What are those?"

One of the crewmen looked up at him. "Those are hits you took. It looks like the Hellcat was able to absorb them. Don't worry, we'll pull the panels off and make sure there isn't any damage behind it. It looks like you got lucky, sir."

Grunting at the statement, Ethan just shook his head in amazement as he turned and headed toward his group's ready room. He told his pilots to head there for a mission debrief. He had some food being catered in for everyone so they could eat while the debrief took place. While all that was taking place, Ethan needed to find out how things were going with the main battle. His pilots would either be given some time to sleep and rest or be given some stims and told to get back in their fighters for another round.

****

Alpha Company, 1st Battalion, 4th Special Forces

Captain Brian Royce looked on in awe at the destruction taking place across the Zodark battleship. He counted himself lucky. That battleship was roughly sixty kilometers away, high in the sky, but he was still able to see the explosions and damage it was sustaining. The ship was large, multiple kilometers in length, and just kind of hovered there in the sky, blocking the Republic's every attempt to overwhelm the enemy forts below.

For a short while, he thought they were about to get zapped by the main guns of the battleship. At first, he hadn't believed it when Major Pilecki had told him about the Zodarks bringing a cruiser or battleship down into the planet's atmosphere to provide close-air support, but then he'd seen it with his own eyes, and it had sent a cold shiver down his spine.

One of his four platoons was working with two RA battalions some one hundred and twenty kilometers away. Like him, they had coordinated to carry out a couple of attacks on some of the smaller

Zodark or Orbot planetary defensive systems. They needed to take those guns and missile systems out before the main invasion force showed up.

Like the battle his platoon was in right now, it was fierce—touch and go at times as to whether they'd come out on top. Then, some forty minutes into the planetwide attack, the Zodark battleship had emerged from the cloud cover and begun to rain down fire and brimstone.

Royce was living through the moment every commander feared. He'd found, in countless battles and campaigns he'd fought in, from that first major battle against the Zodarks to the capture of that star carrier near New Eden at the start of the war to the horrific battle on the Zodark station in orbit of the planet Rass, that the enemy always got a vote no matter how many times you tried to deny them one.

What he saw happening right now to his platoons, and what he knew was happening to the remaining RA battalions, was not just awful, it was an unprecedented slaughter. He'd never imagined a battleship or cruiser could descend into the atmosphere of a planet and utilize its main batteries to zap entire bases and troop concentrations. There was, literally, no defense against such a tactic. One second, Royce had been talking with one of his lieutenants, then the line had gone silent, and he'd seen the streak of light stab the ground in the direction where he knew the young officer and his men were located.

Just as Royce was about to call off the attacks and move for everyone to scatter and try and get underground, back into the caves and tunnels, he saw tiny little dots in the sky. Then those few dots grew to multiple dots and soon it was a swarm. Battles were breaking out all over in the sky. Then some of those dots started firing weapons at the battleship.

Royce saw one explosion. Then he saw three or four explosions across the side of the ship. These weren't small explosions; these were giant plumes of flames that didn't dissipate after the initial blast. Whatever had hit that battleship had done a real number on it. Yet despite those explosions, a couple beams of light stabbed down to the forest in the direction of Second Platoon.

All that damage and that ship is still operational…

"Captain Royce, one of my companies has broken through the enemy lines. They're advancing further into the base. I think this would be a good time to release your C100s," Major Pilecki shouted over the radio.

"That's a good copy, Major. Releasing the terminators!" Royce paused for a moment before adding, "I'm going to have Third Squad follow in behind them while Second and Fourth Squads assault the northern perimeter like we talked about."

"Excellent, is your overwatch squad in position?"

"Yes, we just arrived on station. We should be providing overwatch fire in the next few minutes," Royce explained. He'd chosen to stay with First Squad, who'd been assigned an overwatch position on the west and southwest sides of the enemy base. Their sole job at this point was essentially to provide sniper coverage for the attacking soldiers.

"See you inside the base when this is all said and done," the major said and ended the call.

Walking the line, Royce checked on his soldiers. They'd taken up positions five to ten meters apart from each other. One by one, they were zeroing in on the base and finding a Zodark or Orbot soldier to drill with a magrail slug. They were avoiding using their blasters so the enemy couldn't easily spot their firing positions.

Every few seconds, his ears registered the crack of an M1 being fired. Each crack ended the life of an Orbot or Zodark soldier. Finding a suitable spot to settle into himself, Royce got comfortable and brought his rifle to his shoulder. Peering through his optics, he scanned the enemy base. The perimeter was being heavily fought over. At times, a handful of RA soldiers would scramble into the base, only to be pushed back by an enemy surge. Then that surge would get taken out by a handful of C100 combat synthetics and the gap was opened once again. The fighting was ebbing and flowing back and forth, leaving more and more bodies strewn across the ground with each push.

Spotting an Orbot soldier, Royce peered through his targeting scope, placing the red targeting dot on the Orbot's head—essentially the only place you should shoot them if you wanted to drop them with the fewest shots. Sighting in on the target, Royce pulled the trigger. The head of the Orbot exploded moments later and its body collapsed to the ground.

Every few seconds, another crack was heard and another Zodark or Orbot went down. This went on for a little while as the squad was doing all it could to help cover their comrades' assault. Then a beam of light stabbed through the sky, practically blinding Royce. The visor on his HUD instantly darkened as much as it could, practically turning black as it sought to protect his eyes from the searing light. His ears registered a crispy burning noise somewhere nearby and the temperature of the air around him spiked immensely.

Ducking down behind the tree trunk he'd been sitting against, Royce waited just a moment for his HUD to normalize. He checked his Blue Force tracker and noted nearly half the soldiers in their attacking force were gone.

No, no, no, this can't be happening...

Third and Fourth Squads were gone. They were there one second and simply blotted out the next. Looking above the fallen trunk he'd hidden behind, he saw a huge swath of the forest around them and along the perimeter of the base was burnt to a crisp.

Looking back to the Zodark battleship, Royce saw the ship begin to erupt in tiny explosions—near the center at first, then they spread across the ship, explosions rippling across its hull until it blew apart. He watched as the ship broke in half and the two giant pieces fell to the ground below.

With the ship gone, Royce knew it was now or never. They had to finish capturing this base. Once it was destroyed, the Rangers would begin their own descent to the ground and assist the Deltas in either capturing or destroying a laundry list of targets. Anything marked red was deemed a priority target that had to be taken out prior to the Republic soldiers' arrival.

****

RNS *Freedom*
Bridge

Viceroy Hunt watched in awe as his ship and fleet fought on. It was almost too much to comprehend. The battle taking place around the planet and closest to the *Freedom* was still going strong, but it was clear they were going to win it. The battle further away, near one of its moons, however, was not so clear. Once the Zodark star carriers were fully engaged, the Orbots jumped in several of their own on the back side of the allied fleet. More than two thousand fighters and bombers had been launched and thrown into the melee.

In a battle involving so many fighters and bombers, one of the most valuable ships to the fleet at this precise moment was proving to be a ship that didn't always see a lot of love or action—the flak cruisers.

These were modified *Rook*-class battlecruisers that had been repurposed to defend the capital ships against swarms of Zodark and Orbot starfighters. These ships had had their main railguns removed and in their place were sixty quad-barreled 40mm flak guns. What made these 40mm flak guns so dangerous was the integration of an improved proximity fuze.

This piece of new tech was akin to the proximity shells first introduced by the British during the 1940 Blitz over London and then further refined by the Americans in the Pacific during World War II. This new fuze meant the shells didn't need to score a direct hit on an enemy fighter—they just had to pass close enough to be triggered and explode. The flak cruisers were also equipped with the newest in long-range missile interceptors. The missiles were packed in reloadable pods of fifty, with ten of these pods scattered across the ship.

Hunt watched as the flak cruisers steered themselves into the incoming waves of enemy fighters. The ship captains were constantly moving and shifting their ships to position them in the best possible path of the incoming fighters, forcing the enemy spacecraft to fly through the ensuing hornet's nest they were unleashing. The cruisers, of course, took a lot of hits themselves. Despite the best efforts of their gunners to intercept the waves of incoming missiles and torpedoes, some invariably made it through.

Turning to look at Wiyrkomi, Hunt said, "We need to finish the battle here and get over to the main battle now. Those flak cruisers won't be able to keep the enemy fighters off the fleet for long."

"I agree, Viceroy. I recommend we dispatch another wing of our own fighters to assist them," Wiyrkomi offered.

"Very well. Make it so. In the meantime, let's try to finish these ships off with our own guns. Move us into firing range," Hunt ordered. It was time to bring to bear the full power of this awesome ship.

As the ship's main thrusters kicked in, they approached a large group of Zodark warships. As they drew closer, the enemy's fire shifted away from the Primord ships they had been battling to focus exclusively on this massive unknown warship headed right for them. Then a squadron of Zodark frigates and corvettes diverted their attack runs on a Primord carrier to likewise head toward the *Freedom*.

For a moment, Hunt felt nervous, maybe even a bit afraid as he saw how many warships were now angling in to attack his ship. In all his years going into fleet battles, he'd never faced this many warships on his own. Looking around the bridge, he saw some nervous looks on the faces of his human crew. But the Gallentine crewmembers didn't seem fazed at all. They even looked calm. In a way, that helped to placate his own nerves. If they weren't scared, then why should he be?

The Zodark battleships opened fire with their lasers, targeting the forward sections of the *Freedom*. The ship was fifteen kilometers in length, which meant it had a lot of surface area to attack. Then came the corvettes—the Zodarks' newest warships. For their size, they were incredibly deadly. Instead of being heavily armored and leveraging large laser batteries, they were fast and nimble ships that packed an incredible array of plasma torpedoes. They swooped in toward the *Freedom* from multiple vectors as they lined up to launch their attack, a nasty spread of plasma torpedoes.

Just as the corvettes were coming in range of their primary weapon, the *Freedom* opened fire.

A light reached out from the *Freedom*'s forward turrets and stabbed the first corvette, then cut right down the side of it. The corvette separated into two parts before exploding. Then the other batteries engaged, and in seconds, the twelve corvettes were nothing more than wrecks adrift, sparks and small fires briefly illuminating the darkness around them before they were extinguished by the void of space.

While the corvettes had been carrying out their attacks, the two dozen Zodark frigates swooped in, unloading nearly a hundred torpedoes at the *Freedom*. They weren't even bothering to get in closer to their intended target, opting instead to fire their torpedoes immediately at the ship they deemed too big to miss. Seconds after the torpedoes had fired, they transformed themselves from guidable missiles into the molten plasma that made them unguidable but deadly weapons. The superheated plasma would plow through nearly any level of armor at incredible speeds, only coming to a halt in the bowels of a ship or blowing a hole right through it.

While the *Freedom* was a massive ship, it did make use of some incredible maneuvering capabilities. They were certainly going to take some hits, but once the forward thrusters kicked in, the front of the warship angled hard to one side while a different set of thrusters elevated the ship upwards by thirty degrees. As the main thrusters blasted to full power, the *Freedom* made an incredible and seemingly impossible maneuver in the eyes of everyone around her.

The remaining Zodark frigates, cruisers, and battleships reacted to the radical maneuvers and changes in vector, focusing their own laser and now magrail broadsides on what they perceived to be the more exposed underbelly of the ship. The frigates opened fire on the large warship with their magrail turrets, sending streams of projectiles at the laser batteries that had just cut their comrades' ships in half.

The enemy frigates were now spewing massive quantities of magrail projectiles at the *Freedom* as quickly as they could. The laser batteries that had just literally cut the corvettes apart were now trained on the frigates. It took only minutes for the laser batteries to decimate the attacking force even while a handful of them got torn apart by the magrail slugs. With this knowledge, the Orbot and Zodark ships that had magrail turrets unleashed a torrent of fire on the *Freedom* as they saw the initial success of the weapons.

"Damage report," called out Wiyrkomi.

The engineering officer on the bridge replied swiftly. "Sir, we lost seven forward laser batteries and two batteries along the port side."

"We're about to be hit by a wave of plasma torpedoes," shouted one of the Gallentine crewmen.

Looking at the monitor showing the image of the forward sections of the *Freedom*, Hunt saw dozens of plasma torpedoes slamming into the front section of the ship. Flashes of light intermixed with geysers of flame, and fluids erupted where the plasma torpedoes had hit. Dozens of these eruptions were taking place across a one-to-two-kilometer section of the bow of the ship. Yet despite these explosions, Hunt didn't feel a thing. The ship wasn't vibrating or shaking beneath his feet the way he had experienced so many times before when his ship had sustained such hits.

Why am I not feeling any of these impacts? Hunt thought privately.

Admiral McKee leaned in from her chair, whispering, "The *Freedom* is so big we can't even feel the impacts in the forward sections of the ship."

"I don't know if that's a good thing or not," was all Hunt said in reply. He was a bit awestruck at how this battle was playing out.

The forward laser batteries were ripping into the Zodark battleships now that they had swept the smaller ships aside. Battleship after battleship had its armor sliced open, exposing its internal guts to the vacuum of space. Still, the Zodark and Orbot ships came at the large Gallentine warship, attacking relentlessly.

"Prepare to fire the CPW," Wiyrkomi announced. "I want that Orbot ship I highlighted to be the first ship we hit."

Hunt stood and walked over to Wiyrkomi, whispering, "Do we want to give away that secret now, in this battle?"

Turning at him, Wiyrkomi replied, "Miles, this is the battle to end the war. There are only seven known ships in the universe that have such a weapon—the Titans. It's time we use it."

Hunt nodded ever so slightly. "OK, let's do it, then. Let's end this."

CPW stood for Craykard Particle Weapon. It was some sort of high-energy weapon apparently more potent than even the *GW*'s plasma cannon. The thing had an effective range of one hundred megameters, giving it some serious reach.

Targeting the Orbot battleship, the massive turret housing the still-experimental superweapon turned and elevated its barrel slightly. When the gun fired, it looked almost like a massive beam of bright white light followed by a circular blue lightning bolt. It crossed the expanse of space in fractions of a second to slam into the Orbot ship. The bright beam of light and the ensuing lightning were so bright, it almost looked like a star going supernova as it temporarily whited out their screens. When the sensors and cameras could refocus, the Orbot ship was gone. It had been blown into millions of tiny pieces.

"Holy Mother of God," Admiral Fran McKee muttered. "What the hell kind of superweapon was that?"

"Once the weapon is recharged, fire on the next Orbot ship. In the meantime, keep our main laser batteries going," Wiyrkomi ordered the gunners.

"That, Fran, is some sort of particle weapon, I've been told. Don't ask me how it works because I have no idea. I just know it's an experimental weapon and incredibly dangerous."

The remaining Zodark and Orbot battleships renewed their attack on the *Freedom*, but this time, they focused their efforts on going after

169

the turret of the gun that apparently had the ability to destroy their ships with a single shot. The turret of this weapon was situated closer to the citadel of the ship, making it significantly more protected.

While the gunners on the *Freedom* continued to tear gashes and deep rents into the enemy warships, Hunt made his way over to Rear Admiral Aaron "Warhawk" Blade, the commander of his ship's flight operations. His little section of the bridge was abuzz with its own activity. They had squadrons in life-and-death battles down on the planet, in its orbit, around the *Freedom*, and intermixed in both major fleet actions taking place. It was an incredible amount of information to keep track of.

"Warhawk," Hunt said, addressing the admiral by his flight call sign as the man preferred. "Give me a status update on how your side of the battle is shaking out."

Taking his eyes off a screen he'd been intently looking at, the admiral replied, "Tough, but a lot better than your side, I gather."

Grunting at the comment, Hunt replied, "That's for sure. How are things going? And don't sugarcoat it."

"Tough, sir. This is our first fight with manned fighters and bombers. Our pilots are learning a lot of hard lessons. Unfortunately, some are learning them with their lives."

Hunt grimaced at that. He had known this would be a tough crucible for their pilots, especially his son, who was leading one of the fighter groups.

"Sir, we're getting a lot of calls for air support from the ground forces on the planet now that they know the invasion is on. I'm not sure if it's possible, but if we could send our ground contingent down, that might alleviate a lot of the problems our guys are facing. I can only spare so many squadrons to assist them while still handling the battles up here."

"That's an interesting question," Hunt replied. "What kind of enemy fighter support are we looking at down on the planet and in orbit around it? If we're going to land soldiers, I want to make sure their landing craft are going to make it."

Warhawk grimaced at the question before answering. "The enemy still has a number of support bases on the surface. They've been scrambling fighters left and right to battle our own. It's been a tough fight thus far and we've not been able to fully establish air supremacy. Ideally, we'd want to pound some of those bases from orbit. I think once we clear more of these enemy battleships from around the planet, we may be able to direct one of our *Ryan*-class battleships to slip into orbit and start hammering some of those bases. Then it should be clear to land the ground forces."

"What if we tried to push the landing force through now, with additional fighter support?" Hunt pressed.

"We could likely do it, but you'd risk losing a lot of the ground force in transit, potentially as much as fifty percent of their shuttles. These Orbot fighters are actually pretty good, and generally speaking, our pilots are still green and learning. I'd rather pull a squadron from the battles up here and have them focus on close-air support until we can better clear the skies and properly protect the ground invasion than go in now and potentially lose half of them on the descent."

Hunt couldn't argue with the logic. He just didn't like leaving his people down on the ground without support any longer than necessary.

Shaking his head in frustration, Hunt said, "OK, let's do this, then. Let's pull half the fighters from the main battles in space and get them fitted for close-air support and fighter operations on the planet. Let's take control of the skies, even if it's just for a day so we can land the Rangers and our additional ground forces. Those three divisions we've got sitting around on the ship could turn the tide of the war on the ground. We can't just leave them hanging like this, not after we asked them to rise up once the invasion started. We aren't going to abandon them midway through the battle."

"I agree, Viceroy. We'll make this work, sir. My fliers will give 'em hell."

The admiral issued orders to his operations officers, who started recalling some fighter wings and having others reorganize their ordnance loadouts. The shuttle pilots were put on alert and the ground forces were told to get ready. They'd be landing now instead of waiting until the battle was over with.
****

1st Ranger Division

"Listen up, Rangers," Colonel Michael A. Monsoor shouted to the four battalions of Rangers standing in formation, waiting to hear him

171

speak. "We've finally been given the call. The Old Man has seen fit to deliver us to the surface of this godforsaken wasteland to slay bodies and collect souls. We're going to retake this place in the name of the Republic. For all intents and purposes, this is our first real combat mission. Sumer was a bit of a bust in that regard for most of us, but don't expect the Zodarks or the Orbots to roll over and play dead."

Some murmurs could be heard in the crowd at the mention of the Orbots. The Rass campaign a long while back was the only real campaign any ground forces had ever fought against the Orbots.

The colonel smiled at the murmurs he heard from his brigade of killers. "That's right, you all heard the word *Orbot*. Those six-legged spider-looking cyborg abominations are here, and by all accounts, there's just as many of them as there are Zodarks. Now keep in mind, when you shoot at those bastards, you need a clean head shot or a lot of shots to the torso and other parts to take 'em out. Unlike the Zodarks, which most of us are used to fighting, these Orbots are a lot smarter and craftier, and like any other cyborg or combat Synth, they know how to aim. Heck, most of the time these damn Orbots shoot better than us. What I'm conveying to you is don't underestimate them."

Major Hiro raised a hand. "Sir, any word on where they'll be dropping us or how you want our battalions to coordinate and fight together?"

At the start of the Sumer campaign, RA Special Forces had formed up a second Ranger division at Fort Roughneck back on New Eden. They'd started the process of running some seventeen thousand new recruits through the final phase of Special Forces training when 1st Division had arrived back home. Once the original division was home, the massive reorganization had begun. Half the officers and NCOs of the battle-tested division had been transferred to the new division to give them some immediate leadership and combat experience. This meant a lot of promotions had occurred subsequently to fill in the gaps.

Major Monsoor had become a colonel and taken over their brigade. Captain Hiro had been promoted to major and had taken over the battalion, and Lieutenant Kranston had been promoted to captain and replaced Hiro. Nearly all the sergeants had seen a bump in grade, with many being asked to consider a commission.

Colonel Monsoor looked at Major Hiro as he responded to his question. "All I've been told is our battalions are being dropped near the four pathfinder groups that went in ahead of us. The Delta platoons have established coms with the RA and Prim units that had been left behind, and they've been carrying out all sorts of attacks on the enemy installations around the spaceports and space elevators. When we arrive on the surface, we'll coordinate our operations with the Deltas and look to carry out the missions they've generated for us. Remember, we're still part of the advance team for the main invasion force. The rest of the RA will start to show up in a few days when the fleeters finish clearing the systems. We've got a tough couple of days ahead of us, but this is what we train for. So let's show 'em what we can do."

"When are we leaving?" called out another officer.

"Everyone's to report to the flight bay in ninety mikes. When I leave, I want everyone to return to your company sections and start getting your kits together. Plan on bringing enough food packs with you to survive ten days. I'm not sure how long it'll take to get a resupply, and chances are the soldiers on the ground we'll be interacting with may need it, so give them half your food if it comes to it. Remember, these guys have been fighting and dying on this frozen rock for nearly five weeks. They'll have been through hell. Now get out of here, and I'll see you all in the flight bay in ninety. Rangers Lead the Way!"

"All the way. Hooah!" came the shouts from the soldiers as they leapt to their feet.

****

Alpha Company, 1st Battalion, 4th Special Forces
On the Surface

"That's affirmative, *Freedom*. I need those reinforcements to arrive at grid Papa Juliet Five-Five-Seven-Eight-Five-Four-Tree-Tree. This is some rough country, so we need their ground support elements to be delivered with them. How copy?" Captain Royce asked as he relayed the coordinates to the Orbot base camp they'd finally secured.

"That's a good copy, Pathfinder Actual. Drop is commencing in ten mikes. Should be at your location in…thirty-two mikes. Out," came the short reply from the operations section of the *Freedom*.

"'Bout damn time those reinforcements got here," Master Sergeant Hanke commented.

Royce pointed to the sky above them. "Judging by what I'm seeing up there, they're in one hell of a fight. I'm just glad they're in a position to send us reinforcements at all."

"If we're going to capture any of the remaining infrastructure of that platform intact, then we need to get a move on. That next objective is sixty-eight kilometers away and I'd rather not have to hoof it that far if we don't have to," Major Pilecki said as he joined the conversation.

Turning to face the regular Army major, Royce asked, "How many casualties?"

Looking at the piece of paper he'd scribbled on, Pilecki replied, "Twenty-six wounded that we need to throw on those birds that land so they can go up to the *Freedom*. We've got another nine walking wounded that can fight. I'll keep them unless you think we should send them up to the ships in orbit. Other than that, we lost one hundred seventy-six soldiers assaulting this piece of real estate."

Royce shook his head in disgust at the casualties. He knew most of them had come when that Zodark battleship had arrived on scene and blasted them. Hell, he'd lost nearly an entire platoon of Deltas. Not to be crass, but losing a platoon of Deltas hurt a lot more than losing a battalion of regular Army soldiers. The training pipeline for a Delta was three years compared to the four months it took for a regular Army soldier.

"I'm sorry for your loss, Major. This was a key base that needed to be taken out. I can't say the next objective will be any easier, but I can say that the unit headed our way is a Ranger battalion. Shock troops. Not quite like having a battalion of Deltas, but not far off. I'm going to have them take lead and do the bulk of the fighting while your group will hold back a bit and assist where needed. Your men have earned a break. Let's let the Rangers get their hands dirty. I know they've been itching for a fight."

"I appreciate that, Captain, but don't sideline us just because we're tired. My guys can still fight."

Before any of them could say anything further, the sound of fighters overhead broke through their conversation. From this distance, it was hard to tell who was who. They saw lots of small dots mixing it up in dogfights. From time to time, they'd see one of the fighters explode. Whoever the fighters were, they were hell-bent on dominating the skies above the ground. Royce and Pilecki just hoped it was Republic forces winning this fight.

****

4th Fighter Group "Death Rattlers"

"Listen up, Death Rattlers. We've been tasked with going back to Alfheim to take the skies back so the ground force can land. This is an important mission as the *Freedom* can only stay in the area for a short while longer before they need to move on to join the greater battle going on in the system. Since our last mission to the surface, intelligence has identified the location of several airfields being used by the enemy. One of them happens to be at the spaceport the ground pounders are going to attack next, so this one's a two-for-one. We get to take out a bunch of enemy fighters and then tear the base apart before the ground forces arrive," Ethan Hunt explained as he went over their next mission. They'd only been back on the ship now for ninety minutes since their last foray into the void.

"For this mission, all fighters will be tasked with going after enemy fighters. We've got a single squadron of bombers coming with us who'll lay a hurt on those enemy airfields. Unless they look like they're in trouble, we're going to focus on the fighters and clear them a path in. So let's get out there and do this thing!"

The pilots all jumped to their feet and started making their way out to the flight bay. Ethan ran up to Lieutenant Pushkin—"Flattop." Walking up next to him in the corridor that led to the flight bay, he said, "Flattop, I'm going to fly with you guys for this mission."

"That'd be great, Paladin. I'll have Jinx fly as your wingman. He's still a little torn up over the loss of Lacey."

Ensign Amy Laceton, otherwise known as Lacey, had been killed on the last mission, the only Hellcat pilot to have been taken down by an Orbot fighter. She'd been a real jokester and just a fun person to be around. Her loss was having an effect on the squadron, which was why Ethan felt he should fly with them for this mission.

"That sounds good. Oh, hey, Pushkin—you gotta push her loss out of your mind, at least for right now. You're the squadron commander. These pilots are looking up to you. We can mourn her loss later, but not right now. Got it?"

Pausing their walk, Pushkin motioned with his head for Ethan to follow him to a room just before the flight bay. In a soft voice, he responded, "I get that, sir. I really do. She was...she was practically a little sister to me and really liked by everyone. I still can't believe she got blown up like that."

Ethan took a breath in and let it out slowly before responding. "I know. I'm not going to lie or try to sugarcoat things for you, Lieutenant. You're going to lose more pilots. You might even lose a few more on this next mission. But you have to compartmentalize that for right now. When the battle is over, that's when we mourn our losses and remember our friends, not right now while we're in the thick of it. Remember, those regular Army guys down on the ground have been battling it out against these bastards for five weeks. Put yourself in their shoes. Imagine the losses they've sustained and what they've gone through. Now pull it together for your pilots and go kick some ass. Let's even the score and get some payback for her loss. Got it?"

Ethan hoped he wasn't being too harsh on the young officer. Pushkin was one of the best pilots he'd trained with. He was a natural-born leader. It was one of the reasons Ethan had chosen him to be a squadron commander.

Pushkin finally nodded in agreement. They left the little side room and joined the rest of the squadron as they were getting situated in their fighters.

Climbing into the cockpit of his own fighter, Ethan noticed something new on the side of his Hellcat. His crew chief smiled. "We thought you might like to see your score. Nine kills on the last mission, sir. Puts you in second place behind Ensign Adler—he scored fourteen."

Shaking his head, Ethan responded, "Thanks, Chief. Everything check out fine from those hits?"

"Yes, boss. We replaced a couple of component parts we weren't sure about, but otherwise, yes—you're good to go."

As his crew chief climbed back down and walked away from the Hellcat, Ethan got the engines turned on and the fighter ready to go. One by one, the fighters of his four squadrons left the *Freedom*. As they re-formed into their squadrons, they started heading back toward the surface.

One squadron broke off to approach the newly constructed orbital platform and space elevator. They took out the few remaining point-defense guns and cleared a path for the assault shuttles bringing in the Rangers that would work to secure it. While that squadron was focused on protecting the upper portion of the platform, Red Squadron dove down to the surface and the spaceport it was connected to.

When the fighters passed through angels ninety, or ninety thousand feet in altitude, the first sign of trouble showed up. Two squadrons of Zodark fighters, called Triads because they resembled a flying triangle, flew up to greet them. A little further away, three squadrons of the Orbot fighters they called Lancers were also being vectored their way. The Yellowjackets and the Greens headed toward the Lancers, which left Paladin and the Reds to deal with the two squadrons of Zodark fighters.

"Time to rock and roll, boys. Let's get some!" shouted Flattop eagerly to his pilots.

Depressing his talk button, Paladin called out, "Linx, follow me in. We're going after that group of fighters that's trying to get around our flank."

As he was talking, the group of six Triads were highlighted on both his and Linx's HUDs. Activating his missiles, Paladin got a solid lock on the first one and saw Linx had a solid lock on a second. He fired and moments later his wingman did the same. Instantly, the six Zodark fighters broke formation and tried to do what they could to evade the two missiles fired at them and engage the fighters that had shot at them.

While the enemy fighters were jinking and taking evasive maneuvers, Paladin got another missile lock and fired. This caused the Zodark to break off his attack on Linx and focus on trying not to get shot down. Then Paladin's warning system kicked on, letting him know he was being targeted by a Zodark missile himself. As he pulled up hard on his flight controls and applied his air brakes, the Zodark fighter zipped past him in the blink of an eye. Paladin closed his brakes and applied more power to his engines, zipping right after the guy. He activated his guns and zeroed in on him. Depressing the firing stud on his flight stick, he sent a dozen blaster shots at the Triad. More than half of them scored hits, blowing the fighter apart.

Then his HUD told him one of his missiles had finally connected with another Zodark fighter, but the other had missed. "Break right, Paladin!" came an urgent cry over his helmet.

As he broke to the right, Ethan saw a string of blaster bolts fly right through the space where he'd just been. Then his fighter shook hard from a couple of shots that did hit him. A couple of alarm bells blared, and some red lights came on, letting him know he'd taken some damage.

"How bad are you hit, Paladin?" came the voice of Flattop.

Checking his readouts, Paladin knew he was in trouble. Depressing his talk button, he said, "Bad. I've lost control of my weapon systems and it looks like my engines are at about thirty percent thrust. I'm going to have to break off and try to head back to the *Freedom*," he replied.

"Copy that. Linx, you stay with your wingman. We've got this, Paladin."

"Thanks, Red Leader. Yellowjacket Actual, Paladin. I'm hit and heading back to mother. You're in command."

"That's a good copy, Paladin. We got this," came the quick reply from his XO.

Turning back to a channel for just him and Linx, Ethan said, "Hey, good job back there. You did well."

A few minutes passed before Linx replied, "Thanks, Paladin. But my wingman still got shot up, again."

Ethan knew Linx was probably blaming himself for the loss of Lacey. He had been her wingman too. He'd have to talk with him once they returned back to the ship. The guy was a good pilot and the last thing Ethan wanted was for him to go and get himself killed trying to prove something. Sometimes you just lose people. The young ensign needed to learn that.

Chapter Sixteen
Rangers Lead the Way

Charlie Company, 1st Battalion

As the soldiers took their seats on the shuttle and got themselves fastened in, the pilot flying them to the surface came on to say, "Good afternoon, *Park* Rangers. I want to welcome you aboard the Polar Bear Express as we make our maiden voyage to the surface. My name is Lieutenant Junior Grade Manny Crawford, though people like to call me Joke. While this is my first official flight to the surface of the North Pole, my copilot and I did stay at a Holiday Inn Express last night. Our inflight meal is surf and turf, served by our James Beard Award–winning chef. Barring any major turbulence, surface-to-air missiles and general laser bolts flying in our direction, we should be on the surface in under half an hour. Thank you for choosing to fly the Polar Bear Express."

The pilot's announcement elicited a few laughs and comments from the soldiers in the back. It helped to break up the tension and nervousness they were all feeling.

"Hey, I'd like my steak medium rare with some twice-baked potatoes, Petty Officer Loring," one of the soldiers called out to the crew chief standing near the entrance to the flight deck. He laughed as he rolled his eyes at them.

Staff Sergeant Paul "Pauli" Smith smiled at the banter going on. He looked at the soldiers he'd be leading into battle and thought, *I miss my old platoon...*

Pauli scanned the faces of his squadmates. Only a handful of them were veterans from the Sumer campaign, and even fewer were veterans from their original unit, the 1st Orbital Assault Division. All the veterans had been separated into the new battalions, companies, and platoons of this newly formed-up Ranger division to bring some battle-hardened experience to the new people.

Shortly after the Sumer campaign, a second Ranger division had been formed up—half the division had been folded into the new one and the empty ranks filled with fresh recruits just out of training. Pauli understood the logic, spreading the combat experience around, but he didn't like them doing it right before a major battle. His new unit hadn't had a lot of time to train together. Yogi was still with him, in another platoon but still in the same company. So was Master Sergeant Dunham—so at least he still had a few people he was comfortable with.

"Listen up, men. In a couple of minutes, our shuttle is going to leave to make history. We're going to land and we're going to assault this spaceport and we're going to take it. Just follow me and I'll lead you to victory," came the voice of their fearless leader, a baby-faced lieutenant fresh from officer basic course.

Great, this guy's going to get us all killed, Pauli thought. He shared a nervous glance with Master Sergeant Dunham, who only shook his head in disgust. He had the unenviable job of breaking in the new lieutenant while Pauli had the unofficial job as assistant platoon sergeant next to Dunham. Their old lieutenant, Atkins, had screwed things up big-time and gotten himself promoted to captain, a job he'd never wanted and had fought hard to not take. He'd just wanted to stay a platoon leader, but the brass had needed him to take over the company once they'd promoted Hiro. Similarly, Captain Hiro had been promoted up to major and taken command of their battalion while Major Monsoor had taken over the brigade as their new colonel. War and casualties had a strange way of moving you up through the ranks faster than you anticipated or wanted.

When the LT finished pontificating on the glorious victory he was going to lead them to, Master Sergeant Dunham turned to the soldiers, making sure he excluded the lieutenant's com link, and clarified, "Listen up. If you bastards want to stay alive, you best stick to me and Staff Sergeant Pauli. Follow your training—fire and move. Don't sit in one spot too long, and aim for headshots if you come across an Orbot. It's the only way to take 'em out."

The soldiers around Pauli all nodded in agreement. A few of them looked relieved to hear his words. The boy wonder who'd joined their ranks just a month ago kept going on about the glories of combat and battle. He hadn't fought one yet or fired a single shot, yet he was lecturing everyone on a subject he knew nothing about.

With the rear hatch to the transport closed, the shuttle lifted off and exited the flight bay. Dozens and dozens of shuttles started making their way toward the planet below, most carrying soldiers. Some of the larger, squattier-looking shuttles were cargo haulers, with an internal cargo bay large enough to hold six fully kitted-out DF-12 Cougar infantry fighting vehicles. Until they got some airfields established and their standard fleet of Osprey assault craft operational, the Cougars were going to be the best way to maneuver around the planet.

A fresh-faced cherry asked Pauli, "Staff Sergeant, how many combat drops does this make for you?"

The other privates next to him stopped talking to each other as they all turned, wanting to hear what he had to say. Smiling, Pauli replied, "Six, Private. You'll get used to it. Just give it time." The soldiers looked at him like he was some sort of war god to have survived six of these combat drops.

What Pauli wanted to tell them was that he was scared out of his brains just like them. But he knew he couldn't say that. They were looking up to him. They wanted their sergeant to be in complete control, no fear, basically the opposite of their lieutenant, who was all bravado and no experience.

As their shuttle continued its descent to the surface, their pilot started to take some evasive maneuvers.

"Are they shooting at us?" one of the soldiers called out.

One of the crew chiefs looked out one of the side windows as he commented, "I don't know that they're shooting at us in particular, but they're certainly shooting at our group of shuttles."

That was apparently all it took for the lieutenant to try and take charge of the situation. What should have been communicated via a private coms channel between him and the pilots was broadcast across the platoon. "Oh my God! They're shooting at us! Pilot, take evasive maneuvers now!"

The pilot countered that they were not being individually singled out. He summarily scolded the lieutenant for creating undue panic and told him to sit back and wait for them to get on the ground.

So much for the bravado. He didn't even make it to the surface before he pissed his pants, Pauli thought privately. His disgust for their platoon leader was growing by the second.

Before the lieutenant could say anything further, Master Sergeant Dunham roared loudly over their coms net, "Everyone calm the hell down! Shut up, keep your eyes forward and wait for the pilots to get us down on the ground. These shuttles are being flown by the best pilots in the Navy. You do your job and let them do theirs—that's how this works."

For the next few minutes, no one said anything. The pilots made a few course corrections, nothing too aggressive to indicate they were being shot at, not like earlier. The crew chief who was standing near the flight deck announced they were approaching the surface. Once they dropped the hatch, everyone needed to get out because they weren't sticking around.

When the shuttle landed, that was exactly what everyone did. They rushed off the back of the shuttle, prepared to wage war. Instead, they found themselves in the center of a shot-to-pieces Orbot base camp of some sort with a bunch of regular Army soldiers milling about.

Just as the lieutenant was about to move forward and embarrass them all, Master Sergeant Dunham placed a hand on the young man's shoulder. "Sir, let me take lead."

Before the LT could say anything, Dunham walked up to the man who looked to be in charge at the moment. "Sir, First Platoon, Charlie Company, 1st Battalion Rangers. How would you like our platoon deployed?"

When the man turned around, Pauli immediately recognized the officer staring back. It was Captain Brian Royce, the two-time Medal of Honor recipient and the man who'd convinced him to go Special Forces when his enlistment had ended.

"Master Sergeant Dunham! Damn good to see you again. I see a few familiar faces—looks like they gave you a new platoon to sort through," Captain Royce replied. Many people forgot that Royce had once been a master sergeant himself, so he had a bit of an affinity for his fellow sergeants.

Dunham shrugged. "You know how it is, sir. Someone has to do it. This is Lieutenant Weideman—he took the place of Atkins, who's now the CO. He's coming in on another bird with our rides."

"You'd do well to listen to anything this man says, Lieutenant," Royce said. "I've known Dunham since the invasion of New Eden. And those two, Yogi and Pauli—hot NCOs you have in your platoon. They'll get you through what we're about to face down here."

"Yes, of course, Captain. I look forward to leading my men in battle soon. It looks like we got here a little late to help," Weideman said glumly.

"All in due time, Lieutenant. Once our rides get here, we've got a bit of a hike to our next objective. I'm hopeful the flyboys will have worked them over pretty good for us, but you can bet they'll likely have a few surprises waiting for us. In the meantime, why don't you have your platoon stay over there until our rides arrive? You've got fresh troops, so you guys are going in the first wave. These guys"—Royce waved over to the RA soldiers, who looked exhausted and beat up—"are coming in the rear with the gear. They've earned their break."

"Yes, sir, we're on it," came the quick reply.

As Pauli got his squad rounded up, they played the age-old military game of hurry up and wait. He told them to drop their gear and sack out if they wanted to. Once they got to the side of some sort of blown-out hangar building, that was exactly what his squad did. They dumped their gear next to the walls and proceeded to get caught up on some sleep or dictate a message to be sent back home. Some broke out a deck of cards since they had no idea how long they'd have to wait for new orders.

Pauli sighed to himself. *Hurry up and get on the planet before you get blown out of the sky. Then wait now that we're down on the ground because we missed the main fight. Once our rides arrive, it'll be hurry up to the next battle.* Pauli seemed to remember his grandfather telling him something about this when he'd fought in the Iraq War back in the 2000s, then his father had said the same thing during World War III. *Damn, I'm getting old talking like this.* Heck, he was almost old enough to have a son fighting in this war with him if he'd gotten married and started having kids right out of high school.

Minutes later, they saw a massive Gallentine cargo ship descending near them. Looking at the ship, Pauli felt the same way he had when he'd seen his first Primord shuttle—awestruck. Each species he'd encountered up to this point had created and designed similar yet distinct ships. Similar in that they largely performed the same functions, yet unique in how they performed them. Pauli was no engineer, but he'd love to learn one day how they built these things, how they were powered and just how they worked.

When the giant ship had settled on the ground, a large ramp opened and out rolled six DF-12 Cougars and four other unarmored transport trucks. The vehicles headed toward their platoon's position and parked nearby. As quickly as the transports with the vehicles arrived, it left again, presumably to go pick up another load.

Instead of piling into the vehicles like they'd all thought they would, the platoons were told to stand fast. They were going to wait for the next load of vehicles to arrive so the entire battalion could make the move at once. Major Hiro wanted them to hit the next objective with their full force and not just throw company-sized elements at the enemy. That sounded like a wise move to Pauli. If the flyboys did their jobs, then maybe there wouldn't be a lot of Orbots left, but if the enemy was still dug in pretty well, then having the entire battalion along for the assault could make all the difference.

As time ticked by, Pauli told his squad to get comfortable. Those who hadn't already taken the chance to catch up on some sleep were doing so now. No reason to let a chance to grab some shut-eye pass them by. If they were needed, they'd be woken up. While he let his guys grab some z's, he wandered over to Master Sergeant Dunham, who was sitting against some rubble, reading something on his data pad.

"Any word on what's going on?" Pauli asked as he plopped down next to Dunham. "I thought we were pulling out of here when the Cougars got here. That was like an hour ago."

Dunham placed his tablet down on his thigh. The toothpick he was chewing on moved to the left side of his mouth as he answered, "I heard Captain Royce talking with the major. He mentioned the flyboys telling him the spaceport we're supposed to hit is pretty hot. They've been called back to the mothership, so to speak, so they can't stick around to provide any CAS for us. With no orbital assault ships in system, that means we don't have any Reaper or Orions to call on for help either. So, we're waiting for the rest of the battalion and our vehicles to get here."

"I figured it must be something like that," Pauli remarked. "At least they're smart enough to wait until we can hit them in force. Nothing worse than having to fight these bastards outnumbered, especially without air support."

"You're going to go far thinking like that, Staff Sergeant."

Pauli chuckled at the comment. Common sense wasn't so common in the military, but when it did rear its ugly head, you tended to get promoted.

"What do you think of this new lieutenant?"

Dunham shot him an angry and worried glance. "I've only been able to spend about a month with him. Either he's going to shape up into a decent officer or he's going to get himself killed really quick. I just want to make sure he doesn't take the platoon down with him." He sighed, then turned to look at Pauli. "As much swagger as he's talking with, I think he's just scared to death about leading a platoon of soldiers into battle and he's talking tough to cover for it. Unless he starts doing something stupid, let's let him learn while we try to guide him to the right decisions along the way. Who knows, maybe he'll turn out to be a halfway decent officer. I mean, look at how well Hiro has turned out."

While Captain Hiro wasn't as bombastic as Lieutenant Weideman, he had his own challenges. His problem was his timidity. He struggled with making decisions that could result in soldiers getting killed. Because of this, he suffered from something called paralysis through analysis. It had taken a lot of coaxing and mentoring from Dunham and Atkins, but eventually he had come around and finally been able to move past his hesitancy.

Pauli nodded at that logic—it made sense. Some folks talked tough or big when they got scared, but it was just an act. The ones Pauli worried about were the quiet ones—the ones that sat there with that blank look on their faces and didn't say much. Those were the guys you had to worry about. One minute they were fine, the next they were raving madmen, charging a Zodark gun position all Royce-like. That video of Master Sergeant Brian Royce charging that horde of Zodarks going on a bloodthirsty killing spree in that enemy carrier still circulated around the net. The guy was a living legend—his personal tactics were taught at the Infantry School along with every Special Warfare School. Violence of action almost always carried the day.

Chapter Seventeen
Kraken

RNS *Freedom*
Above Alfheim

The battle raging around the planet and the system in general was as intense as it was sprawling. Several squadrons of Zodark warships had spread out to avoid the Republic's relentless magrail fire. If the Republic could, they leveraged the Primord ships and their lasers for the longer-range engagements while the *Ryan*-class battleships and Rook battlecruisers did their best to get in close to deliver their devastating hammer blows. Intermixed with all of this were hundreds of P-97 Orion fighter drones, Prim starfighters, and the countless Zodark and Orbot fighters and bombers, all hammering away at each other.

The fleet is getting too spread out. We have to get a better battle line formed up, Hunt thought.

Turning to look Wiyrkomi, he said, "We need to tighten the fleet formations. I also want our fighters and bombers to start focusing on that Orbot star carrier. We have to start thinning out these enemy fighters or they're going to pick our support ships apart."

The Gallentine ship captain started issuing orders to the fleet to tighten their positions. The battle had been raging for sixteen hours and cost them nearly fifteen percent of their fleet. This wasn't a sustainable loss ratio. At the same time, they'd destroyed the enemy warships at a rate of nearly two to one. The kill ratio would likely be higher if the *Freedom* had been able to get into the main fight sooner—they'd been detained longer than they should have over Alfheim, clearing it of enemy fighters and deploying their ground contingent. Finally, Hunt had had to call an end to those operations and get his flagship into the main battle.

"Give me a status on the damage we took earlier. How are we holding up?" Hunt called out to his engineering section on the bridge.

The Gallentine officer in charge motioned for his human counterpart to go ahead and answer the question. They weren't in a direct battle right this moment, so he was doing his best to let his trainee do more of the talking. "Sir, we still have extensive damage to the forward section of the ship. It's primarily located in sections A through C but contained to just deck one and some portions of deck two."

"Are we going to have any of those weapon systems back online soon?"

This time the Gallentine officer answered, "Some, just not all. Several of the laser batteries were taken off-line because their power couplings had been severed. Those batteries are operational again. We lost another twelve that will need to be repaired in a shipyard. In general, while the damage looked severe at first, it was largely superficial. It never really got into the guts of the ship or the inner decks."

Hunt sighed, more out of relief than anything else. He thanked them for their efforts and turned his attention back to his flight operations. Until his ship got closer to the main battle, the only thing they could do to help was continue sending squadron after squadron of their advanced fighters to assist the rest of the fleet in the main battle.

****

RNS *Battleaxe*

Commander Amy Dobbs grabbed the arm of her captain's chair as the ship shook hard from yet another blow. Sparks rained down on the bridge and a few of the screens momentarily went black before rebooting.

"Damage report!" she barked to be heard over the chaos of the scene.

"One of the plasma torpedoes hit portside, near the launch bay. We're venting oxygen and fluids. We need to seal deck eight, section nine now!" replied her damage control officer.

Damnit, that section has a lot of people in it. "Fine, do it. Get that fire under control and stop the leaks or that fire will spread rapidly," she ordered. At least twenty-six people worked in that section of the ship she'd just ordered sealed off. If she hadn't, the flames would have spread and reached the fuel stores for the flight line, which would blow an even larger hole in the ship than that last torpedo just had.

"Tactical, what's the situation on those enemy fighters heading toward the *Hood, Sussex,* and *Yorkshire*?"

"We got at least half of the bombers and a quarter of the fighters as they passed us. It looks like they still delivered a serious blow to the *Hood.* I don't think she's going to make it. The other two ships appear to have taken some damage, but nothing like the *Hood*—she took the brunt of the enemy barrage," Lieutenant Commander Joe Wright replied.

Dobbs returned her gaze to the main monitor, where the three battleships she was assigned to protect were being shown on the screen. The *Hood*, situated in the center of the battle line, looked like it had taken eight or more torpedo hits. She was bleeding oxygen and fluids at a rapid pace. Then a series of explosions erupted from deep within the ship before its entire electrical system failed and it broke apart. Tiny little pods were being launched, but far too few for the size of the ship's complement.

The other two ships took a couple of torpedo hits but looked to still be in fighting shape. The remaining enemy fighters and bombers were doing their best to get out of the battleships' weapons range and back to their motherships.

Ensign Waldman, her coms officer, asked, "Captain, we're being asked by the *Sussex* if we can assist in recovery of the *Hood*'s life pods. What should I tell them?"

Turning to look at her most junior officer on the bridge, Dobbs replied, "Tell them we'll assist. Also, please advise them that we recommend they look to tighten their formation back up with the main fleet."

Their squadron of four, now three ships had drifted to the outer edge of the main fleet. If they were going to maintain some level of group protection, then they needed to get back in with the fleet. With this last wave of fighters and bombers having completed their attack run, the bulk of the fleet action was now taking place on the other end of the battle line, some eight hundred thousand kilometers away. Well outside any of their weapon systems' effective ranges.

"Commander Wright, you have the bridge. I'm heading down to sickbay to check on the wounded," Dobbs announced as she got up to leave.

"XO has the bridge," Wright said loudly in reply as he moved to take the seat she'd just vacated.

When Dobbs reached the lift, she finally had a moment alone with no one around. When the door closed, she let out a yell of frustration before closing her eyes and taking several deep breaths to regain her composure. As the decks moved by, she took a deep breath in, held it, then slowly let it out. She repeated the process a few more times until the lift reached the level she'd selected and the door opened.

When it had become clear her previous ship, the *Brandenburg*, was still too severely damaged to join this fight, she'd been transferred to take command of the *Battleaxe*. The ship's CO had died the week prior from an aortic aneurysm. His sudden death had left an opening that needed to be filled immediately. Since Dobbs had worked on the design of the *Battleaxe* many years ago, they'd pulled her from the *Brandenburg* and made her the new CO. This had given her just five days to get to know her crew and officers before they left for battle—not a lot of time.

With the new Altairian-Human hybrid ships starting to come online, the *Rook*s, being the oldest class of warships, were slated for retirement. When she had worked in the R&D and procurements directorate, she'd gotten the idea of taking the now largely outdated warships and repurposing them as antifighter support ships—a role that was proving to be more and more important. Her own ship, the *Brandenburg*, was slated for this fate next year.

The antifighter support ships had integrated sixty quad-barreled 40mm flak guns to go with a larger battery of antifighter missiles. This gave the support ships an incredible defensive punch and was ideal for protecting the capital ships against enemy fighters and bombers. This did mean they had to sacrifice their offensive capabilities in the refit. It also meant the ships were a lot more vulnerable in a straight battle with a Zodark or Orbot ship since they didn't carry their offensive magrail turrets. Instead, these antifighter support ships only traveled in large battle groups. If push came to shove, they still maintained an inventory of fifty one-megaton nuclear-tipped antiship stealth missiles. The missiles were slow by modern war standards, but in a pinch, they could deliver a real blow to an enemy ship if they managed to score a hit.

Walking off the lift, Dobbs made her way through the corridors, passing from one section of the ship to the next until she reached the medical bay. Wounded spacers were being brought in from the damaged sections of the ship. The medical personnel were attending to them and seemed to have things under control. It wasn't like the horror she had seen on the *Brandenburg*. She still had nightmares about her wounded crewmen. Some had been badly burned while others had had missing limbs.

Still, she felt it her duty as their captain to come check on them personally. The battle wasn't over with, far from it. But there was a lull.

"Ah, I heard you were on your way, Captain," her chief doctor said.

"There's a break in the fighting—this is the only time I feel I can get away. How are our people doing?" she asked, concern in her voice as she looked behind him at the injured spacers.

"I think we lucked out, Captain. That torpedo hit could have been a lot worse. How is the battle going?" The doctor had a nervous look of his own.

"I'd say we're winning, but these guys just keep throwing ships at us. Good news is the *Freedom* looks to finally be moving in to join the main battle." She paused for a second as she briefly shook her head. "You wouldn't believe the damage that single ship could cause. It took on twenty Zodark and Orbot ships by itself and wiped them out. Most of the ships were hit by a single superweapon of some sort. I think the battle will turn once they get in range of that weapon."

The doctor was visibly relieved. "That's good to hear, Captain. It can be a bit frightening down here, not knowing what's going on. If you'll excuse me, I'm going to get back to the patients. I just wanted to check on you and the ship."

She smiled as he left, then made her way over to a wounded spacer. He looked young, likely just nineteen or twenty. "How are you holding up...Spacer Tupol?"

"I'll make it, Captain. Did we get the bastards that hit us?" the young man asked through gritted teeth. His lower torso had severe burns. She could tell he was in immense pain even after having been given some meds.

Placing a hand on his shoulder, she squeezed lightly. "We sure did. You guys did outstanding. You helped save the ship."

A tear ran down the young man's face. "It hurts, ma'am. I'm scared I'm going to die."

"Can I get a nurse over here?" Dobbs shouted. Seeing it was the captain yelling, one of the nurses raced over to her.

"Nurse, can you give him any more pain medication? He's clearly in a lot of agony."

The nurse had a look of sorrow on her face but nodded. She pulled out an injector and gave him another dose of fentanyl. The young man's

190

eyes started to get a little glassy and he didn't look like he was in as much pain. The nurse then motioned for Dobbs to follow her for a moment.

"Ma'am, he's dying. He's not going to make it."

The news hit Dobbs like a sledgehammer. She reached for something to stabilize herself.

"Are you all right, Captain?" the nurse asked.

"I'm...I'm fine. It's just, he doesn't look terminal."

The nurse pursed her lips before responding, almost trying to figure out what to say or how to say it. "His legs, his lower extremities...they're scorched to the bone. We've pumped him full of medical nanites—they're the only thing keeping him alive right now, but an injury like this is just too much for the nanites to repair. Maybe if we had more cryobeds, we could put him into stasis and let the nanites rebuild his body. These old battlecruisers only have three on board, and we've got them occupied with folks who came in before him."

Dobbs caught herself wiping a tear away before asking, "Nurse, I know you guys are doing what you can. My last command, the *Brandenburg*, we nearly lost the ship in our last battle. We had a similar situation. Our doctor came up with a slight workaround. He wrapped the injured spacer's body in nanite paste and then ran a nanite blood transfusion until we were able to transfer him to a medical facility on Kita. I know it sounds crazy, but it worked. Can we at least try it here? If we don't, this kid's going to die."

The nurse looked surprised by the treatment but immediately got the doctor. Dobbs explained it again to him. He looked relieved to have learned of something new that might save more of his patients. In minutes, the nurses and doctors were wrapping the worst of the patients in medical nanite paste and setting them up with transfusions. They put the patients into a medically induced coma and would then hope for the best. It was about all they could do.

As the doctor was walking toward her to thank her for sharing this with them, her communicator chirped. "Captain, you're needed on the bridge. We've been given a new tasking by the fleet commander."

"I'm on my way, XO. Get the ship ready for whatever the new tasking is. I'll be there in ten minutes. Out."

"Before you go, Captain, thank you for sharing your experience on the *Brandenburg*. I don't think I had ever heard of that technique being used, but it makes complete sense. I think you just saved the lives of at least six of our patients."

Dobbs nodded, her eyes starting to moisten. "Just keep doing what you're doing, Doc. I'm needed on the bridge; we're likely heading into another fight."

She turned and headed down the hall toward the lift that would take her back to the bridge. She almost hadn't come down to sickbay since they didn't have a terrible number of casualties, but she was glad she had. A few spacers would likely live because of it.

****

4th Fighter Group "Death Rattlers"

"Commander, your ship just isn't ready. We've got to completely change out the engine. We need another three hours for that. Then we'll need at least another hour to test it and make sure it'll function properly with the other one," the Gallentine chief mechanic tried to explain to Ethan Hunt.

Pulling the man aside, Ethan asked, "Talocan, what's going on? Why are more than half my birds down for maintenance? There's a life-and-death battle going on out there and I need these fighters flying."

Talocan was the chief maintenance officer for Ethan's fighter group. He had a crew of ten Gallentine mechanics overseeing one hundred and ten human mechanic trainees.

"Ethan, we are doing the best we can. I would normally have a crew of one hundred and ten highly skilled mechanics working on maintaining your squadrons. Instead, I have trainees who need at least another year of experience before they can work on their own. They just aren't ready yet. My guys are having to check and double-check everything they do and sometimes it's not done right and then it needs to be redone. The best I can tell you to do is start consolidating some of your squadrons until we can get more of your damaged birds repaired and tell your pilots to stop getting their fighters shot up."

Turning to look at a group of six humans and a single Gallentine pulling the port engine out of his fighter, Ethan saw the problem. He just couldn't do anything about it. They hadn't had enough time to get their human crew fully trained up on how to operate and maintain the *Freedom*, and the skeleton crew the Gallentines had given them to act as trainers just wasn't enough—not during a full-fledged battle like the one they were in. The ship wasn't supposed to be ready for combat for at least another year, maybe even two.

Taking a breath in, Ethan calmed himself before responding. "OK, Talocan, I understand. Find a way to have the humans work on the problems they have the skills to handle without supervision and put a few more of your skilled mechanics on some of the birds that require the higher-level skills. This battle isn't over with yet."

Walking out of the flight bay, Ethan made his way over to flight operations. If he couldn't get himself back in a fighter, then he'd at least do what he could to observe and manage the battle from flight operations. When he walked into the room, he saw a couple of new battles picking up in intensity. It was clear the Orbots and Zodarks knew they couldn't take on the *Freedom* directly, so they were doing their best to take down as many Primord and human battleships as they could.

"Hellcats still down for maintenance?" one of the flight ops officers asked.

"We just don't have enough trained mechanics to handle everything," Ethan grumbled just loud enough for only them to hear.

"I remember my dad telling me, 'Son, you go to war with the army you have, not the army you need.' That seems to have rung true my entire time in the military fighting these blue bastards," Commander Reagan offered as he pulled a chair out for Ethan.

"My dad says the same thing. I know the urgency of this mission, this rescue mission for the guys on Alfheim, but I think we really rushed ourselves coming out here. We aren't ready to do battle with this ship, not even close," Ethan replied quietly.

He and Reagan were good friends. They'd gone to the Academy together. Reagan had gone into the world of fighter drones and flown the Reaper ground assault drones. He was now doing his obligatory tour in flight operations, a prerequisite for group commander after commanding a squadron.

His friend leaned over. "I know it's frustrating, Ethan, but put yourself in the shoes of those poor saps on the planet. Imagine being left behind, likely to die a horrendous death at the hands of the Zodarks. We couldn't just leave a quarter of a million people like that. Oh, and by the way, you're an Ace three times over now. So are like half your fighter pilots. Congrats. Even with a quarter of your birds either down for maintenance or destroyed, your group is leading the ship in kills."

Ethan grunted at the news and smiled. He was proud of his pilots. He'd pushed them hard trying to get them ready for combat. He probably should have pushed his maintenance section just as hard. He hadn't made a plug for them to get the improved neurolinks or brain stims like he had his pilots—a mistake he was paying for now.

The Gallentine fighters were simple to fly but incredibly complex to maintain. The technology was so advanced compared to anything they'd previously worked on; it was just taking time to get people up to speed on them.

"I'm glad I'm in flight ops right now and not a group commander."

Lifting an eyebrow at that, Ethan asked, "Oh, why's that? You always wanted command far more than me."

"In flight ops, I'm getting to see all the different mistakes you, the squadron commanders, group, and wing commanders are making," Reagan explained. "I'm learning from your successes and failures, so when I take command, I hopefully won't make the same mistakes."

Ethan laughed. "You did like to use me as a guinea pig."

"That's because your last name is Hunt. If you got in trouble at the Academy, you survived. We learned a lot by watching you, my friend," Reagan replied with a grin on his face.

The two laughed some more. It broke the tension Ethan was feeling right now. He was glad his friend wasn't out there flying right now. He knew you lost friends in battle—that was just the way war was. Still, he wanted Reagan to stick around for as long as possible. He didn't have a lot of close friends. Being the son of the Viceroy had its disadvantages. Namely that you didn't know if people were genuinely wanting to be your friend or if they had an ulterior motive. In either case, Ethan counted his friends from the Academy as his closest—they had known him back before his father had become famous.

"Seriously, though, how is the battle looking from your perspective?" Ethan pressed.

"I believe it's going good, but how can I really tell? We're certainly thinning those enemy fighters out. We just need to finish off more of their battleships, get a blocking force in behind them so they can't make a break for the gate," Reagan replied.

"I'm honestly surprised they haven't made a run for it. They know they can't defeat the *Freedom*, so why stick around any longer than necessary?"

"Easy—they want to bludgeon and degrade our joint fleet to a point where we won't be operationally effective. Then they'll withdraw what forces they have and regroup, knowing we can't threaten them further. It's honestly not a bad strategy."

Ethan shook his head in frustration; he knew his friend was likely right. "I guess we'll have to see what the Viceroy cooks up," he offered before standing up and heading back to the flight bay to ride his maintenance crews a bit more.

Chapter Eighteen
Spaceport

Charlie Company, 1st Battalion

"We're at the rendezvous point," the vehicle commander announced as the Cougar came to a halt.

Pauli stood and made his way over to the man's position. "How's it looking?"

The corporal turned the monitor slightly so Pauli could get a better view. "We can't see too much with our direct cameras. Too many trees in the way, but it's clear from all the smoke that it's been hit pretty good. This is the most recent drone footage we got of the place before it got zapped."

The image showed a lot of burned-out vehicles, warehouses on fire and smoldering, charred marks around the flight line and taxi ramps from laser bolts and bodies. Lots and lots of Zodark and Orbot bodies were strewn about the area. Around the perimeter of the base, some bunkers and towers had been destroyed, but many others appeared to be intact. Many of the fortified positions appeared to be manned. They were expecting an attack.

The monitor Pauli had been looking at suddenly brought up a different screen. The vehicle was being fed targeting data for their smart missiles. "Looks like we're going to soften that place up before you guys hit it," the vehicle commander said.

"Yeah, that makes sense." A new set of orders arrived in Pauli's HUD, telling him they'd reached their destination. The platoons were supposed to prepare for their next mission: the assault on the spaceport itself.

As the platoons exited the vehicles, a few officers and sergeants barked some orders for them to move away from them and into the woods. Master Sergeant Dunham motioned for everyone to follow him and Lieutenant Weideman. He led them away from the vehicles, pointing for everyone to take a seat for a moment.

Master Sergeant Dunham explained, "Here's the deal. The battalion is going to assault this facility en masse, but first things first. Our surveillance drones have identified some solid targets for the Cougars to hit. Once our platoons get dispersed in the woods and move closer to our objective, the Cougars are going to rain holy hell on them. That'll be the cue for us to launch our own attack. Once our attack is underway, the Cougars are going to race forward to join the fray and provide us with direct fire support with their turret-mounted guns."

While he was explaining things, Lieutenant Weideman had brought up a holographic representation of the perimeter their company was going to assault. He then added, "Once we approach our staging position, I want Staff Sergeant Yogi's Fourth Squad to set up our mortars here." He pointed to a spot maybe a hundred meters behind the rest of their positions. "Yogi, when the Cougars missiles start to hit, I want you to expend your two smoke rounds. Dunham said this should give us some cover when it comes time for us to launch our assault. Once your smoke rounds are complete, I want you to drop your remaining HE rounds. At this point, your squad's rounds should be expended. That's when I want to race and catch up to the rest of the platoon."

Dunham added, "Staff Sergeant Holland, your squad needs to hit this point here, taking out this bunker if the Cougars don't. Then push on to this point here once you've done that. Staff Sergeant Ramirez, your squad's going to hit this section of the line and push through to this location here. Staff Sergeant Smith, I want your squad to hit this bunker complex. It looks to be a command post or something. Take it out and secure this portion of the lines. Then I want your guys to set up on top of the facility and proceed to provide sniper coverage for the platoon and the company as we advance further into the base."

"Hooah," came the single-word reply from the squad leaders.

Pauli made sure his two junior sergeants stayed on top of things with their soldiers. Half his squad was fresh from training—they'd never seen a Zodark or Orbot, let alone been shot at by them. No matter how good their training was, until the lasers started to fly, you never fully knew how someone would react.

Moving through the underbrush of the forest, Pauli took a moment to look up at the individual trees. These things were tall. Not as tall as in the forests they had patrolled through and fought in on the Primord planet of Intus. Those trees were insane, some reaching as high as three hundred meters. The tallest trees on Earth were the redwoods in California. Some of them measured ninety-three meters in height. Pauli's HUD was telling him these trees appeared to be one hundred and forty meters, not nearly as tall as the ones on Intus but definitely taller than what you'd find on Earth.

The squad was doing a good job of maintaining their spacing and staying quiet. If someone had to ask a question, they communicated via their internal squad channel or their neurolinks. As they continued to advance, one of their scout drones exploded in the air. It was hit by something and blew apart. This sudden detonation caused everyone to hit the ground, rifles up and ready to lay waste to whatever came next.

Instead of a roar from a Zodark soldier or the skittering noise from an Orbot's spiderlike feet, a strange silence hovered over the area as the human soldiers all along the line lay in the prone position, their rifles facing forward as they waited to see what would happen next. Pauli scootched himself up against a tree trunk as he sought to get a better view of what was happening in front of them.

Nothing...what the hell blew up the scout?

Then he saw it. Movement. Maybe two hundred meters in front of him, he spotted a lone Zodark moving cautiously through the woods. Then he saw something else—a single snowflake. Then he saw a second, then the field of vision in front of him was filled with snow as it fell from the low-hanging clouds above them. The Zodark slowly faded away from view.

Damn this snow...it's obscuring our vision, Pauli thought angrily. Normally he loved the snow. He liked to lie on his back and watch the white fluffy cotton balls of love descend from the heavens above. But not today. The snow was cutting his visibility from a few hundred meters down to barely a hundred.

"Viking Actual, Viking One-One. I've got movement to my front. Blue bastard, roughly two hundred meters. How copy?"

Pauli was hoping someone else along the platoon's line had spotted the blue guy as well—that or maybe another platoon in the company.

"One-One, that's a good copy. Three-One spotted movement along their side as well. Have your squad prepare for contact. Out," came the terse reply from Master Sergeant Dunham. Pauli noticed it was him taking charge of the situation and not the lieutenant. He was likely showing the lieutenant what to do and guiding him through the process of his first contact with the enemy.

One day, it's going to be me teaching some baby-faced lieutenant what to do...

At this point, the snow was falling even heavier. Pauli told his squad to get ready for contact. They were going to let the Zodarks walk into their field of fire, then take 'em out. Switching over to his thermals, Pauli saw that the single Zodark figure he'd been watching earlier was actually at least three or four dozen figures. Whatever force was walking toward them, it was at least platoon-level. Something had caused the spaceport commander to dispatch ground forces in this direction. They'd probably figured this was the most likely approach the human soldiers would take, so they wanted to position some soldiers out here just in case.

"Stand by," came the voice of Dunham over their radios.

Whoosh…whoosh…whoosh…

The sound of the Cougars' smart missiles launching in sequence was barely audible over the snowfall, which was only picking up in intensity. One unmistakable sound they could hear was the rushing and parting of air as the missiles streaked over their heads, zeroing in on their predetermined targets.

A few Zodarks lifted their heads to the sky, obviously hearing the same sound. That was when Dunham roared over their coms, "Open fire!"

In that brief moment when the Zodarks had looked to the sky and their brains suddenly registered what was happening, the entire place erupted in magrail and blaster fire. Some of the Zodarks managed to drop to the ground and dodge the barrage being leveled at them, but many others did not.

Pauli saw at least thirty Zodarks get riddled with magrail and blaster bolts, their bodies dancing a strange jig as the projectiles punched their bodies over and over again until they finally collapsed to the ground. Not all the blue beasts had been killed outright, though. A handful had managed to survive the initial ambush and tore into the human lines. Some of the Zodark fire was wild and inaccurate, meant more to cause the human soldiers to duck. There were a few Zodark sharpshooters that were delivering some accurate return fire, however.

"Ah, damnit! Medic! Medic! Noah's hit!" cried one of the soldiers in Pauli's squad. Checking his Blue Force tracker, he saw it was Private Cholesky calling for the medic. Noah's suit, however, showed that Noah was dead.

A couple of Zodarks started laying into Noah and Cholesky's position, looking to exploit the newly created hole in the line. *I need to get over there...*

Pauli jumped out of his covered position and sprinted in their direction. A couple of blaster bolts zipped around him, forcing him to take cover. Pauli wasn't a medic by any means, but Cholesky's position was in trouble.

I'm up...he sees me...I'm down, Pauli said to himself as he ran forward a few meters while shooting before dropping behind some cover again.

As he neared Cholesky, several laser bolts zipped around him. The heat from them was intense in comparison to the near-zero temperature of the air around them. A piece of tree bark slapped his visor as it blew off the side of the tree he'd just run past, momentarily scaring the hell out of him. Sliding behind the base of another tree, Pauli heard a handful of blaster shots hit the other side.

Damn, that bastard has really zeroed in on me...

Looking to his left around the large trunk, Pauli saw Noah's body lying motionless on the ground, Cholesky cradling his head and torso in his arms. Cholesky hadn't been responding to Pauli's hails over the squad or platoon net, and now he knew why. He'd taken his helmet off. The man had streaks of tears running down his cheeks. Either Cholesky was oblivious to the Zodark closing in on him or he'd given up on living and just didn't care.

"Cholesky! I need you to pull it together and shoot at the Zodarks. One of those bastards is angling to kill you right now and he's got me pinned down! I need you to see where he is and either shoot at him or take him out. Got it?"

As Pauli yelled at the private, the soldier looked like he didn't hear him or at least wasn't acknowledging him. The private continued to hold his friend in his lap and rock slowly back and forth, mumbling something only he could hear.

"Cholesky, damnit! Pull it together! I'm pinned down and I need your help. Look for the bastard and at least distract him while I move to your position!"

Meanwhile, a series of battle cries and screams erupted deeper in the woods. It sounded like some sort of angry mob, only in this case it was an unknown number of Zodark warriors whipping themselves up into a frenzy. From all the years of fighting these bastards, Pauli knew what was about to happen: the Zodarks were about to charge their positions.

"Everyone, stand by for contact. We have a major Zodark and Orbot formation headed right for us," came the calm yet reassuring voice of Master Sergeant Dunham.

"Get the squad's heavy blaster set up ASAP and tighten up our positions. We're too spread out right now," Pauli called out to his two fire team leaders. "Cholesky, snap out of it! We've got a much larger enemy force headed toward us. We're going to collapse our lines back to a tighter position. We have to fall back!"

More blaster shots hit the tree he was hiding behind, only this time they were practically walking themselves around the trunk in search of him. *Holy crap! Where has he moved to now?* Pauli thought as a twinge of fear started to grip him.

Damnit, I'm going to have to do this on my own, Pauli realized. Cholesky wasn't going to snap out of it and cover him.

Grabbing for one of his frags, Pauli pulled the pin and gave the grenade a toss around the right side of the tree. He then moved to the left side and waited for the bang.

Boom.

Once he darted away from the tree on the left side of the trunk, Pauli had his rifle up and his body in a half-upright position as his eyes and the targeting AI built into his HUD looked for that Zodark that was stalking him. Several laser blasts zipped right past his head, his ears registering the slight sizzle and crackle of the air near his head. The Zodark's shots had just barely missed him. Chances were, if he hadn't been wearing his helmet, the side of his face would have been burned.

Pauli dove into the underbrush in a somersault tumble and then rolled to the left, not sure how close the Zodark was. When he came out of his roll and popped up on one knee with his rifle tucked in his shoulder, his finger on the trigger, his eyes registered the blue bastard no more than forty feet away from him.

With a sinister growl on its face and his canine teeth bared, the Zodark raised two handguns up and fired. It was already in a full sprint, running right for him. Pauli fired his M1, sending multiple shots into the center mass of the blue beast that was practically on top of him at this point. The Zodark stumbled, losing its footing and falling to the ground.

It dropped the two swords it had been carrying to break its fall. Then it looked up at him, bluish blood dripping from its mouth, a burning hatred in its eyes.

Pauli had his rifle leveled at the beast's face, and without hesitation, he pulled the trigger, sending several blaster shots right into it at point-blank range. The beast collapsed to the ground, dead, mere feet from him.

I can't believe I just lived through...what the hell is Cholesky doing?

As the fighting around them intensified even more, the anger building up within Pauli grew. *I don't have time to deal with this right now! These bastards are going to be on top of our platoon soon.*

Plopping down next to Noah's dead body and Cholesky, Pauli took Cholesky's helmet and practically threw it at him. "When I call out for help or give you an order, you best do it! Now fall back to the platoon's position with me before you get more people killed!"

"We can't just leave his body!" Cholesky shot back angrily, tears still streaming down his face.

Pauli got back up and punched Cholesky across the face. He then grabbed his helmet and yanked him to his feet by his chest rig and pushed him toward the area of the woods that their platoon was rapidly turning into a defensive position.

The stunned Cholesky seemed to snap out of whatever his mind was stuck in. He placed his helmet back on and started running toward the rest of the guys. Pauli did the same but made sure to annotate where Noah's body was on the map so they could recover it later.

"Staff Sergeant, have your squad tighten up our center position," ordered Lieutenant Weideman. "Fourth Squad is readjusting their mortars and should start hitting in front of us soon. Then they'll move up and reinforce you, got it?"

"Copy that, sir."

Pauli barked some orders to his squad and fire team leaders. They got their heavy blaster set up along with their squad automatic weapons. The other squads of the platoon were doing the same as it looked like the company was preparing for what was about to happen. The howling and screeching from the enemy off in the distance was picking up in intensity. It was terrifying to hear it and know what was coming for them.

I thought we were supposed to be attacking them.

For whatever reason, the remaining soldiers at the spaceport had decided to launch a counterattack instead of holding up in their defenses. This had thrown the Ranger battalions for a real loop. Their prebombardment of the spaceport and the Cougars' smart missiles had likely hit empty bunkers and forts. That meant they were about to get hammered.

Five stressful minutes went by, then he got a message that changed everything. "Pauli, come join us ASAP!" said the text message across his HUD. It had originated from Captain Atkins.

As Pauli approached, he saw it wasn't just Captain Atkins; it was *all* the platoon leaders and sergeants. Something was going on.

"Ah, there you are, Staff Sergeant. Let's get started, everyone," Atkins said. He then displayed a digital topographical map of the area on their HUDs. The map showed the spaceport off in the distance, along with their battalion and vehicles. It also showed several large clusters of red dots not far from the perimeter of the spaceport. Some of those clusters had been moving toward them, but not the entire group—at least not yet.

"This is a much larger force than our initial intelligence led us to believe. It would also appear that our previous air and missile strikes hit empty bunkers and buildings. Colonel Monsoor is ordering us to withdraw to this point here before we get bogged down and can't extricate ourselves."

Atkins surveyed the faces of his officers and NCOs before continuing. "The new location the colonel wants us to set up in is located at the mouth of a valley that leads to the TorTor bridge and then the city of Kalnaz some twenty kilometers further into the valley. This is one of the few sizable cities with any sort of population left on the planet, so the brass would like us to try and protect them."

Highlighting something on the map, Atkins explained, "This is a blocking position we're establishing, not some long-term fort or FOB. Instead of 2nd Battalion moving to reinforce us for our attack, they've moved into the valley. Once we're en route in the Cougars, we'll get our new platoon assignments. Right now, I want First Platoon to stay in place while the rest of the company falls back to the Cougars. Lieutenant Weideman, your platoon needs to buy us time to withdraw if the Zodarks attack. If they don't, then awesome—haul ass to the Cougars and we'll all get out of here. Now get back to your platoons and let's make it happen."

Atkins pulled Weideman, Dunham, and Pauli aside. "If the Zodarks attack, then do what you can to bloody them up and carry out a fighting retreat. Do not let yourselves get bogged down. I'm not trying to be a dick about this, but if you get stuck or allow yourselves to get flanked or surrounded, we'll have to leave. The whole battalion is under orders to get to this new location. Apparently, the Orbots and Zodarks are willing to make this their last stand if necessary."

"Don't worry about us, Cap'n. We'll make it to the Cougars," Dunham assured him. Pauli wished he had that same level of confidence. He wasn't sure how they were going to hold off an attack long enough for the rest of the company to get to the Cougars and get away.

Moving back to the area their platoon had set up in, Dunham ordered, "Pauli, I want you personally to take your squad's claymores and start setting them along this path I'm going to highlight for you. Place them in a pattern covering this field of fire and stretch them across five hundred meters. When it comes time to retreat, this is the route we're going to take."

Dunham told the other squad leaders where he wanted them to place their antipersonnel mines as well. With all the howling and shrieking going on off in the distance, it didn't sound like they had a lot of time to get things ready. It wouldn't be long now. The enemy tended to whip themselves up into a frenzy, fueled with either the blood of their enemies or some sort of stimulant. It was one of the worst things any soldier had to endure before a battle. The sadistic ritual they ran through before a planned battle was brutal.

****

Placing his patrol pack on the ground, Pauli grabbed a claymore and attached it to the side of a tree, roughly a meter and a half above the ground. There was a small membrane mesh one could place on top of the mine that allowed it to mimic its immediate surroundings. This made the little buggers incredibly hard to see. So far, he'd placed maybe ten of these things and the enemy still hadn't attacked yet. By this point, the other platoons of the company had made it back to the Cougars. It was their turn to head back. Looking down at his patrol pack, he saw he only had one claymore left.

Then there was an odd peaceful calm that descended across the forest. The war dance and howling had ended.

"That's it. The other platoons have made it to the Cougars. It's time to bug out," Lieutenant Weideman ordered. "First and Third Squad, move. Head back to the Cougars. Second and Fourth, prepare to fall back. For the moment, hold your fire. Let's see if we can slip out of this place without having to fire a shot."

Pauli's squad caught up to him as he finished attaching the last claymore to the side of a tree. Everyone hurried to the Cougars just in time to hear Second and Fourth Squad open fire. At first, it started with a couple of shots, then it became a loud roar as everyone joined in. The deep bass sounds of the heavy blaster joined in next, as did a few claymores. Then a handful of the nasty little buggers went off, likely the ones Fourth Squad had set up a hundred or so meters in front of their positions.

"Hurry up! Get inside!" called out the vehicle commander, standing at the bottom of the ramp.

Once in the vehicle, the VC closed the rear hatch, sealing them up. The driver got the engine started and waited for the order to go.

Pauli made his way over near the commander's seat. He sat behind the right front seat, which was where the soldier who operated the vehicle's turret gun rode. They could let the vehicle's onboard AI manage it, but while they were stationary, most of the operators liked to manage it themselves.

"Staff Sergeant, activate your first batch of mines now. Our guys just rushed past them," Lieutenant Weideman called out.

Pulling the remote access to the mines up on his HUD, Pauli turned them on, adjusting so that the Zodarks and Orbots would trigger the mines, but a human or a C100 would not. No sooner had he activated them than they started going off. Not waiting to be told otherwise, Pauli went ahead and activated the three other lines of claymores he'd placed. It didn't take long before they were detonating as well.

"Hang on, we're getting out here!"

The Cougar lurched forward and to the right as it raced through the snow and the trees. The road was a short distance away when the double-barreled gun in the turret started firing. Something had clearly gotten in range of their vehicle, and the gunner wasn't having any of it. This was his chance to get into the action and kill some Zodarks, and he wasn't about to miss out on that opportunity.

To Pauli's surprise, their Cougar took some hits on the way out. He heard more than a few blaster bolts hammer their rear hatch. Each time the hatch got punched, it caused the soldiers to jump. The new guys had no idea the hatches had been reinforced many years ago. When the Cougars had first deployed, the hatches had been made of a lighter material to make it easier for the soldiers to operate manually should the hydraulic system get damaged. The problem with creating a lighter door was it became a huge liability. More than a few Cougars and the soldiers riding in the back had been killed when the Zodarks figured that weakness out.

Jumping onto the paved road, the driver floored it. At least, he tried to. They drove as fast as the slowest vehicle in front of them. Then came the mortars. The Orbots or maybe the Zodarks started lobbing them in the general direction of the road, hoping to score a lucky hit or two and somehow create enough of a bottleneck on the highway to stop the human soldiers from escaping. Thirty minutes later, they made it to the outskirts of the TorTor bridge. Now came the fun part—preparing for the counterattack the enemy seemed determined to launch.
****

Two hours after arriving at the bridge, Pauli heard over the command net that a large enemy force was no more than twenty kilometers away and closing. He also heard that an orbital strike was going to take place any minute.

Calling out to his squad, Pauli told them all to come join him. They were standing on the edge of a hastily prepared fighting position. They had a good view of the road leading toward the TarTar bridge that connected to the spaceport they had originally been going to capture.

"According to my HUD, in fifteen seconds you all are about to learn why controlling the high ground, in this case orbit, is critical to the capture of any planet. It's why our guys left behind had to scatter and hide underground. It's why the Zodarks and Orbots will likely end up doing the same thing," Pauli explained. Moments later, they saw a couple of blurred objects slam into the ground along the road and forested area where they had just been a few hours earlier. The explosions were enormous. Whole sections of the forest were flattened by the shockwave from the impacts.

"Wow…is it even possible some of them survived that?" asked one of the new soldiers.

Another veteran commented before he could. "Possible? I'd say maybe. These were kinetic strikes, not nuclear. If they somehow managed to survive the overpressure, then, yeah, it's feasible."

"Who cares? There isn't a swarm of them about to attack us anymore. We all get to live at least one more day, and to me, that's what matters most," Pauli commented to his guys before curling up near his fighting position and going to sleep. It had been a long day and a half, and right now the only thing he wanted was some rest.

Chapter Nineteen
Pyrrhic Victory

RNS *Freedom*
Sirius System

"Viceroy, it looks like the Orbot ships are pulling back. They appear to be disengaging," exclaimed Hunt's tactical officer. As he was speaking, the Orbot battleships, cruisers, and star carriers started to change formation and they broke from the Zodark battle line.

Hunt turned and looked at Wiyrkomi with a puzzled look. His Gallentine ship captain shrugged, unsure of what to make of this recent development either. After the first sixteen hours of battle, most of the enemy fleets had pulled away but not left the system. They had reorganized themselves into a series of new battle lines and resumed their attack the following day. Their new offensive had devastated the human and Prim fleets until the *Freedom* had moved into a blocking position to allow its enormous size to block and absorb the enemy fire.

Once in range, the *Freedom*'s superweapon, the Craykard Particle Weapon, tore the Orbot and Zodark capital ships apart. They'd destroyed all but one Orbot star carrier and wiped out all seven of the Zodark carriers. Now the Orbots appeared to be pulling away.

Then Hunt had an idea. He turned to Lieutenant Ted Roberge. "Lieutenant, hail that Orbot star carrier. Let's see if we can open a dialogue."

He then turned to Commander Eric Schreck, his weapons officer, ordering, "Have the CPW stay focused on the Orbot ships. They may be trying to leave, or maybe they're up to something else, but I want their remaining battleships turned to slag."

Interrupting him, Lieutenant Roberge announced, "Viceroy, I'm receiving a message from the Orbot ship. I think it's their fleet commander."

"Put them through," Wiyrkomi said, not waiting for Hunt.

"Agreed, put them through, Roberge."

Moments later, an image of an Orbot appeared. Hunt made sure he was standing next to Wiyrkomi as he spoke. "I am Viceroy Miles Hunt, the head of the Milky Way galaxy appointed by the Gallentine Empire. To whom am I speaking?"

There was a momentary pause before the Orbot spoke. This was one of the first times Hunt had actually spoken directly with an Orbot. "I am Admiral Garkeh, the senior commander for the Orbot force."

"Admiral Garkeh, I would like to talk with you further about a cease-fire and putting an end to the war between our people. Is that possible?"

Hunt wasn't sure what was and wasn't possible with the Orbots. Considering they were cyborgs, he wasn't even sure how their hierarchy worked. He wasn't sure anyone knew for certain.

Then the Orbot responded, "If you will cease your attacks on our ships, then we can talk further."

Hunt turned to his weapons officer and signaled for him to stop attacking the Orbot ships.

"Very well. I have just ordered my fleet to stop attacking your ships. We will stop attacking the Zodark ships once they agree to stop as well."

"We are not in command of the Zodark vessels. You will need to speak with them if you wish to obtain a cease-fire with them."

"Very well, then let's discuss how we can put an end to the hostilities between our sides."

While Hunt and Admiral Garkeh had talked, Wiyrkomi had managed to get through to the leader of the Zodark fleet. When the *Freedom* had destroyed five Zodark battleships in quick succession, the NOS in charge of their fleet had finally agreed to a pause. For the first time since the battle had started, the shooting between the two sides had finally stopped.
****

RNS *Freedom*
Wardroom

The large monitor in the wardroom had an image of the Zodark NOS in charge of their forces, Admiral Garkeh for the Orbots, Admiral Bvork Stavanger from the Prims, Admiral Fran McKee and Viceroy Hunt for the Terrans, and Captain Wiyrkomi for the Gallentines.

"This war has gone on long enough. It is time for us to come to terms and bring about an end to this conflict," Viceroy Hunt said confidently. He wanted to make sure the Zodarks saw strength, not exhaustion or weakness on his part.

Bristling at the comment, the NOS named Ha'mock spoke. "You speak of peace. Of bringing an end to this conflict. But you forget…it was *Terrans* who started this war. It was *Terrans* who invaded *our* territory. Clovis was a mining colony under *our* control for hundreds of years. Then you Terrans invaded it, slaughtering our people. Now you want peace?"

Hunt felt his face flush as anger swelled up from within him. He wanted to reach through the monitor and choke this NOS out, but he couldn't.

Admiral Stavanger pounced instead. "Do I need to remind you, Ha'mock, how the Zodarks invaded our own mining colonies some one hundred rightars ago? Your people went on to invade dozens of our worlds and enslaved hundreds of millions of our people. The Zodarks are no saints in this war!"

Interrupting them all, Admiral Garkeh pointed a finger at the monitor, demanding, "Why are *you* here, Wiyrkomi? Why have the Gallentines broken the Treaty of Yanooth and entered our galaxy? This breach of the treaty has been brought to the attention of the Collective."

No one spoke for a moment as they waited to hear Wiyrkomi's response. When Hunt heard the words *Treaty of Yanooth*, it suddenly brought forward a flood of information. Until those words had been spoken, he had no recollection of this event. Now his mind was being inundated with data as his advanced neural implant pulled up all relevant information on the topic—information that would take more than a few seconds to digest and understand.

Wiyrkomi leaned forward in his chair as he responded, "The Treaty of Yanooth has not been violated. The Gallentine Navy has not entered this galaxy, nor do we have plans to do so."

"Oh, then explain to us the intrusion of your warship. Its mere presence along with you and its crew is a violation of the treaty between the Gallentines and Amoors, in which your people promised to leave Sector Seven alone," Garkeh interrupted, his flat-toned cybernetic voice sounding even more emotionless, if that was possible.

Hunt's brain heard "Sector Seven" and suddenly realized the universe had been broken down into sectors, with each sector containing a cluster of galaxies. This was what the Treaty of Yanooth was—a territorial breakdown of the known space that the elders of the two main superpowers, the Gallentines and the Amoor, now known as the Collective, had agreed upon.

"This warship is not part of the Gallentine Navy," Wiyrkomi countered. "Admiral Miles Hunt was appointed by Emperor Tibus SuVee to replace the Altairian Viceroy and caretaker of the Milky Way, just as Yarkeh, the leader of the Orbots, is the Amoor's representative. This ship is no different than the ship the Collective gave your own people. My crew and I are only here long enough to train the Terrans on how to use it. The treaty is still intact."

There was a short pause as the two stared at each other. "Very well, then per your explanation the treaty is still intact," Admiral Garkeh replied, emotionless. "Then let us discuss terms to bring about an end to this war."

The Zodark roared back, "No! We are not ready to end this war, not like this."

"You will do as you are told, NOS Ha'mock!" the Orbot interrupted angrily.

"You had best watch what you say next, Garkeh. We have been aggrieved and we are not ready to accept peace with these Terrans."

The interplay between the Orbots and Zodarks was fascinating. It almost made Hunt believe there might be a way of leveraging that mistrust further down the road. He filed that away for the moment.

The Orbot Admiral Garkeh ignored the threat and returned his gaze to Wiyrkomi. "What are the terms you wish to discuss?"

"I am not here as a representative of the Gallentine Empire to settle this dispute, Admiral Garkeh," Wiyrkomi replied. "My people and I are, as I said earlier, here to facilitate the training of our Terran counterparts. This is a question best answered by our Viceroy, who represents this galaxy." He then turned slightly to Hunt, asking, "What do you believe is an acceptable way to end this war?"

There it was. The very thing he had been pursuing for more than a decade. But what would make this a fair and equitable peace that could stand the test of time?

Hunt began, "First, we need to call a halt to all the fighting in the Sirius system and on Alfheim while we work out the bigger details of a galaxy-wide cease-fire. Is that initial request agreeable?"

"It is. I will issue an immediate systemwide cease-fire and order all ground forces to comply as well. What else?" Garkeh asked.

"Admiral Garkeh, now that we are talking, I would like to take this time for us to work out some details for how all our parties can go about living in the Milky Way in peace, much like the Gallentines and the Amoor have done with the Treaty of Yanooth. Would you be amenable to us meeting in person in, say, three Terran days' time so we can lay out our initial requirements?" Hunt proposed.

The Zodark NOS looked like he wanted to reach through the monitor and slash his face off, but he held his tongue. The Orbot seemed to be thinking for a moment, if a cyborg could think rather than calculate. Finally, Garkeh responded, "I believe that would be acceptable. When we meet, I will lay out our list of requirements for an end to the war that will be satisfactory to our leader. NOS Ha'mock will do the same. We will then begin discussion on these terms. Is this acceptable, Viceroy?"

"It is. Would you agree to meet on the *Freedom* for our meeting?"

"Yes, NOS Ha'mock and I will travel to your ship, the *Freedom*, during these initial talks. Depending on the length of these talks, we can continue them down on the planet at a mutually agreed-upon place. One day before our meeting, please send over the details for our arrival. That is all." And then the connection between the Orbot ship and their own was severed.

Hunt turned to look at Wiyrkomi. "That went surprisingly well."

"It did. But I believe you and I should spend some time talking about the Treaty of Yanooth and how something like that might look here in this galaxy. We should also talk over the kind of terms our side should push for and the terms they are likely to demand."

"I agree. We should also send a message to the Altairians and let them know what's been achieved. I'm sure they will have their own needs they'd like met."

Chapter Twenty
You Are Relieved

Alfheim

Columns of thick black smoke rose into the air like pillars from heaven, marking a Pyrrhic victory. Corporal Eva Jorgenson removed her helmet and placed it down into the snow, letting the cold air crystallize the sweat that had formed on her brow. It had been two days since the orbital platform had been attacked. The invasion, from what she could tell on her continent, was a success.

After the counterattack had been called off and a cease-fire had been declared, the officers—what remained of them—had met with the battalion's commanding officer and learned that the Republic and her allies had obtained some sort of cease-fire with the Orbots and Zodarks. Surprisingly, it seemed the blue menace was done fighting. That brought up a lot more questions for Eva than answers. Sure, they were winning planets and campaigns against them, but the cost of those battles was astronomical in the grand scheme of things. Even when they did win, it felt like a loss. Kind of like how she felt now.

She wanted to continue being mad at Mac for the death of Abba, but she knew it was wrong and he wasn't at fault. That made facing him all the more annoying. She did, though. A day after the battle, and after a lot of sideways glances and avoiding one another, she finally approached him. He made a stupid joke about punching him again, and like an idiot she laughed. He always made her laugh, and that was that. They went about like nothing had happened. They both mourned the loss of their friend and helped carry her flag-draped stretcher into an Osprey heading off-planet with the casualties. It was a bittersweet moment, and she was glad to have shared it with Mac.

Ospreys continued to ferry fresh-faced troops to the planet to replace the ones who had fought to their deaths. As she watched another one soar into the sky and into space, she smiled. She had somehow survived another campaign in a war that seemed to finally be drawing to a close.

The next Osprey to land was going to be her ride as she accompanied the wounded to the RNS *Mercy*, one of the many hospital ships in the fleet. From there she would make the short trip to the RNS

Valkyrie and then back to their home base on the planet of New Eden. It wasn't Earth, but it was a start.

She looked down to the stretcher beside her as the sonic boom of an approaching Osprey echoed in the distance. "You made it, Kodiak, we're getting the hell out of here."

Kodiak had come out of his coma shortly before the battle over the orbital platform. He wasn't the least bit happy with being told to stay behind and had to be sedated before he ripped out his IVs. "I always told her I'd beat her out of this mess."

Staff Sergeant Angeline Moreau's death had hit Kodiak hard. They had been very close from basic training to Alfheim, and although their journey had taken them on different paths, they still could be found talking each other's ears off or gambling over a deck of cards. Kodiak was always the bright-eyed ferocious brute with a southern drawl and a sharp sense of humor—the man everyone always found themselves gravitating toward during a barracks party. Looking at him now, Jorgensen couldn't see that spark—only the shell of a man she used to know.

The Osprey spun around as its thrusters leveled out the craft and set it down nicely into the snow. The ramp opened and medics poured out, collecting the stretchers. Eva and Mac both knelt to lift the stretcher up when Kodiak raised an arm.

"No," the man protested. "I'm walking off this damn planet." He grunted as he lifted himself upright.

"Now, now, Kodiak, we know you're a tough bastard, but let's make this easy, yeah?" Mac said, trying to push him down.

"Just because you beat me in one fight doesn't mean you can do it again, Irish. Let me walk."

Jorgensen saw Kodiak's icy glare of determination and knew that if he could do this, he would be all right. She nodded to Mac in approval, and both medics took an arm and helped lift the hulking man to his feet. From the wobble in his knees, they were going to have to lead him to the ramp, but he didn't protest. With each step, Kodiak grunted in pain, his stranglehold on the medic's arm helping to stabilize him. After they reached the ramp and went inside, they handed him off to the flight surgeon.

"Don't get in any more trouble. Got it?" Mac laughed as he walked past Kodiak and took a seat in the back.

"Oh, I'll see you on Eden, Irish. Bet on it."

Jorgensen smiled as she watched the others load onto the shuttle and take their seats next to her. The ramp slowly closed, and as it did, she hoped she never saw Alfheim again.
****

Private Andre Bastille sat on a box toward the rear of the transport compartment. The last remaining mech had been locked into place and the two lone mech pilots sat in silence. They were saying it was a victory, but it hardly felt like one. Before Alfheim, Andre had never been in combat; now he dreaded having to face it again. The actual act of fighting wasn't hard for him. He was quite surprised at how well he'd reacted to the flow of battle. It was the aftermath that was hard. For a day, he'd helped pick up the bodies of people he had known, and those he hadn't. He imagined what would happen if he actually knew some of these soldiers more intimately, like Takata.

Andre shouted curse words as he launched a piece of a metal pole across the compartment.

"Hey, stow that, Private!" the loadmaster screamed from across the way.

"It won't happen again, Master Sergeant." Jones came over, grabbed Andre by the shoulder and dragged him to a darker corner of the Osprey.

"Sorry," Andre muttered.

"No, you're not," Jones scoffed, "but that's all right. You think I was right as rain after my first scrum? Intus was a hellish world. Don't get me wrong—it was beautiful like New Eden, a carbon copy, even, but the animal and plant life were just as deadly as the Zodarks."

Andre looked up at Jones. "Stop it." He shook his head.

He understood what she was trying to do, but comparing the Zodarks to a bunch of animals and plants was absurd. He had watched Zodarks rip a Republic soldier in half in hand-to-hand combat, armor and all.

"It's true." She took a seat next to him. "You know those dog animals we call Ravagers the Zodarks use? Those are native to Intus. I remember going out with a bunch of buddies—Krauss and Abede were there, surprisingly enough. We were headed into a nearby town to shop in their market or eat at one of their restaurants."

Andre cut in, "You guys went to markets and restaurants?"

"Yeah." Jones laughed. "After securing a lot of these worlds, sure, there was some resistance on different continents of the planet, but for the most part, life went on like normal for the Prims. I know you got the short end of the stick heading here immediately after basic, but I promise it's not like this all the time."

Andre had no idea if she was being honest. Sure, his drill sergeants had talked about it being a possibility, but they'd also made this war sound like it encompassed the entire galaxy, so that it seemed impossible he'd have a chance for rest and reprieve.

"So what happened?"

"What?" Jones asked, looking back to him, lost in her own memories.

"You, Krauss, and Abede were headed into town—"

"Oh, yeah," Jones cut him off. "Right. So, we were headed into town when a pack of Ravagers came out of nowhere and attacked our group. Five of us were either ripped apart or dragged off into the forest before the town guard came and got rid of them. It was the last time they let us leave base without our weapons."

"Holy hell," Andre whistled.

"Well, look on the bright side, Andre—it looks like the war with the Zodarks is on hold for whatever reason. Maybe you'll get to experience New Eden properly after all." Jones lay back into a hammock she'd stretched from one hook to another, hanging just above the compartment floor.

Andre thought about that for a moment. It had been jarring to hear that the Zodarks had sued for a cease-fire. He had been taught through basic that they were the end-all, be-all warrior class and he had witnessed it firsthand. They pushed into enemy fire, knowingly heading to their deaths solely in the hope of getting their arms around a single human to rip apart. They were much smarter than a lot of people back home had given them credit for. They were just as skilled in the use of their tandem blades as they were with two blasters. The thought of them just giving up like this in the end baffled him. Unless they saw the alliance the Republic had formed with the other alien races as too much to overcome...

"You think it's over, Tahlia?" He used her first name impulsively, like she had used his.

Jones smiled and lowered her sunglasses. "I haven't a clue, Andre, I'm too busy fantasizing about the pool on base back on New Eden or those greenish-turquoise waters along the beaches of Anzaria."

"Pool...Anzaria?" Andre turned in shock. "I can't wait for a private tour," he said with a smirk before Jones punched his shoulder.
****

Private First Class David Roberts was not leaving Alfheim like his old unit, Apollo Company, was. He had been sent here with the reinforcements and would remain with them. He still had unfinished business, however, as he made his way toward the staging area near the landing pads. Overcast clouds had found their way back over the valley and a light snow began to fall. Without the explosions and laser fire, it was startlingly beautiful.

Making his way across the powdered landscape, he began to search for his old team. He had been separated from them, and despite it not being his fault, he still felt the need to find them and say something. O'Connor and Valdez were following behind him, which at first he'd found exceedingly annoying, but he'd soon gotten used to it. Sergeant McAfee had been killed and their team leader had yet to be replaced. For the moment, he was the acting team leader, and they were his soldiers.

"Hey, do you know where Alpha Team of First Squad is?" he asked a soldier sitting on the ground beside a fire.

The soldier looked up and pointed to his left. "What's left of 'em," he responded coldly.

David didn't take it personally. Apollo Company had been through hell and more, and all the soldiers wanted to do now was leave Alfheim behind. In a weird twist of fate, the wait for their Ospreys probably felt like the longest wait they'd ever had. He thought it would rival his own wait aboard the *Valkyrie* after it had jumped out of the system, but he kept that to himself.

He spotted the group sitting around a small fire, talking and joking with each other. Their helmets and gauntlets were off their armor, allowing the heat to warm their skin directly. The heavy armor was great protection against the enemy as well as certain planetary elements, but sometimes it felt amazing to just strip it off and take in the clean air.

"Hey," he managed to say sheepishly.

Private First Class Aleksei Dmitriev turned and almost looked as if he didn't recognize David, but then his stone expression lightened and he smiled. "Cherry."

Aleksei stood along with Corporal Yeva Petrosian. The two of them walked right up to David and enveloped him in a tight hug. He'd honestly had no idea how they would respond, and he was glad they'd welcomed him with an embrace.

"It's good to see you, David." Yeva smiled warmly.

David sat down next to the two and removed his own gauntlets with a click. He held out his hands to the fire to warm them. "You both have no idea how good it is to see you all."

"Where have you been, David?" Aleksei asked.

At first he was taken aback by Aleksei's tone. "That's an understandable question."

Yeva cut him off. "No, it's not." She glared at Aleksei.

"Well, where has—" Aleksei started to ask, but David interrupted.

"After I was shot, I was taken to the RNS *Mercy* to rehab. I had just been transferred back to the *Valk* and was preparing to go back to the surface with the company CO when suddenly the ship left Alfheim's orbit and then jumped to the rally point. Less than thirty minutes later, we jumped out of the system entirely. There was literally nothing I could do, Aleksei." David shook his head as he fought to control his emotions. A tear ran down his cheek, followed by several more. "I...I tried to get back to you. I really did. I...I didn't know what was happening. Everything was just out of my control...I failed you guys."

At this point David was sobbing uncontrollably at the memory of being forced to abandon his squad. Yeva got up and moved over next to him, placing her arm around his shoulder. "It's OK, David. We know what happened. It wasn't your fault. You didn't abandon us," she said in a soothing and reassuring tone. "Right, Aleksei?"

Aleksei nodded. "I'm sorry, cherry. It's just...it's been really rough down here. We could have used you. Then again, you may have ended up like so many of the others. Maybe it was fate trying to save you for something greater."

David wiped away a few remaining tears, and for the first time, he really looked around and noticed the missing faces. "Duncan?" He knew the answer before he had even asked.

"Killed when his Cougar was hit." David's heart sank. "Moreau punched her ticket with him, along with the guy who came to replace you—Linchman, I think his name was?"

"His name was Lancaster." Yeva smacked Aleksei in the back of the head.

"Yeah. Doesn't much matter now."

Although the reception had been warm, the continued conversation had grown significantly colder. Yeva was trying her best for David's sake, and he appreciated it greatly, but Aleksei was clearly not in a good headspace. David motioned to Yeva to walk with him. She stood and followed.

"Who's your shadows?" she inquired.

"What?" He looked behind him and saw O'Connor and Valdez still awkwardly walking with him. "Oh, that's O'Connor and Valdez. They're in my team."

"Your team?" Yeva seemed surprised.

"Well, momentarily my team. Our team leader was killed during the counterattack. I took control from there."

A small smile came across Yeva's lips as she gave David another hug. "I'm proud of you, David. From when we first met on the *Valkyrie* to who I see now"—she paused and sighed—"I'm just really proud." She turned and looked to the two shadows behind David. "You listen to this guy. Even if you end up getting a new team leader, you listen to him. He saved our squad leader's life before getting wounded. That's how he was injured. He's a good man."

"Yes, Corporal, we know that." O'Connor nodded with pride.

Yeva smiled. "Good." She turned to David. "You take care of yourself down here. If you want to come back to Apollo after your rotation, let me know and I'll start looking around for you."

That was all David needed to hear to make this conversation worthwhile. "I will. It was good seeing you, Yeva."

"It was good seeing you too, David."
****

First Lieutenant Adam Singletary watched as what was left of First Platoon loaded up on the last Osprey leaving the planet. Amazingly enough, the construction of a new forward operating base was already underway for the soldiers replacing them. He was glad he wasn't going

219

to be involved in any of that. Judging by the type of construction underway, it looked like this base was going to be a permanent FOB and not a temporary one. It made sense. With combat operations ending, it was time to build something more comfortable for the soldiers that would be staying behind. All Singletary knew was that he wasn't going to be part of the occupation force, and that suited him just fine.

He knew some sort of cease-fire had apparently been agreed upon, but he didn't trust it—not for one moment. But he kept those feelings to himself. What was really rubbing him the wrong way at the moment was all these officers in fresh clean uniforms disembarking from the Ospreys and transports who seemingly didn't have a job to do or a purpose for being here. These were the officers who wanted to get their Alfheim campaign medal by stepping onto the planet before hostilities officially ended and the peace treaty was signed.

The officers were walking around amongst the troops, trying to bring cheers of victory and inspirational speeches or pausing to take some photos as proof that they were here. They were completely unaware that their pristine uniforms with no sign of wear and tear on them stood out like a sore thumb among the masses of soldiers around them. Like a bunch of preening peacocks, they strutted about.

Suddenly, a voice called out from behind him. "Adam! There you are."

Turning to see who had called out to him, he smiled and snapped off a crisp salute.

Captain Fenti returned the salute and walked right up to him. "I'm glad I found you, Adam. I wanted to personally tell you that you did an outstanding job in my absence. It's a shame Magnussen isn't here to be a part of this."

Apollo Company's CO, Captain Fenti, had been aboard the *Valkyrie* when it had jumped out of the system, stranding his unit on a planet he could no longer get to. That was when Magnussen had stepped up as company commander, and then eventually Singletary, when Magnussen had been killed.

"I appreciate that, sir," Singletary managed, struggling to hide his contempt for the man. What else could he say? He understood that Fenti hadn't purposely left them. It wasn't *his* fault the ship and fleet had jumped away. Still, Singletary didn't like how he would leave the company as often as he could to go back up to the *Valk*. It was like he was always looking for a reason to get off planet rather than staying with their company at their forward operating base's HQ. But he wasn't in a position to call him out for it, so at the end of the day, he just had to accept it.

"In case you didn't hear, the powers that be are transferring me to Luna because of all this." Fenti waved his hand about. He looked sad and dejected.

Singletary was shocked when he heard that. "Wow, that hardly seems fair. Did they tell you why? It's not like you did anything wrong."

Fenti sighed. "I was away from my command when they needed me the most. It doesn't matter that something out of my hands forced me to be on the *Valkyrie*. They don't see it that way...and I guess neither do I." Fenti paused before adding, "I failed you and the company, Adam. I'm not proud of it and I'm going to have to live with it for the rest of my life." Fenti turned and put his hand in his pocket, removing a piece of silver. "I can still try and do some good, though."

Captain Fenti placed a captain's insignia rank in the palm of Singletary's hand and shook his other hand. Singletary looked down at the rank. "I don't understand."

"Congratulations, Captain Singletary. You have been given command of Apollo Company. I'll still be hanging around for the change-of-command ceremony back on New Eden, but the company is going to be yours. I *know* it will be in good hands. You were thrust into a position you were not prepared for, and you still accomplished the mission when many would have failed." Fenti leaned in closer and smiled. "I even heard the little birdies talking about putting you in for the Medal of Honor given it was your command that took out the orbital platform."

"I want to make sure Private Takata is awarded the Medal of Honor. He was the one who took the nuke from their disabled vehicle and personally ran it up to the space elevator and delivered it to orbit. I don't really care about getting the medal myself, sir, but he certainly deserves it."

Fenti jabbed a finger into Singletary's chest. "And that right there is why you deserve it," he insisted. "Don't worry, the battalion commander and the brigade commander are also pushing for Takata to get the medal."

Singletary suddenly felt himself becoming overwhelmed by his emotions. Trying to choke them back down, he stammered, "Thank you, sir. It'll mean a lot to the soldiers."

Singletary would get his official insignia etched onto his armor by the armorer once they returned to the *Valkyrie*. In the coming weeks, Apollo Company would be on its way back to New Eden and their garrison home base. They'd go through the same process they did after every campaign. Receive new replacements, train fresh faces, promote old ones, and get ready for the next great adventure the universe had to offer. Singletary didn't know if he was ready to lead an entire company, but if Alfheim had taught him anything, it was that he could persevere through the worst, and that was good enough for him.

Chapter Twenty-One
An Uneasy Truce

Twelve Days Later
RNS *Freedom*
Wardroom

"Did we just achieve what I believe we did?" Hunt asked his Altairian friend, Pandolly.

"It would appear so."

The two of them sat there in the wardroom alone after everyone had left. "Miles, I need to tell you something," said Pandolly. "Many people in my government, and especially the ones on the war council, were not pleased with you being appointed Viceroy. Taking that role and position away from our people has caused much animosity among the powerful and influential people within our military and government."

Pandolly held up a hand to forestall Hunt's attempt to say something as he continued, "Please, let me finish. What I mean to say, Miles, is that what we have achieved today—or I should say what *you* have been able to achieve today—will greatly smooth things over with my people. It goes to show that once again, Emperor Tibus SuVee is a far better judge of character than we are. I am not sure how he does it, but the Emperor seems to have an ability to view people and situations with more clarity than most."

Hunt breathed a sigh of relief at Pandolly's words. He knew there was a lot of angst amongst the Altairian people about his sudden rise to power. It hadn't been his choice to assume such a dominating role as Viceroy, but he hadn't felt he could say no to it either. With every decision Hunt made with these superior alien species, he was always trying to keep in mind how it could impact the people of Earth and humanity writ large. It was a heavy weight knowing the wrong word or decision could doom one's entire species.

"Thank you for this, Pandolly. I appreciate it. I'm glad we were able to maintain control of the planet. Even if we had to agree to allow the Zodarks to maintain a small mining presence on their side of the planet, we're still the ones who will govern it."

Pandolly canted his head slightly as he replied, "I'm going to assume you know what they are mining, right?"

Hunt blushed slightly as he nodded.

"I think the bigger question is do the Zodarks know why the Orbots are continuing to make them mine it? If not, that may be a wedge issue you should consider using down the road to drive the two species further apart."

"Pandolly, you know we're going to integrate that material into the construction of our own warships. It will change the dynamics of even our relationship down the road."

"I know—or rather our military leaders know. Miles, our navy consists of more than five thousand warships spread across one hundred and thirty-two star systems. Our empire is vast, and you Terrans are but a small blip in that existence. You have bought yourself some time, a reprieve, if you will. I suggest you use that time wisely to grow and scale your own empire and navy to protect it, because this peace we have just achieved...will likely last for but a brief moment. In time, the Zodarks will rebuild, and they will come out swinging again. And the next time they do, you can bet their warships will be better prepared to deal with yours."

The two sat there for a moment, not saying anything. Hunt knew Pandolly was right. Humanity needed to grow fast and spread out. They needed to start making babies, *lots* and lots of babies, if humanity was to have a chance at being an interstellar species and not going the way of the ancient Humtars. But something was still nagging at him—something he had to press Pandolly on.

"Pandolly, you and I are friends. We have known each other since our species first met, but there is something I need to ask you."

"All right, ask."

"When we first met, you lied to us about the origins of humanity, and you lied to us about the comet hitting Earth and the Great Flood. You played into some of our religious beliefs and used that to cover up your transporting humans to Sumer and what we're now calling the Qatana Belt of systems that connect to Sumer. What we don't understand is, why?"

The Altairians rarely showed any emotions, so it was a surprise when Pandolly placed his leathery-looking hand on Hunt's forearm. "Miles, today is a great achievement for you, your species, and everyone who has fought against the Zodarks and Orbots. Let us bask in this well-earned victory and peace and not blight it with uneasy questions and answers that might detract from this great achievement."

Shaking his head, Hunt replied, "Pandolly, as much as I would like to celebrate this great victory—and believe me, we will—there are some serious questions that will need to be answered by your people. Answers that I would like the two of us to handle privately before they're made public."

"Fine, we will talk about them. But first let us celebrate this moment with our allies. They are waiting for us. We can discuss this in the coming weeks. Agreed?"

"Agreed. Now, let's go enjoy the party with the others. My wife has prepared a wonderful party for everyone. Today is a day to celebrate. Nearly fourteen years of war has finally come to an end."

****

Charlie Company, 1st Battalion
Planetside

"You really believe the war may be over?" asked one of the privates. A group of them were sitting in a semicircle around Pauli, cleaning their rifles.

Pauli placed his cleaning tool down and looked at the faces of the Rangers who were staring back at him. He recognized half of them from their original unit, the 1st Orbital Assault Division. Some had been with their unit when they'd liberated Sumer, but many of them were new, Alfheim being their first combat deployment.

Pauli blew some air past his lips. "Maybe," he replied. "All I know is we've gone thirteen days without a single shot being fired at us."

Sergeant Aioli chimed in, adding, "It just seems odd that they would give up like this. I mean, sure, I could see them eventually giving up the planet, but ending the war entirely? I don't buy it. My brother is in the fleet. He's an officer on the *Gettysburg*. During my last R&R, he told me it was believed the Zodark and Orbot empires contained more than one hundred star systems. I mean, if that's true, how could our little navy have defeated such a force? My money says they're just going to use this time to regroup and attack us again in a few years."

Pauli put his rifle back together, then stood and addressed his squad. "Listen, maybe the rumors are true and the war is going to end, maybe it's just that—a rumor. What I do know is this: complacency kills. We've all gone through too much and fought too hard to get dusted during what could be the final days of the war. So, I want everyone to continue to stay frosty, heads on a swivel. In five hours, our squad is heading out to the OP to relieve Third Squad for the next twenty-four hours. Fire team leaders, have your soldiers ready for inspection in three hours. I'm going to go meet with the LT and see if I can find out any more details on this rumor for you all. Aioli, you're in charge while I'm gone."

Pauli turned and headed off further into the woods and down a little in elevation toward the company headquarters section. Since taking up station around the TorTor bridge, they'd dug in. If the Zodarks and Orbots wanted to take it or push their way into the valley, they'd have to go through them and their sister battalion. Thirteen days had given them plenty of time to turn the place into a well-defended redoubt.
****

"There you are, Staff Sergeant. I was just about to call you," Master Sergeant Dunham said.

"I guess it's a good thing I stopped by," said Pauli. "I'm here to check on my squad's orders. We're still replacing Third Squad at the OP in a few hours, correct?"

Captain Atkins then walked into the tent. "That's what I'm about to discuss with everyone."

"So, it's true? The war is over?" Lieutenant Weideman asked.

Atkins made his way over to the small field table that had a thermos of coffee sitting on it. He grabbed himself a cup and looked at them, not saying anything for a minute while more squad and platoon leaders from the company walked in to join them. The place was starting to get a little crowded.

"Here's the deal, men. I just received word from Colonel Monsoor. It's official. A peace treaty has been signed between the Orbots and their alliance and ours. As of two hours ago, the war between our sides has officially ended."

Many of the NCOs and officers let out a few shouts of joy and sighs of relief. More than a handful gave each other hugs and handshakes. Some even had tears of joy streaming down their faces while a couple of soldiers just sank to the ground and cried. They'd made it. They'd survived this horrible war, having fought not one but two angry and nasty alien races for more than a decade.

Atkins tried to regain control of the scene after a few minutes. Even he had a hard time covering the emotions on his own face. "Colonel Monsoor told me that our troops are to remain a safe distance from the enemy forces still left on the planet. Those forces are now going to pull back and make their way to a piece of territory being given to them. While I don't have the full details of the peace treaty, what the colonel told me was the Zodarks and Orbots were being given control of a small part of Alfheim to continue mining whatever resource it is that's mined here while we and the Prims retain control of the rest of the planet. With that in mind, we're pulling everyone back from the OPs and staying tight in our own positions. I was also told that in a few days, a regular Army unit will be replacing our Ranger brigade. We'll be returning to the *Freedom* for some much-earned R&R. What I want you all to do now is go tell your men. Make sure they don't do anything stupid and get themselves killed between now and when we get off this frozen planet. Let's do what we can to keep everyone safe until our replacements arrive and we go home."

****

Two days later, Pauli and his men had finished packing things up around their area. They'd pulled in their claymore mines and repacked them in their storage containers. They also brought the other booby traps and tripwire devices they'd placed around their perimeter. The squad was doing their best to make sure they didn't leave behind anything that could inadvertently kill some unlucky person who happened to be wandering by. It was all part of the process of getting ready to get out of there.

When a fresh regular Army unit showed up, the wave of emotions hit many of them again. The RAs coming to replace them hadn't been part of the initial invasion. They hadn't seen combat on Alfheim, but here they were, coming in to take over the planet and manage the peace that had been achieved. Pauli didn't envy these soldiers. Sure, they'd missed out on some of the most brutal fighting of the campaign, but they had a much harder mission to accomplish now—garrison duty on a frozen planet still being occupied by Zodark and Orbot soldiers—while he and his squad would head back to New Eden and Fort Roughneck.

A change-of-command ceremony was held, such as it was. With the new soldiers now in charge of the TarTar bridge and the entire river valley, Pauli and his battalion loaded up on trucks. As they advanced past the forested area they had just fought in, the same forest Noah had been killed in, Pauli felt a wave of anger that Noah had died just before the war had ended and relief that it hadn't been him or Yogi. So many people had died during this godforsaken war. The last thing anyone wanted was to be the last person to die in it.

When they reached the spaceport, they got a good glimpse of the fortifications still left and of the damage and carnage their side had inflicted on it. The elevators largely appeared to be in good working order, but none of the nearby buildings or hangars were anything close to functional. Pauli could tell from looking at the entire place that it would have been a tough battle to capture it. In a way, he was glad they had essentially been chased out of the area and had retreated to the bridge. A lesser battalion or brigade commander would have ordered them to seize it, and while they likely could have, it would have been costly in terms of lives. It would have made the end of the war that much tougher to accept, knowing that if they had just waited twelve more days, their friends wouldn't have died. He was glad that hadn't been their fate.

"Are we riding up the well on that thing?" asked Private Cholesky skeptically, eyeing the closest elevator.

"Yeah, Staff Sergeant, that thing doesn't exactly look all that stable," chimed in another soldier.

Before he could say one way or the other, a transport descended out of the clouds and settled between a few of the blown-out hangar buildings. "No, I think we'll load up on that thing."

As the transport opened its massive frontal doors, the vehicles carrying the Rangers headed toward them. It didn't take long for the soldiers to pile into the giant craft. A few forklifts took care of getting their gear loaded. Less than forty minutes after arriving at the spaceport, they were in the air, on their way up to the *Freedom*.

Since combat operations had ended, the *Freedom* had unfolded its docking arms, essentially transforming the giant warship into a mobile logistics base. Pauli had tapped his HUD into the transport's external sensors, allowing him to see the giant ship they called home for the first time in almost a month. A couple of *Ryan*-class battleships had attached themselves to the docking arms along with at least a dozen transports and freighters of various sizes. Not being a fleeter, Pauli found it a strange concept to wrap his head around, how this giant warship could suddenly transform itself into a fifteen-kilometer-long logistic base, capable of transferring large numbers of soldiers and millions of tons of cargo from multikilometer space freighters down to the smaller hundred-meter-long transports like the ship they were now riding in.

One of these days, I'm going to sit down and study up on the different ships in the fleet and what they all do, Pauli thought.

Once the transport had docked, the entire company was ordered to report to the troop deck and the main auditorium. The division commander wanted to address them and give them a heads-up on what would be happening next. Many of the soldiers had started speculating about that. With the war over, what would come next? They'd been in a life-or-death battle for the survival of the species for so long that they hadn't really considered what life would like if that threat were suddenly lifted.

****

Auditorium

Viceroy Miles Hunt stood at the podium, scanning the faces of more than five hundred Spacers and twenty-five hundred soldiers, Rangers, and Delta operators seated in the auditorium. He also knew his image and words were about to be beamed to the rest of the fleet and the planet below. In a few seconds, every monitor on the fleet would play what he was about to say.

He'd spent several hours trying to craft exactly what he wanted to say for such an occasion—the end of a war of survival. This battle had cost the lives of millions upon millions, and in comparison to the losses of their allies, those numbers were low. In Hunt's eyes, a single loss of life was too much, but if one died or if ten million died for a common cause or purpose, such as the preservation of one's species, then that was a loss that could be celebrated, honored, and remembered.

As he stood before these soldiers and fleeters, the two military factions that had fought this war, Hunt observed that some of them were in their dress uniforms, just as he was. Many others who'd just returned from the surface or duty were in their utilities or battle dress uniforms, all looking at him, waiting to hear what the Old Man was going to say.

229

Reaching into his breast pocket, he pulled out a small note card. He'd written down a few bullet points he wanted to make sure were covered.

"Soldiers, spacers, the war is over. Some of you participated in the first and second battles of New Eden; some fought on the moons and other planets in the Rhea system. More than a handful of your units fought on Intus to liberate a Primord world while others invaded Rass, our first true invasion of a Zodark world. In all these operations, you fought fearlessly. You fought with honor. You fought with dignity and respect—something that was not afforded to our own forces by either the Zodarks or the Orbots. But regardless of that, we never compromised our own moral values."

As Miles spoke those last words, images of the atrocities committed by the Zodarks against captured RA and Prim soldiers flashed across his mind. That terrifying night on New Eden after the *Rook* had been destroyed gave him nightmares to this very day.

"While the war may be over, the battle to maintain the peace has just begun. Per the new treaty we just signed, a contingent of Prim, human, and Altairian soldiers along with Zodark and Orbot soldiers will remain on the planet to administer our regions of the planet. A landmass roughly the size of the state of China will be managed by their side. None of their forces or people are allowed to leave that area, just as none of our forces will be allowed to enter it. They are going to establish their own space elevator and a small station connecting to it. I won't go over more of the details as the treaty will be made available for all to read on your own. What I want everyone to understand about the treaty is that it doesn't mean we won't see a Zodark or Orbot in the future. We likely will. This is why I said the battle to maintain the peace has just started. We need to make sure this peace lasts.

"Now to the question I'm sure most of you want answered: when are we leaving and going home?"

A lot of heads nodded, but no one spoke.

"Our contribution to the Alfheim occupation force is fifty-five thousand soldiers on the ground and no more than seven warships in system at a time. This part of the treaty will go into effect in three weeks, which gives us time to finish recovering our newly liberated forces from the surface and carry out salvage operations around the battle sites in the system. When our ship leaves, we'll be making a pit stop in the Primord system of Kita to drop off their forces.

"We'll then continue to Earth to do the same with a fair number of our own ships and soldiers. The Chancellor and Admiral Bailey have also come to an agreement for a planetwide celebration to take place. Nearly every Earth city of more than seventy-five thousand people will have a parade with at least one company-sized element of soldiers and their equipment. I encourage you all not to grumble about this but look at it as a victory lap. We all earned it, and I'm glad that after so many years of war, we'll be able to celebrate its end with the very people and communities we have fought so hard to protect.

"In closing, I want to tell you all how proud I am of you—proud of what we all have accomplished as a people and species. Until we leave the Sirius system, I want your units to focus on a couple of final tasks. First, awards, promotions, and administrative tasks. Let's get these knocked out. Second, medical. Everyone's body and mind have taken a beating. Everyone is going to be evaluated. If the doc determines you need to go through the PTSD protocol, then do it. All awards, promotions, and future orders will be held back until that's completed. Third, assignments. If you've ever wanted a transfer to a new unit, base, or even planet, this is likely your only shot for a very long time. Many of you have served in the same unit since the start of the war, and that's commendable, but if you want a transfer or an assignment to a better place, now is the time to put in for it."

Hunt paused for a second as he looked at his people. When he'd first started speaking, he had seen looks of uncertainty. Now he saw looks of hope and a renewed sense of purpose—exactly what he wanted to accomplish. His eyes drifted over to his pilots. Not all of them could be there, but one pilot in particular was—his son, Ethan. They locked eyes for a moment, his son giving him a nod and a smile.

"Group! Atten-shun!" he called out in the most authoritative voice he could summon. "Dismissed."

As soon as he was done, the soldiers and sailors all let out a bunch of hoots and howls of excitement. The entire room erupted in joyous happiness. Hunt had to assume the same scenario was playing out across the fleet. The war had ended.

Chapter Twenty-Two
Decisions

Two Weeks Later
RNS *Freedom*

"Wiyrkomi, how bad is the damage to the ship and will we be able to repair it in any of our current shipyards?" Miles asked. Near the end of the last battle, the *Freedom* had sustained a fair bit of damage. Nothing critical—at least, not that he was aware of—but getting the ship repaired by their shipyards might not be possible.

The Gallentine naval officer looked at Miles for a moment before responding. "We can accomplish about ninety percent of the repairs needed in the facilities at either Mars or New Eden. A couple of the areas that can't be repaired by your own yards can be repaired in Kita. I estimate the time needed at the Kita yard to be around three weeks. If you want, we can stay in Kita during our transit to Sol. It'll save us from having to come back to complete our repairs. We can wrap everything up in around a month if we do all the repairs there."

That's not a bad idea. We can spin it into a goodwill victory tour of the alliance, Miles thought privately.

"Talk with the Primords and see if they can have what you need waiting for us when we arrive in system. We'll be there in another week. I'll see if they'd like some of our soldiers to participate in their victory parades or just hang out on the ships. I know everyone wants to get back to Sol—I do too, but we need to get this ship repaired and ready for anything," Miles ordered.

Wiyrkomi nodded and said something to one of his officers. "Viceroy, we need to determine where the *Freedom* is going to be homeported out of. Then we can begin construction on a more permanent repair facility to service it and other Gallentine warships in the future. We also need to step up our training program. Our ship sustained far more damage than it should have.

"I need to admit that I was more overly confident than I should have been, Miles. The lack of a fully trained crew was far more devastating than I imagined, and we almost lost the ship. You are the Viceroy and are ultimately in charge, but in my opinion, this cannot happen again. Many of the ship's capabilities were not able to be properly employed, and we exposed vulnerabilities in the ship that our enemies may try to exploit in the future. As your liaison officer, while I understand the justification for bringing the *Freedom* into this particular conflict, I cannot advise or support taking it into battle like this again until we are fully staffed and trained."

Wiyrkomi had a point. Hunt knew that, which was why he wasn't upset by his comment.

"You're right, of course," Hunt replied with a sigh. "This was a one-off situation. But you're correct, we need to call off any future deployments with this ship until we have a fully trained crew and fighter corps. How long do you believe that'll take to achieve…now that the war is over?"

"Given how well I saw your people perform during this battle, I'd say we should have a fully trained crew within three years. From then, it'll just be a matter of making sure we keep a steady pipeline of trainees being assigned to it."

Hunt looked at the couple of aides in the room with him and Wiyrkomi's people as well and asked them to go ahead and leave. He wanted to speak privately with Wiyrkomi.

"Stay, Fran. This will likely concern you as well."

Rear Admiral Fran McKee had been by his side during this invasion and now peace situation. He'd come to rely on her as a soundboard these past few weeks. With the *George Washington* still down for repairs at Kita, he had her temporarily assigned to his ship for the moment.

When everyone had cleared the room, Hunt lowered his gaze as he spoke. "Komi, Fran, I want to make it clear that I am not deceived by this peace treaty we just signed. I know this is likely just a pause in the war between our sides. Komi, I am going to need two things from you as my Gallentine liaison officer as we move into this next phase of human history."

"I am here to help and guide as best I can," Wyrkomi replied somberly. When in private, they talked very candidly and informally.

"First, I need you to advise me how best to prepare our human worlds and fleets for the next war with the Zodarks, but also the rest of the alliance. I found the Primords to have a large enough navy, but they didn't seem willing to risk it in any sort of large-scale battles. Same with the Altairians. Pandolly bragged to me about their five-thousand-plus-ship navy, but I kept asking myself if that's true, then why hasn't it been deployed to fight and win this war? In contrast, the Tully are willing to fight, but their territory is so far away from the front lines, it would take them more than nine months to join a friendly fleet, let alone stick around for a few years and fight. We have to find a way to make this a more unified effort."

"I agree, Miles. The people of Earth have been asked to carry more of the fighting than they should have. I am certain we can come up with a better strategy for the future."

Turning to face Fran, his former tactical officer from his days on the *Rook* and his XO on the *GW*, Miles said, "Fran, I'm going to need your help as we rebuild the fleet and prepare to face off against a much better prepared Zodark and Orbot Navy. We've held our own against them because they haven't had time to retool and adjust their force to counter us, but you can bet that'll be the first thing they do now that we aren't fighting each other. Those damn corvettes and frigates they introduced in the last couple of years completely changed the dynamics of our fleet battles. In a future conflict, they'll have more of that kind of ingenuity ready and waiting for us."

"Miles, not that I mind the offer or don't want this position, but isn't this something Admiral Halsey should take on? She's more senior than I am and has more experience as an admiral," Fran offered.

"That's true, Fran. However, you are the admiral with firsthand experience fighting these new Zodark and Orbot ships. Besides, Abi would serve the fleet far better in an administrative role now that we have a peace treaty. The administrative state of the fleet and Space Command writ large has to change and become more nimble and better suited for future conflicts. We're still tied to our historical operational structure of that last century. Who better to lead that kind of institutional change than someone who had to fight it as a fleet admiral?"

McKee opened her mouth to say something, then bit her lip. Hunt had an idea of what she was about to say, so he said it for her. "You're concerned her little grudge against you will only grow and negatively affect your future career in the admiralty."

Seeing her cheeks flush, Hunt confirmed his assumption about them.

"I'm not sure what I said or did, Miles, but for some reason she's kind of had it out for me from the word go. I'm just not sure how she'll take this move you're proposing. I mean, when Admiral Bailey eventually retires, which he might do now that the war is over, she's likely to be his successor."

Hunt held a hand up to stop her from going further. "First, I doubt Chester is going to retire anytime soon. That man has dreamed about this position since he first joined the fleet. He'll hold on to it for many, many more years to come. Keep in mind, he's only been the fleet admiral for twelve years now. Sanchez had held that position for more than twenty before he retired. Second, I think Abi is jealous of you."

"Jealous? Why would she possibly be jealous of me?"

"Think about it. You served on *Rook* with me, then survived the planet fall to New Eden when our ship was destroyed. You were then *my* XO on the *George Washington*. When I was sent to the Altairian home world, it was you who got command of the ship, not her. Then when she assigned you command of JTF-2 under an RA general, she thought she was giving you a backwater assignment that would allow her star to shine when we invaded Sumer. You took that assignment and practically created a docuseries out of allowing the people of Sol and Alpha the chance to see the daily operations of several ships and then the invasion of Alfheim all the way up to the final battle, when they returned with an even larger force to retake the planet and kicked you out. Your little documentary of what transpired over that nearly yearlong experience gave humanity a glimpse into what it is we're doing out here. It was brilliant! It also completely overshadowed what JTF-3 was doing on Sumer and stole humanity's interest."

Hunt paused for a second before adding, "Keep in mind, Fran, Abi rose through the ranks the old, slow way. You've risen through the ranks from attrition and being at the right place at the right time. She's jealous, Fran—jealous of what you've been able to achieve, which is extraordinary. But that's OK. We can work with jealousy, Fran. I'll speak with her."

The three of them spent the rest of the day talking about what would have to happen next once they returned to Sol. Ensuring humans didn't get steamrolled by the Zodarks when they eventually resumed the war could prove difficult.

****

Four Days Later

JTF-2 Headquarters
Hiltantor, Alfheim

Major General Veer Bakshi extended his hand to the Viceroy as he entered his office. "Thank you for visiting, sir. I hope your trip to the surface was smooth."

"I'm sure it was a lot smoother than the ride when you guys first showed up. How are things going? Is there any other help you need from us? We pull out of the system along with the enemy fleet in three days."

"Aside from more supplies, we're fine. We should be able to make do with what we have until a steady supply system is established," Bakshi replied. He wasn't happy about being stuck on the planet with this small a contingent of soldiers and a similar-size enemy force.

"It's going to take some time to get the gravy train rolling, but rest assured, once it's going, there'll be a steady flow of materials. How is the mining operation?" Hunt inquired. This entire campaign had been fought over this very rare and hard-to-find material, so he was eager to see it succeed.

Bakshi leaned forward in his chair. "Can I be blunt, sir?"

"By all means, General."

"I don't get it, sir—the entire focus on mining this one material. I mean, this entire planet, this frozen wasteland, is so far outside of anything important to us or the Primords, yet we traveled all this distance to seize it from the Zodarks. I lost more than one hundred and fifty thousand soldiers to capture and hold this planet. Is this material really worth so much blood and treasure?"

Bakshi was fighting back tears as he tried to keep his emotions in check. The tragic losses had really taken its toll on him. The fact that he now had to share the planet with the enemy further grated on him.

The Viceroy looked at him, compassion in his own eyes as he replied, "General, I'm not going to pretend I know or understand what it was like down here on the planet. I can assure you, if there had been a better way to acquire this Bronkis material, we would have pursued it. As it is, this material is of great strategic importance. It is part of a very complex building block used in creating an incredibly tough, almost impervious armor for our new ships. If humanity is to have any chance of holding our own in this galaxy, then we'll need this stuff."

Bakshi looked at the Viceroy. "My soldiers didn't die in vain, then?"

"Absolutely not. If anything, they may have just guaranteed our very survival."

Bakshi felt mildly better. "If I'm limited in the number of soldiers I can have on the planet, does that also apply to C100s or private security contractors? We may be able to find a workaround that allows us to plus up our numbers in case the Orbots or Zodarks decide to get a bit feisty on us or if they scrap this treaty as soon as you guys leave. I really hate the idea of having to go back to living in caves and running guerrilla operations like we just did."

"Believe it or not, they didn't put a limit on those. Just soldiers. We'll be leaving you roughly two hundred thousand C100s. I'd hide them well and keep them out of sight. If things go south, you have a good number of them to fight with. I know you're concerned about the security situation down here and rightly so. But aside from that, your most important mission, General, is getting these mines running at peak efficiency and then expanding them. I can't stress enough how important it is that we start obtaining large quantities of this material. The fact that this place is so far removed from our industrial centers doesn't help either. It does mean you will have a steady supply of transports, though, so request whatever your mining chiefs know you'll need."

They were nearing the end of their meeting. The Viceroy was set to take a tour of a few of these mining facilities and some other aspects of the city before he returned back to his ship. Bakshi asked one final question. "Sir, how long is a rotation or tour going to be on Alfheim, and will this be considered a hardship tour? I only ask because some of the soldiers do have families and they'll want to know if their families will be joining them."

Judging by the look on the Viceroy's face, it didn't look like he'd considered that yet. It was probably a good thing Bakshi had brought it up directly with the man in charge. He'd likely get a direct answer.

"That's a good question, General. I'm married myself, so I understand where your soldiers are coming from. Let's do this—let's give it a year to make sure this treaty is going to hold up. Go ahead and plan on allowing your married soldiers to bring their families if they like. Once this first year under the treaty is up, we'll make a rotation to Alfheim a three-year hitch. This place is too far out to make it any shorter, but I don't want to subject anyone to being here any longer than they want. I will do this to help—we'll add a sizable hardship bonus pay for Alfheim. See if that doesn't attract a steady supply of volunteers." The Viceroy stood. "General, I appreciate the time and your bringing some of these issues up. I've got to head off to a couple of these other tours before we leave. If you need anything, you let me know. I'll do my best to get it for you."

As the Viceroy left his office, Bakshi had to admit, the guy was likable. He seemed to care about the people who served under him. He also struck Bakshi as the kind of leader who wouldn't bat an eye at sacrificing hundreds of thousands of soldiers or fleeters to win a battle. Bakshi wasn't sure if he liked that side of the man or not.

Chapter Twenty-Three
BSL-6

Gaelic Outpost
Nonaligned Space
Sol

"I don't like it. Not one bit," Sara Alma protested.

"No one from the outpost can gain access to the facility or vice versa. It's about as safe and self-contained as we can make it," countered Gunther Haas at the sudden roadblock Sara was trying to throw up to his well-orchestrated plan.

Sara shook her head in disagreement. "It's not that, Gunther. It's what you all are doing that has me on edge. What if that stuff leaks out?"

Gunther seemed a bit taken aback by that statement. *Leaks out…what do you think we're doing there?*

"I understand your concern, Sara, but with all due respect, you are not privy to all that is going on in this lab, nor do you have a need to know," Gunther countered as diplomatically as he could.

Liam finally jumped into the conversation. "Gunther, how does the signing of the new peace treaty affect this project? We don't want our outpost to somehow get caught up in some sort of interstellar problem or investigation because we've allowed you guys to run some off-the-book bioweapons research facility or something."

Who in the hell is talking about this project? No one should have a clue that that's what we're studying here, Gunther fumed privately.

Gunther stared at the two of them for a moment, trying to figure out how much he could or should share with them. If he didn't require their help and support to get this lab up and running, he wouldn't bother, but he did need their help *and* their station.

"What exactly do you think we're going to be doing at this facility and why are you so confident in what you think we're doing there?" he pressed.

Sara looked at Liam as if asking permission to share something with him. He nodded, so she told him about how one of the cargo haulers bringing some of Gunther's materials had filed a suspicious items report with the station security. When he saw the items weren't heading to the Gaelic-run government, he became suspicious that something might be up. Sara, being the engineering person she was, looked into what the items were and determined that the equipment was used in the development of vaccines. She also learned it could be used for other alternative programs, like biowarfare.

"OK, look, I don't know how much I can or cannot tell you. But there is a lot we do not know about the Zodarks' physiology. We've had Zodark prisoners we've been able to study, and we get a few new ones after each battle, but we're still trying to learn all we can about their bodies and how they function. For instance, we know the Zodarks have a third lung. That extra lung allows them to breathe in several different types of atmospheres without the help of specialized equipment. It's incredible."

"What you're saying, Gunther, is your facility is going to be studying these beasts?" Liam interjected.

"Yes. That's why this facility needs to be separated from the outpost or any other base. It's also why we don't want this type of facility on a planet. If it's in space, they can't escape."

"You mean anything you develop can't escape either," Sara cut in.

Gunther sighed at the hostile tone he was constantly receiving from Sara and tried a different tack with her. "Sara, there is much we don't know about these creatures we call Zodarks. What we do know is they are an insidious species hell-bent on expanding their own empire and control. While I'm not at liberty to say exactly what we're researching, I can tell you if the treaty fails, and in all likelihood it will in a few years, then we'll be in a better position to defend ourselves because of this research."

Sara shared a nervous look with Liam. She wasn't sold on this. "Sara, Liam, I'm not trying to be cagey with you. There are some things I just can't share with you because of the NDA I signed and because of the Viceroy's specific instructions. We want to understand everything we can about these beasts because we want to be as ready as possible to fight them when the war resumes." Pausing, Gunther further explained, "I'm not sure if you've seen the final casualty numbers from the Alfheim campaign. In all, we lost over one hundred thousand soldiers. That was in a ground battle that went on for less than two months. Since the start of that invasion, our total losses for the Army were around one hundred and fifty thousand, with another nineteen thousand fleeters. This has been a brutally costly war. I can assure you, if the Zodarks invaded Sol and landed soldiers on Earth, the casualty count would be astronomical."

"Gunther, why is that? Are they really that much better than our soldiers?" Liam asked.

"It's not that they're that much better than our soldiers—these creatures are three meters tall. That's nearly ten feet. They also have four functional arms and hands. In many of the ground battles, they'll have a weapon in each of them. They're also hard to kill, even when you do hit them—they don't always go down with the first shot. I know you're curious about what we're doing, and I know you want to know what's going on, but that wasn't part of the deal you worked out with the Viceroy for your new planet. Plus, in all honesty, you just *don't* need to know."

Sara appeared to deflate when she saw Gunther wasn't going to share anything more than what he already had. Liam then stood, extending his hand. "Thank you, Gunther, for agreeing to meet with us and discuss things with us. You are right, we're trying to push for more information than we need. In this particular case, ignorance really is bliss, and we should be embracing that. I'll speak with my security people and make sure any suspicious delivery reports are sent directly to me. Thank you again for answering our questions and meeting with us. We'll let you get back to it."

Upon leaving the meeting, Gunther made a beeline to their lone office space on the outpost. He needed to speak with his procurement manager and find out what was going on with the packages. This was the kind of unwanted attention he didn't need.
****

"You were a little harsh on the man, don't ya think?"

"Harsh? I don't think so. What if whatever it is they're working on somehow spreads? There's a reason that kind of research has been banned. It's not safe—it's not natural," Sara countered in her thick Irish accent, blowing some air out her lips. "I don't want to argue about this. We have too much else on our plate." She sighed and changed subjects. "When do we plan on launching our first colonization ship? The people are growing restless with excitement."

Liam smiled at the mention of this new charter. They'd be colonizing a world they'd be able to call their own and build up the way they saw fit. "One month. We're waiting on a few last-minute agricultural items to arrive from Earth. It'll also give us time to finish constructing one additional transport for the journey."

"Excellent. I got the sale of those two space liners completed the other day. They'll arrive at the station in a week. I've got crews on standby to get them ready for an extended journey."

"The fun part now is going to be the lottery, seeing who all is going to get to come with on this first trip," Liam opined.

Shaking her head hesitantly, Sara replied, "I think the lottery system is a terrible idea. We could end up with a real imbalance in skills for what we're about to embark upon, Liam. Have you thought that through, or did you just want to do what would make you popular?"

Wincing at the comment, Liam said, "It's not about being popular. Everyone knows I run the show around here."

Sara lifted an eyebrow at that comment but held her tongue.

"OK, everyone knows *you* run the show," Liam admitted with a chuckle. "Oh, and it's not a complete lottery for all the seats. I've broken the lottery down into specific skill sets. Each skill set gets a certain number of lottery winners allocated to it. *If* a lottery winner is a person with a family, then a certain number of lottery numbers are reduced from the general lottery pot," Liam explained. He was trying to allow for a broad number of people to come, not just those with a critical skill. One never knew what skill you might suddenly need out of the blue on a foreign planet.

Wrapping her hands around Liam's neck, Sara looked him in the eyes. "I'm just excited that this is finally going to happen. I only wish you could come with us on this first trip."

Liam gave Sara a soft peck on the lips before pulling away. "I know. I wish I could. My concern is if we're both away, things may not get done on this end—or worse, someone may try to assume control of things. You saw what happened just a few months ago with Devlos Creed and his crew."

Canting her head to the side, Sara countered, "I think we handled that in a fashion that ought to leave no one challenging our position again, don't you?"

Liam didn't say anything right away. He turned and looked out the floor-to-ceiling windows of his office. "I never thought something like that could have happened in the first place, but it did. It got me to thinking that maybe we've either become too soft or naive enough to think that people will just fall in line with what we're trying to achieve. Clearly the second most powerful faction in the Belt felt they could take us on. They nearly succeeded too."

Sara walked up to Liam, placing her arms around him. She burrowed her head under his arm, so he was holding her. "Kira will be out of the hospital soon and Friederic, he's tying up loose ends on Delvos station. Plus the Republic just canceled several of their security contracts and handed them to us. It's going to increase our annual revenue by at least thirty-two percent. Not bad if you ask me."

Shaking his head dismissively, Liam said, "I don't care about the money. I care that one of the factions out here thought they could do this to us. After all we've done for the Belters, this is how they repay us? I kind of thought we'd be shown a bit more gratitude."

"If that's how you feel, love, then perhaps we need to find a way to either include the other factions more in what we're doing or instill a bit more fear in them, so they won't think to challenge us again."

"I heard the RA is going to allow some of the soldiers who've been stop-lossed for the war to finally be released from service. If that's true and it happens, then I want to see if we can hire a few thousand of them, maybe more. They'll be fully trained and flush with combat experience. They'll be good blokes to have around."

"Yeah, with those new security contracts we just picked up, we could use them," Sara admitted. "Getting back to the expedition, do you believe we have everything we'll need? I mean, once we arrive, it's going to take us a long time to get a resupply if we're missing something." The transport time between the Gaelic and their new planet was four months.

Liam turned around to face her. "I've acquired eighty industrial-grade 3-D printers as you requested, along with four hundred synthetic workers. We'll have enough base materials for the printers to manufacture just about anything you need for at least a solid year based on the modeling and plans we've agreed on for our first city and spaceport. I'm also looking into setting up an I2 warehouse and shipping hub on Sumer. This might help us cut down on the supply challenges we're likely to face. My understanding is that traveling to Sumer via the gates will only take about two weeks."

"That's a great idea, Liam, but when did you start calling Immrama Industries I2?"

Liam shrugged. "It's just shorter, easier to remember for foreigners, I suppose. Keep in mind, once we get an office on Sumer, we're going to be an interstellar corporation," he said with a wink.

"I'm going to miss you when I leave."

Grabbing her firmly by her waist, he replied, "Not as much as I'm going to miss you." The two kissed as they sought to make up for what would be a long dry spell in their love life soon.

Chapter Twenty-Four
Assignments & Reorgs

1st Battalion, 4th Special Forces Group
RNS *Midway*
Kita System

Captain Brian Royce had just sat down at his desk and opened his computer terminal when the AI announced he had a visitor.

"Enter," he shouted just loud enough to be heard.

He'd just brought up the file that said Performance Reports when Major Jayden Hopper plopped himself down in the chair opposite him and placed two small glasses on the table and an unopened bottle of twenty-five-year-old Pappy Van Winkle bourbon whiskey. Royce stopped typing as soon as his eyes caught sight of the bottle.

"I thought you were saving that for when you made colonel."

Jayden opened the bottle and proceeded to make a show of smelling the brown liquid before pouring the two of them a glass. "It's not official yet, but I think I made the list."

Royce raised an eyebrow but didn't say anything. He didn't want to burst the man's bubble or ruin it for him. Plus, he really wanted to try some of this whiskey. He had to know why this bottle was apparently worth more than a month's salary.

"Yeah, it seems Wild Bill, after some seven decades of being on the blacklist, has finally earned his star. He's going to be staying behind on Alfheim as the deputy commander of the allied force," Jayden explained.

Royce grunted at that. "I wouldn't exactly call that getting off the blacklist. That planet is utterly miserable. I don't envy anyone that gets stuck there."

"Who cares? He got his star. He outlasted that old bastard in the Senate."

"I'm just glad none of our units got stuck having to pull garrison duty on the planet."

Lifting the glass of fine alcohol in his hand, Royce examined the hazy copper color. He lifted the glass to his lips and tasted the rich, intense caramel, toffee, and peppery brown spice flavor as he swirled it around in his mouth. Then, as it made its way down his throat, he felt the long, complex, evolving fade of spice and wood notes as it reached his belly. Pulling the elixir of the gods away from his lips, he examined the contents of the glass more closely now that he knew what he was holding. He turned to look at Jayden. "This…is perhaps the finest whiskey I have ever tasted."

"And it's worth every penny I paid for it," Jayden added before downing the rest of his glass and then refilling it.

"The list comes out tomorrow, doesn't it?"

"It does."

"Shouldn't we have waited until tomorrow?"

"I thought about that. But you know what? Even if I end up not making it, you and I have survived nearly fourteen years of the most insane battles and missions one could possibly imagine. I honestly never thought I'd make it to see an end to this war, but here we are."

"Ha, you really think this is the end? Hell, I think this is an intermission," Royce said as the alcohol started to hit him. "Those bastards are just going to use this time to reposition forces and hit us where it hurts. My money says they'll break the truce and we'll be back at war within the next three to five years. You mark my words."

"Let's hope not. But before either of us become too drunk to talk business, I need to have all your final award recommendations completed by COB tomorrow," Jayden said with a grunt. "The colonel wants to get them all approved before there's some sort of reorg or major assignment changes. I also need all your officer and NCO performance reports, recommendations for promotion, or any other administrative functions done ASAP. We're going to reach Sol in three weeks, and once we do, the colonel is going to release everyone for a solid thirty-day R&R after we get done with some of these victory parades we've been selected to participate in."

"Crap, just when you think you've caught a break, the Army hits with you something else," Royce bemoaned. This was the one thing he hated most about being an officer—all the damn paperwork involved. He assigned a lot of it to his internal PA, but many of these reports needed to actually be written by him.

Chuckling, Jayden commented, "This is why you do a little bit each day, my friend. How many years have I been telling you that?"

"Yeah, yeah, I know. I'll get it done—oh, what the hell is this new award for? The Dominion Medal. I saw everyone is being awarded this."

Jayden only shook his head at the mention of the new medal. "Apparently, it's Space Command's service medal they came up with for all those who served during the war with the Zodarks and Orbots. So anyone who served from the start of the war until the treaty was signed is being awarded it. Crazy, isn't it, all these awards? I think it's a way for the rear echelon to feel like they did something if you ask me."

Royce snickered at the comment as he finished off his glass of Pappy Van Winkle. "Honestly, I don't care. If they want to make up a bunch of new medals and service ribbons for folks, let them. You and I know the only medals that matter are the valor ones and Purple Hearts. Speaking of valor medals, I have a total of twenty-three Silver Star recommendations from across the platoons, two of which I want upgraded to Medals of Honor if possible and three to the Distinguished Service Cross. Aside from those, I've recommended everyone in the company for a Bronze Star with Valor device. We and Bravo Company are the only Delta units to have done a low-orbit HALO insertion into an occupied planet. I figure that's worth a valor medal."

Jayden held his drink next to his lips as he listened to Royce. He downed half the liquid before commenting, "If that's what you think they earned, I'll back you on it. I'm sure Wild Bill will as well. He seems to have a special place in his heart for you."

Giving Jayden the stink eye, Royce replied, "What's that supposed to mean?"

"It means the Special Forces legend thinks you're such a badass that he actually thinks of you as his equal. Hell, I think he actually looks up to you," Jayden joked good-naturedly.

"Whatever. Just so long as my soldiers are taken care of, that's all I'm after. Speaking of which, any word on whether the Army is going to downsize or where our brigade or group is going to be home stationed? We've been deployed since our inception, so I don't even know where home technically is anymore."

Refilling his glass for the third time during their conversation, Jayden looked at his friend. "I've heard some rumblings about them ending the draft and keeping the Army at the current size, but who knows? If we aren't fighting the Zodarks, then I suspect they'll start to deploy a lot more soldiers to the different moons and planets we've recently acquired and look to build up more permanent facilities on them. As to 4th Special Forces Group, not sure. We've been operating out of

New Eden with 3rd Group, but I don't know if they'll keep us all together there or relocate our group to Sumer. I know 1st Group is going to have a battalion permanently stationed on Alfheim, while 2nd Group will have one on that Prim world, Intus."

Jayden took another sip from his glass. "Have you given any thought to how long you may stay in, Brian? You've been in the Army now, what, going on thirty-eight years?"

Royce looked down at his hands for a moment before replying. "Thirty-seven years. I joined on my eighteenth birthday. When I joined, I had no idea what I wanted to do with my life, and at the time, all I wanted to do was get out of my parents' house. The military gave me the way to do it, and frankly, I'm pretty good at this stuff. Right now, at this point in my life, it's all I know, Jayden. I mean, I've been in Special Forces now for thirty-one years. I'm damn good at this job. I don't know what I could possibly do outside the military. I mean, look at the two of us. We're augmented supersoldiers. I think I'm just going to stay in for a while."

The two sat there for a few minutes, sipping their whiskey and enjoying every minute of it.

"I'll probably stick around long enough to qualify for retirement and then take it. I've been banking nearly all my money since I joined, Brian. I've built up a nice little war chest too. Once they figure out where they're going to home station us, I plan on purchasing some prebuilt homes or buying some tracts of land and developing them into homes. With all the people looking to expand beyond Sol, there's going to be a huge housing boom. I'd like to cash in on that if possible."

"Sounds like you have it all worked out. But, as much as I want to sit here and get sloshed on some of the best whiskey I've ever tasted, I have a mountain of paperwork that needs to get finished," Royce said as he unlocked his computer terminal.

"Oh, fine—you're no fun, Brian. Have at it with the reports. I'll see you at breakfast tomorrow."

Chapter Twenty-Five
The Halsey Plan

Allied Headquarters
Lakish, Capital City
Sumer
Qatana System

Abigail Halsey looked at the latest supply convoy arriving from Earth. Republic forces had been on Sumer for several months and still didn't have power fully restored to all the cities that had people living in them. The convoy arriving from Earth was bringing with it thousands of 3-D printers and materials needed to print off the parts and components needed to get the power plants back up and running.

"Admiral, Hadad is here to meet you. Shall I send him in?" asked one of her aides.

"Yes, please bring in some coffee as well. Tell General Modi it's time for our meeting."

The door to her office opened a few minutes later, and in walked Hadad Nasr.

"Admiral, it's great to see you. How have you been?" Hadad asked. After living on Earth and then working as an aide to the Governor of New Eden, he had developed a good understanding of how Earthers spoke and greeted each other.

Halsey smiled as she walked toward him, taking his hands in her own. "I am doing well, my friend. Congratulations again on your election victory. You will do a great job blending our two societies together."

"I will try, Admiral."

"Please, just call me Abigail or Abi." She pointed to a set of very nice plush chairs and a table situated between them.

Lieutenant General Chandra Modi walked into the office with one of his assistants. He made his way over and joined them. It was time to get the meeting going.

"If it's OK with the two of you, I'd like to briefly go over a couple of military items and then leave you all to discuss the civilian items without me. We have a fair bit going on, so I'd like to excuse ourselves once we've brought you all up to speed if that's all right?" the general explained as he set the tone for the meeting.

"Of course, General. Please proceed," Halsey offered as she sat back in her chair, sipping on her coffee.

The general's aide placed a small black puck on the table between them. Moments later, it activated and a holographic image of the stargate leading to Zodark space appeared. A little red symbol next to the gate said *The Forge, Alpha-219*. Abigail might be an admiral, but she didn't understand the stargate naming convention the Altairians used in the least. She just went with it.

"As discussed in our previous meeting a few months back, we have moved forward with the idea of establishing a series of listening outposts and forts around critical stargates and systems leading to the Qatana system.

"We've successfully completed the listening posts on the opposite side of our gate," General Modi explained. "We're finalizing construction on the five platforms around the gate and should have them fully functional by the end of the year. If a ship jumps into the system, we'll know pretty quickly who it belongs to. If that ship jumps to the gate leading to the Qatana system, then they'll have to pass through the next layer of defensive platforms. But before either of you get too excited about these things, please understand they will not stop an invading force. They're designed to slow them up while our forces in the system have time to react and prepare." When no one asked any questions, he pressed on. "Once they jump into our system, they'll run into this."

The aide brought up a different image of the same type of defensive platforms, only there were double the number of them ringing the gate. Each platform was three hundred and sixty meters in length, sixty meters tall and forty meters wide. Positioned on the top of the platform were eight twin-barreled thirty-six-inch magrail turrets. On either end of the platform was a pod of forty-eight plasma torpedoes. Interspersed across the top and bottom of the platform were sixteen quad-barreled 20mm point-defense guns or PDGs. Not to be outdone, along the bottom of the structure were eight turbo laser turrets. The entire platform was going to be operated by one hundred and ten enlisted sailors and officers and one hundred and ten C100s.

In addition to the four platforms, there was a fifth platform anchored near the center of them, slightly larger than the others. Instead of hosting a slew of weapon turrets, it boasted a flight bay, capable of launching up to six squadrons of P-97 Orion fighter drones and two squadrons of P-99 Raider bomber drones. This platform gave the defensive structures around the gate the ability to provide fighter cover for the gun platforms as they hammered the hell out of any Orbot or Zodark ships that tried to jump into the system.

"Are these the same type of defensive platforms you had proposed we build around Sumer and our two other colonies in system?" Hadad asked. A big part of Hadad's political campaign had been built around securing the Qatana system and making sure the Zodarks could never again occupy their planet.

The general turned to face the newly elected governor. "They are. Now that the base structure of the platforms has been completed, the workers will transition to sealing it up. The next work crew will take over and work to finish the platforms. I've ordered them to start construction on the platforms around Sumer next. As you requested, we'll build out seventy-five percent of the requested platforms above Sumer and then look to get the ones around Hortuna and Tallanis next. Then we'll circle back and finish the rest of the platforms around Sumer. Once these are in place, it will be very hard for the Zodarks or Orbots to attack Sumer should they break the peace treaty."

Hadad seemed satisfied with the information. Abigail thought privately, *Promise made, promise kept.* "General, what about the planetary defenses? If they do break the treaty, are we in good shape?"

"Yes, we've built more than sixty ground-based laser turret systems. They won't stop an invasion, but they'll certainly hurt them," General Modi said. "Once we're able to couple this with the orbital platforms, it'll be a highly effective combined defensive system. On the ground, we're also placing some three hundred thousand C100s in strategic bunkers around the planet. These can be turned on and used to carry out a variety of missions against our shared enemies, should that need arise." Modi was nearing the end of his military update and appeared ready to leave.

That was when Hadad leaned forward and asked his own question. "General, what is the likelihood that we can begin training a Sumerian-led defense force?"

It looked like the question had caught the military man off guard. Finally, he replied, "I don't think we're ready for that yet. We're still establishing permanent bases on Sumer and the other two colonies. I can authorize some recruitment posts in some cities if you'd like. If an applicant meets the enlistment standards, they'll be shipped either to a training base on New Eden or back to Earth. From there, they'd be integrated into a regular RA battalion and assigned to either a ship or a unit stationed across the Republic. They might get lucky and get an assignment to a unit here, or they may get assigned somewhere far away."

"Why not create a force here? One where they wouldn't get shipped away from us," Hadad pressed.

"That's not really how things work in our military. Hadad, please keep in mind, Sumer is a part of the Republic. It's not its own world—you're part of us now. The Senate back on Earth has made a two-decade exception to the draft policy to allow your people time to heal from this event and for Sumer to grow and prosper. Frankly, there isn't a need for a separate security force here. We have ninety thousand soldiers stationed on the planet and more than half a million C100s for support. Even with a pared-down fleet, we still have a substantial force here. Once these orbital platforms are completed, you'll be cocooned in. Is there a reason you feel you should have a separate force beyond what we've provided?"

Abigail watched this all play out for a moment. She wanted to see what Hadad was getting at; maybe she was missing something.

Finally, Hadad countered, "General, it's not that I don't trust you or your men. I just think our people would feel more protected if there were a force made up of just Sumerians. Perhaps we can create some sort of enhanced police force or special unit that could act like a military in times of war."

General Modi thought about that for a second before replying. "How about this? How about we help you form up some sort of militia or civil defense force? I don't want this to become some massive sprawling force with its own navy and air force, but we can train up some ground forces. I'd recommend working with Admiral Halsey and her civilian advisors on establishing some sort of rules for how you'll use them and such, but yes, we can work with you to get something like this going." The general paused for a moment, looking at the time. "If I may, I'd like to head back to our offices. We've got a few more things to work on before the day's done."

Abigail stood and extended her hand. "Thank you, General. I believe I can handle anything else with Hadad. If not, I'll send you a message and we'll get it sorted the following day."

The general stood and left, leaving Abigail alone with Hadad.

Turning to face the newly elected governor, a man Abigail had known since her task force had liberated his prison camp so many years ago, she asked, "What's bothering you? You've been in a funk ever since you won last week."

Hadad took a seat, looking deflated as he did. "When I returned to my home world, I was burdened with grief at what had happened. Then I was overjoyed by the discovery that my wife and two of my four children were found alive. I ran for governor because I felt I needed to do something to protect my family and make sure they were never threatened with the yoke of slavery again. I felt, having lived amongst your people for more than a decade, that I could best bridge the gap between our societies as we look to merge our people."

Abigail saw by the look on the man's face as he spoke that something was deeply troubling him. He looked like he was aching emotionally. She wanted to help; she just didn't know how yet.

"Now that I'm the leader of my people, of my entire home world for that matter, I feel like I've bitten off more than I can chew. I don't know if I can do this, Abigail—be governor, be responsible for the lives of what's left of my people."

When he paused for a moment, Abigail walked over to her desk and pulled out a bottle of bourbon she'd brought with her. She poured them a couple of glasses and placed the auburn liquid next to him and then sat down.

He reached for the stiff drink and took a couple of sips. Then he finished it off in a couple of gulps. "Abi, what am I to do? I don't know the first thing about being governor."

Taking a sip from her own glass, she thought about that for a second. "That is something only you can answer, Hadad. I'm not a Sumerian. I don't fully understand your culture and I don't have a clue what your people need or want. What I do know about people in general is that they have basic needs that need to be met. I know they also have wants and desires beyond those basic needs. Given the situation your people have gone through, they'll be craving the basics: food, water, shelter, and security. That's being provided for right now.

"Next, you need to work on building your global economy and once again getting your planet self-sufficient. This is also going to start happening in the coming months. Just this morning, I received word that our shipment of 3-D industrial-grade printers is on the way. We're talking about three thousand of these units. Once we have them up and running, they'll start mass-producing more printers. Soon, we'll have all your power generation on the planet running at full speed. With the arrival of more than six million civilian synthetic models, we'll have your agriculture lands producing food once again. Then we'll be on to the major reconstruction efforts next."

"This is most appreciated, Abi, and I don't mean to make light of it. But you are accomplishing all of this with or without me? How do I be a good governor? What do I give my people? We still haven't heard back from the Viceroy or the Zodarks about whether they'll be releasing all the children they took from our planet or any of the other people they took in tribute. I was hoping I could have that as a victory for my own people in this peace settlement with them."

Abi saw the look of desperation and fear in his eyes. He was desperate for an answer, any answer, and he was afraid of letting his people down should he fail.

Smiling a warm smile at the man, she said, "Hope." She let the word hang there for a moment as it sank in, then added, "You give your people hope. Hope for a better future now that they are free of the Zodarks. Hope that they can now have children and know they will live to grow old and see their grandchildren and great-grandchildren. That is what you give them, Hadad. Hope."
****

Two Weeks Later
Central Spaceport
Lakish, Capital City
Sumer
Qatana System

"This way, Admiral. You'll be able to see the new arrivals as they exit the shuttles," Zara announced as she motioned for Abi to follow her to the floor-to-ceiling windows that looked down to the ID booths. All people entering the planet needed to enter through one of the approved planetary points of entry.

Joining Zara at the window, Abi looked on as the newest wave of immigrants arrived from Sol. She enjoyed watching their faces as they got their first glimpse of a foreign planet. Every Thursday, a wave of sometimes a few thousand, sometimes tens of thousands of new immigrants would arrive in search of a new life, adventure, and future for their families.

Before the immigration spigot had been turned on, Sumer and the two colonies had to settle the property rights issues left in the wake of the Sumerian genocide. Billions upon billions of people had been either killed or taken captive by the blue beasts, leaving entire cities and neighborhoods vacant. It was quickly becoming a postapocalyptic hellscape.

To address this enormous problem, a system had been put in place to identify and locate, if possible, a living relative among the survivors who could make a legal claim to the property left behind. If no living relative could be located, then the property, such as it was, became owned by the local government. It would be either repurposed or sold at auction to the new immigrant arrivals. The government had also put into place a resettlement program to ensure many of these new arrivals didn't end up congregating in compact sections of the now-empty cities and neighborhoods. They wanted to spread the immigrants out and help repopulate these neighborhoods and cities.

Zara, the immigration director, began to explain, "The new immigrants are brought to this area over here, where they are assigned a temporary apartment to live in for the next five days. It's during this period they are given some safety briefings on the planet—you know, like what can hurt you and what can't. They are also given some information on the different regions of the planet and shown some potential regions they can choose to settle in. They're given a few days to acclimate to Sumer and look around the capital before they have to choose where they want to go. Once they've decided on a settlement area, they are given a few cities or neighborhoods to choose from. From there, they'll participate in the next auction. When their new home has been purchased, they and their belongings are sent to it. It's a pretty straightforward process once we got the kinks of the program worked out."

As the head of immigration, Zara was the Sumerian who had worked with a few Earther counterparts in getting the entire system up and running. At the current pace, upwards of thirteen thousand people on average were arriving a week. That number was expected to swell into the hundreds of thousands or even millions once they had things sorted out a bit more.

"You've done an incredible job, Zara. I don't know that we would have gotten this entire immigration process up and running if it hadn't been for you," Abigail complimented.

Blushing at the praise, Zara replied, "I am pleased that so many people from your own planet want to immigrate to ours. How could we say no?"

"In any case, I think this system you created is great."

When Abigail finished touring the immigration center, she headed back to her office. She was glad Hadad would be taking many of these functions over from her soon. As more and more of the civilian government got up and running, she'd be able to transfer these kinds of duties back to them. It wasn't that she didn't like learning about these kinds of things or technically being in charge of them; she just wanted to return to being a fleet admiral rather than an administrator.

With most of her fleet transferred to the Sirius system and the war at long last over, she felt kind of lost. This was probably the first time she hadn't had a ship or fleet to command in more than a decade. She was busy, of course, but she missed the fleet. She still felt too young to retire, and if she was being honest, she didn't think the Zodarks would abide by the peace treaty any longer than they had to. When, not if, they broke the treaty, she wanted to be as ready for them as possible.
****

A few hours later, when Abigail got back to her office, she saw a message was waiting for her from Admiral Bailey. It informed her that her flagship, the RNS *Voyager*, was to be brought back to the naval shipyard in Sol to be decommissioned as a warship and redesignated as a science research ship. A new warship was awaiting her command when she returned.

I wonder if they're giving me command one of the new hybrid ships, she thought. She enjoyed the *Voyager* immensely. She'd been in command of it for the better part of fifteen years. Ultimately, however, the ship was becoming more and more outdated technologically compared to the newer ships rolling off the assembly line.

The orders told her she was to make arrangements to leave for Sol in seventy-two hours. It was just enough time for her to get the crew pulled off their R&R and other duties they'd been assigned down on the planet.

****

Space Command Headquarters
Jacksonville, Arkansas
Earth, Sol

Chester Bailey looked at Miles Hunt, not saying anything for a moment. Finally, he acknowledged, "I'm not disagreeing with you, Miles. But it's going to be tough to keep the draft going and keep producing the same number of warships now that the war is over. After nearly fourteen years of fighting, the Senate wants to transition the economy back to meet the growing domestic needs and focus on expansionism into other systems and planets. The biggest thing holding us back in that regard is transport ships of various kinds and deep space explorer ships."

Miles sighed at the news but wasn't surprised by it. The people were weary of war and wanted to go back to the way things had been before the Zodarks. "I get all of that, Chester, I really do. This treaty has bought us a much-needed reprieve. We need to use that time to continue to ramp up production of warships. My suggestion is since we're short explorer ships, let's look to leverage the frigates for that kind of work. With the new Type 001 Destroyers coming online, we can phase the *Viper*-class frigates out of front-line duty and place them in an exploration capacity. What we can't do right now is slow down the production of cruisers, battleships, or carriers. These ships take time to construct, and we need time to train the crews on them."

"I know, I know, Miles. You're preaching to the choir. There's also an enormous demand for transports and haulers. If we're going to expand our population to these other planets and continue to mine for the materials needed to build these ring stations, then we need to allow some of the shipyards to resume civilian construction."

Miles knew Chester was right. They could only keep all the shipyards on a war footing for so long. They did need to start building more of the interstellar infrastructure if they were going to grow as a people and empire of their own.

"Let's do this, then, Chester. The primary Navy yard continues to build warships just as they are. Let's release the Gaelic from their contractual agreement to build frigates for us and allow BlueOrigins' Earth yard to resume civilian construction along with one of the Musk Industry yards. They can choose either the Earth or Mars yard, but one of them needs to keep building warships. Do you think that'll be a good enough compromise for the Senate?"

"It'll have to be. I mean, technically you are the Viceroy, so you can kind of set policy for that kind of stuff, and we have to accept it."

Miles hated that part of being the Viceroy. What he tended to offer as a solution or suggestion was more often than not taken as an order. The Prims had reacted that way; so too had the Tully. The Altairians by contrast had insisted they had enough warships to handle whatever got thrown at them.

"Oh, by the way—what are you doing with the *Voyager*? I heard you had put her in for decommissioning as a warship," Chester inquired, a little annoyed that Miles had unilaterally done this.

"I'm giving the *Voyager* over to Dr. Johnson and DARPA. They've been making some incredible archaeological finds regarding the ancient Humtars as of late, and I'd like them to keep pursuing that for us. As such, they're going to need a ship to move around in. I figure the *Voyager* is one of the oldest warships in the inventory. It won't be missed, and we have newer ships coming off the assembly line. Rather than placing it in the mothball or reserve fleet, let DARPA have it."

"OK, that makes sense, but maybe next time consult with me before you go and take one of my warships like that."

Miles's cheeks flushed a bit. "You're right. I should have and will next time if it's needed."

"So, what's next on the Viceroy's agenda?"

Grunting at the question, Miles replied, "More than I care to admit. In a few days, I need to head back to the Altairian home world and finish relocating the war council. I've transferred everything to New Eden to give it and everyone on it a fresh start. Somehow, someway, I have to get this alliance functioning a lot better, a lot more in tune with each other and what's going on. I won't allow it to keep functioning the way it is. No one group of people should have to bear the entire brunt of the war effort. If we're to be a true alliance, then we need to become an alliance that functions as one and not many."

"Yeah, I don't envy that part of your job, Miles. I have a hard enough time handling our own force. I can't imagine what it must be like trying to manage multiple species' armies. Speaking of multiple species, do you think you could put the word out there that if any of these species would like to set up some cargo-hauling businesses in our space, we'd gladly welcome it? The biggest impediment we're going to have in our expansion into the stars is going to come from a lack of cargo and passenger ships to move everyone about."

"That's not a bad idea. The Tully are a big-time trading race. I'll bet they have a lot of cargo haulers and such that might want to get in on some of this. I'll bring it up to them when I see them. But before we break up our meeting, how do you think Admiral Halsey is going to take her new assignment?" Miles asked, not sure if his old mentor would like it or be angry about being taken away from the fleet.

Chester shrugged. "She won't be happy, but if she wants to sit in my chair one day, then she needs to do some time at headquarters and be seen by the right senators and political leaders. That and we could really use her help in trimming down the ballooning bureaucracy that seems to have taken root over the last decade. I was so focused on the war I missed seeing how cumbersome we were becoming. It'll be good to have someone on staff who has real combat experience—someone who can help change the system from within and improve upon it. We're now going to have a lot of space to not only explore but also protect. That means we need to establish logistical bases in a dozen new places and make sure we have a supply system in place to support and sustain them and the various ships and squadrons that'll be on patrol. I'm sure she'll take to her new post."

The two talked for a bit longer about some finer details of the Navy and how they were going to keep growing it. When Miles left, he wasn't sure when he'd be back again. His next set of duties would take him and the *Freedom* away from Sol for an extended period of time.
****

Republic Naval Yard

Sol

Admiral Abigail Halsey watched the monitor as the *Voyager* dropped out of FTL. It had been a long time since she'd been back to Earth. So long, in fact, that she was caught off guard by the size of the Navy's new shipyard. The last time she'd seen it, it had been just a couple of slips and some small support structures. Now it appeared to house more than a hundred slips and multiple warehouses intermixed between them. The area was abuzz with activity. If she zoomed in, she could make out the army of synthetic humanoid construction workers relentlessly building the individual ships of war.

Once the *Voyager* was back under their own power, the naval yard began to hail them. They were instructed to head toward a specific slip and then wait for a tug to finish pulling them in. For better or worse, this once-proud warship was now going to embark on a new mission—a mission so classified even Admiral Halsey was being kept in the dark about it. All she knew was that the *Voyager* was being taken away from her.

It took nearly a day for the *Voyager* to finally slide into the slip that would be her new home for however long it took to carry out her transformation. The crew spent the next several days offloading everything from emergency rations to missiles and magrail ordnance. Even the Ospreys and cargo shuttles were being offloaded. Abigail felt saddened every time she left her quarters or the bridge and walked around the ship. Everywhere she turned, there were construction crews and synthetic workers either removing more equipment from the ship or working to take her corridors and rooms apart. It was obvious the ship was being remodeled, but for what purpose, she wasn't sure.

Still, it dismayed her to see the ship that had guided her through so many battles being stripped of everything that made her a warship. It just didn't feel right. But orders were orders and she'd been sent to the naval yard for a reason.

"Ah, there you are, Admiral. I've been trying to track you down for some time," a naval commander said.

Abigail turned to face the man who had called out to her. "Hello, Commander. As requested, the *Voyager* is here and being dismantled as we speak. Do I have new orders as of yet?"

"As a matter of fact, that is precisely why I'm here. These were sent to us from Admiral Bailey."

Taking the tablet from the officer, she held her own data pad next to it and completed the handoff. Her new set of orders was now on her own tablet. She entered her access code and then used her biometrics to unlock them. As she read them over, her first instinct was to petition Chester for a new assignment. Then she saw his signature at the bottom of the orders and realized there was no way he was going to change them. He'd clearly had something in mind when he'd selected her for the assignment.

"Do you need any help moving any of your personal belongings, ma'am?"

She'd been mumbling her discontent for these orders and had forgotten the commander was sitting there until he spoke. "Actually, yes. I have my belongings packed in my quarters. If you can arrange for them to be brought to the single officers' barracks at Space Command Headquarters, that would be appreciated." She then turned on her heel and headed for the corridor that would take her out of the ship.

****

The following day, she was on a small military transport headed to Earth. As they approached the planet, she caught a glimpse of the new ring station being built around the planet. It was still years away from being completed, but still, seeing the massive structure under construction was incredible. Once she'd arrived at the Space Command HQ building, she made her way over to Admiral Bailey's office. The two of them spent most of the afternoon talking about her new position. While she wouldn't be commanding a starship for at least a couple of years, she'd help to streamline the Republic's ever-growing bureaucracy instead Instead of being lean and nimble during the war, it had grown and become cumbersome to navigate. She attributed this to the sheer size of the organization more than anything else, but she certainly saw the reason she'd been picked for this job. Bailey needed a hatchet man to come in and shake things up. Once she'd thoroughly pissed everyone off and gotten the bureaucracy trimmed down to where it should be, she'd then take command of a new flagship and depart as quickly as she'd arrived.

Chapter Twenty-Six
Mukhabarat

Six Weeks Post–Treaty Signing
Mukhabarat Headquarters
Sumer

Dakkuri was a seasoned spy and a vicious assassin when the need arose. Since being recruited into the Mukhabarat at the age of seven, he'd been groomed for the roles he'd played over the years. On several occasions, he'd been sent to Zincondria to undergo specialized training in on- and off-world communication technologies he might have to employ at some point. He learned how to use every Zodark and Sumerian weapon created, along with how to employ explosives and even build rudimentary explosives from everyday materials found in a town or city. By the time he was eighteen, he had been proficient in hand-to-hand combat and just about every weapon there was. He'd even been sent to a special school to learn how to properly eat at a fine dining restaurant and all the proper etiquette involved in hobnobbing with those above his station. He'd been groomed to become what they were calling a "gray" man, meaning he had been taught how to blend into his surroundings and become invisible while hiding in plain sight.

For his twenty-first birthday, he had been given his first real assignment. He'd been sent to the planet Regalis, one of many human-populated worlds the Zodarks had been cultivating and grooming. When he'd arrived, he had been given the task of infiltrating a terrorist cell that had sprung up on the planet. Some factions had grown tired of being governed and ruled by the Zodarks. They were looking for a way to escape their rule, which Dakkuri knew was impossible. Still, they persisted in sowing chaos and carrying out bombings and IED attacks against Zodark targets and buildings.

The infiltration of this group was the capstone to Dakkuri's espionage training. It was a task that would require every bit of training he'd received and every skill he'd been taught thus far. It would also give him experience in communicating vital intelligence off-world while not being detected. To ensure mission success, his Zodark handlers had made sure no one on Regalis, human or Zodark, knew who he was or that he'd be operating on the planet. They wanted this to be a tightly controlled circle of only those with a need to know.

Dakkuri had gotten himself settled into a crappy little apartment and found a menial job that afforded him the flexibility he needed for his real mission. In his first few weeks, he had seen firsthand what one of these terrorist attacks looked like. He'd been walking home from his shift when he saw two Zodarks climb into a vehicle. When they turned it on, a massive explosion consumed the vehicle and blew out the windows of nearby buildings.

It was shortly after that blast that he was able to make his first contact within the terrorist organization. From there, he was put through a few of their loyalty tests. Once he passed them, he was officially inducted into a cell. For the next six months, Dakkuri carried out a few errands and other miscellaneous items for his group. It was during this tryout period that he learned who all was in his cell and what their job functions were. In time, he came into contact with other cells and likewise did his best to identify who they were.

Dakkuri knew if he was to catch the eye of the leader or leaders of this terrorist organization, he was going to have to do something spectacular. He was given permission by the Mukhabarat and his Zodark handler to carry out an assassination of a senior-level Zodark administrator on the planet. The administrator in question was also under investigation by the Zodarks for misappropriating money, so his loss was not going to bother anyone save for his family.

Knowing he needed to make an impression with this task, Dakkuri set about studying the administrator's schedule and routine. It was during his second week of surveilling his target that he found his opportunity. Each morning, the Zodark administrator would stop at a particular store to get something to drink. It was during one of these stops that Dakkuri, while kneeling down to tie his shoelace, placed the IED underneath the passenger side of the administrator's vehicle. When the administrator got into the car and started driving down the road, Dakkuri pressed a button on his watch, sending a signal to the IED. Fractions of a second later, the entire car exploded right in the middle of a busy intersection. The fireball was enormous. The overpressure from the explosion blew out nearly every window within a one-block radius and injured dozens more Zodarks. When the dust had settled, Dakkuri knew he'd made his mark in the organization. He'd demonstrated his ability to find and surveil a target and then build and place an IED on said target's vehicle.

While Dakkuri was excited to see his handiwork, he did feel bad for the number of fellow humans who had been killed or injured in the process. *That explosion was too big. I need to learn to make them a lot smaller if I'm going to repeat this tactic again.*

Within days of carrying out his assassination, Dakkuri was told the leader of the organization wanted to speak with him personally about a special mission. This was the meeting he'd been trying to get for nearly a year. Prior to the meeting, he made sure to wire himself up. Because he'd likely be searched for bugs, he used a specially designed eye lens. It was incredibly thin and looked natural but would record everything Dakkuri saw or heard and store that information until it was told to transmit. It also had a fail-safe. If the wearer died, it would automatically transmit its data to a preset link.

When the day arrived, Dakkuri placed the special lenses in his eyes and set about meeting the leader of this terrorist organization—an organization that had been causing problems on the planet and for the Zodark administrators now for going on nine years. When Dakkuri finally met the leader, he was surprised to learn this fabled legend was a thirty-two-year-old woman. She was strikingly beautiful, almost to the point of distracting him from his mission. For the next three hours, they talked. She inquired a lot about him and why he had decided to join their ranks. She asked about how he had learned how to build the type of IED he'd employed. He was honest with her the entire time, telling her he'd been recruited into the Mukhabarat at a young age on a different planet, but when he saw his mother and father killed by the same organization he was working for, he could no longer justify being a part of them. He'd quit and relocated to Regalis under a new identity. He wanted to exact his revenge on the very people and system that had killed his family.

The leader of the organization appeared to believe his story. She invited him into her inner circle and shared with him some of their grander plans. When Dakkuri reported what he'd found, his handlers congratulated him and said they'd execute a raid shortly to take them into custody. Dakkuri, however, had another idea in mind. He proposed letting him stay on the inside and allowing the cell to run a little while longer, wanting additional time to locate other members or at least figure out how many other cells there were and where they were located.

Fortunately, his handlers agreed to his little plan, but they told him time was not on his side. They couldn't let more of these attacks continue while he collected intelligence. He had to move swiftly to identify who the cell leaders were and where they were holing up.

Dakkuri proposed to the terrorist leader having him teach at least one person from each cell how to build both large and small IEDs, depending on the mission set. The leader loved the idea, and soon enough he was teaching his technique to more than fifty different cells. While this was taking place, his Zodark handlers had placed all of these individuals' images and biometrics into their surveillance systems, and within days, they were tracking anyone and everyone they were coming into contact with throughout the day.

For the next four months, Dakkuri worked tirelessly day and night, teaching them how to build IEDs. He made sure each cell member that was sent to him knew how to build them and eventually could teach others. This was the part of the mission Dakkuri was most uncomfortable with. He didn't like the idea of teaching these terrorists how to build actual bombs, but his Zodark handlers insisted the training needed to be real if he was to keep his cover intact. At this point, they'd scrapped their earlier plans to round the cells up right away because he was uncovering so many new ones they hadn't known existed. Dakkuri could tell from the questions his handler had been asking that they were truly concerned that this wasn't just some small terrorist group but rather something more akin to an actual freedom movement—something that would be a lot harder to suppress if it spread. They also needed to know who all was involved so they could restrict their travel to only this planet. The last thing they wanted was for the spark of freedom to make its way to other Zodark-controlled human worlds.

One day, when Dakkuri was teaching a small group how to build an IED known as an explosively formed penetrator or EFP, a device designed to punch right through the armor of a vehicle, the warehouse he'd been teaching inside was raided by a mixture of Mukhabarat and Zodark soldiers. The raiding party knew what Dakkuri looked like in advance, so they knew not to harm him. They made a show of arresting him and beating him up in front of the others. Then they carted him off to Sanju prison, a large, dour-looking building on the outskirts of the capital city.

Once the roundup was complete, a show trial was put on, with Dakkuri being the first to be paraded before the court and the 1.3 billion humans on the planet. It was also being broadcast to the other human planets to act as a warning to others who might get the same idea. His trial was short, only a day. The evidence against him was overwhelming. A couple of the terrorists themselves had struck plea deals in exchange for their lives, agreeing to narc on a few other individuals of concern. When he'd been pronounced guilty, he was to be summarily executed later that day.

It was at this point that Dakkuri was whisked away from Regalis while another person took his place at the gallows. Dakkuri had completed his mission and was rewarded with a three-month vacation to any planet he wanted. Ten years later, he found himself one of the lead spies on Sumer, where he built up the spy network on the planet. Now, after a decade of hard work, the entire thing had been blown up when a new group of humans had stumbled onto the Zodark penal colony of Clovis.

At first, Dakkuri hadn't known what to make of this newly discovered group of humans. Like the Sumerians, they were a spacefaring race. However, unlike the Sumerians, this group of humans also had warships and an army, something the Sumerians lacked. What frustrated Dakkuri's Zodark masters was that they had no idea where these new humans were from. That was when he'd come up with the plan to have as many of their deep-cover spies as possible look to infiltrate this new group of humans and locate their home world and core systems.
****

NOS Heltet looked at the faces of the operatives milling about in the room. "You are sure this will work, Dakkuri?" he asked skeptically.

"If you want to find out where this Terran world they call Earth is, then yes. This is the best course of action."

Staring at his lead Sumerian spy, Heltet asked, "How do you know that once they are free of this planet, free of our control…*your* control, they won't go and turn themselves in? We must assume this system these Earthers are from is a beautiful place with billions of people living in it. Their loyalties may change."

"That is a possibility, one I have considered—and so I've put in place certain measures to keep an eye on it."

Heltet grunted at the comment. "You are assigning watchers to them?"

Dakkuri only smiled.

"Where will you be in all of this?"

"I am going to take charge of the small cargo hauler the *Wawat*. I'll captain the ship with the help of four others I've chosen. Each of them has a specialty that I believe will come in handy over the coming years."

"I see. What will *your* objective be on the *Wawat*?" Heltet inquired, still very skeptical about this proposal.

"I've had the ship outfitted with a variety of electronic scanners and detection equipment. Basically, as we fly through a star system, we'll absorb as much of the radio chatter and communications going on between the different civilian and military ships in the system. In time, I hope to obtain some contracts to haul some cargo to and from some of their shipyards or other military installations. This will allow us to map where everything is and what kind defenses they have," Dakkuri explained confidently.

Heltet could tell his human spymaster thought he had it all figured out. He just hoped Dakkuri was right and his teams were able to smuggle the much-needed intelligence from these Terran worlds back to him.

"Dakkuri, I have one other question. How are your teams going to deliver all this collected data without being detected?"

"Couriers. As you know, the new Sumerian government recently opened a civilian transportation line that will now allow citizens to travel from Sumer to Clovis, the one they now call New Eden, a planet named Mars, their home world, Earth, another planet called Alpha Centuari, and a Primord world named Intus. As we collect information on their systems, we'll have it loaded on data sticks and sent back via human couriers. I know this may sound old-school or low-tech, but it's the safest way to transmit our intelligence activities without risking a communiqué being intercepted."

Shaking his head, Heltet countered, "No, Dakkuri, the data sticks will not be the safest way to transfer the data. They could be lost, stolen, or destroyed in transit. I believe the safest, most efficient way to transfer the data back and forth would be through the cranium upload port."

A slight look of concern appeared on Dakkuri's face at the mention of the cranium port. It was not something any of the humans liked or wanted in their bodies.

Dakkuri countered, "I know that may *appear* to be the safest way to transfer the data. But surely you are aware of the problems many of the human couriers have experienced with these in the past."

Heltet waved one of his hands, brushing aside Dakkuri's concern. "That has already been solved. Here, let me show you."

A second later, a holographic image appeared showing a human head. What came next was a bit gruesome. It showed a Zodark cutting into the skull of a Sumerian and then inserting a small device just under the skull between the brain and the bone. When the piece of skull was reattached and the scalp placed back over the wound, you'd never know a data stick had been added. The device utilized a small wireless capability to transfer information to and from it. It was seen as a clever way of hiding and transferring data in plain sight.

Looking at Heltet, Dakkuri nodded. "I agree. This will be the best way to transfer the data. I am glad to see they found a better way to insert this device. The previous way was barbaric."

Heltet shrugged. To him, human discomfort didn't register as a concern. "When will you begin this operation?"

"We will start immediately. I'm going to start handing out their assignments today. It is going to take some time for everyone to get to their assigned locations and begin the infiltration process. There is a lot to set up, from establishing safe houses on each of these human planets to developing areas where we can meet to pass information off. This is going to be an enormous undertaking, Heltet. I hope you understand this will not happen overnight; it will take time to do it right."

"So long as your spies begin to provide the necessary information, that is all I care about." Deep down, Heltet was concerned with the timeline he'd been given to get this operation going. He knew, perhaps better than most, that intelligence operations like this could take the better part of a decade to start yielding the kind of results his masters were likely to demand. They wanted intelligence on where the Terran home world, Earth, was located along with their other colonies.

As long as Dakkuri comes through for me, everything should be fine.

Chapter Twenty-Seven
Alliance Anew

Altairius Prime
Alliance War Council

The briefer finished presenting the information to the members of the war council and stood by, ready to take questions. The first came from one of the Altairians, named Jandolly, a councilmember who was routinely at odds with many of the non-Altairian members.

"If the Orbots and Zodarks are going to maintain a presence on Alfheim, then why did we just agree to a peace treaty with them?" he queried. "My understanding was you *humans* and *Primords*"—he made a point of overenunciating both names—"had sought to liberate this long-lost mining colony from their control, not share it with them."

The Primord Senator Bjork Terboven explained, "That was our initial goal at the outset of the operation. When the opportunity to put an end to not just the fighting but the entire war presented itself, the partitioning of part of the planet to facilitate continued talks and dialogue with the Dominion did not seem like a bad deal."

Several councilmembers nodded in agreement. A few scoffed. Not everyone was happy about this treaty.

Jandolly turned to look at Senator Terboven when he asked, "Are the Primords really OK with this peace treaty? The Zodarks are still in control of five of your worlds."

"We are aware of the worlds the Zodarks are still in control of," the senator snapped before adding, "We have been given a chance to pursue a truce and hopefully a lasting peace between our alliances. If that means we must share parts of Alfheim and accept Zodark or Orbot control of these five worlds, then my people will learn to accept it."

A few of the members grumbled. Then General Atiku Muhammadu, representing the Tully, added his opinion. "I agree with Senator Terboven. We have been given an opportunity to put an end to this war—a conflict that has gone on for hundreds of years. Why are any of you upset that it has come to an end? We've all lost enough people in this war. It is time for peace."

"I am upset that this peace treaty was negotiated without consulting the council," Jandolly shot back, "No one was allowed to provide feedback on its parameters. Maybe some of the members of this alliance are not ready to accept their peace deal. Did you think of that?"

The tension in the room was thick. The members were starting to separate into two different camps—the ones who were excited by the treaty and those who were not.

Senator Terboven countered, "The alliance members who are doing the fighting and dying in this war agreed to the peace terms on behalf of the alliance. Perhaps if you wanted the war to continue, Jandolly, then the Altairians should have joined in its fighting. Had you been part of this grand fleet and military action, you would have been present when the talks began. But once again, the Altairians like to provide technology to fight in these wars—you just don't like to get your hands dirty and do the actual fighting yourselves."

Viceroy Miles Hunt finally held a hand up to stop the bickering. Jandolly was about to launch into one of his tirades when Hunt slapped his hand down hard on the table. His metallic ring made a loud cracking noise that echoed across the room, ending the sidebar conversations and grabbing people's attention.

"For the time being, the war is over," Hunt declared, eyeballing everyone at the table. "I, for one, do not believe the fighting is done. I believe the Orbots forced this peace agreement on the Zodarks when their pride would not allow them to accept a peace treaty. It is my belief that the Zodarks will use this period of peace to reposition their forces to launch a surprise attack once they feel they have the upper hand. That is why we are going to think of this treaty as a pause or cease-fire and not an end to hostilities."

Hunt looked at Jandolly. "You should have been consulted about the treaty. That is my fault. I saw an opportunity to stop the fighting and bloodshed and I took it. During our talks with the Dominion, it was clear there was a dislike, or at least some frustration, between the Zodarks and the Orbots. The cyborgs felt the war had gone on long enough and they had lost too many ships in a war they did not feel they should be fighting. The Zodarks, however, wanted to keep fighting. From my perspective, they looked like they could continue to absorb the losses and showed no concern about the losses their allies the Orbots were taking. I may not be able to read minds, but it was clear there was a bit of a problem between their two factions. I believe we may be able to exploit that tension down the road."

Jandolly seemed a bit more relaxed at this admission. Holding his chin up, he replied, "Thank you for acknowledging your mistake, Viceroy. Going forward, let us try to do a better job of coordinating things like this. With the military losses the Orbots had been sustaining, we had been on the cusp of launching an invasion into their own space that borders ours. Prior to your reinvasion of the Sirius system, we had observed large numbers of warships leaving the border systems. They were likely on their way to join your battle given the number of Orbot and Zodark ships in the system. That is why we are upset about the peace treaty. It meant we could not launch our invasion, an invasion we had spent years preparing for."

He paused for a moment before turning to the briefer. "If we can, I'd like to look at the ship losses from the battle again," Jandolly said as he motioned for the briefer to continue.

Hunt motioned for the briefer to bring those details up but then added, "Jandolly, you brought up something very important. As an alliance, we have done a terrible job of coordinating what's going on with this war. We may be one alliance, but we are, in reality, a combination of many little coalitions. Case in point, you just said your people have been preparing for years to launch this invasion of Orbot space. But no one else in the alliance knew this."

"That is not true," Jandolly insisted. "The Ry'lians knew." Hunt shot a look at Senator Nom Eblith, the representative of the Ry'lian people; he nodded ever so slightly. The Ry'lians had not been big players thus far in the alliance—they were new additions, joining slightly before the Earthers. Jandolly continued, "They were going to participate in the invasion with us. One of the systems we were going to liberate was a system they had lost nearly twenty years ago."

"Yes, our system, PX-201, has six planets and twenty-six moons in it. We had settlements on five of the moons and two planets. Nearly one hundred and eighty million of our people have been held under Orbot captivity for almost ten dygrills," added Senator Eblith. His race was very stocky, almost twice as wide as a human although they were roughly the same height, and they all had prehensile tails that were usually blunt but that could activate with a deadly spike when in battle.

A brief thought appeared in Hunt's head, letting him know that a dygrill was approximately two human years.

"I understand that, Senator Eblith. But this proves my point. Aside from you and the Altairians, no one else had a clue this invasion was about to take place. This has to stop. We need to start working together as a more unified alliance. Every military operation should be coordinated in advance. As the Viceroy, even I was not told about this offensive, when it was going to start, or what its objectives were. As an alliance, we cannot continue to operate like this," Hunt exclaimed in frustration.

Senator Eblith countered, "To be fair, Viceroy, you and the others were not included because at the time, no one else was going to be involved, so we did not want to burden the council with what we were doing."

Hunt shook his head as he responded, "It's not about distracting the other members of the council—it's about keeping people informed so we can better coordinate our activities. For example, if we hadn't agreed to a peace treaty, then after we had secured the Sirius system, I could have had the *Freedom* jump to PX-201 to assist you in liberating that system from Orbot control."

Pausing for a moment, Hunt continued, "This is one reason why I am insisting on us moving the alliance council to New Eden. The alliance needs a reset. We need to refocus our efforts on working together for the good of all members. This means we need to coordinate what we're doing and why we're doing it. We need to expand and open more interstellar trade between the alliance members, and we need to find ways to grow together. But before I go further into those details, Jandolly has asked that we look at the ship losses from the Sirius campaign, so let's go ahead and bring those results up."

The briefer typed something on his data pad and then up came the battle figures, which then floated in the center of the table. Each person was able to see the floating data and images as if they were being presented just for them.

The information was broken down into two columns. One showed the Dominion, the Zodark and Orbot ships broken down by ship classes. Underneath each class of warships, it showed the number of each ship present in the system and then the number of ships destroyed. The information was laid out the same way on the Galactic Empire or GE side, with Primord and Terran ships.

The Orbots had brought eight of their capital ships, the venerable base stars, into the system. These ships were enormous. They acted almost like the *Freedom* in that they were essentially mobile bases. The ships were nearly six thousand meters in length and bristling with weapons. The main weapon these massive ships brought to bear was their complement of six hundred fighters and bombers. The ship even had the ability to self-replicate fighters and bombers to replace the ones being lost during battle. They were incredibly scary ships to face off against. Of the eight base stars deployed, five had been destroyed. The other three had sustained some level of damage.

Similarly, the Zodarks had moved ten of their own star carriers. While not as large as their Orbot counterparts, their ships packed more ship-to-ship weapon platforms. The lasers on the ship were significantly more powerful than even those on their battleships. While they couldn't launch six hundred fighters and bombers, they could launch four hundred. No small number. The Zodarks had started the battle with ten of these terrifying ships, and by the end of the main battle, a total of six had been destroyed.

In total, ninety-three Zodark and seventy-two Orbot warships had been destroyed over the nearly three-day battle. In comparison, the Primords had lost seventy-six warships while the Terrans had lost fifty-one. It was a stinging loss that would have been even worse had the *Freedom* not been present and able to leverage its super gun. Being able to one-shot many of the Orbot and Zodark battleships and cruisers had turned the battle in their favor.

When they looked at the ground forces, the number of losses was staggering. The Republic Army's official casualty count showed a little more than two hundred and thirty-six thousand soldiers and another four hundred thousand C100 had perished during the ground campaign. Most of these losses had actually occurred during the Dominion invasion and occupation. Similarly, the Primords had lost forty-six thousand souls. There were no official numbers for the Orbots or Zodarks, but it was estimated they had collectively lost a little more than four hundred thousand of their own soldiers. The battle for the Sirius system and Alfheim would go down as one of the costlier battles in the nearly fourteen-year war.

When they had gone over the alliance losses, Hunt made it clear that these kinds of losses were not acceptable in the future, nor should they happen again. No one race should have to bear the costs of a single battle so heavily on their shoulders. He used these stats and this battle to further emphasize to the Altairians their own need to be more involved in any future conflicts—no more sitting on the sidelines and providing technology while observing from a distance. They were either going to contribute to the alliance or find themselves on the outs. Hunt had made it clear to Jandolly and the other Altairians that the Gallentines knew they had been using the Terrans and Primords as cannon fodder in this war. They were now on notice that the Gallentines would keep better tabs on what was going on in the Milky Way through Viceroy Hunt. The consensus among the Gallentines was that the Altairians needed to more involved in this war.

Before he ended the council meeting, he turned to Pandolly and Jandolly, saying, "Before we move on to other business, there is something I would like your help in understanding."

They both nodded and said they'd do their best to help. They had taken his not-so-subtle hints that they needed to be better team players.

"I believe you had mentioned there was some friction between the Orbots and Zodarks. I picked up on that during my peace talks with them. I was hoping one of you may be able to elaborate more on that. I'm specifically interested in anything we can use to drive a wedge between them," Hunt explained.

Jandolly stood and motioned for everyone else to stay seated while he paced the room. In a soft but confident tone, he explained, "There is some intelligence I would like to make you aware of about the Zodarks. It is something I have been meaning to discuss with you when you returned from Sirius, and now seems like a good time."

Hunt kept a neutral look on his face. Beneath his calm demeanor, he was starting to fume that the Altairians had once again held back another piece of valuable intelligence.

"The Balloll, our intelligence organization, has provided some stunning yet unverified intelligence about the Zodarks for the last twenty years. I say stunning because, if true, it could be the very wedge issue you are seeking. Unfortunately, we have not been able to verify it independently or through a second source, so this is only one agent providing us this data," Jandolly began to explain.

"Viceroy, before you Earth humans discovered Clovis, the planet you now call New Eden, the Zodarks had been steadily moving to replace the Orbots as the dominant race in their alliance. In general terms, the Zodarks despise the Orbots as they are cyborgs. They are part biological, but at this point mostly just machines. The Zodarks do not trust them. They feel they do not have souls or fight with honor. That's not to say the Zodarks won't work with them or accept, leverage or outright steal Orbot technology. The Zodarks are, if nothing else, masters of manipulation. As you already know, the Zodarks have been taking humans from Sumer in the form of an annual tribute. What the Sumerians did not know was what was happening to them. Some feared they were being eaten, while others feared they may be sacrificed to some god.

"The fact is none of those assumptions are right. We know the Zodarks use some of the Sumerians as pets or slaves, particularly for their NOSs or commanders. But what they are really using them for is much more sinister than that. The people they are taking in tribute are being placed on a series of planets in the Orinda and Valencia systems." Jandolly then brought up a star map. He highlighted the Zodark-controlled space and then highlighted the two systems in question. They were both deep within Zodark space. The two systems also happened to be at a dead-end chain of systems, roughly three jumps away from the critical Zodark junction and industrial system of Tueblets—the system Viceroy Hunt had been advocating to seize for more than a decade.

"The Orinda system has four planets capable of supporting human life while the Valencia system has two. For the past several hundred years, the Zodarks have been populating these six planets with humans taken during these tributes. The Zodarks have gone out of their way to help grow and cultivate these human colonies so their populations would expand exponentially. With some additional medical help, the average woman on these planets will bear thirteen children. This high level of childbearing has enabled the populations on these planets to grow at unprecedented rates compared to even your own planets and colonies."

Viceroy Hunt was somewhat surprised that the Altairians were coming forward with the same information that he had heard from Captain Wiyrkomi. He wanted to test their statements further to see how the narratives compared. "Excuse me, but with a population growth like that, what can they possibly be doing with all these humans?" he pressed.

Jandolly explained, "That is a question we had been asking ourselves for many years. The women are obviously groomed to produce children, *lots* of children. However, the men are largely put to work.

There are several shipyards in these systems, and while we are not sure what specifically they are building, it is clear they are building a lot of something. Equally of note is that a large number of these men are enlisted into some sort of human army—our agent who has infiltrated into this area has told us he believes the army is being trained to assist the Zodarks one day in fighting and taking over the Orbots' territory and planets."

Hunt had to bite back the look of surprise on his face and a sharp comment he wanted to make right then. The Altairians had intentionally withheld this vital intelligence. Taking a deep breath in, Hunt exhaled slowly. Regaining his composure, he stated, "Jandolly, this is critical information that should have been shared with all of us many, many years ago. Why have you kept this a secret?"

Speaking for the first time, Pandolly tried to intervene. "Viceroy, as Jandolly said earlier, we only have a single source providing us with the information. We cannot verify what he is telling us is actually true and not just a disinformation campaign by the Zodarks or even the Orbots."

"Then you need to find a way to verify this information," Hunt exclaimed. "Perhaps you could speak with some of the Sumerians on Sumer. Some of them may have information that might help point you in the right direction. I mean, what if that human army is real? What if they're now looking at turning that human army on us and not the Orbots? That would be a really big deal, something we would need to be prepared for well in advance."

"Perhaps now that the war is over with, we may be able to verify some of this information by establishing additional sources to infiltrate these systems," Jandolly offered optimistically.

Sitting back in his chair, Hunt thought about a way to share Wiyrkomi's information with the group. He cleared his throat. "Around seven hundred and fifty years ago, the leader of the Ottoman Empire, a man by the name of Sultan Orhan, established an army of soldiers called Janissaries. This was a slave army created to serve the leader of the Ottoman Empire, and it did so for many hundreds of years. The Ottomans created this army by taking young boys from their conquered territories and placing them into military service. The young boys were groomed and conditioned to be warriors and to have unwavering loyalty to the Sultan whom they served. For hundreds of years, this slave army grew

276

in strength and in reputation. If what your source has told you is true, then it is possible that this is what the Zodarks have been working toward—creating a massive slave army that they will be able to use to conquer the Orbots and then the rest of us."

Many of the councilmembers seemed caught off guard by this possible use. Others were still skeptical about any sort of rift between the Orbots and Zodarks. The two species had been fighting well together for hundreds of years. Still, the idea of the Zodarks grooming and growing these planets full of humans didn't paint a very good narrative.

For the next hour, the council discussed the idea of humans being integrated into the Zodark army or potentially doing their fighting for them. Ultimately, they all agreed that more effort needed to be put into collecting intelligence on these worlds and what the Zodarks were up to. This peace treaty had been forced on them—that meant they'd likely had something big in the works beforehand. The question was what?
****

Later that Evening

Miles Hunt walked through the Altairian capital with Pandolly, his four-armed bodyguards doing an exceptional job of blending in and all but disappearing.

It always impressed him to see how advanced this city was. On the ground level, there were hover vehicles that traveled just above the street. Intermixed were hover buses and lorries that moved people and goods about the city. About thirty feet above the street was a see-through plexiglass tube of some sort. Every few hundred meters there was a station, where people would get on and off. An elevator and escalator system allowed people to traverse up or down the system rapidly. Every five minutes, an eight-car train would travel through the tube, ferrying passengers to the station closest to their destination. Connecting to the station was another station about a hundred meters higher. This tube didn't have nearly as many connecting stations. It was designed to move passengers further and at higher rates of speed. It was an incredibly efficient way to move large numbers of people and goods about the city and other connecting cities nearby.

I hope we're building transit systems like this on New Eden and Earth, thought Hunt. *It would really revolutionize public transportation.*

Approaching a very chic-looking restaurant, Pandolly guided them into the upscale establishment. They were led to an outdoor table on the second-floor patio. The patio had a great view of the bustling city below. If you looked up, you'd see the multilayer hyperloop system. One could also see the aerial highway with hover cars moving about in a well-choreographed dance.

The maître d' approached, a member of an alien species Hunt hadn't seen before. He was going to ask Pandolly about them when a menu was handed to him. To his surprise, it had several well-known human foods listed on it—comfort food items like shepherd's pie and bangers and mash, along with more upscale dishes like beef Wellington and duck confit in a red wine reduction sauce. It was clear this restaurant catered to the small human expat community in the city. It was probably the reason Pandolly had brought him here.

The maître d' brought a glass of fine wine for Hunt and a similar drink for Pandolly. Once he'd taken their dinner orders, he left the two of them alone so they could talk in private. Pandolly saw this as his moment to broach a sensitive topic and took it.

"Miles, several weeks ago on Alfheim, you had said we Altairians had not been entirely honest with your people. I wanted us to talk about that and explain some of this to you. Will you allow us that opportunity?"

"Yes, Pandolly," Miles replied as he reached for his glass of wine. "Part of building an enduring friendship and alliance is being truthful and honest with each other. That is something that I feel has been lacking between our people for far too long.

Miles turned to Handolly. "When we first met, you told us a story about an ice comet heading toward Earth. You said this comet would have been an extinction-level event that would wipe out humanity. That, however, was not true since there were humans on other planets. I would like you to be honest with me about what really happened. Why were some humans taken from Earth and transplanted to Sumer? I would also like to know what other planets humans from Earth had been placed on and why," Miles asked. He leaned in, hoping that just maybe he'd be able to get some real facts from the Altairians this time.

Handolly seemed to sigh. He slowly nodded his head in acknowledgment of their past dishonesty. "Miles, you have to understand something. We Altairians did not set out to intentionally deceive you out of malice. There were some things your people were just not ready to know. Some of these things I'm about to reveal to you would have caused some serious unrest within the people of Earth."

"I understand that, Handolly, but you built our relationship on a lie—a lie that has caused my people and my government not to trust your people like we should. So again, please tell me how many times have you Altairians or other species taken humans from Earth and either kept them on your ships or transplanted them to other moons and planets?" Miles demanded in a soft yet deliberate tone.

"I cannot speak for the other alien species and what they may or may not have done on Earth and to your people, so I will only speak about what *we* have done. When I mentioned that ice comet, I was not entirely truthful. I mean, it did happen; it just didn't happen in the time span I had originally told you. This occurred much earlier. At the time the comet hit, your species was still developing. Dinosaurs still walked the land, and the Earth was a very, very different place. We had been monitoring Earth and your species' developments for hundreds of years, documenting your progress and observing your development. What caught our attention was how fast your people were evolving and how rapidly you were able to learn. This told us that your species, if given a little help or guidance, could advance swiftly. We also observed how prolifically your species could procreate if you could improve your infant mortality rates.

"Prior to the ice comet hitting your planet and subsequently wiping the dinosaurs out, we did abduct some humans to study and conduct experiments on. This helped us to better understand your species and what kind of planetary and atmospheric conditions you required to survive. We learned what kinds of extreme conditions your species was resilient to and how your bodies could or couldn't adapt. When the comet headed toward Earth, we did try to stop it. We succeeded in melting large amounts of the ice, and we had tried to change its course—ultimately, what we succeeded in doing was breaking it down into smaller chunks. Most of the comet missed Earth, but the piece that did hit destroyed the semicrystalline firmament around the planet. The damage to that enclosure dramatically changed the atmosphere of Earth and was responsible for changes in the landmass structures on your planet."

"Are you talking about the splitting of Pangaea into the different continents?" Miles asked incredulously.

"Yes, exactly," Handolly replied. "When the comet hit, it caused an enormous amount of volcanic activity across the planet as the impact shifted the tectonic plates. With the firmament around the planet now gone, the greenhouse effect it had caused on your planet was suddenly removed. This also resulted in a dramatic atmospheric pressure change. For example, when you are at sea level, each square inch of your surface is subjected to a force of fourteen point six pounds. When you go underwater, that pressure increases by roughly one atmosphere for every ten meters of depth. When the atmosphere changed, your bodies were suddenly subjected to an entirely different level of pressure. It changed your development, the way you walked, the physical strength of your species. Most importantly, you evolved, and your species learned how to change with the environment, something the dinosaurs and many other species were unable to do."

Miles held a hand up. "Handolly, you are talking about evolution, and while I find that subject interesting, I am not an expert in it. I cannot confirm or disprove what you are saying or implying, and frankly, it isn't important to what I am after or what you and I need to talk about. This is what I mean—you bring up something interesting, something not pertinent, and you use that to deflect away from what we need to be talking about. Like when did you first transplant humans to other worlds, how many worlds, and most importantly…why? Why did you guys do it? *This* is what we need to be discussing, not hashing over evolutionary theories that don't advance our talks."

Altairians generally didn't have many facial expressions, something that made it hard to understand them or judge what was going on during a talk. But Miles could see a noticeable change in Handolly's face. It looked like it was tensing up.

He lowered his chin as he replied to Miles, "It *is* important to this conversation. It sets the foundation for why we interceded."

The two of them stared at each other for a moment, not saying anything. Finally, Miles relented. "OK, please continue, Handolly. I'll do my best not to interrupt again."

The Altairian's facial expression appeared to soften as he returned to his previous thought. "As I was saying—when the comet was headed toward Earth, we were not sure if your species would survive. We also didn't want to let your species go extinct from something like this, so we intervened. We began to abduct thousands and thousands of your people.

We largely did this at night, when we could sedate them and move them without hurting them or causing severe emotional reactions. Once on our ships, we got them sedated for the journey to Sumer. The Qatana system was the lead system to a chain of planets that held suitable habitats for human life to flourish on. As you know, the Qatana system leads to four additional systems. Each system has one planet capable of sustaining life. However, the system you have named the Agora system had three planets capable of sustaining humans. We placed small groups of humans on each of these planets. Unfortunately, the humans we had originally placed in the Agora system were unable to cope with the natural predators on the planet and were killed off. In the end, only three of the seven planets of humans managed to survive to this date."

"So these three systems in the Qatana region are the only systems the Altairians populated humans on?"

Handolly paused for a moment before adding, "These are the planets *we* repopulated with humans. That is not to say humans have not been taken either from Earth or any of these other systems by other species and either studied or repopulated on other moons or planets. The Zodarks are a case in point. During our first war with them, they captured the Qatana region and a few other systems. They learned of the humans on these planets and eventually developed some sort of initial relationship with them. From what we can gather now that we have access to Sumer again, it appears the Zodarks chose to show themselves in the form of some sort of gods or magical deities. They provided the humans on Sumer with radical technological developments that caused them to skip hundreds, maybe even thousands of years of evolutionary development.

"Medical technologies provided by the Zodarks reduced the infant mortality rates to nearly zero. Agricultural improvements enabled them to produce enormous quantities of food that could be grown and harvested through the use of machines. All they asked for in exchange was a small tribute or sacrifice if you will. There was a period of time when the Sumerians actually refused the tributes. The Zodarks stopped operating the equipment they'd provided and essentially turned every piece of technology on the planet off. The Sumerians went through a terrible three-year period of famine, disease, and ultimately death before they determined life was better under the tribute system than it had been before. In their eyes, it was an easier thing to live with than what they had just gone through."

Miles for his part sat and listened with rapt attention. He finished his glass of wine off and asked for another. During his days at the Academy, he'd taken a course in authoritarianism, something every officer studied in the post–World War III recovery days. In the class, they'd talked about how people would invariably suffer through, or even accept in some cases, authoritarianism so long as their basic needs and desires were being met. Some of those desires ranged from enough food to eat to security and safety. When a government could implement a form of classical conditioning, which was often referred to as the Pavlovian conditioning effect, people would invariably be willing to accept edicts and rules that most people would otherwise find revolting or completely unacceptable. In the case of the Sumerians, the Zodarks had conditioned the people through the providing of technology, food security, and physical security but made that contingent on their willingness to adhere to this tribute system they had put in place.

Handolly continued to explain, "For the longest time, we had no idea what the Zodarks were doing with the Sumerians or any of the other human-populated planets. We eventually learned about this tribute system, but again, we were unaware of their designs or what they intended to do with these humans they took in tribute. Now, it would appear they have been populating additional planets with humans to cultivate some sort of army they had intended to use in their conquest to supplant the Orbots. Ultimately, I believe they would eventually turn that army on the rest of us, but not until they had succeeded in removing the Orbots."

"Let me ask you something, Handolly. What is so special about the Orbots? Why do you believe the Zodarks would have to supplant the Orbots before they unleashed this human army they've trained? Why not just introduce this new army and unleash them on our alliance right now?"

"That is a complicated answer. As you already know, the Gallentines are our patrons. They have appointed you to be their Viceroy, representing them and their will in the Milky Way galaxy. Similarly, the Collective have essentially made the Orbots your counterpart in our galaxy. Because of this, the Zodarks must tread carefully. If they were going to challenge the Orbots, then they would need to accomplish that conquest incredibly rapidly or face a potential problem from the Collective. It is likely they may not get involved, but it is also likely that the Orbots would ask the Collective for help. My own opinion is the Zodarks will likely use this peace treaty to rebuild their military and better position their ships to defend against and deflect your weapons. You were right to point out those new frigates and corvettes they had introduced recently. I would wager they will start producing more of these kinds of ships and integrate more of them in a future conflict. In either case, many of us Altairians believe the Zodarks are going to emerge from this conflict in a much stronger position than when they first started."

"That is my thought as well," Miles replied. "This is why I believe we need to massively reorganize the alliance and our fleets. When I was with the Gallentines, they offered to help us build several of their warships. If I am not mistaken, they're even more powerful than the ones you use. Our problem is if we choose to build them, there are several key minerals and components that are not easy to source or produce. One of those minerals is Bronkis-5, a mineral that we have learned is found on Alfheim. It's the reason we fought to capture that planet and why the Orbots joined the Zodarks in battling us for it as well. I have survey teams starting to spread out across every known and friendly system we can enter, looking to find more of it, but this will take time. Then there is this other mineral called Toriander crystal. It's apparently the fuel source for these Gallentine reactors. It's also used in the lenses for the ships' laser batteries. I'm not sure how that all works, but it's another resource we're now scouring to find."

Miles sighed, then continued, "For the time being, at least until we can identify additional sources for these materials, I believe we're going to need to stick with building more of these Altairian-Human hybrid ships. I had originally wanted to move in the direction of the Gallentine warships, and I think we'll build them as we are able to, but for a standard across-the-board alliance warship, we're going to need to stay with what we can currently build."

Handolly nodded in agreement. "I think that would be a wise move, Miles. Your suggestion to create versions of the ship to best meet the crew demands of each race was brilliant. It will make the adoption of these uniformed ships across the different species of ships much easier to implement."

"Handolly, going forward, our two people need to be able to work together a lot more effectively than we have. I know my promotion to Viceroy, essentially taking that position over from your own people, has not sat well with many Altairians. This was not a position I sought or wanted, but when the Emperor chose me for it, I accepted. I made a commitment to the Emperor that I would seek to bring unity to our alliance. I also vowed to either put an end to the wars or achieve some sort of peace. We have now achieved peace with the Dominion; how long that peace may last will depend on the enemy. With one of those goals achieved, I want to focus more on unifying the alliance. This is why we're going to move forward with moving the alliance seat of power to New Eden. We're going to start fresh, if you will. It'll almost feel like a brand-new alliance, full of optimism and hope. This new alliance city we're building is going to be amazing."

"So you are still wanting to move forward with that?" Handolly asked.

"We are. The city isn't completed yet, but once it gets a bit closer to being done, we'll look to relocate the councilmembers and their immediate staff and families. As more of the city and the supporting buildings for the alliance are complete, we'll transition the rest of the alliance's functions. We've also just started construction on five of the new ring stations, just like the one you have around your planet. When those stations are complete, the number of warships we'll be able to produce will be staggering," Miles explained proudly.

When their meal finally arrived, they paused their business conversation and moved to family. Handolly opened up more than he had previously to Miles. He told him that he was nearly four hundred years old. His age astonished Miles, who was still getting used to humans now living into their midhundreds. His Gallentine doctor told Miles that theoretically, as long as he continued to receive medical nanites, he could live well into the high hundreds. In a way, that sounded amazing—being around long enough to see how humanity continued to evolve.

Handolly shared with him that he had been coupled a total of four times. Coupling was what the Altairians called marriage. His first coupling had lasted forty-six years. He and his wife had six children during that period. Sadly, they had grown apart from each other and eventually had just become roommates. They had ended their coupling on amicable terms. His second coupling ended when his wife had been killed in an accident during their fourth year of marriage. They didn't have any children, which Handolly said made it easier to recover from. In total, Handolly had sixteen children—those children had gone on to have seventy-eight grandchildren. It was fascinating to Miles to think that he could live long enough to watch his own kids have children of their own and then watch the process repeated with subsequent generations. He and Lilly could live long enough to see multiple generations of Hunts.

When they had finished their dinner, Hunt circled back to one piece of business: logistics and trade. The Republic was in desperate need of transports, for both civilians and goods. By the end of their meeting, Miles was able to secure a shipbuilding agreement that would net the Republic some five hundred cargo haulers and three hundred and fifty civilian transports. It wouldn't completely end the chronic shortage the Republic was facing, but it'd certainly put a dent in it.

Chapter Twenty-Eight
Earthly Ceremonies

Earth, Sol
Three Months Post–Peace Treaty

If there was one thing Brian Royce hated, it had to be military dog-and-pony shows, from change of command ceremonies to now victory parades. His company of Delta operators had thus far performed in no fewer than eight of these parades since arriving on Earth more than a month ago. The Republic had been putting these victory parades on every weekend and planned on hosting them for at least another two months. They were doing their best to have a parade take place in each city with a population greater than a hundred thousand people. With more than ten thousand company-sized elements involved, they were averaging twenty thousand parades around the world each weekend. By the time the three-month victory tour was over, they'd have done one hundred and twenty thousand parades.

Royce's company was among the most decorated in Special Forces, so naturally they had been selected to receive the public's accolades and show the tax-paying people of the Republic just who they had been supporting. Try as he might to get them out of this boondoggle, they were stuck. Not only stuck having to perform them, but they also had to parade around in their dress uniforms, medals, and all. The only saving grace was that he'd somehow managed to land them on a tour of North America. For many of the members in his unit, this was home.

During each of these parades, one or two of his soldiers would receive one of their valor awards with the citation being read aloud for the crowd's sake. He found this kind of an awkward way of honoring their bravery, but as he had been told by Major Jayden Hopper, it was all part of the public's way of honoring them and showing just how vicious and tough this war had been. One of the good things that came out of the parades and even some of the medal presentations was they never had to buy a drink or pay for a meal in any city they traveled to. If you asked his soldiers, they'd tell you they were getting laid on a daily basis by the locals, who wanted to show a bit more of a private "thank you for your service."

Following the conclusion of one such parade in Idaho Falls, Royce found a sports bar that was airing the Sunday afternoon football game. He was still in his dress uniform, his rows of medals on full display, but right now he was hungry and wanted to watch some football. His first sergeant and platoon leaders had things covered, so he figured he'd get a burger, drink a few beers, and watch some football. He'd downed his first beer and was nursing his second when the waitress brought his dinner. He'd ordered a fat, juicy buffalo burger with a bacon-mayo jam of some sort, three slices of peppercorn bacon, two slices of cheddar, pickles, onion straws, lettuce, and tomato. On the side, he had baked beans and some fries.

Biting into that burger, he felt the hot juices from the meat run down his chin as he wiped it away with a napkin. *Oh my God, that tastes so good...*

"I'll bet they don't make burgers like that on a starship, do they?" a redhead sitting a couple seats down from him said.

Royce looked to his right, suddenly conscious of himself eating. "Uh, no, ma'am, they sure don't."

The redhead slid over to the empty seat next to him. She was attractive, likely in her thirties, but then again, with the medical nanites it was hard to tell how old someone was these days unless they were a Luddite.

"That was a nice parade today."

Royce had just taken another bite, so he couldn't respond just yet. That was likely a good thing. Washing his food down with a sip of his beer, he said, "We're all just doing our part. The public deserves to see the brave men and women fighting for them."

"That's true. But I'll bet you're more than a little tired of doing this every weekend."

Royce wasn't sure what she was trying to get at with her line of questioning. "You a reporter?"

She blushed at the question. "Would that be a bad thing if I was?"

Oh great, just what I need. Becoming a story for tomorrow's headlines.

"Well, if you are, then I'm not really at liberty to say one way or another. The people of the Republic have financed and supported us for nearly fourteen years. They are entitled to see the folks they've been supporting. Besides, many of my soldiers are from North America, so they're using this opportunity to see friends and family who they haven't seen in years."

"That's great for them. Just so you know, I'm not a reporter, soldier boy. I work for a company that provides some component parts to Walburg Industries. We help to build those C100 combat Synths you guys have been going through like mad."

Breathing a sigh of relief, Royce let his guard down a bit. "Well, I'll tell you this. Those terminators have saved our bacon on more than one occasion."

"Terminators?" she asked, her left eyebrow rising a bit.

Shrugging, he said, "Yeah, we have a few nicknames for them. Synths, Toasters, Terminators, Bots—it's just nicknames. Some of the guys will actually name the C100s themselves. I'm not a big believer in going that far. The fact is most of them end up getting destroyed in one battle or another. Some manage to make it through an entire campaign, but not many. We're pretty hard on them."

"Honestly, it's nice to hear they're making a difference. We don't hear a whole lot about the war. I mean, we all watched that woman admiral, Fran McKee, for a while. She had some incredible footage shot of the invasion of Alfheim and the battle that took place in the system. That was really the first time most people in the Republic had seen stuff like that on a regular basis."

Royce had heard about Admiral McKee leveraging a film crew to do some bi-ops on her crew and some of the soldiers down on the planet. She thought it'd be a good way for the people back home to learn what kinds of struggles the fleet and the RA were going through. She was right too. The nation was becoming seriously war-weary. The drafts of young men and women just kept coming, and so too did the names of those killed on far-flung planets light-years away from Earth.

"Are those Zodarks really that tough?" the woman asked.

"What's your name?"

"Silly of me, I should have introduced myself. I'm Jane Burton," she said, blushing, as she stuck her hand out.

Royce noticed she didn't have a ring on her hand either. "Nice to meet you, Jane. My name is Brian Royce. I'm a captain, a Delta operator."

Suddenly her eyes went wide. "No way, you're *the* Brian Royce? Of Special Forces?"

"Uh, yes. That's me. Why?" Now he was confused. *Why would she be impressed by meeting me?*

"Um, wow. You're like a national hero. I remember watching your video of you fighting all those Zodarks on your own when you guys captured that Zodark carrier. They showed us that video at our work, telling us this is what the Zodarks looked like and this man, Master Sergeant Brian Royce, needed our help in producing combat synthetics if we wanted to win the war. I didn't know they had promoted you into the officer ranks."

"Ah, OK. Yeah, once we secured that carrier, I was promoted to lieutenant. Then through natural attrition, I was promoted again to captain, where I'll likely stay for a while now that the war is over with."

"Yeah, I'll bet you're glad it's over. You guys can all come home now."

"Come home? No, I doubt that. We've got more than a handful of moons and planets to colonize. I suspect they'll keep us Special Forces busy for a while doing missions on those planets and moons. Besides, I think this peace treaty is just going to be a lull in the fighting. Those Zodarks will never accept our people or surrender."

"Oh yeah? What makes you think that?"

"Um, fourteen years of fighting them. Besides, it was the Orbots that demanded they accept the peace treaty. The Zodarks had no say in it," Royce explained in between bites.

As he worked on finishing his burger, he regaled her with tales of some of the planets he'd seen. He told her about a couple of the moons and how unique and different they were from Earth's own moon or some of the moons around Jupiter or Saturn. She was fascinated by what he was telling her. They ended up spending the entire afternoon and into the early evening just talking.

"So, Brian," she started out, acting all coy, "how long are you in town before you have to head out again?"

"Unfortunately, we're only here until Wednesday. Then we head out to the next city and get ready to do this dog-and-pony show two more times over the weekend."

Royce was now thoroughly getting ticked off about constantly being on the move. Jane could see he was disappointed. "You know, if you'd like to come over for dinner tonight, I can make you a homemade meal. I could even whip up some breakfast in bed, food for a real war hero."

Wow, a homemade meal, and breakfast in bed...how can I say no?

"That, Jane, would be marvelous. Do I have time to change out of this and into some more comfortable clothes?"

"Oh, but then I wouldn't get to see you wearing all your medals," she said with a flirtatious smirk. "But yeah, that works. I'll send you my address. Be there at eight?"

Once she'd sent him her address, she gave him a brief hug and left, presumably to get whatever she was going to prepare in the next couple of hours. Brian settled his tab and left to find his hotel so he could change and get ready.

When he showed up that evening, his senses were bombarded by the most incredible smells. Whatever she was cooking, it smelled great. Once he was inside her house, she guided him back to the kitchen. She had thrown a roast into one of the one-pot wonders. The pots had evolved over the years but by and large, it was the same concept. You placed your protein in the center of the pot along with your diced vegetables and all the herbs and spices and let it cook for a few hours. Jane had already opened a bottle of red wine and had a couple of full glasses waiting for them. Since the pot roast needed a little while longer, they grabbed their wine and moved over to the family room.

Sitting in the family room like this, sipping on some wine, did start to make him miss home. He'd been gone for so long and moved so often he'd never really had the opportunity to call any place home. His longest stint on Earth had been as a drill sergeant at Fort Benning. Unfortunately, that kind of job literally sucked the life right out of you, so he had little time for dating or finding someone to fall in love with. Then the war had started, and needless to say, his life had changed once again.

The following morning, he woke up to the sight of a beautiful woman nestled against his chest. He didn't want to wake up. He wanted to savor this moment right there. Just as he was about to try and slide out of bed to scrounge up some breakfast for them, he got a message sent through his neurolink. It was from his first sergeant. Opening the message, he saw a police blotter report. Last night, four of his guys had had a bit too much to drink and gotten in a fight with some locals.

Oh, this ended poorly, he thought as he finished reading the message.

His soldiers were being held in the county jail. His first sergeant told him he'd have to be the one to sign for them and post the bail. Royce woke Jane up and explained what had happened. He told her he'd have to take a rain check on the breakfast in bed.

Before he got dressed and left, they vowed to stay in contact and spend as much time as they could together as they could while he was still on Earth. With the hyperloop transportation system and air travel, it was pretty easy to get from one point of the country to another. It also helped that Royce was sitting on more than ten years of salary and bonus money he'd made along the way. He'd also wisely invested a lot of his money into Walberg Industries when he had seen the first use of the C100. He'd known right away the government would be buying these things in the millions if not tens of millions, and he planned on riding that stock for as long as he could.

Chapter Twenty-Nine
Jackpot

Three Months Post-Treaty
Free Trader *Wawat*
Rhea System

Sitting on the bridge of the *Wawat*, Dakkuri waited for his sensors to come back online. They had just exited the stargate, entering the Rhea system.

"We're being hailed by a nearby destroyer, Dakkuri," Namtar, his communications operative, announced.

"Connect me through to them."

A moment later, Namtar gave a signal he was connected.

"This is the Free Trader *Wawat* en route to Emerald City Spaceport. How copy?"

A momentary pause ensued before the radio came back to life.

"Free Trader *Wawat*, this is the RNS *Donald Jones*. Please transmit your travel log and passport papers," came a stern voice.

"Transmitting now."

For the next five minutes, they just sat there, floating in space maybe twenty thousand meters from the destroyer. Dakkuri had to admit, that Republic destroyer looked menacing. It had some actual gun turrets mounted on it, and at this precise moment, they were trained right at them.

"Free Trader *Wawat*, your information checks out. You are cleared to travel to Emerald City Spaceport. Please report to Space Operations once you are within one million meters of the station and wait for clearance to approach. It's a busy spaceport. Out."

With permission to finally move forward, Dakkuri told Sadat to get their engines spun up to maximum and set course for the station. Once their ship had cleared the gate and the defensive platforms around it, Sadat jumped the ship in the direction of Clovis, or New Eden as these Earthers now called it. Dakkuri was still having a hard time wrapping his head around how this supposedly inferior species had bested their Zodark overlords. It almost made him wonder if he was serving the wrong side.

Pushing those negative thoughts aside, he did his best to stay focused on the mission at hand. Once they arrived at the spaceport, he'd offload his forty-two passengers, all members of his spy network. Each of them would then arrange their own travel to their assigned planets and cities. Then they'd look to establish a series of safe houses, forged documents, money, and other necessary pieces of tradecraft for the others who would follow behind them in the coming weeks and months. Once the *Wawat* was docked, he'd try to find some shipping contracts that would allow him to travel to other planets, specifically Earth.

"We're coming out of FTL now," Sadat announced loudly. Dakkuri could hear the excitement in the young man's voice. They were all enthusiastic; this was the first time any of them had seen a non-Zodark-controlled world. They had no idea what to expect or what they might encounter.

When the FTL bubble collapsed around their ship, it took just a moment for their scanners to pick up what was going on around them. What they saw once the sensors were operational again nearly took their breath away. The planet they had known as Clovis had been transformed into a hustling, bustling Mecca of ships coming and going.

Both Sadat and Namtar looked back at him in awe. This was not what they had been expecting to see. This was not what they had been told they should see.

Picking his own jaw up off the floor, Dakkuri announced, "OK, everyone, let's get back to doing what we came here for. Sadat, bring us into the station. Make contact with Space Operations and get us clearance to approach and park. Namtar, activate our passive sensors and let's start absorbing as much of the activity going on around us as possible. Oh, and, Namtar—activate the Lanish and give it three pings. That should give us more than enough data to map the system."

A chorus of "yes, sirs" rang out as his two crewmen went to work. While that was happening, Dakkuri pulled up his own computer monitor and started sifting through the initial pieces of information they were already getting returns on. One thing he noticed immediately was the number of warships near the planet and its two moons. It wasn't a small number. More concerning was the size of some of these ships.

The tonnage on some of those larger warships is astronomical. Those must be their battleships, Dakkuri realized. Seeing the massive warships also made him a little concerned about using the Lanish scanners. He'd been told it was an advanced piece of Orbot technology that was strong enough to scan damn near an entire star system so long as you stayed in the system long enough to receive all the signal returns.

For the next twenty-four hours, they continued their approach to the Emerald City spaceport. It was a large space station connected to a space elevator tethering them to the planet. From their vantage point, the station looked to be about twenty decks in height. At the top and bottom decks of the station were sets of docking arms or spokes that extended outwards from the station for about one kilometer. Many of the docking arms looked like they had ships tethered to them. It was a very busy spaceport.

"Do you suppose those are all transport or cargo ships?" Sadat asked as they continued to get closer to them.

"I think those ships there"—Namtar pointed to a group of ships near the top of the stations docking arms—"look like some sort of cruise liners. The entire side of the ship has multiple decks full of windows like a passenger liner would. If that was a cargo ship, it wouldn't have nearly as many windows."

Namtar's explanation made sense. Dakkuri made a mental note to include such astute observations into his own report. Judging by the number of ships they were looking at, either a lot of people were coming to New Eden from somewhere else, or they were on their way to another planet—maybe Sumer or one of their other holdings. In either case, it only reinforced his private assumptions that these Earthers were the real deal. They hadn't just gotten lucky against the Zodarks; they'd beaten them solidly.

As they neared the station to dock at the slip they had been directed to, Dakkuri was able to use their shipboard camera to get some good close-in camera shots of a ship he was assuming was a battleship. It was enormous. Aside from the gigantic front-mounted turrets, both the underbelly and top of the ship appeared to be armed with hundreds of what he had to assume were antiship missiles given the size of them. Then he saw something small fly out of what looked like a launch tube near the front left side of the ship. Several additional smaller objects flew out, joining the first one. Doing his best to zoom in and follow them with his camera, Dakkuri suddenly realized what they were—fighters.

Namtar turned to Dakkuri. "I count at least six of these large warships here."

Dakkuri didn't reply; he just nodded in acknowledgment. Something new had caught his eye. When he zoomed his camera in on it, he nearly lost his breath. He saw a massive structure being assembled further away from the station. Right now, it just looked like a giant flat platform that was being rapidly expanded upon. In some areas of the large platform, it appeared that walls and rooms were being built. But what caused him to nearly lose his breath wasn't the construction of this structure; it was the small army of humanoid machines working in the vacuum of space on it. He'd seen images of what the Earthers were calling C100s or combat synthetics, but he'd had no idea they had worker versions like this. He now understood how these Earthers had been able to build all their warships in such a short time. They had an army of machines building them around the clock.

This is something the Zodarks are definitely going to want to know about.

Once the *Wawat* had docked, they were met by an inspection team. The inspectors came aboard and looked around the ship. They checked their cargo hold against the manifest, making sure they were in fact hauling what they said they would be. They were carrying twenty tons of material from Sumer to New Eden. From there, they'd take twenty tons of Andorra meat from New Eden to Earth, then they'd grab another supply contract and move goods from Earth to Alpha Centaurus. Finally, they'd make their way back along the same route until they ended up back on Sumer. All told, they should be gone for roughly seventeen months, scouting and mapping the Earthers' core systems for what would surely be an invasion of epic proportions.

Now that they had cleared customs, their cargo hold was unlocked, and half a dozen synthetic dockworkers began the process of unloading the specialty items they'd brought with them from Sumer to be sold. Dakkuri told his human cargo it was time for them to disperse and start their own operations. The operatives left the ship in small groups of no more than two or three at a time, so it wouldn't appear like they all came from the same ship. They'd now do their best to infiltrate their assigned targets and disappear in plain sight until they were activated.

Sadat walked up to Dakkuri. "Everyone has left the ship. It's just us. Would it be OK if Namtar, Chryssoula, and I took a couple of days and went to the surface? We have a lot of places we need to try and visit before we head out on our next contract." They had five days until their shipment of Andorran meat would be ready to load.

"Yeah, I can manage things here at the station," Dakkari answered. "But I'm going to need Namtar back here in two days, so make sure you tell him. I'm going to check out some of the stores on the promenade here and look around the place."

"Hey, why don't you see about grabbing us a couple of those worker synthetics? I think Chryssoula could use a hand in engineering, and we could use them to help us with loading and unloading this thing when we reach Earth," Sadat offered.

Dakkuri snickered. "A strapping young man like you should not have any trouble loading and unloading the cargo hold."

The two of them laughed for a moment before the rest of the team arrived. Dakkuri made sure Namtar knew he had to be back in forty-eight hours. Once the group left, Dakkuri did as well. He locked up the ship and then secured the docking bay door as well. With everything safeguarded, he made his way to the trolley system situated in the center of the docking arm. All along the trolley route were warehouses that connected to freight cars and the cargo vessels themselves.

The more Dakkuri saw of just this part of the operation, the more impressed he was with these Earthers. The docking arms along the sides of the station extended close to two thousand meters from the station and were about four hundred meters wide, giving them more than enough room to have a two-lane trolley system that would ferry passengers and crewmen from their ships all the way to the station and back. Next to the civilian trolley system was a more complex system for cargo. This line ran much closer to the warehouses. Along this route, if a particular slip was taking on a large load, they had a secondary parking lane, allowing additional freight to still move on the mainline while the load was transferred to the ship.

The way they could take on or unload cargo from the station was incredible. He suspected they made heavy use of synthetic workers because they could work around the clock, and they never tired. When Dakkuri had made it off the docking arm and into the center part of the station, one of the first things he did was consult a map of the station. Prior to leaving the *Wawat*, he had made sure he had his special contact lenses in. He wanted a recording of everything he was about to see.

For the next six hours, Dakkuri walked the station. He checked out every deck and every position he was given access to. Sadly, at least a quarter of the station was off-limits to civilians. Not that it mattered much; he was still able to see most of the station.

Once on the promenade, Dakkuri found a shop for Walburg Industries and made his way in. This was the storefront he had been told would sell him the synthetic humanoids. When he walked in, he saw the standard four versions one could purchase, but none of the combat versions. When he asked about them, the store proprietor just laughed. He told him no one could purchase a C100. He ended up buying an engineering Synth and two general-purpose ones they'd end up using for loading and unloading their ship.

Since he had a couple of days until Namtar returned, Dakkuri figured he'd spend some time at a handful of the bars on the station. He wanted to try and gain a better understanding of his new adversaries. When he spoke with some people and asked what they thought of the Zodarks or how they felt about the war, he got an earful. The people he talked with were scared of them. They'd seen a lot of video footage of them inflicting carnage, but they also knew they could be defeated. The people were extremely confident in their fleet and Army's ability to battle the Zodarks and even the Orbots, anywhere, anytime, and reign victorious. When Dakkuri asked why they were so confident about defeating the Zodarks, the answer they gave him was a surprise. He was told that outside of a few battles, the Republic Army had never been defeated by them.

When Dakkuri heard this, he had to stifle his desire to probe beyond what they were casually providing. A few folks showed him images of their sons or daughters, fathers or mothers or siblings in uniform. They were proud of what their family member was doing, and they told him about the battles they had fought in. A few of them even had some combat footage they had managed to smuggle past the censors. They played a few of the video clips for him. Dakkuri had to admit, it was terrifying seeing the Zodark soldiers in combat. Even as a member of the Mukhabarat, he'd seldom seen them fighting like he had in these short video clips. But what he found more interesting was these people's family members. The way they moved and fought unnerved him. Between their incredibly effective infantry assault rifles and their exoskeleton combat suits and body armor—it was remarkable to watch.

Dakkuri asked how the soldiers' helmets worked. One of the people at the bar then asked him, "Why all the questions? Have you never seen any of this equipment before?" More than a handful of people suddenly start to eye him suspiciously.

Holding his hands up in mock surrender, he countered, "My name is Dakkuri. Sorry for all the questions. I am Sumerian, from the planet Sumer. We were recently liberated from the Zodarks. I have only seen limited numbers of your soldiers. I know they are brave, and I know they show true compassion and concern for noncombatants, something the Zodarks do not."

The folks nearest him at the bar suddenly relaxed. One of them bought him another round of beer as he started to talk. "My name is Glenn Cronkite. I served in the Republic Army for thirty-two years and likely would still be serving if I hadn't lost both my legs." Glenn turned his chair a bit to face Dakkuri and pulled up on his pants a little bit to show off a pair of metal prosthetic legs. "They got ripped off right above the knees when our Osprey started taking enemy ground fire. I'm not totally sure how it all went down. Some of my buddies with me said it was chaotic and hectic when our Osprey got hit. It all happened so fast. One minute I was going over the battle plan with my half of the platoon, and then next thing I knew, we had crashed. Then I woke up on a hospital ship and they told me I had lost my legs."

"I'm sorry for your loss," Dakkuri offered. "If I can ask, do you regret attacking the Zodarks all those years ago on Clovis?"

"Regret *attacking* them? Whoa, you got your facts mixed up. We went to New Eden in peace. I was there. We sent our ambassador forward to speak with them and *they* attacked *us*. They kidnapped the ambassador and did all kinds of terrible things to her. That's when we went in and smashed their base and the war started." Glenn paused for a second before adding, "All we wanted was to start a dialogue. Instead, we were viciously assaulted. Now we're taking the fight to them. Personally, I don't think this peace will hold out much longer. I think the war will be back on in a couple of years."

This comment kind of surprised Dakkuri. He was curious why this Earther would think that. "Do you think the Republic will restart the war?"

Glenn took a sip of his beer. He then shook his head in what appeared to be frustration. "You know, prior to losing my legs, I had spent almost nine years fighting the Zodarks, and to a lesser extent, the Orbots, so I'd like to think I have a little bit of an understanding of how these two species operate. The Orbots appear to just be focused on technological advancements and chasing something called transcendence, whatever that means. The Zodarks, on the other hand— well, they're just bloodthirsty animals that want to conquer the entire galaxy. They seem to operate with no rules, or at least without the standard rules most species govern themselves by, like trying to provide a safe environment for their people to thrive and grow within.

"This may come as a surprise to you, coming from Sumer, but the God's honest truth is the Republic doesn't want war. We never have. What we want is peace—peace to expand into the stars and colonize new worlds and moons. We want to explore, to establish colonies free of Zodark threats. My personal opinion, Dakkuri, is that the Zodarks will find a way to restart the war. But God help them if they do."

Dakkuri spent another hour at the bar talking with Glenn and a few others, completely fascinated by their perspective of the Zodarks. Having spent his entire life living inside the Zodark empire, Dakkuri had never been exposed to any opinions outside of what had been determined acceptable. What he was hearing from all these people was hard for him not to comment on. He felt he should say something or defend the Zodarks, but he knew if he did, it would likely blow his cover. He had to keep reminding himself he was here for a reason, a mission. He needed to stay focused on that and not allow himself to get distracted.

Once his ship had been fully loaded with Andorran meat and his crew had completed their individual missions, they pushed off from Emerald Station. They'd now been given the official coordinates for Sol, and soon enough they'd catch their first glimpse of Earth, the seat of power for this upstart starfaring species called the Republic.

Chapter Thirty
A Return to Normalcy

Four Months Post–Peace Treaty
Space Command Headquarters
Jacksonville, Arkansas
Earth, Sol

Fleet Admiral Chester Bailey stared at Chancellor Luca and Senator Chuck Walhoon and a few other senators from the Defense Committee and Ways and Means Committee, in shock at what they had just proposed for his budget.

"I know what you're thinking, Chester—we're cutting the budget at a time when we should be spending more," said Chancellor Luca. "But frankly, we can't afford to keep spending money on the military like this. We have to start building up an interstellar infrastructure to support our growing presence in these other systems." She was obviously trying to soften the blow.

Chester countered, "Chancellor, I know we have to put resources into building our infrastructure, but we also need to put resources into building up our Navy. That last battle in the Sirius system cost us eighteen percent of our entire fleet. We're short hundreds if not thousands of warships—ships that take time to build and time to train up their crews. This treaty with the Dominion has given us the time we need to get our Navy built up and ready for whatever may come next down the road. Please don't let us squander this opportunity."

"Admiral," Senator Walhoon said in his thick Texas drawl, "we aren't trimming back on the size of the fleet you want for the Navy. We're just slowing its pace of construction down so we can rein in government spending. These ring stations the Gallentines are helping us build are enormous. They're sucking up tremendous amounts of resources. The government just doesn't have the funds to build all these different things at once. We have to start picking our priorities better."

Chester shook his head in frustration. "The first two ring stations are being financed by the Gallentines," he insisted. "Plus, as we get more trade going between our alliance allies, we'll bring in the needed tax revenues to keep things running as they are."

"The Gallentines are covering the costs of the first two ring stations, but as you know, we're building three additional stations," Chancellor Luca reminded him. "This is all part of our infrastructure plan. I'm afraid we can't afford to keep producing warships at the same pace we have been and still fund the construction of these stations. We also need to let some of the shipyards return to civilian construction. The demand for freighters and cargo haulers of all sizes is enormous. The yards need to start filling those orders so we can get that trade between our allies moving again."

Chester knew this was going to be a losing battle. He let out a deep sigh. Then an idea popped into his head. "OK, I understand we're in a pinch for cargo haulers for the civilian market. Right now, the fleet has eighty-six cargo haulers with another fourteen still under construction. What if I released half the cargo haulers for civilian use? We can charge whatever the prevailing cargo rates are, but whatever moneys they earn would be plowed back into our coffers. Could that work? My transport fleet can help fill the current void and the moneys we earn will go toward covering the reduction in our budget."

Several of the senators seemed to like the idea. Chancellor Luca turned to Senator Walhoon. "Well, Chuck, what do you think? This could be a win-win for everyone."

The senator thought about that for a moment. The gears in his brain were clearly crunching through numbers and data. "I'm generally not a big fan of using military assets like this because if we're not careful, you guys could seriously undercut legitimate civilian businesses. How about this—you create a separate command or squadron that'll run these ships and then we assign a government contracting rep to be their deputy to help oversee things and make sure you guys aren't undercutting other civilian freight shipping companies. Fair enough?"

Chester knew this was about as good as he was going to get. He readily agreed. He'd offer up the Navy's small mining fleet he'd built over the years to keep the materials for his warships coming, but frankly, he needed those resources himself. The freight transportation would have to suffice.

Then, just as they were about to wrap the meeting up, one of the senators commented, "Admiral, if I'm not mistaken, in addition to cargo haulers, you also have a large troopship transport fleet built up. Do you think you might be able to part with some of them to complement the

301

cargo haulers? Being able to move large quantities of civilians to these new worlds is also something we desperately need."

Chester was kicking himself for not thinking of that earlier. They had seventy troop transport ships—vessels that could transport upwards of fifty-five thousand soldiers for months on end.

"Thank you for bringing that up, Senator. I'd honestly completely forgotten about them. I agree, though, we should look to include some of them," Chester conceded. "Let me get with my logistics folks and find out how many we can part with for an extended period of time. My planners are still trying to figure out where we're going to base all of these soldiers and how many soldiers we want forward-deployed on our new colonies."

"Speaking of new colonies—outside of Earth, where are we going to keep most of our forces at now that we're not going to be using Alfheim as a forward staging base?" Senator Walhoon asked.

Chester pulled up some information and then shared it to the holograph puck on the center of the table, which projected an image for them to look at. "As of right now, the Army stands at eight million, six hundred thousand strong. Of that, we have two Ranger divisions with a strength of twelve thousand five hundred each. Special Forces are broken down into four Special Forces groups. Each group comprises roughly five thousand Deltas, and there are another fifteen thousand support troops. We have Groups One and Two stationed on Earth, with Groups Three and Four currently on New Eden. Elements of each group have been dispersed on other Moons or planets, but these units rotate back and forth, so we don't have one battalion deployed all the time.

"When it comes to the ground forces, that's an entirely different conversation. We have one million on New Eden, five hundred thousand on Sumer, three hundred thousand spread across the other moons and planets in Sol, a million five hundred thousand on the Primord planet Intus, and another million and a half on Alpha Centaurus, leaving the remaining three million two hundred thousand on Earth. We also have two million still in various stages of their military training here on Earth."

Chancellor Luca chimed in, "That circles us right back to the ongoing draft. Is it really necessary to keep it going now that the war is done?"

The draft had been very unpopular. People were still volunteering for military service, so not nearly as many people had to be drafted. The biggest challenge they had with the draft was the information black hole. The battles were being fought so far away that it took time for any news or casualty reports to finally make it back to Earth. Sometimes people were finding out their loved one had been killed three or four months after the fact. They had tried to improve upon that notification process for years.

Chester knew this was a question that would have to be answered soon. At the end of the month, they were going to announce the next quarter's draftees. "I've been struggling with this question myself. Prior to the cease-fire, we had been preparing to launch an invasion into Zodark-controlled space once Alfheim had been secured. There's a planet named Tueblets; it's a critical system for them. That invasion called for no less than four million soldiers.

"With that kind of operation on pause or likely never to happen, I do propose we modify the draft. I'd like to lift the stop-loss on the soldiers who have already served their enlistments. To do that, we'll need to replace almost a million soldiers. I'd also like to allow anyone who was drafted and served at least eight years the opportunity to join the reserves. In time, I'd like to get our military reserves built up to about the same strength levels as our active force. This way, if war does break out again, we have an army ready to be mobilized to deal with it."

"OK, I can work with that," Chancellor Luca responded. "How large do you want the active Army to be, then?"

"I think we should maintain an active force of no less than eight million, with a reserve of between ten and twelve million. This will allow us to bring a lot of people back to active duty should the need arise without having to resort to a massive draft again like we just did."

"I like that idea," Luca replied. "I'll couch it that way—that we're only looking to raise a few million more so we can allow those who have been stop-lossed to transfer to the reserve. But if we're going to create a reserve force, then we need to make sure that force continues to stay trained and equipped. I don't want these to become weekend warriors with no skills or equipment should the time come to reactivate them." As she spoke, she looked at Senator Walhoon, the man who controlled the purse strings of the Senate.

Chester held his hands up in mock surrender. "You won't hear any disagreement from me. I think this is a great idea. We can look to do this with the Navy as well. Figure out how many ships we absolutely need to maintain on active duty and then move the others to long-term storage and just maintain them. This way, we continue to build our forces up but don't have to keep shelling out money on a monthly basis to keep them fully manned and functional."

"What about Special Forces? Will you create a reserve function for them as well?" asked one of the other senators. "With the war done, I don't know what we'd use this many Deltas for."

Chester thought about that for a moment before responding, "I suppose we should look at that. Maybe we keep two of the groups on active service and we place the other two in the reserve."

"Just make sure if you do that that those operators are still able to keep their skills sharp, or as sharp as they can," commented Senator Walhoon. "Maybe we find a way to integrate these Delta operators into that new Interstellar Marshall Service or IMS group you wanted to form up or find someplace for them in the intelligence community, or heck, even in civilian law enforcement. They're augmented supersoldiers—we need to make sure they don't end up becoming mercenaries or guns for hire or something like that," Senator Walhoon commented.

When they'd created the augmented supersoldiers, they'd never really had a good solution as to what these guys could do once their twenty-year enlistments were up—not many had made it to that mark. The few that had usually went into government contracting as trainers for the military.

"I'm sure we'll figure something out, Senator."

The group talked budget items for a few more hours. The senators grilled Admiral Bailey on which ships were still going to be built and which ones would have to be pushed to the outyears. They had more than a hundred thirty hulls under construction, with another four hundred and fifty still slated to be built. By the end of the meeting, they had agreed to take those four hundred and fifty hulls and spread their construction from five years to ten years. This would help cover down on Space Command's budget cuts. What none of them realized just yet was how much revenue this new logistics command would start to bring in for the Navy. They were about to receive a windfall of cash once they started moving freight and people around. Admiral Bailey might just be able to get his ships built before the Zodarks had a change of heart about this peace treaty.

****

1st Ranger Division
Five Months Post-Treaty
New Eden

Staff Sergeant Paul "Pauli" Smith was nursing a beer at the NCO club with Staff Sergeant Yogi Sanders and Master Sergeant Jason Dunham as the three of them talked over their futures in the military. It was official: the military was going to do a major realignment, allowing millions of soldiers to transfer into the reserves. The 1st Orbital Ranger Division was no exception, nor was the 2nd Division. The plans to create a 3rd Division had immediately been scrapped once the treaty had been signed. This new reorg called for two of the four brigades in each division to be placed in the reserves.

Earlier that morning, during a division-wide all-hands briefing, their commander, Brigadier General Isaac Isaacson, call sign I2, had laid out their options. If they wanted to go into the reserve, they'd still get to keep any bonus money they had headed their way, and they'd only need to serve a total of forty years, at which point, they'd be allowed to retire and immediately collect their pension. This was actually a big deal because the standard military pension required you to serve fifty years to receive fifty percent of your salary. That said, if the majority of your military time was in the reserve, your pension wouldn't be as large as an active-duty pension.

"I don't know about you guys, but I've got forty-four years of active service," Dunham said. "I'm only six years away from a full pension, so I'm going to stick it out. Heck, I might even stay in longer and go for that seventy-five percent retirement." He finished off the last of his beer and signaled for the bartender to bring everyone another round, adding, "Drinks are on me, fellas. You've done an incredible job over the years. Heck, I still remember when you and Yogi were so fresh from training, we could smell it on you guys. Now you all are hard-chargin' combat veterans."

Coming from Dunham, this was high praise indeed.

"Thanks, Jason. That means a lot," remarked Yogi. "What about you, Pauli? You going to stick it out to get the full pension?"

Pauli kind of snickered at the thought. He'd met with his CPA and investment advisor two days ago. He was happy to learn that he'd likely never have to worry about money again. "Right now, I'm leaning more toward going the reserve route," he explained. "I've only got fourteen years in, so I'm a long way off from the fifty-year mark. If I stay, I need thirty-six more years to collect my pension. Whereas if I go into the reserves, I only need sixteen years, then I can be completely done with the military. The reserves would also allow me to start my own business here on New Eden, something I'd love to be able to do."

Dunham's left eyebrow rose quizzically. "Oh? What kind of business are ya thinking?"

Yogi jumped in before Pauli could say something. "You should see, Jason. Pauli here is like some kind of land baron entrepreneur. He's going to go into all sorts of businesses."

"Really? You come from a rich family?" Dunham asked sarcastically. "I hear land prices have gone through the roof, at least around any semblance of civilization, that is."

"Nah, I wasn't born rich, Jason. A long while back, Yogi and I bought into an up-and-coming Andorra ranch. I also bought as much stock as I could afford in a tech company called BlueWorld Technology. They have a patent on a very specific type of computer chip used in those new Tesla hover vehicles they came out with like ten years ago. When the war ended five months ago, General Motors, BMW, and Toyota were freed up to produce civilian vehicles again. The very next day, they announced a partnership with BlueWorld to provide them their component parts needed to manufacture hover cars. This is a *big* deal. I don't know if you can wrap your head around how big of a deal that is."

"Oh yeah, that sounds great. Maybe I should have bought into it a while back. What did you buy in at and where's that stock now?" Dunham asked, his curiosity piqued.

"When we bought in, the stock was valued at 18 RD a share," Pauli began to explain. "Since I'd hardly spent any of my military pay for most of the last decade, I was able to dump 150,000 RDs into the company, which netted me 8,334 shares. The week before the peace treaty was signed, the stock price had hit 800 a share. The day before they announced this massive deal with GM, BMW, and Toyota, they did a four-to-one stock split, which dropped the price down to 200. I then had 33,336 total shares. When they announced the new deal with the three automakers, it sent the stock up from 200 a share to over 1,223 in a week. That meant my 33,338 shares suddenly became 40,772,374 RD."

"Wow. So all this time, you've been a badass entrepreneur, Pauli," Dunham commented, truly impressed with his squad leader.

"Well, that's just my investment holdings. I sold all my stock in the Andorra farm and plowed it all into three large tracts of land. I plan on developing them into some luxury home communities, maybe plop a couple of golf courses on them."

"Yeah, Jason. Pauli's got it all figured out. Maybe I'll get out and go to work for him," Yogi joked as he downed his second beer. Their chicken wings finally arrived, along with another round of beers.

Dunham suddenly turned very serious. "Pauli, I know you may want to get out, and I wouldn't blame you if you did. You clearly have a better backup plan than most. However, with your combat record and list of valor awards, you'll easily rise through the ranks, even in a peacetime military. I mean, I know you'd likely make more money on the outside, but you could have a really good career in the military too. You're a hell of a soldier and NCO, and I'd hate to lose you. But again, I'd understand if you wanted to get out."

The three of them ate their wings in silence for a moment. This was kind of tough for Pauli. He enjoyed the military. He liked his job and was good at it. Hell, he'd racked up three Purple Heart medals, two Bronze Stars with Valor devices, a Silver Star, and the Distinguished Service Cross. Their battalion and brigade commander were in the process of trying to upgrade his Silver Star to the Medal of Honor. One part of him would feel terrible about leaving the Rangers to go into the reserves, but at the same time, he wanted to live his life. He wanted to find a nice woman to marry and settle down with, have children and a career that allowed him the flexibility to do what he wanted when he wanted. It was a real conundrum.

"When do we have to give our decisions by?" he asked Dunham.

"We all have until next Monday—so five days."

Pauli sighed, then nodded his head. "OK, I'll have it figured out by then. Right now, I just need some time to think about it."

****

Officer Housing
Fort Roughneck
New Eden

Captain Brian Royce had been accused of a lot of things in his life, but getting married to a woman after only dating her for eight weeks was certainly falling into the category of reckless abandon. Back on Earth, he and Jane Burton had started out as a one-night fling, which had quickly grown into a whirlwind romance that had ended with them getting married his second-to-last night on Earth. Once married, he'd filed the paperwork to have a travel visa issued for her to live on New Eden. Next, he went to base housing once he arrived back at Cantonment. If his name hadn't been Brian Royce, two-time Medal of Honor recipient, he likely would have had to wait months for an on-base house to come available. As it was, he was able to secure a large, beautiful single-story house. This type of house was typically reserved for colonels and above, but being a two-time MOH awardee had some additional perks, namely that he got one of the nicest houses on the base.

Once Royce had secured his housing situation and gotten everything ready for his bride, he felt he was ready to settle into his command position. As the company commander for Alpha Company, 1st Battalion, 4th Special Forces Group, he figured he'd spend the next couple of years as commander before transferring to do an obligatory staff or joint staff tour so he could get selected for major and eventually have a battalion command of his own.

Then, out of nowhere, Royce got a new set of orders. All they said was that he was being assigned to work in the Defense Attaché Office or DAO shop for a Major General Alfred Bates. He would apparently work at the Republic's office within the Galactic Empire or GE headquarters staff. By all accounts, this should be the cushiest of all joint billeted assignments he could have hoped for, but something told him there was more to this story than met the eye.

Who the hell is General Bates? he wondered. *He's clearly not Special Forces or I would have heard of him by now. I'll bet he works with Ambassador Nina Chapman.*

"You are to report to your new duty assignment on 22 September," Royce said aloud to himself. At least he had a month before he had to report—plenty of time for a change of command and some time to help Jane get acclimated to military life.

When she showed up at the spaceport a few days later, he was there to greet her with some flowers and a sign that read "Welcome Home, Jane" on it. They embraced and kissed for what felt like an eternity before they climbed in his vehicle.

Jane was enthralled by everything she saw. "The sky looks so different from Earth," she remarked in wonder. The system had two suns, and New Eden had three moons that orbited it. It made for an incredible contrast in scenery. Then there were the buildings. Every city on New Eden was a deliberately designed city. There was nothing just thrown together like so many cities on Earth. On New Eden, everything was planned, all the way down to the size and number of roads, subways, streetcars and hyperloop stations. Even the skyscrapers looked impressive. Many of them were as high as three hundred and fifty floors; a few of them went even higher. The structures themselves were encased in a glass-like substance that gave off a slight green hue when the sun hit them directly. Many of the skyscrapers also had connecting sky bridges or direct access to the hyperloop system.

Before Royce drove Jane to the base, he took her to a restaurant that had an overview of the ocean. They ate some food that was local to New Eden and got caught up on things. When they arrived at their new house on the base, she couldn't believe how large and nice it was. Brian had to assure her twice that this wasn't a joke, this really was *their* house. He mused with her that they'd need to start work on filling all these rooms with babies. She gave him a mischievous look that said they should get to work on that right away.

During the first weekend Jane and Brian were together, he took her out to enjoy one of his favorite parks nearby. He wanted to show her as much of this world as he could before his new job would invariably pick up. They'd spend Saturday exploring one park, then take a trip to the beach to enjoy the water while soaking up some sun.

For so much of Royce's life, Special Forces had been all he'd known. Between all the schools, training, missions, and then the war, he hadn't had time to know anything other than war. These last couple of months with Jane had made him realize how much of life he'd been missing out on. He realized for the first time since he'd joined that there *was* life outside the military. With Jane here, she immediately turned the house into a home. She had pictures of herself and her family on the walls and newly taken pictures of them doing fun stuff back on Earth and now on New Eden.

While Royce had a couple of weeks left before he had to report, they took advantage of the time to get a lay of the land and explore what there was to do around the base and the Emerald City. Jane had them trying a new restaurant at least two or three times a week, just to get out and meet new people and explore more of their surroundings. Brian had to hand it to her—he was seeing more of this planet now with her than he had in the last number of years he'd been stationed here. Prior to getting married to Jane, he'd been tethered to his work. He just hadn't taken a lot of personal time to go exploring or do things. His dedication to the job was all-consuming, but Jane was changing that.

Jane joined a few social groups on some message boards, and before Royce knew it, she had them meeting up with other couples on the weekend for BBQs and other fun outings. They'd become part of a hiking club, going out at least once a week to explore some of the nearby parks. It was such a stark departure from the world he'd known and worked in for the last thirty-one years. Looking at the glow of her face and the new friends and couples they were meeting had brought about a strange satisfaction with his life he hadn't previously felt. It was refreshing.

****

Imperial Headquarters
Emerald City, New Eden

When Captain Brian Royce walked into the office to report for duty, he was immediately led to the office of Major General Alfred Bates. He stood outside the door, knocked, and waited to be called in.

"Enter," came the voice from the other room.

Royce closed the door behind him and walked to the desk before he snapped to attention. "Captain Brian Royce, reporting as ordered," he said in a crisp but firm voice.

"At ease, Captain. Please take a seat," the general said as he motioned to an empty chair.

Eyeing the general sitting opposite him, Royce couldn't quite place where he'd seen him before. He didn't recognize his voice, but his face looked vaguely familiar, which seemed odd since he was obviously a former Delta.

I thought I knew all the general officers in SF.

"My name is Alfred Bates, and yes, my name really *is* Alfred. You may call me Al, or General Bates, whichever suits you. Do you like to go by Brian or Captain Royce, or do you have some other moniker you like to go by?"

"My friends call me Brian. Um, you can call me whatever you'd like, sir."

"Excellent, Brian. I think you and I are going to get to know each other pretty well over the coming weeks and months. But first, let's get down to business. I'm sure you're wondering exactly what your job is and what you'll be doing here and probably who the hell I am?"

"I won't say I haven't been a little curious this last month," Brian admitted. He'd been so busy enjoying his time with Jane that he really hadn't researched Major General Alfred Bates. "I figured you'd clue me in once it was time. If I may—when did you serve in the Deltas? I thought I knew most of the general officers. Kind of a small number and all."

Alfred grunted. "Let's just say I'm a lot older than I may appear. I'm OG. One of the few remaining 1st Special Forces, Detachment Delta guys still around from the old days, back when the United States of America was still a thing. However, you have a hell of a reputation and combat record yourself. It's why I handpicked you for this next assignment."

Now Royce was really curious who this guy was. He was still in the service given his rank, but who he worked for was another question entirely.

"OK, I'm all ears as they say. What can I do for you, sir?"

Alfred smiled. "Good, then let's get down to it. First, I'm not an operational operator anymore—not since I lost my left leg and my right eye during the battle for this planet nearly twelve years ago. I now head up a newly created outfit called Task Force Orange. We face some new and growing threats, Brian. We need a new force that can deal with this, which is why I'm putting this task force together."

"This sounds…interesting. What exactly is it we'll be doing?"

"We've been given two mandates, Brian. The first is a thorough FID assessment of our allies. Seeing how things played out during this last war, the powers that be would like to have a better understanding of what our allies' true capabilities may be. Either they're a lot weaker than we were led to believe, or they used us and the Primords like cannon fodder in this last war. In either case, we need to have a better idea of who our allies really are.

"Our second mandate is to hunt down and exploit the remnants of the Zodark-Sumerian Mukhabarat." Alfred held a hand up to stop Royce from asking a question. "I know what's been said about them, but I can assure you, they have not been destroyed."

Alfred handed him several pieces of paper before adding, "Yeah, I know. This is old-school, but some things are best kept off the electronic file system and dealt with the old-fashioned way, with paper and pen. What you are holding is a highly classified report from some of our OGA guys on Sumer. Apparently, in our zeal to wrest control of the planet from the Zodarks and dismantle the Sumerians' secret police, we caused the Mukhabarat to go dormant for a while, and we seem to have missed a few of them. Why don't you take a moment to read over the report? Then we'll talk about it."

As he dug into the pages before him, Royce started to realize they had a serious problem on their hands—one he wasn't sure how to resolve. When he finished reading the report over, he handed the document back to Alfred.

"When you landed on Sumer with Hadad Nasr and found his family, his daughter Diyana's friend, Sadat—he was an active member of the secret police at the time. Do you remember him?"

"Remember? Of course!" Royce confirmed. "When we captured him and showed him there were other planets with billions of people who weren't subjugated by the Zodarks, we eventually managed to flip him. He helped us identify a handful of Zodark bases. Then we lost contact with him. We figured he might have gotten himself killed. Are you saying he's still alive?"

Alfred nodded. "It would appear so. He's the one who provided the intelligence in that report you just read."

"Really?" Royce asked. "That's incredible. So, we have a source not only working inside the organization for us, but he's a part of this infiltration team?"

"That's what it looks like. That was another reason why I wanted you to be a part of this task force. You guys recruited Sadat—you know his motivations for doing this and what he's hoping to get out of working for us. That's invaluable insight and it'll go a long way toward validating his reporting."

"Wow, this is incredible. If these guys are able to infiltrate across the Republic…my God, the Zodarks could tear us apart," Royce lamented. "I mean, one of the biggest advantages we had in the last war was that the Zodarks didn't have a clear view of where Earth or our shipyards and bases were. All they really knew about was New Eden, and that was because of the stargate. If the Mukhabarat is able to establish a network of spies across the Republic and map our entire territory, this may be the precursor to them restarting the war. They'll know exactly where to attack and how strong our defenses are." He'd fought too hard, lost too many friends to see everything they had worked for be wiped out by this insidious species known as the Zodarks.

"Exactly. That's why I've brought you onto my team," Alfred replied. "What I'd like you to do over the rest of this week is help me identify additional team members you believe will be helpful in tracking these bastards down. Don't just think about fellow Delta operators. Figure out skill levels you are missing, and I'll get new orders cut assigning them to our unit. Oh, and by the way…" Alfred pulled a small box out from his desk drawer and slid it across the desk toward him. "You're going to need these. I can't have the tip of my spear being a lowly captain."

Royce took the small box and opened it. Inside was a pair of gold oak leaves—the insignia for major. He'd just been promoted.

"Wow, sir. I don't know what to say. I'm still a few years out from going to the board."

Alfred waved his wrist like the board was no big deal. "While this task force is technically a part of the Alliance DAO office, we report directly to JSOC. Promotions within our group are a little easier to come by, but I think you already knew that."

A grin spread across Royce's face. "All right, so aside from assembling a team to hunt these jokers down, do you want me to assemble a dozen or so FID teams as well, or do you have another person covering down on that?"

"No, I've got another officer I'm going to tap for that," Alfred explained. "I want you focused on finding these infiltrators. Keep in mind—the information in that report you read is at least a week old. That means they're likely already on their way here or possibly have already arrived."

The two of them spent the rest of the morning talking and strategizing how they were going to find a specific needle in a stack of needles. With the formal induction of Sumer into the Republic nearly two months ago, these would-be spies and saboteurs would now be able to enjoy unfettered access and travel throughout the Republic. Royce needed to get his new spy-hunting team built rapidly and put them to work ASAP.

When Royce left Alfred's office, the general's aide led him down the hallway, where they turned toward a large empty room with a placard above it that simply read J2/3/5 Operations, Plans, & Policies. The aide typed a code on the door lock, which activated a palm reader. When the aide placed his right hand on the reader, the biometric scanner verified the match it had on record and popped the door open with a slight hissing noise.

The young lieutenant turned. "We tried to make your team room about as nondescript as possible, but as more of the alliance staff begin to arrive, it'll be incumbent on your team to keep what you're doing in here a secret."

When they walked in, what Royce saw was a massive empty room. There were no desks, chairs, computer monitors—nothing. It was a blank canvas to design as he saw fit. "This'll work."

"Good, because there are no other rooms close to the size of this one. Once you have figured out how you'd like it laid out, send me the specs, and we'll have it built. In the meantime, you can use any of those terminals over there until your office space is completed." The aide paused for a moment. "Oh, before I go, once you've figured out who you want to recruit to your team, send them over to me ASAP. I'll have them transferred immediately."

Before the lieutenant officially left, he made sure Royce knew the keypad code and that they'd registered his biometric data for the locks.

As Royce stood there alone in this massive empty room, a single thought kept cropping up. *I've been out of JSOC for seventeen years...and just like that...I'm back*, he thought. *I guess it's time we put the band back together.*

From the Author

I hope you've enjoyed this book. If you'd like to continue the action in the Rise of the Republic series, you can preorder your copy of *Into the Calm* on Amazon.

Because I wanted to continue building out more of the Rise of the Republic universe, I am partnering with one of my veteran co-authors, T.C. Manning, to bring you an exciting new series, Apollo's Arrows. The first book, *Cherubim's Call*, follows Harrison Kodiak and two of his battle buddies as they go through training and get in on the beginning of the conflict with the Zodarks. It's a whole different perspective on the ground level of the Republic Army. Visit Amazon to reserve your copy.

In addition to the military sci-fi series you've been reading, we are also producing new books in our military thriller series, The Monroe Doctrine. You can join that series by purchasing *Volume I* on Amazon.

If you like to listen to audiobooks, we have several that have recently been produced. The first three books of the Rise of the Republic series are actually available for your listening pleasure, as is Volume One of our new military thriller series, The Monroe Doctrine. All five books of the Falling Empire series are now available in audio format, along with the six books of the Red Storm Series, and our entire World War III series. *Interview with a Terrorist* and *Traitors Within*, which are currently standalone books, are also available for your listening pleasure.

If you would like to stay up to date on new releases and receive emails about any special pricing deals we may make available, please sign up for our email distribution list. Simply go to https://www.frontlinepublishinginc.com/ and sign up.

As a bonus, if you sign up for our mailing list, you will receive a dossier for the Rise of the Republic Series. It contains artwork of the ships we've written about, as well as their pertinent stats. It will really help make the series come to life for you as you continue reading.

As independent authors, reviews are very important to us and make a huge difference to other prospective readers. If you enjoyed this book, we humbly ask you to write up a positive review on Amazon and Goodreads. We sincerely appreciate each person that takes the time to write one.

We have really valued connecting with our readers via social media, especially on our Facebook page https://www.facebook.com/RosoneandWatson/. Sometimes we ask for help from our readers as we write future books—we love to draw upon all your different areas of expertise. We also have a group of beta readers who get to look at the books before they are officially published and help us fine-tune last-minute adjustments. If you would like to be a part of this team, please go to our author website, https://www.frontlinepublishinginc.com/, and send us a message through the "Contact" tab.

You may also enjoy some of our other works. A full list can be found below:

Nonfiction:
Iraq Memoir 2006–2007 Troop Surge
Interview with a Terrorist (audiobook available)

Fiction:
The Monroe Doctrine Series
Volume One (audiobook available)
Volume Two (audiobook available)
Volume Three
Volume Four (available for preorder)

Rise of the Republic Series
Into the Stars (audiobook available)
Into the Battle (audiobook available)
Into the War (audiobook available)
Into the Chaos (audiobook available)
Into the Fire
Into the Calm (available for preorder)

Apollo's Arrows Series
Cherubim's Call (available for preorder)

Crisis in the Desert Series (co-authored with Matt Jackson)
Project 19 (audiobook available)
Desert Shield
Desert Storm

Falling Empires Series
Rigged (audiobook available)
Peacekeepers (audiobook available)
Invasion (audiobook available)
Vengeance (audiobook available)
Retribution (audiobook available)

Red Storm Series
Battlefield Ukraine (audiobook available)
Battlefield Korea (audiobook available)
Battlefield Taiwan (audiobook available)
Battlefield Pacific (audiobook available)
Battlefield Russia (audiobook available)
Battlefield China (audiobook available)

Michael Stone Series
Traitors Within (audiobook available)

World War III Series
Prelude to World War III: The Rise of the Islamic Republic and the Rebirth of America (audiobook available)
Operation Red Dragon and the Unthinkable (audiobook available)
Operation Red Dawn and the Siege of Europe (audiobook available)
Cyber Warfare and the New World Order (audiobook available)

Children's Books:
My Daddy has PTSD
My Mommy has PTSD

Abbreviation Key

4FG	Fourth Fighter Group
ACLS	Advanced Cardiac Life Support
AI	Artificial Intelligence
AO	Area of Operation
AOR	Area of Responsibility
ASAP	As Soon As Possible
ATV	All-Terrain Vehicle
BSL	Biosafety Level
CAS	Close Air Support
CCP	Casualty Collection Point
CIC	Combat Information Center
CO	Commanding Officer
COB	Close of Business
COP	Combat Outpost
CPW	Craykard Particle Weapon
DAO	Defense Attaché Office
DZ	Drop Zone
EFP	Explosively Formed Penetrator
EKIA	Enemy Killed in Action
ETA	Estimated Time of Arrival
FID	Foreign Internal Defense
FOB	Forward Operating Base
FRAGO	Fragmentary Order
FTL	Faster than Light
GE	Galactic Empire
GEU	Greater European Union
GW	George Washington
HALO	High-Altitude, Low-Opening
HE	High-Explosive
HQ	Headquarters
HUD	Heads-up Display
HVI	High-Value Individual
HVT	High-Value Target
IDF	Indirect Fire
IED	Improvised Explosive Device
IMS	Interstellar Marshall Service

318

IR	Infrared
JTF	Joint Task Force
JSOC	Joint Special Operations Command
KIA	Killed in Action
LT	Lieutenant
MOH	Medal of Honor
NCO	Noncommissioned Officer
NDA	Nondisclosure Agreement
NOS	Zodark admiral or senior military commander
OGA	Other Government Agency
OIC	Officer in Charge
OP	Observational Post
OP2	Overwatch Position Two
PA	Personal Assistant
PDG	Point-Defense Guns
PFC	Private First Class
PNN	Private News Network
QRF	Quick Reaction Force
RA	Republic Army
RD	Republic Dollars
RNS	Republic Naval Ship
RPD	Remotely Piloted Drone
SAM	Surface-to-Air Missile
SF	Special Forces
SITREP	Situation Report
SOCOM	Special Operations Command
TPA	Tri-Parte Alliance
VC	Vehicle Commander
XO	Executive Officer